Authors featured in T

Steve Berman

Holly Black

Bill Congreve

Charles de Lint

A. M. Dellamonica

Jeffrey Ford

Gregory Frost

Nan Fry

Neil Gaiman

Bruce Glassco

Hiromi Goto

Nina Kiriki Hoffman

Tanith Lee

Kelly Link

Gregory Maguire

Patricia A. McKillip

Delia Sherman

Ellen Steiber

Katherine Vaz

The Faery Reel

Tales from the Twilight Realm

Edited by

ELLEN DATLOW & TERRI WINDLING

Introduction by

TERRI WINDLING

Decorations by

CHARLES VESS

FIREBIRD

AN IMPRINT OF PENGUIN GROUP (USA) INC.

Ellen Datlow and Terri Windling would like to thank their editor, Sharyn November, for all her support and help.

FIREBIRD
Published by the Penguin Group
Penguin Group (USA) Inc., 345 Hudson Street, New York, New York 10014, U.S.A.
Penguin Group (Canada), 90 Eglinton Avenue East, Suite 700,
Toronto, Ontario, Canada M4P 2Y3
(a division of Pearson Penguin Canada Inc.)
Penguin Books Ltd, 80 Strand, London WC2R 0RL, England
Penguin Ireland, 25 St Stephen's Green, Dublin 2, Ireland
(a division of Penguin Books Ltd)
Penguin Group (Australia), 250 Camberwell Road, Camberwell, Victoria 3124, Australia
(a division of Pearson Australia Group Pty Ltd)
Penguin Books India Pvt Ltd, 11 Community Centre, Panchsheel Park,
New Delhi - 110 017, India
Penguin Group (NZ), Cnr Airborne and Rosedale Roads, Albany, Auckland 1310,
New Zealand (a division of Pearson New Zealand Ltd)
Penguin Books (South Africa) (Pty) Ltd, 24 Sturdee Avenue,
Rosebank, Johannesburg 2196, South Africa

Registered Offices: Penguin Books Ltd, 80 Strand, London WC2R 0RL, England

First published in the United States of America by Viking,
a division of Penguin Putnam Books for Young Readers, 2004
Published by Firebird, an imprint of Penguin Group (USA) Inc., 2006

1 3 5 7 9 10 8 6 4 2

Decorations copyright © Charles Vess, 2004
Copyright notices for individual contributors appear on the last page of this book.
All rights reserved

THE LIBRARY OF CONGRESS HAS CATALOGED THE VIKING EDITION AS FOLLOWS:

The Faery Reel: tales from the Twilight Realm / edited by Ellen Datlow and
Terri Windling; introduction by Terri Windling; decorations by Charles Vess.
p.   cm.
Summary: A collection of stories and poems about faeries
in all parts of the world by a variety of authors.
ISBN 0-670-05914-5 (Hardcover)
1. Fairies—Literary collections. [1. Fairies—Literary collections.] I. Datlow, Ellen.
II. Windling, Terri. III. Vess, Charles, ill.
PZ5.F18 2004   808.8'0375—dc22   2003023537

ISBN 0-14-240406-3

Printed in the United States of America

To Merrilee Heifetz, who was "midwife to the faeries" (to borrow the words of an old folktale), or at least to this book about them. Thank you, Merrilee, for all you've done for this book and so many others.

—*E. D. & T. W.*

Contents

∾

Preface

~

Ellen Datlow and Terri Windling

Faeries and similar nature spirits can be found in folktales all over the world. They inhabit woodlands, moorlands, rivers, oceans, deserts, and rain forests; they're found in the crannies of human dwellings and in the shadows of city streets. There are few places where they *can't* be found, unless they're repelled by iron, pins, salt, or other protections against them. In parts of the world, belief in faeries lingers to this day.

Some say that the earliest known faeries in Europe were those who appeared when children were born, to bless or curse their destinies, much like the three goddesses called the Fates in Roman myth. The word *faery* comes from the Latin *fatare* (meaning "to enchant"), and over the centuries they've been known by many related names such as *fée*, *fai*, *fey*, *fai-erie*, *fayre*, *faery*, and *fairy*. The latter two names are the ones used today, and either spelling is historically correct. (We've allowed the authors in this book to use whichever spelling they prefer.) *Faërie*, in modern usage, is the name of the realm where faeries live, and the faery race is often referred to collectively as *the Fey*. Many folklorists, however, will tell you that you shouldn't say any of these names out loud, that it's dangerous to call the faeries by name and thus catch their attention. One still finds country people who instead refer to faeries as the Good Folk, or the Good Neighbors, the Wee People, the Hidden Ones, or Them Ones . . . speaking quietly and carefully so the faeries won't take offense!

If you think of faeries as tiny winged sprites flitting prettily from flower to flower, you might wonder why such excessive degrees of caution are necessary. How dangerous, after all, can dainty faeries like Tinkerbell be? But the faeries of folklore are far more varied than the ones found in most children's books and cartoons. They can be male or female, lovely or ugly, with human features or features borrowed from birds, animals, minerals, and plants. Some faeries are good, some are bad, and the vast majority are unpredictable—helpful one moment, mischievous the next, downright dangerous the moment after that. Even Tinkerbell, it's wise to remember, tried to have Wendy Darling shot.

In folklore, faeries come with a bewildering variety of names, shapes, sizes, customs, habitats, and local histories—from the tiny portunes of old English manuscripts to the human-sized Sidhe of Ireland; from the humble barstukken in German tree roots to the elegant ladies of the French faery court; from the lonely urisks who haunt Scottish pools to the merry salvanelli of Italy; from the domoviks who protect Russian hearths to the wicked als of Armenia. Faeries are enchanting *and* terrifying, charming *and* exasperating, elusive to find *and* impossible to get rid of, shifting shape from country to country, story to story, and moment to moment.

In this book about our Good Neighbors, we've asked a number of our favorite writers to travel into the Twilight Realm (an ancient name for the land of Fäerie) and to bring back stories of faeries and the hapless mortals who cross their path. "No butterfly-winged sprites," we pleaded. "Read the old folktales, journey farther afield, find some of the less explored paths through the Realm. Bring us tales set in Fäerie and in the past—but also tales about faeries today. Let's see how these spirits of nature are getting along in the modern world."

The results of their travels through legend and myth can be found in the stories and poems that follow: tales of changelings, undines, a tengu, an oakthing, fox faeries, and a shapeshifter or two. Tales of faery enchanters, faery seducers, and yes, even Tinkerbell.

The bewitching cover and interior art is by Charles Vess, who is no stranger to the Twilight Realm. He's illustrated such classic faery stories as William Shakespeare's *A Midsummer Night's Dream* and J. M. Barrie's *Peter Pan*. He created the illustrated faery novel *Stardust* in collaboration with Neil Gaiman, and faery lore can be found in his various comics from Green Man Press.

In an old Celtic story (and folk ballad), a mortal queen is whisked away underground by the amorous Faery King, and her husband, King Orfeo, must journey to Fäerie to win her back. He leaves his knights and his archers behind, disguises himself as a poor harp player, and travels to the faery court to play before them all. First he plays a joyous song, then one so sad that the whole court weeps. Last, he plays "The Faery Reel"—a tune so lively and captivating that even the Faery King leaps up to dance. As the last notes die away, the Faery King tells him to choose his reward. "Name your heart's desire," says he. "Gold . . . silver . . . fame among men?" But the humble musician straightens his back and reveals himself as King Orfeo. He wants neither wealth nor fame, but only to take his dear lady home. "Choose something else!" the Faery King roars. King Orfeo stands silent and firm and the Faery King, bound by his word, must let the mortals go.

In this book, you'll find stories as joyous, painful, and magical as "The Faery Reel." May they open the door to the Twilight Realm . . . and bring you safely home again.

Introduction: The Faeries

∾

by *Terri Windling*

Where do faeries come from? Folklorists, philosophers, historians, mystics, and others have debated this question for centuries. No one really knows how faeries originated—unless it's the faeries themselves, and they're not telling. What we *do* know is that tales of the faeries can be found on every continent around the globe, and that belief in the existence of the "Hidden People" is surprisingly widespread even today.

Some scholars see the vestiges of pagan religions in tales about the faeries, who are, they say, the diminished remnants of once powerful gods and goddesses. Other scholars insist that faeries are really just the early, indigenous peoples of each land, who may have been viewed as magical and otherworldly by conquering tribes. Many people once thought that faeries were fallen angels who'd been ejected from Heaven but weren't quite wicked enough for Hell, or that they were the wandering souls of children who'd died unbaptized. Some read the following words from the Bible as proof that God created the faery race in addition to mankind: "And other sheep have I that are not of this fold." (John 10:16). The most widespread belief, still prevalent today, is that faeries are simply nature spirits and thus as ancient as wind and rain. In this view, they're the manifestations of the living spirit in all organic matter.

In the fifteenth century, an alchemist named Paracelsus divided faeries into four elemental groups: Sylphs (air), Gnomes (earth), Undines (water), and Salamanders (fire). They are made of flesh and blood, he said, and procreate like human beings but are longer lived than man and do not possess immortal souls. In the seventeenth century, a Scottish minister named Robert Kirk wrote that faeries "are of a middle nature betwixt man and angel," with "light changeable bodies, like those called astral, somewhat of the nature of a condensed cloud, and best seen at twilight."[1]

In the nineteenth century, the physiology of faeries was of great interest to the Spiritualists,[2] who divided them into two basic types: nature spirits tied to features of the landscape (a river, a pool, a copse of trees), and higher spirits who lived on an astral plane between flesh and thought. In the early twentieth century, a Theosophist[3] named Charles W. Leadbeater developed an elaborate system of faery classification inspired by Darwin's theory of evolution. Leadbeater maintained that faeries live on an astral plane divided into seven levels. He believed the faery race to be the original inhabitants of England, driven to its margins by the invasion of mankind, and he drew elaborate diagrams showing how the faeries had evolved. His chart began with mineral life and then rose upward through water and earth, and through seaweed, fungi, and bacteria. Further up the evolutionary ladder he showed how faeries developed through grasses and cereals, reptiles and birds, sea flora and fauna, until they matured into nature spirits linked to each of the four elements. But evolution didn't stop there; these nature spirits would in turn evolve into Sylphs, then Devas, and then into angels. On the top rung of the ladder the faeries would become what he called "solar spirits," where they'd join with evolved humans in a more enlightened age.[4]

Another Theosophist, Edward Garner, argued that faeries are allied to the butterfly genus, and are made of a substance lighter than gas, which renders them invisible to human beings (except clairvoyants). The function of faeries in nature, he said, is to provide a link between plants and the energy of the sun. He wrote that the "growth of a plant, which we regard as the customary and inevitable result of associating the three factors of sun, seed, and soil, would never take place if the fairy builders were absent."[5] Franz Hartmann, a medical doctor, believed that faeries have a role in human psychology, explaining that "the spirits of nature have their dwellings within us as well as outside of us, and no man is perfectly master of himself unless he thoroughly knows his own nature and its inhabitants."[6]

While the Spiritualists, in their journals and lectures, argued how many faeries could fit on the head of a pin or swim through the higher astral plane, unlettered country people were taking great pains to avoid the faeries' notice. Charms, talismans, and spells were used to keep troublesome faeries at bay—to chase them away from the house, the livestock, newborn children, and unmarried girls.

Although faeries had been known to give aid to mortals, more often they were seen as irksome creatures, quick to take offense and dangerous when riled. Faery bargains were notoriously tricky things, and faery treasure was often cursed. Mortals who stumbled into Faeryland could end up trapped in that realm forever, or emerge from it aged and withered, even though it had seemed that little time had passed. Faeries were blamed for soured milk, blighted crops, and barren cows; for illness, madness, birth defects, and other mysterious ills. Even good faeries followed rules and taboos that could be unfathomable to humans, thus it was wise to be scrupulously polite and to treat all faeries with great caution. Folklore is filled with cautionary tales outlining the perils of faery encounters. Do not eat faery food, they say, or you will be trapped in Faeryland. Avoid using a faery's name, and don't ever tell your own. Don't bargain with the faeries or join their dances or spy on their courtly revels. Wear your shirt inside out and carry iron to avoid abduction.

Many stories tell of faeries who steal human children, particularly newborn babies, and sometimes adults as well, particularly midwives and musicians. When babies are snatched, a faery changeling is left behind in the child's cradle. In some tales the changeling is just a piece of wood "glamoured" to look like a child; in others it is a sickly faery baby, or an old and peevish faery. The young human changelings who are spirited away to Fäerie will be petted and cosseted for a while—until the faeries grow tired of them. Then the humans are banished from the realm (for which they'll pine from that day forward), or else kept on as household slaves for the rest of their mortal lives. Some say the faeries are required to pay a blood-tithe to Hell every seven years, and that they steal mortals for this purpose so as not to sacrifice one of their own. A human knight named Tam Lin was destined to be the tithe in one old tale, until his true love tricked the Faery Queen into releasing him on All Hallows' Eve.

Some faeries can be alluring creatures, but woe to those who seek their kisses, for few amorous encounters between faeries and mortals ever come to good. A harp player named Thomas the Rhymer kissed the Faery Queen under the Eildon Tree, then paid for each of those kisses with seven years of servitude in Fäerie. Thomas was one of the lucky ones, because many hapless lads and maidens sickened and died after twilight encounters with sweet-talking lovers who turned out to be faeries in disguise. There are stories in which faeries wed mortals, but such marriages rarely turn out well, whether it is a woman with a faery husband or a man with a faery bride. Irish seal people who marry human men and women always return to the sea, and Japanese fox faeries make dangerous brides, stealing the life essence from their husbands. The children born of such unions are often lonely, melancholic creatures, too mortal to live comfortably in Fäerie and too fey for the human world.

Some faery lore makes a clear division between good and wicked types of faeries—between those who are friend-ly to mankind and those who seek to cause us harm. In Scottish tales, good faeries make up the Seelie Court, which means the Blessed Court, while bad faeries congregate in the Unseelie Court, ruled by the dark queen Nicnivin. In old Norse myth, the Liosálfar (Light Elves) are regal, compassionate creatures who live in the sky in the realm of Alfheim, while the Döckálfar (the Dark Elves) live underground and are greatly feared. Yet in other traditions, a faery can be good *or* bad, depending on the circumstance or on the faery's whim. They are often portrayed as amoral beings, rather than immoral ones, who simply have little comprehension of human notions of right and wrong.

The great English folklorist Katharine Briggs tended to avoid the "good" and "bad" division, preferring the categorizations of Solitary and Trooping Faeries instead. She noted that the faeries in either group "may be evil, dealing death or sickness to every man and creature they pass on their way, like the Sluagh of the Highlands; they may steal unchurched wives from child-bed, or snatch away unchristened babes leaving animated stocks [pieces of wood] or sickly children of their own in their place, or they may be harmless and even beneficial—fertility spirits watching over the growth of flowers or bringing good luck to herds or children." Solitary Faeries are generally those associated with a certain location: a bog, a lake, the roots of a tree, a particular hill or household. The Trooping Faeries, by contrast, are gregarious creatures fond of hunting, feasting, dancing, and holding court. "This is perhaps particularly true of the British Isles," writes Briggs, "though in France, Italy, Scandinavia and Germany there are the same tales of dancing, revelry and processions."[7]

Other folklorists divide the faeries by their element, rather than by their temperament, harking back to Paracelsus's classification system of earth, air, water, and fire. Faeries associated with the earth are the most numerous type in tales the world over. Earth elementals include those who live in caves, barrows, and deep underground, and who often have a special facility for working with precious metals, such as the coblynau in the hills of Wales, the gandharvas of India, the erdluitle of northern Italy and Switzerland, the maanväki of Finland, the thrussers of Norway, the karzalek of Poland, the illes of Iceland, the various silver-smithing dwarfs of Old Norse legends, and the gans of the Apache tribe in the American southwest. Forest faeries and tree spirits are also associated with earth, such as the shy aziza of West Africa, the mu of Papua New Guinea, the shinseen of China, the silvanni of Italy, the Oakmen of the British Isles, the skogsra of Sweden, the kulaks of Burma, the hantu hutan of the Malay Peninsula, the bela of Indonesia, the patu-paiarehe of the Maori, and the manitou of the Algonquin tribe in Canada. Other earth faeries guard standing stones, such as the tiny, web-footed couril of Brittany, or thrive in desert sands, such as the Ahl Al-trab of Arabia.

Faeries associated with the air element include various winged faeries and sylphs, and those whose realms are in the sky. Air faeries are less common than earth faeries in the oldest faery stories, though they've become the most popular type in modern faery paintings and children's books. Examples of air faeries include the luminous soulth of Ireland, the Star Folk of the Algonquin tribe, the atua of Polynesia, the Light Elves of Old Norse legends, and the peri of Persian lore, who sleep on clouds and dine on perfume. Faeries who account for weather phenomena, such as mistral winds, whirlwinds, and storms, are associated with the air element, including the spriggans of Cornwall, the vily of

Slavonia, the vintoasele of Serbia and Croatia, the rusali of Romania, and the mischievous folletti of Italy.

The most common type of fire faery is the salamander, an elemental spirit much prized by Renaissance alchemists. Also associated with fire are the djinn, the wicked faeries of Persian lore, and the drakes (or drachen), fire faeries found in the British Isles and western Europe who resemble streaking balls of fire and smell like rotten eggs. Luminous, will-o'-the-wisp type fire faeries are famous for leading travelers astray, such as the Ellylldan of Welsh marshland, the Teine Sith of the Scottish Hebrides, the spunkies of southwest England, Le Faeu Boulanger of the Channel Islands, the candelas of Sardinia, and the Fouchi Fatui of northern Italy. The various faeries who guard hearth fires are also associated with this element, such as the gabija of Lithuania and Natrou-Monsieur of France. The muzayyara are fiery, seductive faeries in old Egyptian tales; and the akamu is a particularly dangerous fire faery found in Japan.

Water faeries are divided between those who live in the sea and those who live in fresh water. Sea faeries include all mermaids and mermen, seal people, and sirens of various kinds, including the selchies (Selkies) of western Europe, the Daoine Mara and Fin Folk of Scotland, the merrows of Ireland, the Nereides of Greece, the havfreui of Scandinavia, the Mal-de-Mer on the coast of France, and Groac'h Vor, a Breton mermaid. Fresh-water faeries live in rivers, lakes, pools, fountains, bogs, and marshes, or are water elementals who can live anywhere fresh water is found. Like all faeries, some are gentle creatures and some are exceedingly treacherous. Water faeries include all the dangerous nixies and kelpies found in English rivers, the dracs in the river Seine in France, the merewiper in the river Danube in Germany, the hotots of Armenia, the judi of Macedonia, the cacce-halde of Lapland, the kludde of Belgium, the jalpari of India, the manii of Italy, the fuath of Ireland, the laminak of Basque folklore, the kappa of Japan, the sweet-voiced nakk of Estonia, and the bashful nokke who appear only at dusk and dawn in Sweden.

Although (as the brief list above indicates) faeries are known all around the world, nowhere are they quite so varied and populous as they are in the British Isles—which is probably why we find so many of them in English literature. Faeries can be found in many of the courtly romances of the medieval period, although they're rarely named as such, "faery" being a relatively late term. These ancient stories are filled with faerylike men and women who wield magic, live in enchanted palaces, forge magical weaponry, and bewitch or beguile innocent mortals—such as the Lady of the Lake who gives Arthur his magical sword, Excalibur. The tales of the King Arthur and his court are particularly rife with faerylike beings, especially in the Welsh and Breton tradi-tions, as are the splendid *Lays* of Marie de France, written for the English court sometime around the twelfth century. In the fourteenth century, the Wife of Bath in Chaucer's *Canterbury Tales* speaks wistfully of an elf queen and her merry court in the old days of King Arthur, when "al was this land fulfild of fayerye"—as opposed to the Wife of Bath's own time, when faeries were rarely seen.

A fifteenth century French epic romance called *Huon of*

Bordeaux was popular among English readers. This sprightly story of King Oberon, Queen Mab, and assorted knights of the faery court is notable for providing inspiration for the faery plays of William Shakespeare. Shakespeare seems to have been well versed in traditional English faery lore, for he borrowed liberally from this tradition to create the faeries who quarrel, scheme, and cavort in *A Midsummer Night's Dream* and *The Tempest*. Along with "Queen Mab" from Mercutio's famous speech in *Romeo and Juliet*, these are the best known and most influential faeries in all English literature—which is why diminutive faeries "no bigger than an agate-stone on the fore-finger of an alderman" are better known today than their human-sized cousins found in many older stories. Faeries are also the subject, of course, of Edmund Spenser's epic poem, *The Faerie Queene*, written in the late sixteenth century, although Spenser's faery court owes more to Italian romances than to homegrown English faery legends.

In the seventeenth century, faeries inspired Michael Drayton's *Nymphidia, the Court of Fayre*, a satirical work featuring King Oberon, Queen Mab, and a hapless knight named Pigwiggen. A series of poems in Robert Herrick's *Hesperides* also features King Oberon, and also has a satirical edge, but this is a darker, more sensual look at Faeryland than Drayton's. In the eighteenth century, the faeries appear in Alexander Pope's arch tale, *The Rape of the Lock*, and also, covertly, in *Gulliver's Travels*, the great satire by Jonathan Swift, for Swift used many elements of faery lore to create his tiny Lilliputians.

It was in this same century that Bishop Thomas Percy

began to collect old English folk ballads, which he published in an influential volume called *Reliques of Ancient English Poetry*. Without Percy's labors, many old poems and ballads might have been lost forever—he rescued one important manuscript from maids who were using it to light a fire. Percy's work had a notable influence on the writers of the German Romantic movement, who in turn influenced such English Romantics as Samuel Taylor Coleridge, Robert Southey, Percy Bysshe Shelley, and John Keats. All of these writers wrote faery poems, but the ones that are best known today are Keats's evocative "Lamia" and "La Belle Dame Sans Merci." By the end of the eighteenth century, many writers were publishing tales and poems about the faeries, including Tom Moore, Thomas Hood, Allan Cunningham, and especially James Hogg. Known as "the Ettrick Shepherd," Hogg was a working shepherd for most of his life, as well as a writer of stories and poems that drew upon Scottish legends.

James Hogg's good friend Sir Walter Scott was another writer who'd been greatly inspired by the ballad collections of Bishop Thomas Percy. Scott's fiction is permeated with the faery lore of his native Scotland, and he was an influential figure in the early nineteenth-century folklore movement. Scott's *Minstrelsy of the Scottish Border* preserved such important faery ballads such as "Thomas the Rhymer" and "Tam Lin," and did much to educate readers about the value of Scotland's folk heritage. In addition, Scott gathered around him a group of poets and antiquarians determined to preserve the old country tales of a nation that was rapidly urbanizing. Scott was fond of faery lore in particular, for he'd believed in faeries in his youth, and never entirely lost faith in "things invisible to mortal sight."

Partially due to Scott's influence, two extensive volumes of faery lore appeared in the early nineteenth century: Thomas Keightley's *The Fairy Mythology* and Thomas Crofton Croker's *Fairy Legends and Traditions of the South of Ireland*. They proved to be enormously popular and kicked off an explosion of folklore books by Reverend Sabine Baring-Gould, Anna Eliza Bray, Joseph Jacobs, and many others. Folklore was still a new field back then—the name itself wasn't coined until 1846—and these publications generated much talk and excitement among Victorian writers and artists. At the same time, the magical tales and poems of the folklore-loving German Romantic writers (Johann Wolfgang von Goethe, Ludwig Tieck, Novalis, etc.) frequently appeared in English magazines of the period. One German story in particular captivated Victorian readers— *Undine* by Baron de la Motte Fouqué, about a water nymph's love for a mortal knight and her attempt to gain an immortal soul. *Undine* inspired a large number of subsequent stories, paintings, and dramatic productions about doomed faery lovers of various kinds (including, over in Denmark, Hans Christian Andersen's *The Little Mermaid*). Such stories were particularly appealing to readers interested in matters of the occult—which was a large group, once the Spiritualist movement crossed the sea from America and took England by storm. These various influences came together to create a widespread interest in the faery race that was unprecedented. At no other time in British history have the faeries been so popular among all types of people, from the working class to the aristocracy, and at no other time have they been so prevalent in all forms of contemporary art.

In visual art, following in the footsteps of the eighteenth-century painters Henry Fuseli and William Blake,[8] artists such as Joseph Noël Paton, John Anster Fitzgerald, Richard Dadd, Richard Doyle, Daniel Maclise, Thomas Heatherly, Eleanor Fortescue-Brickdale, and many, many others created an entire genre of Victorian faery paintings, which were hung in prestigious galleries and Royal Academy exhibitions. These were paintings for adults, not children. John Anster Fitzgerald's faery imagery, for instance, was often dark and hallucinatory, full of references to opium pipes and opium medicines.[9] Richard Dadd's obsessively detailed faery paintings were created in a mental hospital where Dadd was incarcerated after he lost his reason and killed his father. Many faery paintings were distinctly salacious, such as Sir Joseph Noël Paton's huge canvases of luscious faery maidens in various states of undress. Faeries enabled Victorian painters to explore the subject of sexuality during the very years when that subject was most repressed in polite society. Paintings of the nude were deemed acceptable so long as those nudes sported faery wings.

The passion for faeries among Victorian adults must also be viewed in light of the rapid changes wrought by the Industrial Revolution, as Britain moved from the rhythms of its rural past toward the mechanized future. With factories and suburban blight transforming huge tracts of English countryside, faery paintings and stories were rich in nostalgia for a vanishing way of life. In particular, the art of the Pre-Raphaelite Brotherhood—who depicted scenes from legend and myth—promoted a dreamy medievalism and the aesthetics of fine craftsmanship to counter what they saw as a soulless new world created by modern forms of mass production. ("For every locomotive they build," vowed artist Edward Burne-Jones, "I shall paint another angel.") The Arts and Crafts movement, which grew out of Pre-Raphaelitism, embraced folklore and faeries to such a degree that by the end of the nineteenth century, faeries could be found in middle-class homes in every form of decorative arts: wallpaper, draperies, ceramics, stained glass, metalwork, and so on. Advances in printing methods allowed the production of lavishly illustrated fairy tale books,[10] ostensibly aimed at children but with production values calculated to please adults (and the growing breed of book collectors). Arthur Rackham, Edmund Dulac, Warwick Goble, the Robinson brothers, Jessie M. King, and numerous others produced wonderful faery pictures for these volumes. Jessie M. King, like William Blake before her, was an artist who passionately believed in the faeries. Her lovely illustrations were based, she said, on visions seen with her "third eye."

In the pretelevision, precinema world of the Victorians, theater, ballet, and opera had greater importance as forms of popular entertainment than they enjoy today, as well as a greater influence on the visual and literary arts. In the 1830s, the new Romantic ballet (as opposed to formal, classical ballet) thrilled large audiences in London with productions that dramatized tales of love between mortals and faery spirits. Aided by innovations in "point work" (dancing on the points of one's toes) and improvements in theater gaslighting techniques, sumptuous faerylands were created in hit productions such as *La Sylphide*, the tragic story of a mortal man in love with an elfin maid. In the theater, faery plays were staged with stunningly elaborate special effects, each new production striving to be even more spectacular than the last.

Faery music was another popular phenomenon, much of it imported from Germany, such as Weber's faery opera *Oberon*, Hoffman's *Ondine* (based on Fouqué's *Undine*), Wagner's *Die Feen* (The Faeries), and Mendelssohn's overture for *A Midsummer Night's Dream*. Faery music for the harp was composed and performed by charismatic musicians as popular then as pop stars are now, and young women swooned and followed their favorite harpists from concert to concert. Magical music and dance reached its height in the works of Tchaikovsky, the brilliant Russian composer who took London—indeed, all of Europe—by storm. The popularity of his fairy tale ballets (*Swan Lake*, *The Sleeping Beauty*, and *The Nutcracker*) fueled the Victorian public's love of all things magical and fey.

In literature—as in art, theater, and ballet—the faeries made their presence known, turning up in numerous books written during the Victorian and Edwardian years. Some of these works were for adult readers, such as Anne Thackaray Ritchie's *Fairy Tales for Grown-ups*, the Arthurian poems of Lord Tennyson and William Morris, and (at the turn of the century) the remarkable faery poetry of "Celtic Twilight" writers such as William Sharp (writing as Fiona Macleod) and William Butler Yeats. But one of the major shifts we see in faery literature from the nineteenth century onward is that more and more of it was published in books intended for small children.

The Victorians romanticized the very idea of "childhood" to a degree never seen before; earlier, childhood had not been viewed as something quite so separate from adult life. Children, according to this earlier view, came into the world in sin and had to be strictly civilized into God-fearing members of society. By Victorian times, this belief was changing to one in which children were inherently innocent rather than inherently sinful, and childhood became a special Golden Age, a time of fanciful play and exploration before the burdens of adulthood were assumed. Mothers were encouraged to have a more doting attitude toward their little ones (following the example of Queen Victoria herself), and this, combined with the rising wealth of the Victorian middle class, led to an explosion in the market for children's books.

Children's fiction in the previous century had been diabolically dreary, consisting primarily of pious, tedious books of moral instruction. But by the nineteenth century, European fairy tale collections from the Brothers Grimm and Hans Christian Andersen were proving popular with English children and their parents. Publishers, editors, and writers took note, and soon homegrown volumes of magical tales set in the British Isles appeared, including tales inspired by faery lore, though toned down and de-sexed for younger readers. In addition to retelling traditional tales, writers created new faery stories for children, using the tropes of folklore in charming and innovative ways. These tales include John Ruskin's *The King of the Golden River*, Charlotte Yonge's *The History of Tom Thumb*, Christina Rossetti's extraordinary poem *Goblin Market*, Charles Kingsley's *The Water Babies*, Jean Ingelow's *Mopsa the Fairy*, George Macdonald's *The Princess and the Goblin*, Rudyard Kipling's *Puck of Pook's Hill*, and J. M. Barrie's *Peter Pan in Kensington Garden*, to name just a few.

In his excellent book *Victorian Fairy Tales*, folklorist Jack Zipes divides the magical children's fiction published from 1860 onward into two basic types: conventional stories and stories written in a utopian mode. Although there were good fantasy tales of the conventional type, such as the faery stories of Jean Ingelow and the ghost stories of Mary Louisa Molesworth, many others were forgettable confections full of twinkly faeries with butterfly wings and good little boys and girls who caused no disturbance to the status quo. Utopian fantasies, by contrast, demonstrated "a profound belief in the power of the imagination as a potent force"[11] to change English society. George Macdonald, Lewis Carroll, Oscar Wilde, Lawrence Housman, Ford Madox Ford, Edith Nesbit (in her later works), and many other fine writers created magical tales that were archly critical of Victorian life, promoting the possibility of a better society. The prevalence of utopian fantasy is explained by looking at the context of the culture that produced it—a society in the grip of great upheaval due to rapid industrialization. Faeries flittered across London stages and nested in bucolic scenes on gallery walls, but the city streets outside were a long way from Never-Never Land, crowded as they were with beggars, cripples, prostitutes (many of them children), and with homeless, desperate men and women displaced by the new economy.

While the upper classes charmed themselves with faery books and dancing nymphs, and clapped to bring Tinkerbell back to life, in the lower classes, both urban and rural, faeries remained a different matter altogether. Rather than the delicate winged maidens depicted by painters and ballet dancers, these were the fearsome creatures of the still-living oral tradition. Throughout the nineteenth century, the British newspapers reported cases of faery sightings, curses, and abductions. The most famous of these incidents occurred as late as 1895, and riveted newspaper readers all across the British Isles. This was the murder of Bridget Cleary, a spirited young woman in Ireland who was killed by her husband, family, and neighbors because they thought she was a faery changeling. Bridget Cleary had fallen gravely ill, and the family had consulted a "faery doctor." He claimed the young woman had been abducted and taken under a faery hill, and that the sickly creature in her bed was a faery changeling in disguise. The doctor devised several ordeals designed to make the changeling reveal itself—ordeals that soon grew so extreme that poor Bridget died. Convinced it was a faery he had killed, Bridget's husband then went to the faery fort to wait for his "real" wife to ride out seated on a milk-white horse. Bridget's disappearance was soon noted, the body found, the horrible crime brought to light, and Michael and the faery doctor and several others involved were prosecuted for murder. Although this was the most flamboyant case of changeling murder in the Victorian press, sadly it was not the only account of brutal mistreatment of those deemed to be faeries. Usually the poor victims were children born with physical deformities or struck by sudden wasting illnesses. It wasn't until the twentieth century that reports of faery abductions began to dwindle—when reports of abductions by aliens began to take their place.

The last major faery encounter reported widely by the British press took place in the tranquil countryside of Yorkshire in 1917, when Elsie Wright, sixteen years old, and Frances Griffith, her ten-year-old cousin, contrived to take photographs of faeries at play in their Cottingley garden. Elsie's mother had the photographs sent to Edward Gardner, head of the Theosophical Society, who then passed them on to Sir Arthur Conan Doyle (the creator of Sherlock Holmes).[12] Although the photographs are rather unconvincing by today's standards, professionals at the time could find no evidence of photographic doctoring. The pictures, championed by Conan Doyle, caused an absolute sensation and brought the faery craze well into the twentieth century. Only when Elsie and Frances were old ladies in the 1980s did they admit that the Cottingley faeries were actually paper cutouts held in place by hat pins. Even so, their deathbed statements on the subject were more ambiguous, implying that the faeries, if not the photographs, had been real after all.

In her fascinating book *Strange and Secret Peoples: Fairies and Victorian Consciousness,* Carol G. Silver points out that the Cottingley incident, despite briefly reviving interest in the faeries, was actually one of the factors that ended the Golden Age of faery art and literature. "Ironically," she says, "the photographs, the ostensible proof of the actual existence of the fairies, deprived the elfin people of their grandeur and their stature. . . . The theories that Gardner formulated to explain the fairies' nature and function reduced them to the intelligence level of household pets and the size of insects."

In addition to this, the massive popularity that the faeries had enjoyed throughout the nineteenth century ensured that they'd be branded old-fashioned by the generations that immediately followed. Those who'd survived the hard trials of World War I had little interest in the faux-medievalism and faeries of their grandparents' day. And yet, it is interesting to note that one of the most popular art prints of the war era depicted a simple country boy playing a pipe and surrounded by faeries. This was *The Piper of Dreams*, a painting by the Anglo-Italian artist Estella Canziani—an image as ubiquitous in England then as Monet's water lilies are now. Canziani's gentle, forgotten faery picture once rivaled William Holman Hunt's *The Light of the World* in popularity, and was said to be a favorite of English soldiers in the trenches of World War I.

During the middle years of the twentieth century, the faeries seemed to go underground, rarely leaving the Twilight Realm to interact with the world of men—except to appear in a sugar-sweet guise in children's books and Disney cartoons. One could find them if one looked hard enough—in Ireland, for instance, in the fiction of James Stephens and Lord Dunsany. But in general, it was not until an Oxford don named J.R.R. Tolkien wrote about elves in a place called Middle Earth that faeries came back to popular art in any numbers. And then they came with a vengeance.

Professor Tolkien was a scholar of folklore, myth, and Old English language and literature, so when he created the elves of *The Hobbit* and *The Lord of the Rings*, he knew what he was doing. He rescued the elves from Disney cartoons and saccharine fables, and restored their height, grandeur, danger, power, and unearthly beauty. Although they were written and published some years earlier, it was not until the 1970s that Tolkien's books dominated the best-seller lists and became part of British and American popular culture. This in turn created an enormous interest in all things magical, wondrous, and fey. Suddenly there were faeries, dragons, unicorns, mermaids, and wizards everywhere. People started seeking out folklore texts, and teaching themselves to speak Elvish. "What is the reason for this preoccupation?" asked Alison Lurie in an article for *The New York Review of Books*. "Possibly it is a byproduct of the overly material and commercial world we live in: the result of an imaginatively deprived childhood."[13]

Lurie believed that college students of the era were embracing Tolkien and folklore with such passion because they had been raised on the thin gruel of television and Walt Disney cartoons instead of the great classics of children's literature. Having been imaginatively deprived in youth, she argued, they had now taken "possession of a fantasy world that should have been theirs at eight or ten, with the intellectual enthusiasm, the romantic eagerness—and the purchasing power—of eighteen and twenty." While this was undoubtedly true of some readers, I find it an unsatisfactory explanation overall, for there were many other readers (and I was among them) who *had* read classic children's literature when young and *had* embraced classic fantasy worlds at ages eight and ten. What Tolkien did was to prove to us that we needn't give up these worlds at age eighteen— or at twenty-eight or eighty-eight, for that matter. Back in the 1970s, this was a radical notion. Tolkien dismissed the post-Victorian idea that fantasy was fit only for children, reaching back to an older adult fantasy tradition running from *Beowulf* to William Morris. He opened a door to Fäerie, and readers discovered this door was not child-sized after all, but tall and wide, leading to lands one could spend a lifetime wandering in.

In the mid-1970s, another book lured adult readers into the Twilight Realm. This was *Faeries*, an international bestseller by the British artists Alan Lee and Brian Froud—a sequel, of sorts, to a book called *Gnomes* by the Dutch artist Wil Huygen. But whereas *Gnomes* depicted cheerful little creatures who had little in common with the dour, clever, metal-working gnomes of the European folk tradition, *Faeries* was deeply rooted in traditional faery lore. Here, in all their beautiful, horrible glory, were the faeries of old British legends: gorgeous and grotesque (often at the same time), creatures of ivy, oak, and stone, born out of the British landscape, as potent and wild as a force of nature. Lee and Froud had taken inspiration from Victorian faery paintings and updated the tradition for a new generation. *Faeries*, in turn, would go on to inspire young artists in the years ahead—indeed, it's rare to find faery art today (or faeries in film, or faery fiction) that doesn't owe a debt, to some degree, to this influential book.

From the mid-1970s onward, numerous other books on

faery lore appeared, including several "field guides," and the peerless folklore studies of Katherine Briggs. In fiction, the great success of *The Lord of the Rings* helped to establish an entire new publishing genre of fantasy fiction for adult readers; as a result, a new generation of writers has turned to folklore and myth for inspiration, in North America as well as in England.[14] Faeries have found their way into a number of their books, some of which are set in days gone past or in the land of Fäerie, and some of which are urban tales of faeries in the modern world. John Crowley, for example, in his brilliant novel *Little, Big,* draws on a host of Victorian ideas about the faeries to create a modern faery tale set in rural and urban New York. Ellen Kushner's award-winning *Thomas the Rhymer* follows a figure from an old Scottish ballad into the halls of the Faery Queen. Patricia A. McKillip's lyrical *Winter Rose* takes a slantwise look at the ballad of Tam Lin, as do Pamela Dean's *Tam Lin* and Diana Wynne Jones's *Fire and Hemlock*. Lisa Goldstein's *Strange Devices of the Sun and Moon* finds faeries among the playwrights of Elizabethan London, while Poul Andersen's *A Midsummer Tempest* and Sarah A. Hoyt's *Ill Met by Moonlight* revisit the faeries of William Shakespeare. Emma Bull's groundbreaking *War for the Oaks* brings faeries to the 1980s Minneapolis music scene, and Charles de Lint's *Jack of Kinrowan* brings them to urban Canada. Holly Black's *Tithe* discovers a faery changeling living on the Jersey shore, while Midori Snyder's *Hannah's Garden* finds a faery fiddler in an Irish bar in the Midwest. These are just a few of the many fine faery novels available in the fantasy genre. Outside the genre, Sylvia Townsend Warner published adult faery stories in *The New Yorker,* which were subsequently reprinted in her sparkling collection *Kingdoms of Elfin.* Numerous works of children's fiction have also been inspired by the faeries, such as *The Folk Keeper* by Franny Billingsley, *The Faery Flag* by Jane Yolen, and the Newbery Honor books *The Moorchild* by Eloise McGraw and *The Perilous Gard* by Elizabeth Marie Pope. All are highly recommended. (See the longer list at the back of this book for further recommendations.)

In visual art, the English painter Brian Froud has been exploring Fäerie for over twenty-five years, beginning with the publication of *Faeries* and continuing on through more recent publications such as *Good Faeries/Bad Faeries, Lady Cottington's Fairy Album,* and *The Runes of Elfland.* As a result, he's probably the best known "faery artist" in the world today. Among the other contemporary artists who have dared to depict these tricksy, elusive creatures are painters Charles Vess, Dennis Nolan, Lauren Mills, Ruth Sanderson, Gary Lippincott, Marja Lee Kruÿt, Virginia Lee, Hazel Brown, Tony DiTerlizzi, Michael Hague, and Amy Brown; photographers Anne Geddes, Suza Scalora, and Rowan Gabrielle; and sculptor/doll-makers Wendy Froud, Lisa Lichtenfels, and Beckie Kravetz, to name just a few. The revival of interest in Victorian faery art led to an important traveling exhibition curated by the University of Iowa and the Royal Academy of London in 1997; in 2002, Abbaye de Daoulas in Brittany presented an extensive exhibition of faery art from twelfth-century manuscripts right up to the present day. I recommend the following related art books: *Victorian Fairy Painters* with text by Jeremy Maas and others; *Fairies in Victorian Painting* by Christopher Wood; and *Fées, elfes, dragons, and autres créatures de royaumes de féerie* (Faeries, elves, dragons, and other creatures of the faery realm), edited by Michel Le Bris and Claudine Glot.[15]

In film, faeries are the subject of two movies inspired by the Cottingley photographs: *A Fairy Tale* and *Photographing Fairies* (based on the novel by Steve Szilagyi). Faery-type creatures can also be found in two children's films by Jim Henson, *The Dark Crystal* and *Labyrinth*, both of them designed by Brian Froud. "Faery fashions" have appeared in New York shop windows, on Paris runways, and in an illustrated book: *Fairie-Ality: The Fashion Collection* by David Ellwand, Eugenie Bird, and David Downton. Traditional faery ballads from the British Isles, Brittany, and Scandinavia have been recorded by many folk bands and musicians, including Steeleye Span, Pentangle, Fairport Convention, Kornog, Martin Carthy, Robin Williamson, Solas, Connemarra, Garmarna, Kerstin Blodig, and Loreena McKennitt. Elizabeth Jane Baldry has recorded Victorian faery music for the harp on *A Wild and Dreamlike Strain*, and Áine Minogue's *The Twilight Realm* is a lovely CD of music inspired by traditional faery lore. The faeries have also appeared in pop music, in songs by musicians and bands such as Donovan, Queen, The Waterboys, and Tori Amos.

In his famous poem "The Horns of Elfland," Tennyson wrote that even the echoes of elfin bugles are growing faint and dying away, as the faeries disappear from the woods and fields, chased away by modern life. This was a favorite theme of the Victorians, who believed that the faeries were taking their leave of us, and that magic would soon vanish from the world forever. Fortunately, as far as I can see, the Victorians were dead wrong. The British Isles and other parts of the world are still thickly populated by the elfin tribes, if the present revival of faeries in popular culture is any indication. In North America, faeries are everywhere— in books and paintings, on T-shirts and teacups, in children's toy shops, in art museums, and flying through the airwaves. If Tennyson's elfin bugles have dimmed . . . well, never mind. The faeries play electric bagpipes now, and the writers in this book have found them in some unexpected haunts indeed.

Instead of Tennyson, I'm more inclined to listen to the poet William Butler Yeats, who knew a thing or two about the faeries, for he believed in them all his life. He said that "you can not lift your hand without influencing and being influenced by hordes of them." They're everywhere. And now that you've brought them into your house inside the pages of this book, you're going to have a devil of a time getting rid of them, I'm afraid.

There's a famous story of a Scottish house faery who proved to be so terribly annoying that the family in the house tried and tried to make him leave, to no avail. Finally there was no help for it. The family packed to go themselves. But as they drove down the road, their worldly goods strapped to the old farm cart, they noticed the faery perched on top, saying, "Ah, but it's a fine day to be moving!" And so they sighed and went back home, knowing they were stuck

with him for good. The faery haunts that cottage and their descendants to this day.

So it is with faeries in literature and art. Faery stories go in and out of fashion. But just when you think they're gone for good, cast out by book and art critics who insist we move on to weightier matters, the faeries are still there, grinning, saying, "Ah, it's a fine day to be moving!"—determined to move right along with us and be a part of whatever the future has in store.

∾

NOTES

[1] Robert Kirk, *The Secret Commonwealth of Elves, Fauns and Fairies*, 1893.

[2] Spiritualism was a practice in which "spirit mediums" provided contact with the spirits of the dead and with supernatural creatures. The movement was started in America by the Fox sisters in 1848, who claimed to communicate with the dead through mysterious knocks upon a table. Soon "table-turning" parties were all the rage in every class of English society, right up to the royal court. Spiritualist societies sponsored lecture tours, opened reading rooms, and published newspapers, and popular spirit mediums developed huge followings.

[3] Theosophy was a Spiritualist and philosophical movement founded by Madame Blavatsky at the end of the nineteenth century. Many prominent Theosophists believed in faeries.

[4] Charles W. Leadbeater, *The Hidden Side of Things*, 1913

[5] Sir Arthur Conan Doyle, *The Coming of the Fairies*, 1922.

[6] From "Some Remarks about the Spirits of Nature," published in *The Occult Review*, 1911.

[7] Katherine Briggs, *The Vanishing People: Fairy Lore and Legends*, 1978.

[8] Painter and poet William Blake firmly believed in faeries, and once wrote about witnessing a faery funeral.

[9] Opium derivatives like laudanum, called "the aspirin of the nineteenth century," were available without prescription in Victorian England, and were commonly used for insomnia, headaches, and "women's troubles." It may be no accident that the Victorians' obsession with fairies and Spiritualism occurred during the same span of years when casual opium use was widespread.

[10] "Fairy tale" is a term commonly used today to mean stories like "Snow White," "Beauty and the Beast," "Little Red Riding Hood," et cetera, regardless of whether they contain faeries or not. I am using the standard spelling of the term here, and reserving "faery tales" for stories specifically about the faery folk.

[11] Jack Zipes, *Victorian Fairy Tales*, 1987.

[12] Sir Arthur Conan Doyle was the son of the faery painter Charles Doyle who, like Richard Dadd, had been confined to an insane asylum and whose imagery came from his personal visions. The faery painter Richard Doyle, by all accounts a sane, sweet-tempered man, was Arthur Conan Doyle's uncle.

[13] Alison Lurie's "Braking for Elves" was first published in *The New York Review of Books* (March 8, 1979) and reprinted in her excellent 1990 book *Don't Tell the Grown-ups: Why Kids Love the Books They Do*.

[14] Some claim that North America has no faeries, which is stuff and nonsense. What it has is a melting pot of faeries and stories carried over by numerous immigrant groups, transplanted to new soil and bearing fruit both familiar and strange. Mixed into this pot are Native American tales from a variety of tribal traditions—including tales about magical little people who live under the hills or deep in the woods, and are sometimes good and sometimes bad, and who tend to play tricks on human beings—faeries, in other words, in everything but name.

[15] You needn't go to France to find this book—copies can be mail-ordered internationally through www.amazon.fr.

The Boys of Goose Hill

Charles de Lint

There's a place called Goose Hill
    and the boys that live there
are such tricksters and foxes
    that none can compare.
Malkin's their mother
    and she's the White Rose of May,
and Mabon's their father
    —tally-ho and away!

When the kettle boils o'er,
    the wheels fall from your cart,
you're pinched from your sleep,
    or the fire won't start,
when the hens won't lay eggs,
    or there's knots in your hair,
be sure that the boys
    of Goose Hill have been there.

They're the bees in the heather
that call up the spring,
when the bonfires blaze
from every stone ring;
they're teasing and canny,
though they mean no great ill,
those Pucks of the midden:
the boys of Goose Hill.

They're the wind in the field
when the harvesters come
and the corn dollys dance
to the songs that they've sung;
there's a hare on the slopes
and a stag higher still
and a wren harping tunes
for the boys of Goose Hill.

Now the boys of Goose Hill
they know all the old tunes,
they can call up a mist,
they can drink down the moon;
take a hag-stone for luck
and a dram for the cold,
turn your coat inside out
if you want your own road.

Here's a health to the horn
that the old man once wore,

and the May, bonny May,
  and the last sheaf of corn.
Here's a health to the Green Man
  and a health to the Moon,
and to the boys of Goose Hill
  that call up the tune.

Charles de Lint is a writer, musician, and folklorist who was born in the Netherlands and now lives in Ottawa, Canada, with his wife, MaryAnn Harris, an artist and musician. *Spirits in the Wires*, *Seven Wild Sisters*, *Waifs and Strays*, *The Blue Girl*, and *Quicksilver and Shadow* are the most recent of his many novels, illustrated novellas, and story collections. The second and third books were named World Fantasy Award finalists. He is also the author of *A Circle of Cats*, a children's picture book illustrated by Charles Vess, and of the faery novels *Jack of Kinrowan*, *The Little Country*, and *The Wild Wood*.

For more information about his work, visit his Web site at www.charlesdelint.com

Author's Note

I love playing music as much as I do writing, and occasionally run across a great melody that doesn't happen to have lyrics I feel like singing. Such was the case with "The Meet Was at Matthews," a traditional Irish song I first heard on a 1979 album by the Cork singer Jimmy Crowley. It has a mesmerizing melody, but the lyrics detail an afternoon of hunting the hare. I decided I'd rather sing about a rowdy bunch of fairies, which is how I ended up getting to meet the Boys of Goose Hill.

CATNYP

Delia Sherman

The story I'm about to tell is a fairy story. It's got genuine fairies in it, and it's about how humans get catapulted into adventure through breaking a fairy law. The difference is that in fairy tales, the humans don't always know what law they're breaking or why.

I should have known better. I did know better. I grew up with the Folk. They stole me when I was just a few weeks old and left one of their own in my bassinet for my parents to raise. So I'm kind of bicultural, human and fairy. A changeling, in fact.

My story takes place in New York City. Not the one in the "I ♥ New York" posters, but the one that exists beside it, in the walls and crawlspaces and all the little pockets and passages of its infrastructure. Call it New York Between. That's what I call it. The Folk don't call it anything—they simply live there. Me they call Neef, which was okay when I was a kid, but now I'm not a kid anymore, I wish they'd picked something a little less lame.

So anyway, once upon a time, not all that long ago, I was sitting in the FolkXChange with Snowbell and Fleet. We were talking about men. Actually, Fleet, who'd just been dumped by the selkie she'd been dating, was talking about men, and Snowbell and I were listening. Snowbell is a swan maiden. Fleet's a changeling, like me. The FolkXChange is an open kind of place. Sometimes you even see vampires there.

Anyway, there we are, drinking nectar and eating fairy cakes and listening to Fleet carry on about her selkie. Her ex-selkie. "We'd been having this fight," Fleet was saying, "about how I didn't understand the stresses of being a shapechanger, and I just said if he wanted me to understand so bad, maybe he should lend me his sealskin, and he. . . ."

Snowbell made a noise that was a lot more swan than maiden. Fleet shook her black braids forward over the cinnamon oval of her face. "It was all his fault," she muttered. "He started it. He was all, 'You're just human, you don't know what it's like, you haven't got any magic.' And I kind of lost it."

I snorted. "You can say that again. How could you be so dumb?"

Fleet sighed. "Love, I guess. It makes you do stupid things."

"Oh. Love. Like you know anything about love," I said.

"I know more about it than you do," Fleet countered. "I've had lots of boyfriends. When was *your* last date, huh?"

She had me there. Having a love life is hard for a changeling. There aren't that many Folk a girl can date. A lot of them are as ugly as a backed-up sewer and would rather take you apart than out dancing. The beautiful ones know how to have fun, but they can be kind of temperamental. And changelings don't date changelings. We hang out together, we talk things over, we're friends, but we don't date. I mean, who'd go out with a human being when there are elves around?

Snowbell stretched out her long, white neck and gave her slender shoulders a swanny little ripple. "You will stop quarreling," she said. "It is not interesting. Neither of you knows anything of love. You are human. You are too frail to bear the intensity of true love. If you felt for one moment the heat of desire the least of the Folk feels, you would turn black and crumble, like toast."

"Dog doo," I said. Fleet stopped sniveling. "You know, I've heard that line before, and to be perfectly honest, I've never seen the slightest proof of it. It looks to me like we humans are the ones who do all the loving around here. All you guys do is eat it up with a spoon."

Snowbell isn't very big. She's all white skin and floaty hair and big, black eyes, wistful and delicate as a paper flower. But she's got a touchy temper and a mean bite. I thought for a minute she was going to go for me, but she laughed instead.

"I have an idea," she said. "You will try to prove that humans know more of love than the Folk."

"Why?" I asked.

"Because you will discover that I am right, and I look forward to watching you lose."

"And what happens if I do?"

"The usual, I think. Service for a year and a day. It's been ages since I had a human servant."

"And if I win?"

"You won't. But I'll give you a boon if you do. Whatever you like. We'll put it to the Genius of Central Park at the Solstice Rave." She got to her feet in a graceful surge and preened her tight black sweater. "Good luck."

Before I could tell her what she could do with her dumb bet, she was out the door. "You're in deep trouble, girl-friend," Fleet said.

"Not even. All I have to do is avoid her for a while and she'll forget all about it. I never said I accepted or anything."

Fleet just gave me a look. "Come *on*, girl. You make the rules around here? I don't think so. If you say you're not playing, she'll just collect anyway, and you know it."

Yeah. I knew it. "You gotta help me, Fleet," I said. "What am I going to do?"

Fleet looked thoughtful. "Well, I guess you could go ask the Genius of the New York Public Library. He knows every-thing, they say."

"Good idea. Thanks, Fleet. You're a peach."

And I walked out of the FolkXChange and took the Betweenways to the New York Public Library to ask the Genius about love.

The proper term is *genius loci*—the guardian of the place. There are a bunch of them, and they're the most New York of all New York Folk. A building or a park or even a street is around long enough, with people loving it and thinking it's important, and a genius appears—Poof! Like magic. The Genius of the New York Public Library isn't as old as the Genius of Broadway or as powerful as the Genius of Central Park. But he's pretty impressive anyway.

The Genius of the NYPL speaks every language he's got a book written in, and he knows everything that's in the library, from agriculture to zoology. He can (and will) go on endlessly about any subject. He's kind of cute, in a lanky, long-haired, short-sighted way, and he rustles pleasantly when he moves.

"Love," he said thoughtfully. "A rich subject. A thorny subject. May I inquire why you are choosing to research it here?"

"I've got this bet with a swan maiden," I said. "I have to prove that humans know more about love than the Folk do."

He sighed. "And how do you propose to go about winning this, er, bet?"

"I don't really know," I confessed. "I thought I'd ask you to help me."

He took off his huge, square spectacles and polished them with a white handkerchief. "*Primus*," he said dryly, "I am no expert on the subject of human love, being myself a supernatural being. *Secundus*, I am not a pedagogue. I am simply a repository of admittedly human knowledge and opinion. In short, I do not answer questions. My books do."

"Oh." This was going to be more complicated than I'd hoped. "Well then, I guess I'll read a few books about it."

The Genius replaced his glasses. "Reading is good," he said. "'Histories make men wise; poets, witty; the mathematics, subtle; natural philosophy, deep; moral, grave; logic and rhetoric, able to contend.'" He fixed me with a bright, expectant look, like a pigeon waiting for a crumb. I nodded like I knew what he was talking about, but you can't fool a Genius. He sighed. "I was quoting Francis Bacon, child. From the essay 'On Studies.' I recommend it."

"'On Studies.' Bacon. Does that have anything to do with love?"

He turned back to his desk. "In a manner of speaking," he said. "Now. The New York Public Library is open to everyone. But you'll need a card, and you'll need to peruse this list of rules. The rules are very important." He opened one of the quadrillion drawers in his huge desk and pulled out a small cardboard rectangle and a sheet of paper, which he handed to me before dipping a long feather pen into an ornate inkwell. "Name?"

He didn't mean my real name, of course—there's a kind of don't-ask-don't-tell policy on names in New York Between, where names are power. "Neef," I told him, and started to read.

Regulations
for use of the New York Public Library Between
Department of Humanities and Social Sciences
DO NOT

1. Deface or write in a Book
2. Bring food or drink of any kind into the Library
3. Remove any Book from the Library
4. Create a Disturbance
5. Enter the Stacks

"Sir," I said, "I don't quite understand Rule #5. If I can't go into the stacks, how am I supposed to get books?"

He turned his spectacles on me. "Consult CATNYP, of course. One of the library pages will then get it for you. Have you never been in a library before?"

"No."

He smiled, showing small, pointed teeth. "Stay out of the Stacks, child. They're dangerous."

I've lived in New York Between all my life; I know a fairy law when I hear one. I put the rules in my pocket and took my library card, which announced, in beautiful spidery lettering, that one Neef was allowed unlimited reading privileges at the NYPL. Then the Genius blew down a brass tube sticking out of the wall by his desk.

A page popped out of another brass tube and unrolled itself at my feet. I moved back so I wouldn't step on it and greeted it.

"Don't bother," the Genius said. "It's deaf."

Unrolled, the page came up to my waist. It looked like a giant paper doll with a smiley-face inked onto its circular head. "Don't tell me," it said. "You're a changeling, and you want to get in touch with your human heritage. What can I get you? A nice romance? Some pop psych? Or maybe something more challenging? Quantum physics? Sigmund Freud?"

The Genius glared at it. "The page will take you to the Reading Room and introduce you to CATNYP," the Genius said. "Good-bye." And he turned back to his desk.

The page was hard to see when it turned sideways, but I managed to follow it up and around and along the betweenways of the NYPL. We ended up in a room with a handful of changelings in it, sitting in comfy chairs with their noses in open books. It was a nice room, just perfect for reading in: plenty of soft, silver fairy light, little desks to write on if you needed to, and the happy hum of minds concentrating on stuff they were interested in.

"CATNYP's in here," said the page. "Come on."

I followed it into a side room, which was furnished, if you can call it that, with a couple of chairs and a lion on a marble pedestal. The lion's eyes were closed and its paws were stretched out in front of it. It was maybe the size of a big dog, and its fur was a grainy white.

The page tickled the lion between its furry ears. It opened its eyes, which were robin's-egg blue, and stared at us.

"This is CATNYP," the page told me. "It knows what books we have and where they're kept. It's a simple, user-friendly system, designed for you to be able to figure it out by yourself. Give it a little pat when you're done. That puts it to sleep." And it left me there, face to face with CATNYP, which yawned toothily.

Okay. I've dealt with enchanted animals before. You ask them questions, they answer. You just have to ask them the right questions. If I only knew what the right questions were.

Well, that was a place to start. "What should I ask you?" I said.

The lion blinked at me. "Title, Author, Subject, Keyword."

This was not very clear, but then, magic animals aren't supposed to be clear. I thought for a while. "Subject, I guess. Love."

The lion shut its eyes and seemed to go to sleep again. I tickled it between the ears, experimentally, which produced nothing more helpful than a slight, irritated growl. I was about to go out and tackle the page when the lion opened its eyes again. "There are 28,073 entries under Love," it informed me.

"Ooo-kay," I said. "How about Romance?"

"13,298 entries," CATNYP said. "Would you like some search tips?"

Well, that was a little more user-friendly. I smiled into its eyes. "Yes. Please."

"Limit your search," CATNYP suggested.

"Say what?"

CATNYP sighed. "Love Poems. Divine Love. Love and Women . . ."

"Oh. Thank you. It's hard to ask questions when you don't know what you're asking, you know?"

CATNYP had no answer to that, unless you counted a twitch of its tufted tail.

"Okay," I said, half to myself. "What I want to find out is—"

"You're never going to get anywhere like that," said a voice behind me. It was a nice voice, smooth and deep as double chocolate ice cream. I turned around and saw it belonged to a guy, maybe a little older than me, brown eyes and brown hair, built like an athlete, and almost too good looking to be human. He was dressed in the changeling uniform of jeans and T-shirt stolen from Salvation Army bins, but it didn't matter. He looked like a prince in disguise as a swineherd, or (because this was twenty-first century New York and not nineteenth century Germany) like a rich boy pretending to be a street person.

"What are you staring at?" he said. "Did I cut myself shaving?"

This wasn't a question I felt like answering, so I turned back to the lion. It yawned and settled its chin on its paws.

"Don't go to sleep on me here," I said. "I haven't found a book yet!"

"Here," the changeling said. "Let me help you."

In one way, it was easier, since he knew how to ask the right questions. In another, it was just about the most embarrassing thing in the world to have to tell the cutest human guy I'd ever seen that I was searching for books about love. Once I got it straightened out that I wasn't looking for *The Joy of Sex*, though, it got better.

The way it worked was, you gave CATNYP your subject, properly limited, and CATNYP gave you mice. They hopped out of its mouth and lined up on the pedestal and gave you their titles, authors, and publication information, one after another, in tiny, clear voices.

The mice the handsome changeling had pulled up for me represented a couple of anthologies of love poetry, a couple of scientific-sounding studies, and something called *Your Love Signs*.

"How many can I choose?" I asked.

"The pages will only bring you two volumes at a time."

I grabbed two mice at random. They snuggled cozily into my fingers. "What if I want the others later?"

"They'll come if you call them by title and author."

"Who designed this system anyway?"

The guy shrugged. "Nobody designed it—it just happened. Typical fairy magic."

"Yeah. Well, thanks for the help."

"You're not home free yet. You have to get a page. I'm Byron, by the way."

"And I'm Neef."

I was also in love. I was ready to can my mice and my bet with Snowbell and ask him if he'd like to cut out for a nice, long walk in Central Park. But he was already heading toward the back of the Reading Room, where there was a long wooden counter. It had a couple of books and a scattering of corn on it, and a small stack of pages.

Byron peeled a page from the stack and skimmed it across the counter. The page shook itself with an irritable rustle, chose a kernel of corn and gave it to me, took the mice, rolled itself tight around them, and dove into a brass tube.

Byron breathed into my ear. "That's your seat number. Okay now?"

I was anything but okay. His whisper had gone through me like an electrical charge. "What?" He tapped the kernel. I looked down, noticed that it had a number printed on it. "Oh. Sure. Thanks."

He flashed me a heart-stopping smile and went off to his own seat. Which wasn't, of course, anywhere near mine. I'm sure the page did it on purpose.

Glamour is usually a Folk thing, but Byron definitely had it. Not megawatt, like a fox spirit or a pooka. His was more subtle, like a couple of candles on a bedside table. It was enough, though, to make me want to go up behind him and run my fingers through his hair and across his shoulders, broad and square under the torn T-shirt.

But that would lead to breaking Rule #4 (don't create a disturbance) and possibly Rule #1 (don't damage the books) as well. So I didn't do anything. But thinking what I'd like to do passed the time until the page brought me my books.

"Here you go, girlie," it said. "Knock yourself out. And, girlie, you gotta quit thinking so loud. You're making us blush here."

I blushed myself. Then I picked up the top book and opened it and started reading.

Since this is a fairy tale, I'm not going to go on about what I learned at the NYPL. Fairy tales don't go into detail about what the characters do between adventures. I'll just say that those books—the poems especially—cast a spell of their own, a powerful enchantment that changed the way I felt about being human. I didn't always understand them, but I felt them curling up in my brain and making me feel stuff I'd never felt before.

The poems were enchanting enough to make me forget about Byron. Almost. I didn't sneak a peek at him more than every couple of pages or so. And when he closed his book and took it back to the book counter and put on a battered leather jacket to leave, I swear I got up and followed him just because I was hungry.

He waited for me by the door. I sauntered up to him—Miss Nonchalance of New York Between. "This part of town's not in my flight path," I whispered. "Where can I go to grab a sandwich?"

Instead of answering, he took my hand and pulled me with him out the door. I don't know how he felt when our hands clasped, but my mouth went dry and my face flamed hot as a sidewalk in August. I checked my symptoms against the poems. Love, for sure. Maybe this bet would be easier to win than I thought.

We ended up at a place I'd never been before: the

Wannabe, under Times Square. It was a changeling hang-out—no Folk allowed—and it served human food, stolen from a deli Outside. It smelled kind of odd to me, but I was willing to try anything Byron liked. He ordered hamburgers and coffee for both of us, and I tried to think of a conversation starter. After about forever, all I could come up with was, "What are you studying?" So I asked him that.

"Magic," he said.

"Oh," I said. "Why?"

He looked around and scooched his chair a little closer to me. "I want to get out of here, get back Outside, where I belong."

I nodded. Just my luck. I meet the answer to every changeling girl's prayer, and he turns out to be loony tunes. Everybody knows changelings can't get out of New York Between, not unless the Folk kick them out. Most changelings wouldn't go Outside if they could. I sure wouldn't. Go to a place without magic, where you need money to live, where the wind will chill you and the rain wet you, where you can't talk to cats or dance with the Vilis or match wits with a lep-rechaun? Not on your life. I was curious about Outside, sure. I read the newspapers and magazines that blew down the storm sewers and listened to the Folk's stories about their adventures with mortals. But no way did I want to live among mortals. They're way too unpredictable.

"I'm like a pet, a toy, and I'm sick of it," Byron said. "Nothing I do makes any difference here. I want to make a *difference*, Neef. I want to be somebody. I want to be a hero."

He might have been loony tunes, but he was definitely adorable. I made sympathetic noises and watched his brown curls flop endearingly over his forehead whenever he pushed them back.

"There's got to be a way. I mean, you know the precedents: Thomas the Rhymer, Tam Lin, Orpheus, Hercules. All I have to do is put it all together. I've got this theory, that it all has to do with chaos theory and alchemy. You see. . . ."

While he talked, I admired how passion lit fires behind his soft brown eyes and wondered whether I could get him to look at me like that. Since I doubted he'd succeed in getting out of New York Between, I figured I'd have plenty of time to try.

I never got back to the Library that day. We stayed at the Wannabe for a while, and then we went dancing at the permanent floating Faerie Rave. I couldn't quite figure out why Byron was sticking with me when there were so many delicious Folk looking at him, but finally, I didn't care. We had a good time. When we got tired of dancing, we swam with the merfolk in New York Harbor and stole clams from the Grand Central Oyster Bar and caught an act of *Song of Broadway*, the Folk's perpetual musical entertainment. We did stuff until we were too tired to do any more, and then we fell asleep. When I woke up, I was in a nest of were-bears underneath the Central Park Zoo, and Byron was nowhere. The were-bears didn't know where he had gone, but I did.

When I walked into the Reading Room, there he was, curly brown head bent worshipfully over a huge book with black covers and red edges. I made sure to pass his chair on my way to the Catalog Room and brushed his shoulder as I went by. He didn't even look up.

That was a disappointment. But then I reminded myself that he wanted to be a hero. Fine. I understand heroes. They go on impossible quests. Byron was just doing his thing. I decided to play with CATNYP for a while, and then I'd see if I could get him to come out to the Wannabe and tell me how it was going.

CATNYP was asleep when I came in, its mane a furry wave over its glistening shoulders. I scratched it gently between its teacup-size ears. CATNYP's fur was soft and springy under my fingers, and it purred like an approaching subway.

"Hey there, CATNYP," I said. "What's up?"

It opened its eyes, shook its mane, and yawned. "Author, Title, Subject, Keyword," it said sleepily.

"Okay," I said. "Today, I'm going to learn to talk to you."

It was fun, really. At one point, I had the room full of mice, nosing all over the floor while I tried to figure out how to organize my searches. Then I discovered how to get a list of titles without the mice, and the Subject Index, and all kinds of cool stuff. CATNYP was incredibly patient with me and, once I learned how to ask, showed me all sorts of useful shortcuts. Finally, I buried my fingers in CATNYP's mane.

"Thanks," I said. "You're the best. Sleep tight, now." I tousled the coarse fur and watched the blue eyes drift shut.

That was when I heard the uproar in the Reading Room.

The first thing I thought was, "There's Rule #4 down the tubes." And then I recognized Byron's voice, and got my butt out there on the double.

Byron was climbing over the counter. There wasn't a

page in sight. The changelings were milling around like a flock of worried pigeons, cooing frantically:

"What's he *doing*?"

"He's breaking all the rules!"

"Come back, you idiot!"

"Somebody call the Genius!"

It took me about two breaths to take this all in, and then I was across the room and on top of the counter myself, by which time Byron was standing in front of a door I hadn't seen before, a wooden door with a frosted glass window in it, narrow, but human-sized. One hand was on the polished brass doorknob, and the other cradled a terrified mouse. He was flushed, determined, and totally, awesomely heroic-looking.

"Byron, stop!" I called. He glanced impatiently over his shoulder, dead set on breaking Rule #5, whatever the consequences. "Just a sec. I'm coming with you."

I was over the counter and through the door before I had time to think whether it was a good idea, then looked around for my dashing boyfriend, who had thoughtlessly dashed out of sight. I thought I heard his boots moving down a parallel aisle. I ran to intercept him, but when I reached the cross aisle, it was empty in both directions.

So here I was in the Stacks, alone. I could go back, but how lame would that be? The Stacks stretched around me, dim and cramped. I could touch the ceiling without stretching and the aisles between the cast-iron shelves were not a lot wider than my shoulders. The air was cool and dry, not at all musty or dusty or book-smelling. It didn't seem danger-ous, although I did notice that the books were all jailed behind iron grilles. I concentrated on listening for the sound of footsteps or breathing, anything to tell me which way Byron had gone.

That's when I began to hear voices.

It was real subtle at first, a vague, low murmuring that was so much a part of the atmosphere I might have been imagining it. But once I noticed it, it got louder. I started getting jittery. I mean, here I was in a forbidden place, a place I'd been warned against, and there were these mysterious voices getting louder by the second, like an invisible mob creeping up on me. I stood there, undecided, getting antsier and unhappier while the murmuring grew. I started picking up words: "psyche"; "death"; "human condition." I put my hands over my ears.

A mouse ran across my foot, which made me jump about a mile and duck into the shelter of one of the side aisles. The mouse scrambled up the grille that covered the shelf, wiggled through the wires, and sat on a book spine. I shrank back to the end of the row and made like a bookcase just before a page appeared and opened the grille. The mouse disappeared to wherever magical constructs go when they're not needed and the page wrapped itself around the book and dived into a brass tube at the mouth of the aisle.

One mystery solved. Several million left to go. Beginning with: Where was Byron and how was I going to keep from going nuts? No wonder the pages were deaf. I wished, briefly, that I was too. And that's when I remembered that I'd already broken one rule that day: Rule #2, in fact. Do Not Bring Food or Drink of Any Kind into the Library. In my pocket was a corned beef and mustard on rye I'd picked up at the Wannabe. I fished it out of the pocket of my sweater and, tearing off two little pieces of fairly unmustardy crust, squished them up and stuck them in my ears. Gross, but effective. The murmuring faded to a faint roar, like traffic through a closed window, easy to ignore for a city girl like me. Now I could think, and so I did.

It was a big library. Running around like an idiot was only going to tire me out, not to mention getting me more lost by the second. What I needed was a mouse. To get a mouse, I needed CATNYP. Which was back in the Reading Room. Dead end.

So much for thinking. I crept out of my aisle and looked right and left. To the right, the corridor disappeared around a bend. To the left, I saw a narrow stair leading to the next level. I turned left.

The Genius was right. The Stacks were dangerous. The only way I can explain it is to say that those books really, really wanted to get my attention. When I didn't respond to their whispering, they sent out fictional characters, metaphors, and dangerous ideas to reel me in. I was pelted with visions: a path between a snowy wood and a frozen lake; a man who was also a tree with a woman twined ivy-like around him; a wild-haired woman with blood on her clothes, brandishing a knife and begging me with terrible eyes to listen to her story.

I'm calm about it now—I survived it, after all—but I wasn't very calm then. I was scared shitless. I knew it was all an illusion, that the woman's knife couldn't cut me or the man and woman break my heart with their beauty, but it felt as if they could. Finally I shut my eyes and crawled, the floor reassuringly cold and stable under my hands and knees, until I got to the stairs. I crawled up a few steps and cautiously opened my eyes. All I saw were dimly lit aisles and the flat black ends of bookshelves. I'd reached neutral ground.

My face was sweating. I wiped it on my sleeve, and that's when I found the hair.

My sweater was black, and the hair, which was white, showed up like print against the dark wool. The were-bears were brown, and I don't have a cat of any color, so I must have picked it up in the Catalog Room just before the upheaval began.

Well. I may not know much about human love, but I do know what to do with a hair from a magic animal. Carefully, I tweezed it up between my fingernails and breathed on it.

"CATNYP brave and CATNYP bold,
Please boot me up before I'm old."

"Flattery," a deep voice remarked at my shoulder, "will get you everywhere. Although I must say I don't think much of the poem."

It was CATNYP, all right, bolt upright on the landing above me. "What happened to Title, Author, Subject, Keyword?" I said a little shakily.

CATNYP looked just as inscrutable as a cat can look. "I can do that, if you like."

"No. That's okay. This is fine. Listen. I need a mouse, big time."

"When you have me?" CATNYP sounded offended. "If you like, but I can move through the Stacks much faster than the mice. And there's really not a lot of time to spare, if it's that tiresome young hero you're looking for."

I couldn't let myself think about what might be happening to Byron. I didn't have time to panic. "You will? I mean, I never expected you'd help me yourself. I'd appreciate that, CATNYP. Really."

"How much would you appreciate it? How much does this young human mean to you?"

No one curses in New York Between unless they're prepared to deal with the consequences. But I came close. I hate unanswerable questions almost as much as I hate bargaining with a magical animal when I'm in a hurry. But what choice did I have? "Name your price," I said, "and we'll see if I can meet it."

"You," CATNYP said.

"Meaning?"

"I will not bargain with you. I'm offering you my help in return for your service. That's the trade. Time grows short, changeling girl."

Oh, boy. At this rate, I was going to be running errands for animal-Folk the rest of my life. "Okay," I said. "Yes. I agree. You help me get Byron out of here, and I'll scratch you behind your ears and bring you milk and whatever else you want."

"For as long as it pleases me."

It wasn't fair, but that's the Folk for you. I sighed. "For as long as it pleases you. But you'll have to wait your turn. There's a swan maiden with dibs."

"I don't think you'll have to worry about Snowbell," said CATNYP. "But it was honorable of you to mention it."

And then we were in another part of the library and I saw Byron.

He was in deep trouble.

He was standing in the mouth of an aisle, with his hair blowing around his cheeks in a wind I couldn't feel. His back was straight, his head was high, his arms were stretched out before him. Beyond him was one of those purple-and-green, gold-tusked demons with bug eyes that look so comical in pictures. In the flesh, it wasn't comical at all. It was as beautiful and deadly as a gun. It was opening a door. Not an ordinary door, of course—a magical door, a dimensional door, a door that should not exist.

I turned to CATNYP. "I thought you said he was in trouble," I said. "It looks to me like he's just about to achieve his quest."

"Look again," said CATNYP.

Byron had moved a little closer to the door. He looked awfully rigid, standing there like a sleepwalker with his arms out. And I realized the demon was looking positively gleeful, which meant that it was doing something that made it happy, which was probably not good news for Byron.

"He conjured the demon to open a door Outside," CATNYP said. "He neglected to specify which Outside he wanted to go to."

"Oh, my." I took a step forward to pull him back, and fell over CATNYP, suddenly blocking my way.

"Touch him and you go with him," it growled.

"Okay," I said. "What do I do?"

"To rescue him?"

"Of course, to rescue him."

"The boy has broken a number of important prohibitions.

He has entered the Stacks, he has Created a Disturbance and Defaced Books. He has sought to go Outside."

"Listen," I said. "I don't care what he's done. He doesn't deserve to go wherever that demon is taking him. I've already said I'll be your servant for as long as you want, which is way longer than the usual arrangement. Help me out here. Please, CATNYP?"

So I started out heroic and ended up pathetic. I'm only human, okay? And I was pretty upset. CATNYP wasn't. It sat down with its tail coiled around its front feet.

"You must break the bond between him and the demon," it said. "Once his concentration is broken, the demon will disappear and the door will close. Provided it is no more than halfway open."

By this time, Byron was about a third of the way down the row, and the door looked to be about thirty-three degrees open. Swirls of darkness were leaping from the gap and flashes of colors I didn't recognize. "Byron!" I screamed. "It's me, Neef. Come back!"

Nothing happened, except for the demon's grin creeping around under his ears. "He can't hear you," CATNYP remarked. "May I suggest a good book?"

It took every bit of self-control I had not to lose it. But I know how these things work. This was a hint. I needed to keep my cool to figure it out. A good book could mean several things. I ran through the possibilities as fast as I could. With a magic book, I could turn Byron into something the demon wasn't interested in—a mouse, maybe. Or I could unsummon the demon. But finding the right book and the right spell would take longer than I had, even using CATNYP's Subject Index. I looked at the books nearest me. *The Art of Toulouse-Lautrec*, *The Architecture of Frank Lloyd Wright*, an illustrated folio edition of *The Canterbury Tales*. What they all had in common was their size. They were big books. Heavy books.

"The door is opening," CATNYP murmured.

There wasn't time to think. I yanked open the grille, grabbed the biggest and heaviest of the books in both hands, took three big steps down the aisle, and bopped Byron on the beezer.

Then several things happened at once. Byron collapsed in an untidy heap on the floor. The demon's grin disappeared into a roar that revealed more than I wanted to see of its crimson throat and knobbly blue tongue. The invisible door slipped from the demon's claws with a screech even louder than its roar and snapped shut with an ear-popping rush of pressure, taking the demon with it. All that remained were a few little eddies of darkness that rippled aimlessly around on the floor until CATNYP pounced on them and batted them still.

"Well," it said. "That was exciting. How's the book?"

I looked at the book—*The Canterbury Tales* by Geoffrey Chaucer, the Kelmscott edition. It had held up very well—better than Byron, who groaned and lifted a hand to his head. I knelt down beside him, laid the book on the floor, and helped him sit up. He winced and felt the back of his head tenderly. He looked a whole lot less handsome than he had, and I loved him so much that my heart hurt.

"Byron," I said softly. "It's over, baby. You're safe now."

He pulled away from me. "What did you do that for?" he snapped. "I was nearly there!"

"The girl saved you," CATNYP said. "The only place you nearly were was a world even more inimical to you than this one."

"I knew what I was doing," Byron said.

"You did not," CATNYP said.

When the Catalog of the New York Public Library tells you something, you can make book it's telling the truth. Byron squeezed his eyes shut very tight, took a deep breath, and let it go. "Okay." He opened his eyes. "Thanks, Neef. You saved my life. I appreciate it."

My heart, which had been standing still, thumped into action again. "No biggie. You'd have done it for me."

He smiled at me, dazzlingly. "Thanks anyway. And you, CATNYP. I owe you one."

"You do indeed."

It wasn't CATNYP's voice, and we weren't in the Stacks anymore. We were in the Genius's office, sitting in library chairs facing his desk. CATNYP was on its haunches beside his wooden chair, staring at us with unblinking eyes.

"I am gravely disappointed in you," the Genius went on. "Gravely. Between the two of you, you have broken virtually every rule in the list. What do you have in your pocket, young lady?"

There are times when it's okay to lie to the Folk and times when it isn't. Besides, I was too tired. "A corned beef and mustard on rye, sir."

"And what were you intending to do with it?"

"Eat it. In the bathroom, where there aren't any books. I get hungry, and I hate having to go all the way to the Wannabe to get something to eat."

"Still," he said. "And you, young man. Why did you enter the Stacks?"

Byron was sitting up, very straight and proud. "I wanted a book," he said, looking the Genius firmly in the glasses.

"The pages would get it for you."

"There weren't any pages available," Byron said.

"That's right," I said. "There wasn't a page in the room."

CATNYP and the Genius exchanged an inscrutable look. "That's no excuse," the Genius said. "As you know very well. You've been told the Stacks are dangerous. You know what danger can mean here. You behaved foolishly." The glittering squares turned from Byron to me. "As did you. With better cause, perhaps, but still foolishly. I'm afraid I must ask you for your library cards."

I fished my card out of my jeans. I was astonished that our punishment wasn't any worse, but I was even more astonished at how sorry I was to be handing over my card. After the wonders I'd glimpsed, it was going to be hard to go back to soggy newspapers and torn magazine pages.

"I don't need it anyway," Byron said, pulling out his own card. "I know what I know. You can't take that away from me."

"Can I not?" the Genius said. His tone was mild, but the hair on the back of my neck rose. He held out his hand, and we gave him the cards.

Byron stood up and headed for the door. "Coming, Neef?"

I stood up, too. I felt tired and sad. "Yeah," I said. "Good-bye, CATNYP. I'll miss you."

"Not so fast," said the Genius. "I'm not done with you yet. Byron and Neef, you have broken the prohibitions and survived the ordeal. If I recall my folklore correctly, a boon is customary in cases of this kind. One wish each, don't you think, CATNYP?"

The white lion nodded.

"Very well," the Genius said. "One wish it is. Byron?"

My jaw dropped. I could see why I'd get a boon—I mean, I rescued Byron and banished the demon. All he'd done was get bopped over the head just in time. In this scenario, he was the helpless one and I was the hero. So why was he getting a reward? I know the Folk aren't fair, but at least you can count on them to follow their own rules.

I was just about to ask this when Byron piped up. He'd recovered from his shock faster than I had, and was all bright-eyed and flushed with excitement and knowing exactly what he was going to say.

"I want to return Outside," he said.

"Very well," said the Genius. "When you go out that door, you will be in the human reading room of the New York Public Library. A hero like you will have no difficulty in finding his way to the main entrance and onto Fifth Avenue. Good luck."

Byron turned toward the door. "Wait," I said. "First of all, how come he's a hero? He didn't do anything but almost get killed. And second of all, do you have any place to go out there, Byron? What are you going to do?"

Byron grinned. "Seek my fortune. Wanna come with?"

The Genius turned to me. "Is that your wish, Neef? To go with Byron and help him seek his fortune?"

You never know what you're going to be surprised by until it happens. Up until about a minute ago, I had thought that all I wanted in the world was to be with Byron and live happily ever after with him in the fairy tale ending I'd earned for us. But then the hero question had come up and Byron had opted for New York Outside, and I suddenly wasn't so sure. What it boiled down to was that I knew I loved New York Between. I didn't know whether I loved Byron.

"Answer, child," said the Genius. "I'm getting bored."

I swear I had no idea what I was going to say. I opened my mouth and this is what came out: "My wish is to have my library card back."

"Let's get go— What did you say?" Byron's double take would have been funny, if I'd been in a laughing mood.

"I'm not going with you, Byron. I'm staying here."

I don't think the Genius would have allowed me to change my mind, but I might have tried if Byron had argued with me. Instead, he nodded sadly. "Good luck, Neef," he said. "I'll miss you." And then he gave me a hug and turned around and squared his shoulders and strode briskly through the door.

"Good riddance to bad rubbish," said CATNYP. "I never liked him."

"I did," I said, sat down, and started to cry. I hate crying. It makes my nose run and my eyes sting and it's so humiliatingly human. The Folk never cry.

I felt a weight on my knee and took my hands away from my face. CATNYP had its head in my lap, like a big dog, and was purring. My library card was in my lap too.

"Wish granted," the Genius said. "Now, one last piece of

business, and we can all get back to work. I believe you have sworn service to CATNYP in return for its help in rescuing that singularly stupid young man from the consequences of his foolhardiness."

I sighed. What a bargain that was. "Yes. I did."

"CATNYP?"

The lion raised its chin from my leg. "I think," it said, "that I'll turn you into a Librarian. Come in and talk to me about it when you've had some rest. But now, I'll take that corned beef sandwich. I've always been curious about human food."

I wanted to kiss it and cry into its mane and generally carry on like the crispy critter that I was, but the Genius cramped my style. So I took the sandwich out of my pocket and unwrapped it. It was kind of smooshed. CATNYP snapped it up, threw it back, and licked its chops with a long pink tongue.

"Interesting," it said. "You shall bring me another next time you come."

I turned to the Genius. "Can I ask you a question?"

"One wish," the Genius said. "You know what happens to mortals who are greedy with wishes."

"It's not a wish, Genius. It's information."

"Oh, very well. Byron is in the kind of tale in which the hero succeeds by attracting the right companions. If you had been his heroine, you would have chosen to go with him and used your superior common sense to help him to success in New York Outside. If the same rules obtain there."

"So what I get for saving Byron is to live happily ever after as a Librarian?"

The Genius blinked, looking momentarily very like CATNYP. "What you get for saving Byron is the chance to be the hero in your own tale. Only time will tell what that will be."

So that's it, really. In the tradition of the oldest fairy tales, Byron got his wish through someone else's help, and mostly I hope it turned out happily ever after for him. Sometimes, when I'm feeling sorry for myself, I hope he's a street person for real, seeing fairies wherever he looks without being able to talk to them. But mostly I'm happy enough, hanging out at the Library, learning the ins and outs of the system, learning how to talk to the pages, feeding CATNYP corned beef sandwiches, and reading. I'm reading a lot: poetry, novels, plays, philosophy, history. And folklore. I was right. Mortals know a lot more about love than the Folk can even imagine. At the Solstice Rave, I'll prove it, chapter and verse, so that even Snowbell will have to admit she's beat. In the meantime, I'm planning what boon I'll ask of Snowbell and figuring out what kind of a tale I want to be in. I don't know quite what it is yet. But I'm getting there.

Delia Sherman was born in Tokyo, Japan, but she grew up in Manhattan, about twenty minutes by bus from the New York Public Library. She has published stories about the magical side of New York in the anthologies *A Wolf at the Door*, *The Green Man*, and *Firebirds*. "CATNYP" is not the end of Neef's adventures in New York Between. There are other stories, and maybe even a novel or two, to come.

In addition, she has published three adult fantasy novels, been nominated for the World Fantasy Award, and won the Mythopoeic Award. She is a consulting editor for Tor Books and president of the Interstitial Arts Foundation (www.artistswithoutborders.org).

Author's Note

When I was growing up, I spent a lot of time in the New York Public Library system, mostly in the children's section of the Seventy-Ninth Street branch. I didn't really know the Research Library until I got to college and needed to look up obscure biographies of Irish poets and studies of the Renaissance theater. The librarians were nice to me, the card catalog system easy to use, the reading room beautifully airy, and the chairs comfortable enough to sit and read in for hours. I fell in love with the place then, and have been in love with it ever since. Since I live in Boston, it is necessarily a long-distance relationship. I keep it up by regular visits to CATNYP online (http://catnyp.nypl.org) and the NYPL lion bookends my father gave me when I was going away to college, which still sit near my writing desk.

Neef and her friends are the result of a disagreement with a friend about whether fairies are comfortable living in a modern city. Having grown up in New York City and having found it a very magical place, I know that they are, and do.

Given the number of people from different nations who have settled there, it only makes sense that the city's fairies should represent a wide variety of cultures. Of course there are indigenous fairies, too, sprung from New York's own brand of magic. They are such fun to play with that I'm writing a novel about Neef's early years among the Folk, to be called *The Changeling*.

Elvenbrood

∾

Tanith Lee

> *How beautiful they are,*
> *The lordly ones,*
> *Who dwell in the hills,*
> *In the hollow hills.*
>
> —"The Immortal Hour," Fiona Macleod (William Sharp)

When they moved to Bridestone, Susie had tried to be very positive. That was the key word, apparently. Positive. What you *had* to be. So Jack tried to back her up. She'd been through enough, they all had. Make the best of things.

He was seventeen and a half, and because of that, she said she *preferred* him to call her Susie, though outside the house, at college, he referred to her, when he needed to, by her true title, which was Mum. Luce still had the unchallenged rights to call Susie Mum, but she didn't either. Luce was fourteen, white-blonde, strange in the way girls suddenly got.

"Susie's a *person*," said Luce, seriously, bossily, "she has a right to have a *name*, not just be our Mum."

"She *is* our Mum," Jack pointed out.

Then Susie had come in, all Positive, and they had to start Positively cleaning the new house up, and unpacking.

It was a new house in every way, as several sections of the sprawling village were, part of a block of houses, all joined up, with big flat glass windows and doors. They were all presumably the same inside, too. One largish downstairs room, kitchen, cloakroom, three small bedrooms upstairs, and a bathroom. The house, though, looked out onto fields and hedgerows, woods. It was all right, better than the flat they'd all been crammed into in outer London, when Dad—Michael—was fired.

The firing had been because Dad drank too much alcohol. Or no, it had been because *Michael* drank too much. Jack could remember a few years before, when Luce had been nine and sweet, and Susie had been, not Positive, just happy, and Dad had been Dad, and brilliant. Michael worked too hard, Susie explained as things ran downhill; he was trying to keep them all going; they must support him. Then he got fired anyway, and they lost the house in Chester Road where Jack and Luce had grown up. They went to live in the flat. Once there, Dad—now truly Michael full time—went on drinking too much. He began to tell Susie, Luce, and Jack that he was sick to death of them and the burden they were, and also he started to hit Susie. One night Jack smashed one of Michael's bottles over Michael's head to stop him. Jack had been crying, just as Luce and Susie were. Michael sat there on the floor looking stunned. Then he just got up, with a trickle of blood from his forehead running down his nose, and walked out. He never came back.

That had been a year and a half ago. Now they were here.

Which was the really stupid part, Jack thought. Mum had had a win on the National Lottery. Oh, not millions, but enough for a decent down payment on a small house, and some left over until, as Susie said (positive enough she'd fooled the mortgage people), she found a job. Being Positive, they'd already found a local school for Luce, and Jack's college was only half an hour away on the train.

Jack couldn't help thinking it was a shame they hadn't won the lottery before all hell broke loose in their lives. Susie said that wasn't the way to look at it. It was wonderful luck. And of course it was.

Bridestone, though.

Jack had stared at the place uneasily, even as the train pulled in. Susie's choice. It was one of those Kent-Sussex villages that had been picturesque, and still was in bits—ye olde smithy, ye olde pub, a church that was built just after the Norman Conquest of England in 1066, even the ruins of a Roman fort and Norman castle nearby. But the village had also grown. It had put on weight since the fifties, got too fat with new houses and estates and silly shops that, Jack thought, sold stuff no one in their right minds could afford, or would want to.

There was a Big Divide here too. There were the Rich, who lived in old timbered houses along the hilly narrow streets or in flash mansions just outside, with gardens like parks. The Rich had huge dogs, rode horses, talked like things yapping to each other. They looked way, way down on "That Common Lot" who'd bought the new houses.

Susie had been an actress once. She'd been on TV and everything, only no one remembered. But she wasn't *common*—she was *un*common.

"Look at the lovely view!" she sang as they saw it first, properly, from the upstairs landing window.

Well, it *was* a good view, Jack had to admit. He was going to be studying photography next year; he was just on his foundation course now. He could take excellent pictures of the green-golden fields, the clouds of dark woods, the sweeps of open land beyond . . .

Why didn't he like that view?

He tried, in a funny way, not even to look at it, not to look out of the windows. Nuts.

Luce *loved* it. She loved the tiny garden, too, with the blue, fake wrought-iron chairs and table Susie bought, the untidy rosebushes and lilac tree. She'd be out there for hours in the evenings, when he and Susie watched TV, alone, singing to herself like she had when she was little. Maybe it was good for her. Over the end fence, the fields buzzed smokily with summer.

At night, the moon sailed white across that countryside, owls eerily cried, and Jack found himself going downstairs about one A.M., not for a drink of juice or piece off the cold chicken, but to check the locks, front and back.

"Susie, do you think these locks are strong enough?"

"They're what we've got, Jackie."

"Yeah, but couldn't I fix for someone to put on better ones?"

"What are you expecting to break in—" she chortled. "A *lion?*"

"Those bloody dogs are about lion size. One of those'd be through that glass in two seconds."

"I *like* dogs. Lucy and I might like to get one ourselves. But listen, Jack, thanks honestly, but we're out of London here. It's much safer, you know."

Luce said primly, "Jack never worried about locks in London. Once he left the front door unlocked all night when he came in."

This had been at Chester Road, so Susie changed the subject.

What *was* it that bugged Jack about this place? A couple of Sundays they went for a walk around the lanes. Susie and Luce chatted about birds and wildflowers. Jack kept looking over his shoulder. Once he heard something following them behind the hedgerow—he got ready to thump it till two crows flew up.

But it wasn't just the wildlife, or the view, or the people here—but—*something*—

Something . . .

Perhaps he was just a city boy, or neurotic, like Susie and Luce were now, a bit. Just that.

The fourth week they were there, Luce ran in one afternoon from school, breathlessly excited to tell them, "I met this *weird* man in the High Street."

Jack and Susie looked up, horrified.

"What do you mean, Lucy?" Susie asked, careful, gripping the edge of the kitchen table.

Jack, home early on what the awkward course tutor called "An Assignment," waited.

Luce said, "I don't mean *that*. He's off his head, out of his skull . . ."

"On *drugs*, do you mean?" demanded Jack.

Luce burst out laughing. She still had this laugh, like silver bells . . . Michael had said that. No, *Dad* had said it. "I just mean crazy. Not dangerous. He just came up and said, 'You be careful, little girl'—as if I was a kid—'careful how you go.'"

"Did you speak to him? Lucy, I've told you—"

"*No*. Of *course* not. Why would I? I just walked on. Then he called after me, 'Just go careful with that hair.' And then something about the Romans leaving the stone, and knights leaving the castle—but I was by the bread shop then, and I went in like you asked and bought this loaf—"

"Forget the loaf. What did he look like?"

"Thin, old. His hair was long. He looked like a woolly sheepdog. His clothes were old, too. Sort of like Victorian for a fancy-dress party—only worn and mucky. But people like that stink. They smell like dustbins and garbage, and he didn't. He smelled . . ." Luce considered, "like grass."

"*Grass?*"

"Off a *lawn*—that sort. And he had green eyes, like me."

Susie and Jack exchanged a worried, brown-eyed glance.

"Tomorrow, Lucy," said Susie firmly, "I will take you in to school. I will collect you in the afternoon."

"Oh, *Mum!*" Luce wailed.

Jack went out after tea, which was their early dinner at six o'clock. He walked down the hill from the grassy estate, past the quaint gate where sometimes cows grazed, and which led to a cornfield. He walked through a couple of narrow streets and into the High Street.

There was a village green with a war memorial on it. The church, with its square Norman tower, was across from the green, and, on the other side, nestled among huge oak and beech trees, the pub. This pub had a strange name. . . . Jack peered round the leaves and past the several posh drinkers gathered outside on rustic benches, with their wine and Real Ale.

The pub sign showed a green hill, and some people dancing together on it under a curved crescent moon. THE LORDS AND LADIES said the lettering.

One of the drinkers had noticed Jack and pulled a face. Ah, Jack could see the man thinking, That Common Lot have now produced a yob intent on underage boozing.

Jack turned his back and strolled on, across the green to the church.

He was looking for the man who had spoken to Luce. In such a stuck-up place as Bridestone, anyone like that, surely, would have been run out of town long ago. Unless—did they still keep a village idiot here? Just for the twee charm of it . . .

What had he meant *Go careful with that hair*? A warning? A threat? Jack badly wanted to see the man, ask him which, and why. And if a threat, tell him that Jack didn't like old tramps threatening his sister, all right?

After a while, Jack left the church. He walked on, up and down roads and through the little between-house alleys. Someone was playing Mozart. Dogs barked, richly, in gardens with not one branch out of place.

Returning to the green, he saw the sun was going. It was

getting on for 8:30. An hour at most, and it would be full dark, and Susie getting anxious because he'd only said he was going for a walk.

The church, too, bothered Jack. The graveyard was packed with ancient leaning gravestones with dates like 1701 and 1590. Age so thick you could cut it in slices.

And what had the nutter meant when he said that about the Romans leaving the stone, and the Norman knights? Jack had never heard that the Romans—or the Normans, for that matter—had left there at all. The air was cooling and the smell of flowers blew over on a breeze. It was getting dark quicker than he'd expected.

When Jack got to the front door, Susie was already flinging it wide. "Jack, Jack, thank God—"

"What is it? *What,* Mum?"

"Lucy's gone!"

Jack stood there, with all his blood turning to sand. It felt like the flat again, those times when Michael . . . the raised drunken voice rising in the other room, accusing Susie of caring nothing for her family, only for the career she'd given up, and then the sound of a blow.

"Are you sure, Susie?"

"Of course I'm bloody sure, you stupid moron!"

Unlike Michael, she was seldom rude. She must be at her wit's end. He read the signal and said, "Yes, okay. You've checked. When did you realize?"

"She was up in her room playing her CDs, quite loud—one of those thump-thump people you both like so much . . ."

"U2."

"And it just kept on playing the same track, so I went up

to say could she turn it down a little . . . Oh God, Jack, she wasn't there. The window was wide open, that was all—she couldn't have climbed out of the *window*, could she? I mean, why would she do that? I mean, she wasn't in the bathroom, and she didn't come downstairs—I was ironing and I had the radio on—but I'd have seen her go by the main room door. . . ."

"Did you check the other rooms? Yes. The garden?"

"I looked *everywhere*. I even—I even looked in the blasted washing machine for God's sake!" Susie cackled weakly. "Am I being daft? It's all right, isn't it? She's probably somehow been up there all the time. . . . Susie turned abruptly, raced along the hall and up the stairs like a slim stampeding elephant. Jack followed. Upstairs, there was no sign of Luce.

They craned their necks out the open bedroom window, gazing down at the small patio below. It wasn't such a long drop.

The air smelled wonderful now, scented with flowers and hay and clean growing, living things—and *night*.

"Mum, *look*! I think . . ."

"Oh, oh there she is! Oh my God, what's she doing out there? Lucy! Luce!"

Across a couple of fields of ripening corn or wheat, or whatever it was, among the tall stalks, a short slender figure stood quite still, showing up with an almost luminous whiteness that must be because of lights shining out from the house backs. Luce, with her pale blonde hair . . .

Go careful with that hair.

Susie was already running downstairs again, throwing

open the back door. He caught up in the garden. By then she was standing by the back fence, nearly crying, like a scared child.

"She vanished."

"The stalks would hide her from down here."

"No. When I got here I could still see her out in the field. And then . . . she just wasn't."

The night felt chilly, or cold. It was moonless, too.

"I'll go and look for her." Jack sprang at the fence and over.

"Be *careful!*"

Jack grunted, and pelted forward into the stinging coarse slap of the wheat or corn. He hated it, smashing it aside with his hands—he'd probably never eat bread or cereal again.

He heard Susie calling when he thought he'd traveled about a quarter mile. By then the dark shadow of the woods was looming through the stalks, sinister in some electric way.

Jack stood, bewildered.

Behind him floated the voice of his mother, vital again with relief: "Jack! It's all right, she's *here* . . ." And then Luce's voice, "Jackieee!"

While in front of him, against the backdrop of woods, motionless as the unshaken grain, a white-skinned, white-blonde creature was looking back at him, smiling—quiet, and amused—with slanting cat-green eyes. Only a second, this. Then it melted away. Into shadow, into night—*into the ground?*

Jack shook himself. Nothing had been there—adrenalin and an optical illusion. He turned and ran back for the house.

"She says she was everywhere I'd just looked, doing something, not realizing I was looking for her. We just kept *missing* each other."

Jack scowled. "That's dumb. We looked everywhere. You can't *miss* someone anyway in a house this tiny."

"It's what she says. She got bolshy and then tearful when I kept saying it couldn't have been like that. She said she's not a liar. But she is. I took the flashlight. There're scuff marks on the table on the patio. She must have got out on the windowsill, swung onto the shed roof—I can hardly bear to think of it. What if she'd jumped all wrong?"

"Yeah. Do you want me to speak to her?"

"In the morning. We've had enough for now."

He wondered how Luce had got back in. She must have sneaked in again when he was out in the fields and Susie at the fence. Crazy.

Crazy like the green-eyed man.

That night, Jack dreamed he was still running. Something was chasing him—a dog, he thought, a white dog. He woke up sweating, because he'd left his window shut.

He wondered if that other thing—that white figure Susie and he thought they'd seen—was Luce's *decoy,* so she could get back unnoticed.

The woman behind the library desk was pretty tasty, but she was also pretty nasty. "The computer's crashed. I'm sorry." You could see she wasn't.

He told her he needed to research Bridestone. She raised

an eyebrow. "You must have heard of it," he said, "one stop up the line."

"I'm from London," she proclaimed loftily.

The promised data hadn't been much anyhow. Just dates on the castle, and a plan of the Roman remains with some altar to a pagan goddess.

As Jack was stalking through the door, a man's voice sounded behind him.

"Were you asking about Bridestone?"

Jack looked around. A young middle-aged man stood there, frowning at him, as if it was forbidden for people like Jack to ask questions. Jack didn't like men of this age anyway. Michael had been one.

"Yes," said Jack shortly.

"Any special reason?"

"I live there. If that's okay."

Jack saw suddenly the man's frown was because he was squinting out into the sun.

"You might try an old guy called Soldyay," said the man. "That's spelled *Soldier*, by the way. He's dotty, but quite harmless. I've known him years, and he knows Bridestone village, the history and so on."

"Soldier? What do you mean, 'dotty'? You mean off his head?"

"Somewhat. But as I say, no danger. Gentle as a lamb. Really, I wouldn't recommend seeing him otherwise. I'm his dentist. He appears before me once a year to show off his truly wonderful teeth. They really *are* wonderful. Like a young tiger's. Not a single cavity."

"Has he got green eyes?"

"That's another thing. His eyes are as clear as a child's. Green? Yes, I think so. Also his clothes are horrible but somehow he's always fresh as a daisy. Anyway, if you want to know about the village, he's your man. Bridstane it used to be. It's in the Domesday Book and all that. Seen the ruins?"

"Not yet."

"Nothing much left. A few crumbling walls. The Roman fort is even less intact, plus it's up a mountain of a hill. I *don't* recommend *that*."

"Was it abandoned—the fort? Or the castle?"

"Sometimes Soldier seems to say so. But then he has times when he just talks in riddles. He's supposed to have a peculiar history himself. My mother used to remember him first turning up. Old then, she said. I don't know his age. He lies and says sixty to my receptionist, but he's well past that. Catch him on a good day, and you'll get some sense."

"When's a good day?"

"Waxing moon. That's today, in fact. You can call at his house, he won't let you in. You'll have to talk to him in the street. Number Seven, Smith's Lane, behind the old—"

"Smithy," said Jack. "Thanks, Mr. . . . ?"

"Tooth," sighed the dentist. "Please *don't* say it."

On the train going back, Jack thought how he hadn't gone in to college to check. He had considered it—the computers there might work. But then a foundation student had practically to walk over blazing coals to get access to them. He hadn't spoken to Luce, either. She'd slipped off early to school that morning eluding Susie's escort, so Susie felt she had to phone the place to make sure Luce had safely arrived. She had. Then the phone had rung again, someone wanting Susie for an interview that day, some job she'd applied for— she hadn't said doing what. "Jack, I'll have to go out. Would you please pick Lucy up this afternoon from school? She'll like it better anyway, her handsome elder brother, not her Mum."

Before meeting Luce, he had plenty of time to run Mr. Soldier to ground. But first, lunch was on the agenda. Or it was meant to be. As he opened the fridge door, there was a multicolored explosion.

Jack yelled, staggered back against the kitchen table, soaked and gawping, as a double pack of colas, two cartons of orange juice and one of cranberry, and a bottle of fizzy white wine erupted their contents all over the room—and all over Jack.

He hadn't the heart to leave the mess for Susie when she got back. His note about the ruined food would be bad enough. Most of the stocks in the fridge were now spoiled— unless you really fancied soggy bread, wet butter, cold sausages in an orange and cola sauce. The fruit and salad might make it, if washed. Could you wash *bacon* though?

Jack was glaring into the fridge again when the milk carton, somehow slower than the rest, also decided to blow its top, right in his face.

Eyes full of milk, Jack swore. Spilled milk stank, too. So, not only cleaning the kitchen now, but another shower and a change of clothes.

He got out of the house again about three o'clock, and ran through the village to Smith's Lane.

The street was cobbled, the houses—drab, old, narrow

oblongs—slotted together like a kind of jigsaw. Most looked uncared for, but Number Seven won the prize for worst. The door-paint peeled in strips, the windows were nearly black with dirt behind yellowed filthy net curtains. No bell. Jack went at the door knocker as if needing to hammer something in.

He thought no one would answer.

Then, silent as the fall of a leaf, the door opened, and Mr. Soldier stepped out to meet Jack in the street.

His eyes *were* green. They didn't slant, though. And, as Tooth the dentist had said, they were incredibly clear, the whites like enamel. The rest of him—he was old and crinkled up, like scrunched paper. His gray hair poured over his shoulders, over his face. His clothing looked more 1970s, Jack thought, than Victorian, but also as if he slept in it, slept too in a refuse sack.

"You spoke to my sister."

"Did I?" He had a good voice, not overeducated and yappy like the Bridestone Rich, more like an actor. So, was he acting now?

"Yeah, you did. Blonde girl, yesterday."

"Ah." Mr. Soldier smiled. His teeth were just as the dentist had said. "That was your sister, then."

"Why did you try to scare her?"

"Did I scare her?"

"No. But . . ."

"I did mean to, in a way. I meant she should be careful. Sometimes . . ." Mr. Soldier hesitated. He seemed apologetic. "Sometimes I'm not very coherent."

"You get *drunk*?"

Mr. Soldier looked surprised at the rage in Jack's tone. "No, not often. I can't afford to. I simply mean I'm not always myself."

"Do the police know about you? Do you have to attend at a hospital for treatment?"

"Not at all. I seldom cause any bother."

"You bothered my sister."

Mr. Soldier said, "I think it isn't *I* that bother her. Perhaps it's already too late. Maybe not."

Jack snarled. His fists rose.

Mr. Soldier did not react. He said quietly, "Something wants her. Something is *interested* in her."

"*Who?* How do you *know?*"

"I was the same. Once they were interested in me."

"*Who are THEY?*"

Mr. Soldier knelt down unexpectedly on the ground. He licked his finger and wrote in his own spit on a large cobble, one word.

Jack stared at it. ELVNBROD.

"Elven—"

"*Don't.*" Mr. Soldier rose. He sounded oddly proud as he said, "Don't name them. They can be called the Lords and Ladies, or the Royalty. In Ireland, you know, they call them the Gentle Folk, or the Little People. Or the Lordly Ones."

Jack goggled. "*Faeries?*"

"Oh, *that* name. Well. Of a kind, maybe. In the faery tales and legends, it's true, faeries do steal human children. And that is what these ones do, the ones we have here."

Jack stood back. "You are out of your tree."

"They stole me. Yes. Though, believe me, I wanted to go

with them. They make you want to go, more than you can
bear. They're old as the hills, fair as the morning. They look
young as children or adolescents, that's why they like the
mortal young. In their country, you stay young too, and
immortal. They live under the hills. It's like paradise there."

"So what's paradise like, then?" Jack demanded.

"Like the best and most wonderful place you can imagine, then better."

The sun beat on Jack's head. The word *Elvnbrod* had
faded from the cobble. He felt dizzy. Did he want to shake
the old man, or was he starting to believe him? Don't be a
fool.

"So, then," Jack said, adult and cool, "These *things* want
to take Luce away with them, like they wanted you when you
were a kid. Only you didn't go."

"Oh, but I did."

"You—you what?"

"Listen. Something gives them the right to take a child.
Myself, then. Your sister now. There is a stone in the old
Roman fort. The Romans put it there, back in the time of
Caesars. It was dedicated to the goddess of light, Brid. They
left it here too, when the empire ended. This area has always
been a center for *Them*. But the Stone keeps the village safe.
Unless . . ."

Jack swallowed noisily.

The old man softly said, "There was a Norman warlord
in the castle. He sold his youngest daughter and son to the
Lordly Ones, in return for riches and luck for himself. He got
what he asked, but later his knights learned of it and gave
him to the church. He was burned as a witch. The castle was

abandoned as cursed. Even the best luck can run out."

"Luck . . ." said Jack, dully. "Money . . ."

"After a long while, one of the warlord's children was returned. The Lordly Ones had to let him go, because the luck had failed. They didn't want to, nor did the boy want to come back. The moment he breathed the air of this world, he became old as the hills himself. Yet he lived on. The power of immortality preserved him, but not his youth. He lives still. Perhaps he always must."

The man's face was like a carved stone. Jack took a step away.

Just then, the church clock struck four. It didn't always strike, but now it did and the chimes filled him with a terror without cause. Then he knew why. *Luce*. He reeled away up the lane and sprinted for the school.

She was gone. The teacher he found in the tree-planted yard told him she'd seen Luce running off. One of her friends had tried to interest Luce in seeing a new foal someone had, but Luce said today she had to be home.

Jack bolted back toward the house.

As he ran, the thoughts drummed in his skull. Normans, Romans, Brid's protective altar stone that gave its name to the village, Luce so mad to reach the fields she jumped out of a window, singing out there all those evenings in the dusk—to herself? Or to *what*? The figure among the grain, amused, patient—*greedy*. And Susie winning the lottery, such good luck.

When he burst into the house, Susie was sitting there with her shoes off, drinking water from a bottle.

"Jack! I didn't get the job, but there's much better news. I met Ken Angel in town—you know, that TV thing I did. He's down here looking for locations. He *said*—now *wait* for it—he'd like me aboard on this production. Oh, just two or three lines but . . . well don't look so astounded. I can still act, you know."

"Is Lucy here?" said Jack.

Susie's flushed face went white. She dropped the water bottle and he watched the water uncoil along the carpet. "*What do you mean?* Of course she's not here—you just met her at school. *Didn't* you?"

Jack explained Luce had been gone, to a mother whose face was now blank with fear.

He thought, even if any of this were possible it couldn't be Susie's fault. She hadn't met *something*, made a bargain. . . .

She was at the phone, rattling it about. "Damn, no line, now of all times. Where's my mobile . . ." the contents of her bag tipped out on the water on the floor. She stabbed at buttons.

"You're calling the police."

"No, a pizza delivery. *What do you think?*"

Something slid into Jack's mind. He thought of foxes in London, on the streets in the early morning, sleeping in gardens—man had taken over so much of the open country, now the foxes had come to live where the people were.

Were *They* like that? Did they in fact like to be close, maybe just in that wood up there—watching their chance, intrigued by cricket on the green, the pub with their name, the trains. Waiting. In case something might become available. . . .

All this was madness.

Jack stood fighting with himself. Then he realized Susie wasn't talking into her mobile. She said, flatly, "I can't get a signal." Then she said, *"Where are you going?"*

What could he tell her? Nothing.

He ran into the kitchen, opened the back door, ran again. Behind him he could hear her shouting in panic and anger. He couldn't let that slow him down.

He was practiced now getting over the back fence. He heard her bare feet beating on the path. The fields were like a wall of dry white fire, into which, like a moth, he flew.

They were there.

Yes, he could feel them all around, unseen but *present*. Some primitive sixth sense had kicked into play inside him, though really, hadn't it done that from the very start?

Jack stopped running. He pushed forward through the grain. There seemed to be eyes behind every group of stalks. *Green* eyes, and hair that blended with the color of the fields. Yet when they *let* you see them, they were luminous.

It was no good now thinking he was mental. He knew this was *real*.

Above the fields, the woods, dark green, with green-gold glitters of sun.

He strode through them, fast, looking everywhere. Birds shrilled warnings, squirrels darted overhead. They were like the heartless servants of what truly lurked here.

The hot, static air seemed full of mocking laughter. Sometimes he called out his sister's name. It had a hollow sound.

This was useless, but somehow it had to be done. A sick weight was gathering in his stomach. He refused to think about Susie. Even though this was no use, he must go on. He wondered vaguely how many times, since people first lived here, someone or other just like Jack had trudged across this hilly landscape, calling someone's name, knowing it was no use at all.

The sun moved west. He would have killed for one of those exploded colas—of course, *They* had done that, too—and messed up the phones? Some sort of electric psi stuff, like a poltergeist.

Jack came to a halt. Suddenly he'd stepped over dark tree roots, mosses, ferns, and come out on quite a wide road going sunlit through the woods.

The sense of being watched and laughed at lessened. Then he saw there was an ordinary man standing under a tree.

"Thank God, there you are."

"Mr. Tooth the dentist," said Jack, confused.

"Thanks for the inevitable joke. Try Alan, if you wouldn't mind."

"A. Tooth," said Jack idiotically. He burst into childish giggling, appalling himself. Then he leaned over and threw up.

When he'd finished, Alan Tooth handed him an unopened bottle of water. Jack gulped; the water helped. He said, "How the hell did you happen to be waiting?"

"It seems everyone comes this route. They used to call it Lordly Way—there's an old track under the fields and trees. You can still find traces if you know where to look. I'm into amateur archeology. That's how I first met Soldier. As for you—well after we spoke, I worked it out—abruptly, during my tea break. I canceled a couple of non-emergencies and called on Soldier myself, this evening. Then I knew."

"Do you know . . . does it *happen*?"

"Yes, I think so. Not often. This is the first for about half a century. The police scoured the place that time. They said it was child abduction, the usual filthy human thing. It wasn't, though, I don't think. My mother told me about it. A boy that time, twelve years old. Very fair hair. *They* like the ones that look the most like they do, you see."

"He—Soldier—said it had to be a bargain."

"No. A certain kind of *wishing* seems to do it. The mother of the boy that time, she'd made a thing of telling everyone she wished she'd never had him, was sick to death of him, wanted a better life instead. And the funny thing is, after this child went missing, the police never had her under suspicion. Then she met a man with a load of dosh and married him."

Jack put his hand on the nearest tree to steady the rocking world.

Now he knew who had made the bargain that involved Luce—or formed the *wish* that wrecked the protective magic of Brid's Stone for her. It was *Michael*. Susie had never *ever* wished her family gone. She had been happy. But Michael invented a new personality for Susie—a woman who hated her kids and only wanted her old life back—and this was the Susie he slapped and punched. And all that time Michael told them all how sick of them *he* was. Sick enough to get up and leave forever. And with that thought he must have changed his loser's luck—and they received the edge of it.

They had also been dragged toward the nearest place where the payment for Michael's luck must be made. Jack remembered the three of them looking at the estate agent's stuff. Susie and Luce had fixed on Bridestone the moment they saw it.

"Come on," said Alan Tooth. "We'd better get you home. Your mother'll need you."

"Then it's hopeless—searching?"

Alan's face fell. He no longer looked particularly grown-up himself. "Let's hope not. But better leave it to the police."

"You said . . ."

"I know. But going on the records, no one ever got them back. Not even a body."

"Unless they came back themselves centuries after—like Soldier."

Someone spoke out of the wood. Both Jack and Alan jumped violently. "It's waxing moon," said the voice of Soldier. "Go we up that highest hill. Go careful."

He came out of the wood, his face holy as that of a knight carved on a tomb. His speech was altered by time and memory, and *he* was altered—strong, perhaps irresistible.

The climb up the hill was hard work. Stony outcrops, beech and elder trees, interrupted the path. The hill was coated in tangled grass. Far behind, the golden sun was sinking into the land, taking away the light.

"See," said Soldier, "she is risen."

The crescent moon was up the hill, still faint in the sunset.

The remains of the fort above seemed one with the jumble of the hill.

"This is where the entrance lies to their domain," said Soldier.

Alan added, "Yes, it's supposed to be under this hill. That's why the Romans had trouble here and brought in the druids—most unusual. They weren't normally friends. The druids suggested the Stone of Brid. Roman soldiers tended to prefer worshipping Mithras. Not here."

Alan was seeming more scholarly, and Soldier more insane. Defensive? Jack had no defense. He didn't even know why they had come up here—but again, the *compulsion* was intense.

Maybe *They* liked somebody to see what they could do, how beautiful they were, how clever. . . .

The last sun was squashed out just as they made the final stretch. Both Jack and Alan were dripping sweat. Soldier wasn't, though he looked three times Alan's age. The darkening light now became actual darkness. Shadow sprawled from rocks, trees, down from the sky itself. The moon, though, brightened, a white rip in the dusk.

The jagged Roman walls were in front of them. Ruin and nightfall robbed them of any shape or logic. A portion of archway stood ahead, and beyond it a kind of grassy court that looked as if sheep had grazed it recently. Down a topple of slope, Jack saw a formless stone.

"There," panted Alan. "There it is. The altar."

"They will always come here," said Soldier softly, "when they have gotten, to show their triumph to the Stone. God wills. *They are already here*."

Jack stared, hair rising on arms and neck.

Through liquid shadow, something pale, that shone—

He could see them. The Lordly Ones, the—

Elvenbrood.

He didn't try to count, but he thought there were four-teen—one for every year of his sister's life. Yes, they were beautiful all right. Their skin was pearl, hair moonlit clouds. Some were male, others female, but their clothes were the same, misty, clinging on slender bodies, but also flowing. There were jewels on them like nothing he'd ever seen or imagined, with great tears of light inside. They had daggers too, and swords of some silvery metal that couldn't be steel. And as he gazed at them, hypnotized, Jack saw Luce, there in the middle of them. Like them, she had flowers in her hair.

He wanted to shout to her. *They* were smiling and laugh-ing, and so was she. Laughter like silver bells and silver dag-gers—

His mind yelled in the prison of his paralyzed body—but he couldn't move, and neither it seemed could Alan.

The Lordly Ones danced their stately dance along the hill, with Luce dancing with them, and coming to the altar they bowed, and their bowing was full of the most exquisite scorn.

Alan croaked something. "D'you see?"

Another thing had formed, beyond the altar, right there. It was a hole into emptiness, but down the tunnel of it was a pulsing, gorgeous glow.

"It's the *gate*, the way into the underhill . . ."

Trying to move, heart roaring, pinned to the spot . . .

Jack's struggle seemed to dislodge something outside himself.

Soldier.

"Here I am. Here, your child that you loved, who loved you hundred on hundred years. The one you sent into exile, lost in this world that, to your heaven country, is hell . . ." Soldier moved among them, with extraordinary grace. He moved as *They* did. Not like an old man in clothes from the garbage in a dustbin. He spoke in some language Jack never heard—almost a twisted sort of Germanic French—yet Jack somehow understood every word.

"Don't take that other child," said Soldier to the Lordly Ones, royally scornful as they were. "Do you really want *her*? Ignorant and unformed and knowing nothing of your glory. No, take me again, out of this bitter world. I love you so. And I have learned all there is to know here. I am like a book you will be able to read for a thousand years."

The beings on the hill had ceased to move about. They looked stilly at Soldier.

Luce, petulant suddenly, cried, "It's only that stupid mad old man . . ."

One of the beings struck her lightly across the face. He did not speak, but turning to Soldier, he reached up and breathed into the old man's mouth. Although there were no words, Jack knew what the being had said: *Let us then remind ourselves of how you were. Let us compare and judge.*

You could make no excuses. It happened in front of Jack's eyes. Age and decay fell from Soldier like a discarded shell. He stood there, straight as a spear, a boy of maybe thirteen, golden skinned, unmarked, sun-gold hair to his waist.

Yes, said the voice that *had* no voice, *he is better.*

Laughing, Soldier looked green-eyed over his shoulder at Jack and Alan stuck there to the ground. "Farewell, men of mud. Farewell, world of dust. Know for always you could not have kept her, had They not loved me better than she."

A dazzle hit the hillside. Treetops and walls flared like neon, faded.

They were gone, the beings from the hill, the old man who had become a boy. Only one last pale shape remained, lying on the grass.

Paralysis left Jack. "Luce!"

When he touched her, she opened her eyes and looked at him, annoyed. "Why did you wake me up, Jack? What time is it?" And then, surprised but not alarmed, "Why am I up *here?*"

Jack couldn't speak. It was Alan who had to spin her some yarn that she'd come up here on a dare. Oddly, as she listened she seemed to believe him, to *remember* the dare—and nothing else unusual at all.

Alan and Jack talked later. It was a secret they had to keep always from Susie, and from Luce too. "It wasn't just they loved Soldier more than Lucy, Jack. It was because you and Susie love her so *much*. That other woman who hated her boy—Soldier could never have made a swap with him—I doubt if he even tried. I think he only warned Lucy to make her more likely to do it—you know how girls can be. Or maybe when he was saner he did try to stop those things. Would she have been happier *there?* Well, yes. But that's not it. We're supposed to live out *here.*"

Jack and Alan often had talks now, since Susie had moved the family to the town, and Susie and Alan became an

Item. Susie was rehearsing for her part in Ken Angel's TV drama—it had nothing to do with faeries.

It was a year later that police in Gloucester found the burnt-out Jeep Cherokee with Michael's body in it. It had gone off a country road into some trees. They said Michael would have been killed at once, the fire had happened afterward. It seemed, from bits of evidence, that Michael had become rich after leaving Susie. No one could find any trace of how, or where. It was a real mystery.

But Jack knew, he and Alan, though *this* they did not discuss: how Michael had come by his sudden money luck, the edge of which had rubbed off on Susie. Knew, too how Michael would not have been dead when his vehicle caught fire. Like Soldier's father, the Norman warlord ten centuries before, Michael had been burned alive.

Tanith Lee was born in 1947 in London, England. She began to write at the age of nine. In 1970–71 three of Lee's children's books were published. In 1975 DAW Books published her novel *The Birthgrave*, and thereafter twenty-six of her books, enabling her to become a full-time writer. To date she has written sixty-two novels and nine collections of novellas and short stories (she has published over two hundred short stories and novellas). Four of her radio plays have been broadcast by the BBC in the UK and she has written two episodes of the BBC cult TV series *Blake's Seven*.

Lee has twice won the World Fantasy Award for short fiction and was awarded the August Derleth Award in 1980 for her novel *Death's Master*.

In 1992 Lee married the writer John Kaiine, her partner since 1987. They live in southeast England with one black-and-white and one Siamese cat.

Her Web site address is www.tanithlee.com

Author's Note

I first had the idea for this story when I was seventeen. It seemed to me that all the wild land in England was being taken over by man. And so, just like foxes, frogs, and owls the faery kind might end up living very close—even in our fields and gardens. The Elvenbrood themselves appeared mentally before me, and have stayed in my mind, therefore, for almost forty years.

Your Garnet Eyes

Katherine Vaz

Papá sobs every night when he thinks I'm asleep. Especially during a storm, when the rain bangs our tin roof, like a bill collector demanding to be let in. All over Brazil, the palm trees wave furiously, like huge rags trying to wipe away the weeping of the sky. I tiptoe across our brown rug, so worn it looks like a balding head. I'm a cat on my feet. Cats are half-faeries too, just like me. I lean my head on the kitchen door, not sure whether to go in and grab the whiskey bottle from Papá. He's floating on a bitter river: whiskey and tears, my mortal father.

My faery mother, Aurora, liked to siphon the rich beauty out of milk, leaving us with just the whiteness.

Aurora would buy beads to string me bracelets, but she'd steal the brightness from the colors.

She sapped the juice out of papayas, the bite out of peppers.

What she robbed, worse than all that, was the strength from my father's bones. Tonight I fried bean cakes with shrimp and sliced pineapple as tender as butter—he didn't touch any of it. He claims that only the touch of my mother will save him. I scream that it's been three years since she left us, and in faery time two months equal two hundred years, and you do the math, I'm weary of it, she's a sprite, a firefly, a belch of swamp gas, an accordion made of sparks that you grasp in both hands and squeeze to hear music, but she explodes in your face. Aurora was born in water; the rain makes Papá wonder if she's splintering into an army of needles hailing down on him.

He showered her with gifts! And she thanked him by running off!

I beg him to visit a *mãe de santo* who'll dance to a drumbeat and put him in a trance, so he'll possess himself again. He says, "I don't want her out of my skin."

Like a salmon swimming the opposite direction from my father's sadness, I return to my room. Salmon are half-faeries, too. They fight against the tide, hoping to protect their flesh that's orange-pink-coral, bold as the tint of roses.

I know an enchantment that will fix my father up with someone new. Mamá told me that wearing the scent of the primrose will attract the first person who comes near, like nails to a magnet.

A bottle of primrose oil hides at the candle factory where I work. Tourists come to my city of Salvador to buy green candles for luck with money, blue for good health. Yellow heals a friendship. We save the primrose oil for a select few of the red candles, for passion; these cost the most and come with certificates of warning. When we pour it into a vat of wax, we must wear a mask and gloves.

I've chosen my friend Xani to help Papá forget my mother. She's a widow who works with me. She's forty, twice my age, but one of the best dancers in the Carnaval parade. Her husband was a handsome cliff diver who could hold his breath for three minutes underwater, and you'd wonder if he was finding a pearl. One day he didn't surface. Xani's black hair used to shine like a waterfall, but now it's flat. She used to wear earrings that swung; she doesn't bother anymore. I'll call across the factory, "Shhaa . . . nee . . ." and sometimes she barely glances up.

I stole the primrose oil off the shelf. The bottle was small and blue with a cork stopper. I tucked it into my purse that's shaped like a straw alligator, and just to celebrate (there's a speck of my mother in me, I admit it), I mixed red and blue dye in a vat of wax to make forbidden purple. Xani giggled and joined in. I was coating some white candles with stripes when our boss, Dolores, blew in and said, "Teresa Silva! What are you doing?" "Being artistic," I said. "Purple is for jealousy, and don't tell me you don't know that!" she shouted, "and why aren't you wearing your hair net?" "Because it's ugly," I said. Another reason is that it reminds me of a fisherman's net, which is how my father caught my mother, but this hag does not need bulletins on my history. "Purple also means royalty," said Xani. "You pipe down," said Dolores. "Leave my friend alone," I said . . . you see what I put up with to earn a living.

Dolores has orange frazzled hair, and her body bulges in

her tight clothing, like bicycle tires stacked horizontally, with her fat head on top. A beauty mark on her cheek reminds me of a beetle. She said, wagging her finger at me, "Tread lightly, Senhora Silva!" and stomped away through the factory, her butt in her stretch pants like two basketballs getting smothered.

It was worth a scolding to see Xani laughing. My alligator purse had a sagging belly, full of primrose oil. I asked Xani to come over for dinner. She was in such a good mood that for once she agreed.

While my father was working at the fish market, tying bands around the pincers of lobsters, I snapped on rubber gloves and dipped the edges of our special lace dinner napkins with the oil and let them dry in the sun, then folded them and set them on the table. When my father and Xani wipe their lips, they will stare at each other and not stop kissing.

I decided to boil crabs and make a palm-fruit salad. A parrot dipped a wing in front of the window and went to converse with the birds-of-paradise in our garden, and my soul was heating up from a joy that felt almost unearthly, until I realized why: I'd forgotten to cover my face, and the perfume of the primrose oil was entering my nostrils.

I stumbled to Mamá's trousseau chest and grabbed the vial of her eye ointment. I never want to fall in love—look what it's done to Papá. I rubbed the salve onto my corneas so I'd have the power to stare through glamour to a person's insides. A faery can do that without any ointment, a human needs a lot of it, and a half-faery needs a thin coating. Usually there's moss, puffed-up feathers, and spiders swinging on threads inside people, and one glimpse of that is enough to make anyone turn and sprint for her life.

(I'm frightened of what I'll do when the ointment runs out. . . . Mamá, you're stupid and wicked. You didn't leave enough behind.)

I smoothed my hand over the lid of Mamá's chest. It's a gleaming cherrywood, red, red, like wood that's run a long way and pumped its blood to the surface.

While chopping hard-cooked eggs and pickles to mix with the cooked crab, my hand shook with the knife. Even with a cloth tied around my nose and mouth, the dinner napkins were like a bellows blowing out perfume. I needed some open air.

At the market stalls near the bay, I bought a tiny paper boat, a red lipstick, and a comb shaped like a peacock from a street boy named Zé, whose black feet were made polka-dot by white blisters.

"Why are you sad?" Zé asked.

"Sad? I'm not sad," I said, my lip trembling.

Zé walked with me to the edge of the water, holding my hand. We put the lipstick and comb into the paper boat and launched it as a gift to Iemenjá, the Goddess of the Ocean.

Making a megaphone out of his hands, Zé called out: "EEEE—MANH—JAAAhhhh!"

The waves answered, "*AAAhhh. . . .*"

Zé asked if I was an Asrai faery. Was that why my eyes stared faraway? Because I missed my home? I said, "No, I'm not an Asrai. But my Mamá was." Once every hundred years, the Asrai faeries kiss Iemenjá farewell and rise from their homes in the sea. They emerge to stare at the moon until they grow. Most of them get greedy and swell until they explode into a million sparks that burn back through the waves. But Mamá, when she rose up, stared just long enough to become human size, and she tore her sight from the moon and captured the eye of my father, alone on a boat, pulling a trap of lobsters from the murk.

Zé and I giggled while walking backward from the shoreline. Never turn your back on Iemenjá! She expects your gaze until you disappear. She's as vain as my mother was, forever admiring herself—that's why the ocean is so often described as filled with glassy mirrors.

Did Mamá run back to her home in the water?

Or did she dart through those slits in the air that connect our hours to the endless time of the other world?

The rumor is that only a person or spirit in love can slip through to the filmy underside of the sky.

On a boat ride down the Amazon River once, the three of us joking and my father's mane of hair blowing and his wire-rimmed glasses throwing beams like light swords, Mamá said, "Time gets split open like wet fruit." She seized a mango from a hanging branch and gave it to me.

I must have loved her then, because I fell through a crack in time. Why else did I feel weightless, in heaven?

I told Iemenjá that I didn't need my mother anymore; I had new plans, and I kissed Zé good-bye and hurried home. I stopped at the view through our window. Sitting at the table, wiping her chin with the lace napkin I'd set out, eating the crab, guzzling white wine, was Dolores, her Godzilla rear end threatening to break one of our cane chairs. My father's glasses were steamy as he kissed her face. She was slobbering something, probably, "Oh, Gil, you old fox! You're so sweet!" She grabbed a hunk of my father's tanned leather cheek and pinched it. This seemed to tickle him. I didn't know whether to faint or throw up.

Xani approached down our cobblestone path, in a sky blue linen dress, like the kind of outfit a lovely but sensible woman wears for her second wedding, this time in a garden.

"You're late," I said.

"Not too late, I hope?" She held out a bouquet of azaleas and smiled. She'd tucked a hibiscus like a trumpet into her hair. "I heard that Dolores was coming over to tell your father about the trouble we cause at work, and I wanted to wait until I figured she'd be gone."

My father's gifts, over the years, to my mother: insects trapped in amber; onyx necklaces; ribbons to tie around her wrist for wish-making; coconut candy; harmonicas; Indian rain sticks; samba CDs.

Stop, Gil, stop, stop! she'd say. But he'd insist.

He bought her a cockatoo costume to march in the Carnaval parade, spangles on a yellow bikini, a headdress the size of an almond tree, shedding its snowflake-flowers.

Stop, stop, stop!

He'd hoist her onto the tabletop so that her head vanished inside the full moon burning through the windowpane. She wore the blazing moon on her shoulders.

All heat and glow, my father holding her there, Aurora would laugh. With joy? With power?

Why not? Gil Silva loved to give her the moon and dress her with the night.

~~~~~~~~~

Xani and I sat on a beach towel. She pretended that a terrible spectacle was not occurring close by. Fiddler crabs opened breathing holes in the sand so it looked pocked, but that was a prettier sight than my father dancing with Dolores; sprays of sand hitting the bare backs of people who were here to enjoy Iemenjá's official feast day and eat shrimp and pork roasted on a spit at one of the little food stands.

Oh, Papá! You're lean and tough, but put a *shirt* on! Dolores was squeezed into a bikini with tassels that swung as the two of them did a bad-on-purpose tango through the forest of towels, and naked guts, legs, and arms glistening with coconut lotion. The sun poured a white, hot syrup over everyone, while schooners and canoes drifted from the shore to deeper waters, carrying tiaras, earrings, toffee, starfish pasted with glitter, and barrettes for Iemenjá. Maybe she'd give my mother the blue metal bracelet I sent out. Paper flowers like Technicolor jellyfish bobbed on the waves, their dye melting and painting streamers on the surface before they sank.

"What a jackass," said Xani.

"I know," I said. "Bad enough we have to deal with her at work."

A column of foam burst skyward; faeries sometimes shoot through the geyser of a dolphin, hoping for a peek around.

"I meant your father," said Xani. "He's lovely, everyone says he's the best lobsterman around, which means he knows how to crack tough things to get to tender things, he's got such nice long hair and kind eyes, but he's acting like— Well."

"A fool?" I said, blushing as red as Iemenjá's lips must be by now, from all the lipsticks dropping like bullets into her lair.

"I'm sorry," said Xani. "I guess I should keep my mouth shut."

I was annoyed with her, but then again, I figured if I wanted her as a stepmother I needed to give her license to see Papá as he was at any given moment. Her black hair was in a shiny braid, and since she was in a cobalt string bikini I noticed a wine-colored stain, in the shape of a star, on her side. How could my father resist that star? Maybe he *was* the jackass. Just then I heard Dolores—singing? Braying? What was that noise from her? Whooping? Or was that my father? I'd have to act fast before Xani got so disgusted that even primrose oil wouldn't work.

I arranged for my father to deliver a lobster to Xani's house and told him he'd have to show her how to break its shell. "What kind of Brazilian girl isn't on a first-name basis with seafood?" he said. "Ever since her husband died in that diving accident, she finds water creatures upsetting," I said solemnly. While he was changing from his fisherman's rubber apron and boots, I oiled the claws with primrose. This time I wore a mask as well as gloves. I looked like a lunatic surgeon.

I really planned to get the ointment out of Mamá's cherry-wood chest and slather my father's eyes, so that he could see that the inside of Dolores is coal while Xani's spirit is clear as a drink of water. I had every intention of neatly removing Dolores from the equation. . . . It's easy to trick him into getting eyedrops; since he's a lobsterman, the sea glare scalds his vision, and I'm always plying a dropper with medicine because he's large and strong but a big baby about such things. The trouble is, with the supply running low, I have to think of myself, don't I?

Okay, I admit it, it amused me to think of two women fighting over him. Sure. Let's just see how nature and primrose duke it out.

While sitting on the steps of the church on Rua Ribeiro dos Santos, I glimpsed, in the plaza, my father with Xani and Dolores, all three of them fighting in a way that was very funny when observed from my perch, the three of them waving their arms and stomping and Xani pushing Dolores on the shoulder and then both the women knocking Papá's shoulders. They looked like a puppet show viewed through a telescope. *No, I love you! You do not! I love him best!* Hilarious!

So tell me this: Why was I cracking with grief?

Was it because I was by myself and far away? Or because they looked like they were underwater—where words aren't heard, and kelp shakes like people in a rage, and where Aurora my mother is dead or alive or whatever it is that creatures become when they slip out of our days?

The Christ lying on a bed of white lace in Igreja Nossa Senhora do Carmo is my favorite, because he combines several worlds. He was carved by an African slave for his Christian master, a priest. The slave worked with only two knives over eight years and used resins to give the skin color a dark brown, just like mine. Just like Papá's. His eyes are closed; his face looks so helpless that it fills me with wonder, that someone knew how to carve with a knife until helplessness looked like a kind of strange beauty.

The priest was so astonished that he gave the slave a sack of two thousand rubies along with his freedom.

The freed slave crushed the rubies and attached every bit of them to the loincloth and chest of his statue. The one thing that had been missing from his masterpiece was the sign of shed blood. He'd only been given resin, wood, and knives.

It was his own blood, of course, that he gave. Not long after gifting the dying Christ with this finishing touch, the slave—or should we call him the free man?—curled up and died.

I went to see the statue again. I couldn't touch the wooden limbs through the glass case, but I wanted to whisper, "Imagine giving a gift so great that you're ready to die. Imagine loving something or someone so much that you'll give the gift that kills you."

Papá didn't fight me. His head was spinning with confusion. "Angel?" he asked me. "Yes, Papá." "I give up." "On what, Papá? Would you kindly sit still?" I was aiming the ointment for his eyes. He was sitting on our lumpy sofa, his head tilted back. Since he's human, I'll have to douse him with all I have left. "I give up on women, witches, faeries, candlemakers, and maybe even female lobsters." "Then we'll starve. Hold still!" I had to wait until the salve sunk into one eye and then I started on the other, then applied a second coating, and a third. "You can support me with your fine wages as a candlemaker." "Dolores will eventually fire me." "Oh, God, don't talk to me about Dolores!" shrieked my father with burning eyes.

The vial was empty.

He looked into Xani, past her lovely exterior, and saw a gorgeous soul. But he also detected that she missed her dead husband, and Papá wasn't the right one for her. Sometimes, he explained to me, you could care about someone enough to go away from him or her; you could give that person up.

Dolores wasn't (whew! close call!) meant for him either, though he told me she was a lonely soul, not an ashy one.

"Teresa?" he said. We were lounging at the table, while the faucet was *plink-plink*ing to serenade us with some morning water music. We were eating bread smeared with honey for our breakfast and drinking coffee thick and sweet, like candy tar. I nodded at him; I was listening.

"I can't stop loving your mother. I don't want to stop." He gripped his espresso cup and took its contents back like a shot. The veins on his arms were like blue ropes from years of hauling traps.

"I know," I said.

Being only half-faery, I hadn't known that Aurora broke one of the rules. Faeries adhere to a strict code of gift giving. They expect a present in return for what they do. A lesser gift in return is an insult, but so is a greater one. "I loved her too much, I couldn't stop giving her things, but most of all, I couldn't stop giving her myself," said Papá. "I upset the balance that keeps life calm and ordinary. Someone had to pay for breaking the rule, and she should have destroyed me, on a whim. But your mother loved me too, and so she decided to destroy herself. She paid with her freedom. She left me a note about throwing herself back into the sea."

At the candle factory, Dolores let me take a canister of the paraffin with lanolin we sell to the beauty salons in Bahia. Ladies stick their hands into the cooling, melted paraffin, and then they peel off white waxy gloves. Their softened skin smells like lavender. The discarded wax looks like the ghosts of their hands. Dolores was wearing a rhinestone butterfly in her orange hair, and I told her it looked nice. She seemed shocked and said, "Thank you, Teresa."

I stuck my hands into the paraffin and peeled off replicas.

My father and I strolled to the bay, carrying my wax ghosts of hands, and we launched them into the water. I hoped Iemenjá would find them and call Aurora over and say, "These are for you."

My ghostly hands will touch either side of her face to say, *Look at us, waiting for you here.*

"Aurora!" called out my father.

My mother's garnet eyes shine in the dark. She shows me the octopus that leads her through crevices on the underwater floor, flattening its head to get where it wants to go.

"Teresa," says Mamá, and holding her is like being in a whirlpool, but without the fear of drowning. She's chopped her hair off in a modern, spiky style; long hair gets tangled in coral. We both laugh at this. I put my head on her spongy shoulder. I have no trouble breathing. Her eyes are red, the color of passion.

I leave my mother and father together and play skittles

with some starfish. A fluorescent snap lights up the deep, and with it a sense that I am awakening, kicking back to the surface.

I need to go back! I need to go back! I forgot to tell Mamá that her eyes are the color of the ruby blood on the slave's work of art.

My human father and I belong to the clockworks of the world. We landed in the midst of Carnaval. Where had the days gone? Xani jogged by, wearing next to nothing. She waved at my father and me and danced off alone, smiling. The twirling, hoop-skirted women, the feet-thumping drummers, the *mães de santo* and *pais de santo* who help people go into trances: I couldn't shake off the one I was in, sick with wanting to see my mother's jeweled eyes. The sequins, the baubles of the costumes, were driving me half-mad with longing.

Is this the danger of love? Now that I don't have the ointment for protection, now that I can't peel people like fruit and inspect their rotten insides, I found myself admiring a man, maybe twenty, my age, in a *capoeira* match. They're our street fighters, our magicians; they leap as if the air holds down invisible ladders; somersaults turn them into white-clothed pinwheels, slapping gravity until it begs for mercy. This boy tumbled with the others, all of them like pointed stars. Long ago, the slaves here taught each other to fight so it looked like dancing, so no one would see clear to the fury within them.

I was finishing a *maracujá* juice. Passionfruit. Pink and sweet. Isn't mischief better than love? I took out my pocket mirror to catch the light. A ray stabbed the boy I liked, and he crashed to the ground.

Every time he spun, I jabbed him with bolts of light, and he fell into the dust. What came over me? After the match, I ran to him and said, "Are you hurt?"

He held his side and dusted off his white trousers. He gave his name as Jaime and smiled, and I thought I was dying. He was so forgiving. "Not my best day," he said, grinning. I was about to say this was maybe my best day ever, but then a girl in a gold tube dress raced over and took his arm. She was upset for fear that he'd broken some bones from falling.

"My wife," he said, drawing her near, his arm over her shoulder.

I gave her a quick good-bye kiss, and one for Jaime.

At home, at night, a rainstorm can cover the sound of my weeping. Tears, of course, are salt water, the realm of our bodies, the realm of the deep sea. That's how my mother floats inside me. How shall I bear her safely, buoyantly along?

My father tiptoes into the kitchen, and I straighten up, wipe my face, and we drink pineapple soda together. We talk about my going back to school, or visiting Rio. We tell bad jokes and groan. He wonders if I want to work in the candle factory for the rest of my days. Would that make me happy?

Happiness! We both giggle at such a word. I get up and wash our glasses. They sparkle. I put them into our splintery cupboards. When will time split open? I visit the statue with its bleeding rubies and must patiently wait for it to inform me how pain becomes beauty. And then one day, I see it—my father rises early to go out to the sea in his boat, trawling for lobster. I wave to him from the shore. As he dips traps and nets, the sparks of Aurora jump up as if slapping his face, and the fierceness of the sun on the water forces him to lift his gaze—and I lift mine—toward the enormous city. It sparkles, too; it glistens like a breathable ocean. Treasures— love and its blinding troubles—await us there, my mother seems to say, there among the living, when we're ready to go and find them.

Katherine Vaz, a Briggs-Copeland Lecturer in creative writing at Harvard University, is the author of two novels, *Saudade* and *Mariana*, the latter published in six languages and selected by the U.S. Library of Congress as one of the Top 30 International Books of 1998. Her collection *Fado & Other Stories* won the 1997 Drue Heinz Literature Prize and her short fiction has appeared in many journals, including *Glimmer Train*, *BOMB*, *The Sun*, *The Antioch Review*, and *Tin House*.

Her stories have been published in the anthologies *A Wolf at the Door*, *The Green Man*, and *Swan Sister*. She lives in Cambridge, Massachusetts.

Author's Note

I have some very distant cousins who emigrated from the Azores to Brazil. I never met them, and I've never been to Brazil, but the place contains for me the lure of legend. One of my relatives, it was whispered, threw herself into the sea.

I'm lucky to have many Brazilian friends who always bring me back the magical ribbon *O Nosso Senhor do Bomfim* from Bahía, in the north. You tie the ribbon around your wrist, and when it breaks on its own, your wish is granted. I was wearing a green one that broke while I was teaching in California, and that was the week that I sold my story collection! (Green represents commerce, luck, money.)

I've long enjoyed the tales of Iemenjá, the Queen of the

Ocean, and the ceremony of sending paper boats filled with lipsticks and other treasures out to sea on her feast day. That image has existed for so long in my imagination that I can just about feel the breezes. So here is a story full of my love and connection to a place I've visited only through friends, talismans, and in my mind and heart.

Tengu Mountain

~

Gregory Frost

Ando met his fate in the form of a priest, while he was climbing up the mountain to his aunt Sakura's house. Ando nearly stepped on him.

The priest lay across his path, like a log that had rolled down the mountainside and come to rest where the path cut between two outcroppings of stone; and at first that was what Ando thought he was seeing. The priest's orange robes looked like leaves or peeling bark in the light of the setting sun. Not until he stood over him did Ando notice the closed eyes, the ridiculously long nose, the gray beard, the small black *tokin* cap topping that slumbering face. From the robes and cap, he knew he was looking at a *yamabushi* priest—an outlaw monk.

His hand went to his sword and he glanced around warily. Had the priest been struck down? Had some irate military governor sent samurai after him? But no blood stained his robes, and his head seemed securely attached. Really, it looked as if he'd just stretched out and gone to sleep with the rocks keeping him from rolling away.

Meanwhile, the sun was setting, and Ando fretted that he still had a long climb ahead of him. He didn't want to leave the path. Besides, if the monk *was* dead, then there was nothing to do. If he was asleep, it was best to leave him alone.

Hefting his pack, Ando raised his foot up over the priest.

A hand shot from the robes, clutched the sole of Ando's sandal and propelled him into the air. He pinwheeled high around his pack, only to land on his feet—although not through any skill of his own.

Now he was above the priest, but the priest hadn't moved. His eyes remained closed and his hand had vanished into the orange folds of his robe again.

"Sir?" Ando said.

The priest didn't stir.

Now what do I say? he wondered. He scratched behind his ear. Across the valley, the sun had almost disappeared behind the ridge. There was no time to puzzle this out. "Thank you," said Ando, and he turned to go.

Behind him, a voice replied, "I stop you from stepping on me and rather than apologizing, you tell me 'thank you'? That's uncommonly strange."

Ando swung about. "I would never have stepped on you."

"Indeed." The priest sprang up like a sapling that had been tied back until the rope snapped. "And I suppose you'd never pour boiling copper down my throat, either."

Ando blinked. "It would never have occurred to me. Boiling copper?"

The priest gestured dismissively. "I've had worse. Evil

shugo sending their samurai to cut us all down . . . You, young man, should not be traveling up this mountain alone with night setting in."

"This from a man who was asleep on this mountain, with night setting in."

"In fact," the monk continued, "it's rare to see humans here at all." He squinted at Ando suspiciously.

"I happen to be traveling to the top of this ridge, below Mount Kurami. My auntie lives there, and I've come to spend the rest of the year with her. So I won't be by myself for long, provided I stop jabbering with you." He hoisted his pack.

"Taught you manners like this in the city, did they? You must have a couple of *tanuki* for parents."

"My—" Ando went stiff with anger—"My parents are perfectly decent. I'm done conversing with you, you vagabond. I should turn you in to the local *shugo* and *let* him have you, boiling copper and all!" He stormed up the path.

Ando's anger fueled his pace. His aunt's house couldn't be too much farther now. But he had been a child the last time he'd seen it. He stared through the darkness, into the trees above for some sign, some light to guide him.

The path snaked from right to the left, at which point Ando stopped dead in his tracks, because the priest stood ahead of him, leaning on a strange staff as if he'd been there for hours. Ando was compelled to look back the way he'd come. Perhaps there were two such monks, playing a trick upon him.

The priest said, "I wish to apologize to you, young man. No business had I casting aspersions upon your good family, who have clearly raised you well. Please, allow me to accompany you—not because you require assistance, no, no. I'm sure you would find your way. But, allow me because I know these mountains better than anyone living here, and can navigate this path in the blackness of a moonless night."

"How do I know you won't lead me right off the edge of a cliff, out of spite?"

The priest tugged at his nose. "Then let me follow after you to guard your back."

"What from?"

"Who can say?"

"I suppose I really cannot stop you, unless I want to walk backwards the rest of my journey."

"It would be difficult."

"But keep your distance," Ando warned. "I don't want you pushing me over the edge, either." Shaking his head, he continued on his way. He glanced back now and again, but the priest came no closer.

"Who is your aunt?" the priest called.

"Aunt Sakura," replied Ando. "She lives in a fine house at the top of this ridge. My parents call it her summer home, although she lives here year-round since my uncle died, and that was long ago. She is my father's sister, and my mother does not get on with her. I haven't visited since I was six."

"Fourteen years absent," the priest said.

"Yes—say, how did you know that?" Looking around, he paused.

"I guessed, young warrior."

"Ha! I'm no warrior. I'm—that is, I'm a . . . a painter."

Soon Ando glimpsed lights through the trees above.

"There!" he cried, and hurried on. The path was only a vague stripe now.

Finally, he stood at the open gate below a plateau on which perched a wide house, sparkling with lanterns. "There it is, you see?" said Ando.

"*This* is your aunt's house." The priest sounded dismayed.

"Quite astonishing, isn't it?"

"Astonishing, yes. And so are you, young . . . man."

"You know my aunt, do you?"

"Not as such."

Politeness overcame Ando's better judgment, and he asked, "You wouldn't care for a meal? You've come all this way with me, surely you must be hungry."

"Hunger," said the priest, "is a concern of the body. I fast on the mountain often to deny such concerns, and to see beyond the surface of things. I mustn't be tempted. No, I must bid you farewell here."

He edged close to Ando, tilted his strangely carved staff and removed one of the iron rings that hung from its tip. Ando couldn't see how this was done. "Here's something for you," and he handed him the ring. Ando thanked him and tucked the ring into his pack. The priest said, "If you need anything, I'm always on the mountain, somewhere." Then he strode back down the path. The gloom swallowed him up.

"If you ask me, you've been fasting too *much*," Ando muttered. He hefted his pack again and entered the gate.

Despite being his father's age, Ando's aunt Sakura was as beautiful as he remembered. Dressed in a scarlet kimono, she embraced him at the top of the steps. She smelled of flowers wet with dew, so clean and fresh that Ando nearly swooned. "Dearest Nephew—why, you've become a man. Has it been so long?"

"Very long, Auntie. Only now I was telling a fellow traveler that it had been fourteen—"

"Another traveler on this mountain at night?" She peered past him into the dark. "And you didn't invite him in?"

"I did. But he declined, as if I wanted to lead him into a trap."

She rolled her eyes. "Who was this fellow of so little discernment?"

"A monk, a *yamabushi* I met. Tall, with a big bulbous nose, and very impertinent."

His aunt stepped away, her fingers at her lips. "You saw *him*?" She rushed forward and hugged Ando tightly. He thought he must invent more reasons for her to hug him so. "Oh, my poor dear nephew, you've no idea how lucky you are. Another hour, surely no more, and it would have been over for you."

"What do you mean 'over'?"

"There are creatures living on this mountain, Ando. They lurk hereabout and you never want to meet them. They're fierce goblins, called *tengu*. They can disguise themselves as anything, including priests. They steal and eat children. They have big snouts, too. That one was surely a *tengu* lord and if he'd had his way, he would have walked you right off the path to your death."

Ando thought, *So, as I suspected.* He said, "He offered to lead me, but I refused him, Auntie. I made him walk behind."

She clutched him again. He could feel her body's hills and valleys against him. "That decision surely saved your life, Nephew. Of course he will not enter here. His kind cannot enter a house unless the owner welcomes them. He could never have come in, and you would have known him for what he was."

Ando rested his chin on his aunt's shoulder. How close a call he'd had! He shivered. The goblin had lain in wait for him, and if he hadn't been so cautious, it would have killed him.

Eagerly, he drank the hot *sake* his aunt served, to ward off the chill of death that had followed him up the mountain. It was the best *sake* he'd ever tasted.

Aunt Sakura had arranged a spare room for him. A candle burned in a paper globe in one corner, making the mats seem warm and friendly. The screens of the far wall opened onto the central courtyard of her huge house.

Comfortable and a little drunk after his meal, Ando sat and massaged his tired feet. As he drew his parchments and brushes from his pack, something clanked on the floor. It was the iron ring the priest—the goblin—had given him. He picked it up. Its surface, he saw in the light, was engraved with odd characters. He started for the door, but stopped with his hand raised to slide the panel aside. It would only upset his aunt further that he'd accepted a gift from the goblin. Better to keep it to himself. Tomorrow he could go off and bury it someplace.

He blew out the lantern, fell back on his mat, and went to sleep.

Exhaustion, the mention of goblins, and the befuddlement of *sake* must surely have worked together on him that night. Ando dreamed that the door of his room slid silently open and a hulking, twisted silhouette shambled inside. As though blind, it sniffed about in the dark, up and down the walls, moving ever nearer. Ando squirmed but seemed to be anchored in place. He could not rise from his mat.

Strange figures flocked to the doorway. Huge eyes followed the progress of the monster around the room.

The monster snuffled to rest above him. He had to tilt his head back to see it, and when he did, it grinned at him, then at the creatures in the doorway. "He's *my* feast," it announced in a voice that screeched like an old iron hinge. Then it reached down to pluck out his eyes.

He sat up with a yelp.

It was morning. No goblins surrounded him. Ando knew the monster had been a dream. He held his head. "No more *sake* for me," he muttered.

The door slid suddenly open. Ando flinched and reached for his sword; but no monster greeted him. It was a young girl. She had a doltish, ashen face. Her black hair hung limply about her dull eyes. Monotonously, she spoke. "Good morning, young master. Your aunt instructs me to bathe and dress you for breakfast."

"Bathe and dress me?"

"Yes."

The girl shuffled in and, as he climbed from the mat, took his arm and led him down the hall and into the bath room. The air swirled with steam. He marveled at the size of his aunt's house. The girl undressed him and helped him into the tub. For all the hot steam, the water was hardly warmer than the air—not uncomfortable, but not hot as it appeared.

The girl knelt and began to scrub him with a brush.

"Hey!" he cried, lunging away from her. He put a hand to his shoulder and looked at his back. "Trying to skin me, are you?"

"I am sorry. Please let me try again."

Reluctantly, Ando moved within her reach. She began scrubbing him much more gently. "A better-fed man would not have been injured so easily by the bristles of my brush," she commented. "It's good you came here. A few weeks with your aunt, and you'll be much healthier."

He glanced back at her, but the girl stared past him as if lost in thought.

After bathing, she gave him a clean *yukata* to wear, then led him through the house to the kitchen, where his aunt Sakura knelt awaiting him. If anything she was lovelier this morning. "I trust you slept well, Nephew."

He thought about his terrible dream, but dismissed it. She should not be burdened with such a thing. "I did, thank you," he said. "It's very . . . peaceful here."

"You miss the noise of city life. People on the streets at all hours."

"I'm used to the noise, it's true. After a while, you no longer notice it's there. Until you leave it."

"Often this is so," she agreed. "You must lose a thing in order to recognize it. Now, however, you must come and eat. You look dreadfully thin from your journey. We must fatten you up."

"That's what the girl in the bath said to me."

"Did she?"

"Yes, although she seemed a very dull creature."

"I keep her on as a favor to her relatives."

He flexed his shoulder. "She scrubbed me like a dirty pot."

His aunt frowned. "I will speak with her. I don't want problems for my dearest nephew." She led him into another room, where the screens were open to the courtyard. On the low table were small bowls of rice, seaweed, fish, eggs, and an assortment of sauces and condiments. It was a feast. "You are hungry?"

His stomach rumbled. "Yes, but who else is eating?"

"Only you, dear. I was up quite early and have eaten already."

"But so much . . ."

"Well, consume what you can. Later you can tell me all about your art." She patted his cheek, smiling, then bowed and withdrew.

After his meal, Ando went off for a constitutional. He hoped to find a view that would inspire him. Great painters, he thought, must be inspired. Once he found inspiration, he would return with ink and brushes and compose great art, for that was what artists did. He intended to return home in the winter with works so beautiful that his parents must find a master to teach him.

The mountain seemed to be etched with paths, as if hundreds of travelers wandered here all the time. Yet he encountered no one. It made him wonder if the *tengu* his aunt described had frightened everyone away. Or eaten them. But the day was far too pleasant for goblins, and he had his sword in any case.

Soon Ando lost sight of his aunt's house. As he walked, he idly spun the monk's iron ring around one finger.

Slowly he became aware of a distant roaring. He followed the sound, working his way down a rocky slope, which required him to stop playing with the ring and pay attention to his footing.

The noise was still some distance off when he came to the edge of a cliff. He stood on a ledge that was nothing more than a plate of rock surrounded by brush. From the ledge he could look out and down upon the graceful waterfall that had drawn him there. It cascaded past him from high above, disappearing in a great cloud of mist far below. Here, he thought, was his inspiration. Capture this view with brush and ink, and he would surely rank among the greatest of all artists who had ever been.

There remained the matter of the iron ring. He couldn't imagine any place where he could throw it farther than this. Yet he hesitated. The lovely filigree of the metal teased his sense of beauty. These goblins must be remarkable metalworkers. Nevertheless, he could not keep a goblin's ring. It might have attracted that monster—maybe the creature had been sniffing around in search of it. Oh, but that was imaginary. A dream. He shook his head. The best thing to do was dispose of the ring before he could change his mind.

With that, he cocked his arm and flung it away.

Except that he threw nothing but air.

He stared in disbelief at his open, empty hand stretched before him, fingers wide. Then something clinked beside his ear, and the tip of a staff came to rest upon his shoulder. Rings dangled from it.

Ando spun about.

The priest stood right behind him. With the staff he had snared the ring even as Ando threw it. The priest raised the staff, and the captured ring slid down into his right palm.

"You are certainly an evil creature," said the priest, "to cast away so potent a magic as this. You don't want it? Does it burn you to touch it? It would burn a demon." He waved it between them, then whacked Ando on the nose with it.

Ando jumped away from the blow, then realized there was nowhere to jump to—he had just stepped off the ledge—and threw himself desperately onto the plate of stone.

"I'm rethinking my opinion of you," the priest commented. "You try to cast away gifts. Then you try to fly after them. Neither the behavior of a harmonious being, nor a particularly rational one. So, what are you then?"

Ando's heart climbed from his throat back into his chest while the priest blathered on. Furious, he sprang up and whipped his sword out. "*Tengu!*" he cried.

The priest studied the sword as if he'd never seen one before. "*Tengu,*" he parroted. "Yes, all over the mountains. It's crawling with them around here. They breed like demons, which is hardly surprising. I've not known one to draw a blade before. You're a curious specimen. Maybe a new breed. . . ." He held the ring out. "Here, take it, hold it."

"I won't!"

"As proof."

"Proof to welcome *you* into our house. You and your horde."

"Horde?"

"Horde, brood, den, nest—whatever it's called!"

"Monastery?" the priest suggested.

"What monastery? I've wandered all over. I haven't seen any monastery."

"It's down there. Far side of the waterfall. I'm surprised you didn't see it just now. Come over here to the ledge again and I'll point it out to you." He turned and gestured toward the waterfall with his staff.

The moment he did, Ando leaped up and ran for his life across the mountain. What a fool that old *tengu* was if he imagined Ando would just walk to the precipice. Demons! They might be everywhere, but they weren't very bright.

Over dinner he related to his aunt the perilous adventure of that afternoon. She gasped as he described how the *tengu* had tried to murder him. "But the monster backed off, Auntie, when I drew my blade."

"My brave nephew. It's a wonder you aren't lying somewhere, a heap of broken bones, while I roam the hillside with a lantern, calling your name, and surely drawing the monsters to me. What a horrible thought." She gestured for her servant to come and refill his plate. "The important thing is, you are here and you've a healthy appetite. We must keep you alive and well. I think you should not stray again."

"But my art, my painting—"

"Oh, you can set up outside and paint my house against the backdrop of our lovely mountains. I should greatly desire to have a picture of my house the way *you* see it. And you have to admit, it's a lovely view."

"Well, yes," he said grudgingly. Lovely, but nowhere near as inspiring as the waterfall.

"Please, Ando. Humor me. Wait to go far. Wait till the leaves have turned on the trees. Then the whole mountainside will be alive with colors, and your painting will prove so much more dramatic. When the snow comes . . ." She reached across the table, and cupped her hand against his cheek. He smelled her perfume and his eyes rolled. Oh, she smelled like no woman he knew. She was so lovely.

"As you wish," he sighed.

"Good, my nephew. I needn't worry about you then."

With that settled, they spoke pleasantly of his life in the city, of his parents and his aspirations. Aunt Sakura plied him with good *sake* and he became more and more loquacious. He confessed his desire to be a great artist, and even admitted that he thought she was the most beautiful aunt anyone had ever had. She did not rebuff him, but smiled demurely, took his hand and bid him tell her everything, which he surely must have done, although he was too inebriated to remember. Finally, she disengaged from his embrace—he did not recall when he'd wrapped his arms about her—and said that she was tired. "Go to bed now, sweet Nephew," she told him. With wounded dignity, he wove an unsteady path down the hallway, which seemed to go on forever. He wished she were coming with him but he couldn't think enough to turn around and invite her.

Somehow he stumbled into his room and collapsed facedown on his mat. He resisted the urge to fall asleep until he'd undressed. Rising up onto his knees, he drew off his *haori* coat, then fumbled with the knot of his *obi* while the room tried to pitch him about. Something thumped on the mat between his knees, and he squinted at it for some moments before realizing that it was the iron ring he'd tried to throw away.

His brow furrowed. How had he acquired it again? He couldn't recall, but he was certain the big-nosed goblin hadn't touched him. "It's cursed, is what it is," he muttered, but then giggled at the idea. He dropped his *haori* over it and then, dressed in his *yukata*, sprawled across the bed. "Lovely, lovely Auntie," he sighed, and his eyes closed.

That night, whatever he dreamt, it remained submerged beneath the vat of *sake* between his ears. Upon awaking, his head hurt so terribly that he couldn't even contemplate nightmares and goblins.

A different girl led him to his bath. This one appeared no less dull, but she conversed hardly at all. He wondered where his aunt found such vacuous servants. Perhaps on the mountain there was little to spur the intellect, and over time the denizens became stupid, passing their dullness down the line like the color of their eyes. He did not wish to become so empty, and charged himself to start painting right away— the moment he overcame his hangover and could open his eyes to the daylight again. Tomorrow.

His aunt cooed over him, her voice and touch so soothing. She spoon-fed him, then put him back to bed.

Ando passed many weeks in his aunt's house. In the morning he was bathed and fed; then as the day warmed, he would sit either on the open porch and paint the valley view, or under the trees and paint the house against the mountains.

Initially, he thought his brushwork quite acceptable. His aunt complimented him on everything he did and encouraged him to continue. As the weeks passed, he found he could look back at his first pieces and see that he had tried to capture too much detail instead of expressing it through the simplicity of lines, the sweep of his brush. Every time he showed her a new illustration, Aunt Sakura crowed to the servants that her nephew was the finest asset the mountain had ever seen. She rewarded him with treats, with meals that approached feasts. His appetite, like his brushwork, seemed to grow daily. At one of these meals, he commented, "I think before I paint the mountain, you will have fed it to me." She laughed and pinched his cheeks.

Ando never tried to throw away the ring again, but kept it hidden beneath his mat. He seemed immune to its evil influence. He ceased dreaming altogether, but rested in dark slumber, weighted down by rich food. Over time he forgot about the capricious monk.

His aunt's serving staff seemed to grow throughout the summer. He encountered new people every day. Some ignored him as they polished the floors or arranged the stones in her garden. Others paused in their duties to nod and smile. They kept to their end of the house—the back end of the house. It must have been full of servants' quarters. When he asked his aunt, she said, "Ah, they're helping me prepare for the harvest festival. Didn't I mention it? In a few days, I shall have a great party for many of our neighbors. So I am preparing the house. You will be the star of our celebration. Your paintings I'll put on display, and I promise you everyone will admire them. You'll be the most important person on this mountain, dear Ando."

He nodded agreeably, his mouth too full of rice cake to speak.

The air was brisk that night. Ando noticed that the leaves had turned color. Looking out from his porch the next, rainy morning, he realized that the whole valley and the mountains opposite were aflame with color. He'd been painting the transformation daily, and it shocked him to discover that he hadn't noticed.

His waterfall would now be bursting with color. It was the view he must paint, he was certain of that. It existed to test his skill, to forge him. Surely after so long he could go there untroubled by the monstrous monk. If it hadn't been raining, he would have gone right then.

When he mentioned it to his aunt, she replied, "Are you certain that's wise?"

"It's not very far. Just the other side of the mountain. It's so beautiful. Besides, no *tengu* have been around in all these months."

When he said *tengu* she blanched. "Not far, but far enough away that you'll be out of my influence," she said. "I wouldn't be able to intervene if anything should happen to you."

"Nothing will happen, Auntie. I have my sword."

"Oh, surely you're right. Still, what would I tell your parents if anything *should* happen?"

His parents—he'd almost forgotten that he had any. He was so safe, so happy here that the thought of returning to the city nearly repulsed him now.

Ando convinced himself that his aunt had bestowed her blessing on his going to paint the waterfall, if only reluctantly. But the next morning it rained even harder. Mists curled across the tops of the far mountains like dragons. The landscape seemed ghostly behind the torrent, beautiful enough in itself to warrant painting. There was, he assured himself, always tomorrow.

It rained the next day and the next, and showed no signs of ever letting up. The valleys must be filling up like lakes, he thought. He became edgy. He couldn't work. Oh, the view was spectacular, but it wasn't the view he wanted. The colors would begin to fade soon. There was nothing here left to paint. He'd captured as many views from her balcony as every artist in history had ever done of Mount Fuji.

He decided that rain or no rain, he must go to that precipice and at the very least gaze upon it, memorize it, let it soak into him like this rain, until every detail burned in his mind. If need be, he would carry it back with him and paint it here.

He intended to tell his aunt of his going, but couldn't locate her. He didn't wish to ask one of the queer servants where she had gone, either, so without a word to anyone, he stole a straw *mino* that was big enough to protect him, and a pair of *geta* to keep him high enough off the ground that his kimono wouldn't drag through the mud. Walking might be more clumsy but he would manage. He poked his head through the raincape, slipped over the edge of the balcony, and hurried off into the rain and mist. He glanced back, but no one appeared to have seen him depart. After a few minutes he lost sight of the house.

The rain stopped.

It happened so abruptly that he looked up, expecting to find a roof over him. There was nothing but cloudy sky. Back in the direction from which he'd come, the rain inexplicably continued to fall.

Ando clambered on across the mountainside until he heard the roar of the waterfall again. Eagerly, he approached the precipice, but also with more effort than he remembered it taking to get there. Then he stood and beheld an explosion of colors more beautiful than he could have imagined.

The trees everywhere burned like flames, more subtle and varied than he could hope to represent. "We can only *speak* of nature," he muttered to himself. It was all he could do to stand and behold, to drink up the scene that he must later try to express.

The waters poured down, glistening through rocky channels green and brown with moss, and erupted at the bottom, so far below him, in a spectrum of spray. Staring through rainbows, he saw, on the far side of the gorge, the walls and peaked roof of a structure—one that could have been a distant monastery.

A sense of unease settled upon him. He hadn't noticed such a building the last time, but the last time he had not seen with today's eyes, which had developed more perception in the intervening months. He would have called it an "artist's vision" then, but no longer. He had come to realize that he was forever a student. He would strive to be an artist his whole life, growing but never grown. His former ability to see was as a charcoal sketch to this vision, as this would be to a future gaze. He began to understand why someone would paint many versions of one view. Each day, one's eyes were as new as clouds.

Hardly daring to blink, Ando sat upon the flat rock and stared. He found moments—light flashing in the cascades, the rainbows dimming as the sun slid behind a cloud, leaves falling listless then perking up again at the breath of a breeze—too many moments to capture in one painting, but that was good.

It wasn't until his skin prickled at the chill of being out of the sun that he realized a shadow had fallen over him, and he turned his head slowly, fearfully. His hand went to the hilt of his sword.

Only a few feet behind him and leaning on the same wooden staff as before, the figure he'd thought to elude contemplated him curiously. He was ready to draw the blade, but the orange-robed priest made no move toward him.

"Why, what sort of jolly fat fellow makes his way so far up the mountain unnoticed by me?"

Bewildered, Ando edged away from the precipice. The priest's gaze followed him. "I must say, you remind me of somebody."

"And who would that be, sir?" asked Ando as he continued to circle away from the ledge.

"There was a creature on this mountain, oh, five months back. A skinny goblin he was."

"Skinny *goblin*?"

"Indeed. I'd given him a ring from my staff." He flicked the remaining ones with a finger. "Initially it was to ward him off if he was evil, or protect him if he was not—at first I couldn't be certain of him. I had my answer when I found him here the next morning preparing to fling it into the gorge. I retrieved it before he could succeed, then slipped it back into his clothes before he noticed. I never saw him again, and so I think it destroyed him. It's surely lying in that haunted ruin where his family no doubt still waits to feast on my bones. He pretended to be a naïf from the city, so I hope yours is a different story, fatso."

"I pretended nothing, you villain! *You* tried to force me into the gorge!"

The priest blinked as he fathomed the meaning of this; then his eyes went wide with shock. He shook his staff in a threatening gesture that drove Ando back. "You! You look like this? How many hapless travelers have you preyed upon?"

"I haven't preyed upon anyone. I'm staying with my auntie, in the house where you accompanied me, only you wouldn't. . . ." He stopped, his brow furrowed. "What do you mean, 'that haunted ruin'?"

"Take off that shaggy *mino*," ordered the priest. "It isn't raining here."

Ando pulled off the straw raincape. The priest clucked his tongue. "Oh, dear, they've fattened you up and you've no idea. I wonder how she did this. Her spell must have traveled all the way down the mountainside to find you, even before we met."

"What are you talking about?"

"Ah, I've been very wrong about you. Very wrong. It's sheer good fortune I'm here. From the look of you, you haven't another week left."

Nothing the priest said made sense to Ando. "I'm not *fat*," he said, and looked at himself.

"I should have guessed, but you see, I thought *you* were *tengu* and that I was to be your feast. When you invited me into her house, I was certain you'd arranged a trap for me. I am her fiercest enemy after all. But, no, no, it was about you, poor fool. I will do penance for my pride later. Right now we must rescue you."

"Rescue me from what?" Ando asked angrily.

The priest swung his staff at Ando's head. With a yelp Ando hunched up in defense against the impending blow, but the tip halted just as it brushed his hair. In his terror, he suddenly saw himself as a bloated figure with sausage fingers and an enormous belly. "Oh, Buddha, I'm huge!"

"She didn't want you to encounter me, did she? Soon it won't matter, as you'll be nothing but bones anyway."

"How did I get like this?"

"You ate yourself like this, idiot. She's been fattening you up for a banquet—haven't you listened to a thing I said? From the looks of you, *tengu* from all over this mountain will be attending to sup on your . . . oh my, yes, from *all* over. You know, I think I shouldn't rescue you after all."

"Not rescue me?" Ando squealed.

"She's planning a party, your aunt, isn't she?"

"Her harvest festival."

The priest chuckled. "Harvest, she calls it." He gazed across the hillside. "You still have the ring?"

"It's under the *tatami* mat, beneath my bedroll." The priest's gaze was so intent that Ando turned to see what was so absorbing, but there was nothing there. He kept watching, expectant. "I never got around to showing it to Auntie Sakura. I thought it might upset her," he said.

"That's your good fortune, for she would have destroyed it and perhaps you along with it. From now on keep it with you all the time you're in the house. When the moment comes, take it from your *obi* and fling it down as hard as you can."

"When what moment comes? What do you mean?" asked Ando. When he received no reply, he turned around.

The priest had disappeared.

In approaching the house again, Ando took care that no one saw him. A curtain of rain still fell around it out of a gloomy sky, and although he knew now the rain was nothing more than a spell, he could not break it nor see his true form any longer—fear seemed to be the only way through her magic.

On the porch he removed the dripping raincape and the *geta* from his feet and hid them. He dried his hair on his kimono sleeve, seated himself, took up his brush and roughly sketched in the misty view of the mountains opposite— the dripping trees, the heavy clouds. Soon he was drawing the waterfall, capturing everything he could remember. The more he portrayed it, the more excited he became, the more lost in the work, casting memory, obsessed with every line and smudge. In it he forgot his peril.

He heard his aunt's voice calling, "Ando! Whatever are you about? We have guests. You must come and let them see you." He glanced around himself. The sky was growing dark. He hadn't noticed the time passing. They had *guests* now. . . .

He stiffened with fear. "I'm—" he concocted a hasty reply as he stuck his head into the hallway "—I must change my clothes. I didn't know there were guests, Auntie!"

He heard her laughter and the words, "I didn't tell him when the party would take place. Surprise is always best."

Yes, he agreed, surprise is best. He hurried to his chamber, removed his damp outer garments, replacing his kimono with a fresh one decorated with chrysanthemums. Then he knelt and reached beneath his bed mat until he touched the large iron ring. Remembering the priest's instructions, he tucked it into his sash, then stood, making sure it was hidden and secure. He considered taking his sword, but wearing it would arouse suspicion.

His aunt awaited him. With her were a dozen people he'd never seen before. They might have been members of a single family. All were tall, with sharp noses and wide dark eyes. They beamed at him, as if overwhelmed with the pleasure of his company. Some nodded in satisfaction to one another. His aunt had set a place for him at the table with his favorite foods laid out along it. She came up to him and pinched his cheek as she liked to do, then turned to the guests and said, "Delectable, isn't he?"

They all nodded in unison. Some clasped their hands. One licked his lips and muttered, "Toothsome."

"What a fine job you've done with him," proclaimed another.

His aunt bowed with the compliment. "Come, come, we must wait for the others," she said.

"Others?" asked Ando. He tried to keep his voice from trembling.

"Oh, many more, yes. You'll see them all. Ah, I must go tend the fire. We want it nice and hot on so cold and wet a day. Why don't you eat something, dear?"

He started to protest that he wasn't hungry, but she'd already turned away.

Left alone with the guests, Ando tried to keep to himself. The man who'd called him toothsome came over and tugged at his sleeve. "Pardon me," he said, drawing back the sleeve in order to push one finger into Ando's forearm. His head seemed to stretch forward on his neck as he watched Ando's flesh respond. His prominent nose quivered. "My, you've taken such good care of yourself. Lovely skin. Pink."

Barely able to keep from bolting, Ando stammered, "Really?" He held steady even when the man turned to a few others and said, "Look, look," as he poked some more.

Auntie Sakura returned then. She parted the crowd. Dozens more followed in her wake, the grinning bath girls among them. The room was full now.

"I believe everyone's here," she said. "And so, Ando my dear, it's time to begin. The fire has warmed the other room, you should come along now."

When the moment comes, the priest had said—and surely this must be it. Ando nodded to his aunt as if in compliance. She turned to go. The crowd's attention fixed upon her. They parted to let her pass. Ando drew the ring out of his sash and hurled it to the floor.

It thumped loudly, bounced, and rolled in a half-circle before falling over on someone's foot. Everyone stared down at it. His aunt turned back. She looked at the ring, then at him, then at the ring again. "What ever is that?" she asked.

One of the guests said, "I believe a part of him fell off."

He had thrown down the ring. Where was the blinding flash of light, the explosion that destroyed them all, the great wind that whisked away their spells? Nothing had happened. "Ha-ha," Ando said nervously, as if it were all a mistake. His aunt bent over to pick up the ring. Before she could touch it, the foot against which it rested burst into flame.

The guest screeched and jumped almost to the ceiling, kicking the ring into the air. It struck his aunt in the forehead. She fell back against the nearest guests. The other hopped madly about as flames climbed his leg. Those nearest him tried to beat out the fire.

Everything changed.

Auntie Sakura glared at Ando—only she was no longer his aunt. Her face was transforming. Her nose became something like a craggy beak, her brows projected forward over her eyes, which had turned black and shiny as stones on a *gō* board. He prepared to dive under the table, but was stopped in his tracks as he beheld the feast she'd laid out for him. The rice had turned to maggots, the meat and seaweed to insects and worms, all alive and wriggling. Was *this* what he'd been fed all along? His stomach churned and threatened to heave. Before he could move, a hand clamped upon his shoulder—a claw, the fingers ribbed like a bird's talons.

Swung about, Ando faced the creature who'd pretended to be his aunt. Her jagged mouth opened wide as if she were about to bite him in half.

Then from the very back of the room a head came sailing over the crowd. It bounced off another guest and landed on the table, rolled along, spilling dishes, and finally dropped to the floor, where it spun slowly at his aunt's feet. It was a black head, leathery, feathered, and horrible. It looked up at her and clacked its angry jaws. She shrieked, and Ando joined her in screaming. He tore loose from her grasp and threw himself against the nearest guests in the hope of reaching the door. The ghastly creatures sprawled every which way and Ando fell with them.

The room rippled as layers of spell were shed. Behind him, a bright light appeared. It was the ring, finally behaving as he'd expected. The guests staggered as he scrambled on hands and knees through them. They had their arms up to ward off the severed heads that were flying about like bees. He lunged for the doorway but it was jammed with fleeing guests. A head dropped between his hands and immediately tried to bite his fingers. Ando sprang away into the corner.

The crowd ran about in a frenzy, toward one exit or another—some right through the walls. Heads shot up on geysers of blood. None of them looked human any longer. Behind them he glimpsed quick flashes of light.

The goblin who had been his aunt found him through the crowd and charged at him. "You!" she screamed. "You're the cause of this!" He cringed against the post at his back. Her talons snipped the air in front of his face. Then, like a line of lightning, a blade flashed across her throat and her own grotesque head toppled from her shoulders. The body crumpled upon it, covering the cold black stare of her eyes, but the head continued to hiss from beneath like a wet log thrown on a fire.

Behind her stood the priest in his orange robes, streaked now with dark blood. He held a slender sword instead of his staff. Other monks like him, all armed, continued to slaughter the remaining goblins. Their actions were lit by the great fire, burning where the next room had been. The house had become a ruin.

This was where Ando had been living all these months. The walls were broken and rotted. Screens hung in shreds. The furnishings were blackened and moldy as from an old fire, and grass poked out of the crumbled weave of the mats. A few of his sketches blew, like dead leaves, through the open corridors.

Over the fire stood a spit big enough for . . . for him, Ando realized.

"My aunt," he said, "my aunt was a *tengu.*"

The priest patted his shoulder. "I doubt it runs in the family," he replied. He wiped his sword on the sleeve of the goblin's corpse before sliding it back into its sheath. "Truly, she was not your aunt. Your aunt likely fell victim to this creature long ago. This spot—this ruin—has been haunted for many years now. Did you happen to send a letter to your aunt that you were coming?"

Ando nodded. "Of course."

"A pity we missed the messenger or we might have saved you much trouble."

"Yes, look what she's done to me."

"Grieve not, young man. Nothing has been done to you that cannot be undone. This time tomorrow, you wouldn't have been able to say that."

The *yamabushi* monks had finished their gory work. They assembled behind the priest, and observed Ando serenely.

"Gather up your belongings now and follow me. You

may remain with us at the monastery until you shrink back to normal size."

Ando waddled through the ruins, fully aware now of the difficulty of propelling his bulk. He collected his drawings, paintings, his supplies and clothes, and then came back. He stepped carefully over the slaughter. Some of the heads hissed at him and clacked their jaws as if to bite his ankles.

"Don't they die?" he asked.

"Depends on who you listen to," replied the priest. He'd retrieved both the ring that Ando had thrown down and his staff, and now fitted the ring onto it again in some clever and seemingly magical way. "Some people even believe they turn themselves into monks."

Gregory Frost "demonstrates his mastery of the short story form in what will surely rank as one of the best fantasy collections of the year," according to *Publisher's Weekly* in its review of *Attack of the Jazz Giants & Other Stories*. The collection includes Frost's novelette, "Madonna of the Maquiladora," a James Tiptree Jr. Award, Nebula Award, Theodore Sturgeon Memorial Award, and Hugo Award finalist. His latest novel, *Fitcher's Brides*, a sinister recasting of the Bluebeard fairy tale, "Fitcher's Bird," was a Best Novel finalist for both the World Fantasy and International Horror Guild Awards.

His shorter work has appeared in many magazines, and in such anthologies as *Snow White, Blood Red, Black Swan, White Raven*, and *Swan Sister*, all edited by Ellen Datlow and Terri Windling; *Mojo: Conjure Stories*, edited by Nalo Hopkinson; and *Weird Trails*, edited by Darrell Schweitzer.

He has been a researcher for nonfiction television ("Wolfman: The Science & the Myth" and "Curse of the Pharaohs," episodes of *Science Frontiers*), an actor in a very "B" horror film ("The Laughing Dead"), and is one of a trio of fiction workshop directors at Swarthmore College.

His Web site is www.gregoryfrost.com

Author's Note

The first hints of "Tengu Mountain" came from the wonderful book *Japanese Ghosts and Demons: Art of the Supernatural*, edited by Stephen Addiss. I've been a student of the martial art of aikido for ten years, and what I know of

Japanese culture I like a great deal. Particularly appealing to me is that the story elements don't adhere to the code of the Western fairy tale at all. Many Japanese tales simply stop; the telling is over. I wanted to bind a Western story arc to such a tale without losing the flavor of it. Many Japanese stories are of travelers coming to a haunted fortress or house and spending the night without realizing that the owners are dead, or worse. The book supplied the notion (and wonderful illustrations) of the *tengu*—the mountain demons—and the rest evolved from there. My interest in "Hong Kong cinema" and anime (especially Miyazaki and Kitakubo) also informed and shaped the story.

The historical background of the *tengu* is at least as interesting as the fantasy. *Tengu* and *yamabushi* monks were inextricably connected. The *yamabushi* had to defend themselves against samurai, who were sent by warlords the monks had offended into the mountains to kill or capture the monks. The monks developed a fighting art of stealth, of blending into the landscape, and they managed on many occasions to rout the samurai. Rather than lose face in defeat, the samurai invented stories about being set upon by powerful mountain demons that could disguise themselves as monks. The *tengu*, it seems, were invented in order to protect the wounded pride of samurai warriors. Unless, of course, they really were set upon by demons. . . . Eventually the *yamabushi* with their covert skills evolved into those invisible assassins, the ninja. But that's for another tale.

The Faery Handbag

Kelly Link

I used to go to thrift stores with my friends. We'd take the train into Boston, and go to The Garment District, which is this huge vintage clothing warehouse. Everything is arranged by color, and somehow that makes all of the clothes beautiful. It's kind of like if you went through the wardrobe in the Narnia books, only instead of finding Aslan and the White Witch and horrible Eustace, you found this magic clothing world—instead of talking animals, there were feather boas and wedding dresses and bowling shoes, and paisley shirts and Doc Martens and everything hung up on racks so that first you have black dresses, all together, like the world's largest indoor funeral, and then blue dresses—all the blues you can imagine—and then red dresses and so on. Pink-reds and orangey-reds and purple-reds and exit-light reds and candy reds. Sometimes I would close my eyes and Natasha and Natalie and Jake would drag me over to a rack, and rub a dress against my hand. "Guess what color this is."

We had this theory that you could learn how to tell, just

by feeling, what color something was. For example, if you're sitting on a lawn, you can tell what color green the grass is with your eyes closed, depending on how silky-rubbery it feels. With clothing, stretchy velvet stuff always feels red when your eyes are closed, even if it's not red. Natasha was always best at guessing colors, but Natasha is also best at cheating at games and not getting caught.

One time we were looking through kids' T-shirts and we found a Muppets T-shirt that had belonged to Natalie in third grade. We knew it belonged to her, because it still had her name inside, where her mother had written it in permanent marker when Natalie went to summer camp. Jake bought it back for her, because he was the only one who had money that weekend. He was the only one who had a job.

Maybe you're wondering what a guy like Jake is doing in The Garment District with a bunch of girls. The thing about Jake is that he always has a good time, no matter what he's doing. He likes everything, and he likes everyone, but he likes me best of all. Wherever he is now, I bet he's having a great time and wondering when I'm going to show up. I'm always running late. But he knows that.

We had this theory that things have life cycles, the way that people do. The life cycle of wedding dresses and feather boas and T-shirts and shoes and handbags involves The Garment District. If clothes are good, or even if they're bad in an interesting way, The Garment District is where they go when they die. You can tell that they're dead, because of the way that they smell. When you buy them, and wash them, and start wearing them again, and they start to smell like you, that's when they reincarnate. But the point is, if you're looking for a particular thing, you just have to keep looking for it. You have to look hard.

Down in the basement at The Garment District they sell clothing and beat-up suitcases and teacups by the pound. You can get eight pounds worth of prom dresses—a slinky black dress, a poufy lavender dress, a swirly pink dress, a silvery, starry lamé dress so fine you could pass it through a key ring—for eight dollars. I go there every week, hunting for Grandmother Zofia's faery handbag.

The faery handbag: It's huge and black and kind of hairy. Even when your eyes are closed, it feels black. As black as black ever gets, like if you touch it, your hand might get stuck in it, like tar or black quicksand or when you stretch out your hand at night, to turn on a light, but all you feel is darkness.

Faeries live inside it. I know what that sounds like, but it's true.

Grandmother Zofia said it was a family heirloom. She said that it was over two hundred years old. She said that when she died, I had to look after it. Be its guardian. She said that it would be my responsibility.

I said that it didn't look that old, and that they didn't have handbags two hundred years ago, but that just made her cross. She said, "So then tell me, Genevieve, darling, where do you think old ladies used to put their reading glasses and their heart medicine and their knitting needles?"

I know that no one is going to believe any of this. That's okay. If I thought you would, then I couldn't tell you. Promise me that you won't believe a word. That's what Zofia used to say to me when she told me stories. At the funeral, my mother said, half laughing and half crying, that her mother was the world's best liar. I think she thought maybe Zofia wasn't really dead. But I went up to Zofia's coffin, and I looked her right in the eyes. They were closed. The funeral parlor had made her up with blue eyeshadow and blue eyeliner. She looked like she was going to be a news anchor on Fox television, instead of dead. It was creepy and it made me even sadder than I already was. But I didn't let that distract me.

"Okay, Zofia," I whispered. "I know you're dead, but this is important. You know exactly how important this is. Where's the handbag? What did you do with it? How do I find it? What am I supposed to do now?"

Of course she didn't say a word. She just lay there, this little smile on her face, as if she thought the whole thing—death, blue eyeshadow, Jake, the handbag, faeries, Scrabble, Baldeziwurlekistan, all of it—was a joke. She always did have a weird sense of humor. That's why she and Jake got along so well.

I grew up in a house next door to the house where my mother lived when she was a little girl. Her mother, Zofia Swink, my grandmother, babysat me while my mother and father were at work.

Zofia never looked like a grandmother. She had long black hair which she wore in little braided spiky towers and plaits. She had large blue eyes. She was taller than my father. She looked like a spy or ballerina or a lady pirate or a rock star. She acted like one, too. For example, she never drove anywhere. She rode a bike. It drove my mother crazy. "Why can't you act your age?" she'd say, and Zofia would just laugh.

Zofia and I played Scrabble all the time. Zofia always won, even though her English wasn't all that great, because we'd decided that she was allowed to use Baldeziwurleki vocabulary. Baldeziwurlekistan is where Zofia was born, over two hundred years ago. That's what Zofia said. (My grandmother claimed to be over two hundred years old. Or maybe even older. Sometimes she claimed that she'd even met Genghis Khan. He was much shorter than her. I probably don't have time to tell that story.) Baldeziwurlekistan is also an incredibly valuable word in Scrabble points, even though it doesn't exactly fit on the board. Zofia put it down the first time we played. I was feeling pretty good because I'd gotten forty-one points for "zippery" on my turn.

Zofia kept rearranging her letters on her tray. Then she looked over at me, as if daring me to stop her, and put down "eziwurlekistan," after "bald." She used "delicious," "zippery," "wishes," "kismet," and "needle," and made "to" into "toe." "Baldeziwurlekistan" went all the way across the board and then trailed off down the right-hand side.

I started laughing.

"I used up all my letters," Zofia said. She licked her pencil and started adding up points.

"That's not a word," I said. "Baldeziwurlekistan is not a word. Besides, you can't do that. You can't put an eighteen letter word on a board that's fifteen squares across."

"Why not? It's a country," Zofia said. "It's where I was born, little darling."

"Challenge," I said. I went and got the dictionary and looked it up. "There's no such place."

"Of course there isn't nowadays," Zofia said. "It wasn't a very big place, even when it was a place. But you've heard of Samarkand, and Uzbekistan and the Silk Road and Genghis Khan. Haven't I told you about meeting Genghis Khan?"

I looked up Samarkand. "Okay," I said. "Samarkand is a real place. A real word. But Baldeziwurlekistan isn't."

"They call it something else now," Zofia said. "But I think it's important to remember where we come from. I think it's only fair that I get to use Baldeziwurleki words. Your English is so much better than me. Promise me something, mouthful of dumpling, a small, small thing. You'll remember its real name. Baldeziwurlekistan. Now when I add it up, I get three hundred and sixty-eight points. Could that be right?"

If you called the faery handbag by its right name, it would be something like "orzipanikanikcz," which means the "bag of skin where the world lives," only Zofia never spelled that word the same way twice. She said you had to spell it a little differently each time. You never wanted to spell it exactly the right way, because that would be dangerous.

I called it the faery handbag because I put "faery" down on the Scrabble board once. Zofia said that you spelled it with an *i*, not an *e*. She looked it up in the dictionary, and lost a turn.

Zofia said that in Baldeziwurlekistan they used a board and tiles for divination, prognostication, and sometimes even just for fun. She said it was a little like playing Scrabble. That's probably why she turned out to be so good at Scrabble. The Baldeziwurlekistanians used their tiles and board to communicate with the people who lived under the hill. The people who lived under the hill knew the future. The Baldeziwurlekistanians gave them fermented milk and honey, and the young women of the village used to go and lie out on the hill and sleep under the stars. Apparently the people under the hill were pretty cute. The important thing was that you never went down into the hill and spent the night there, no matter how cute the guy from under the hill was. If you did, even if you only spent a single night under the hill, when you came out again a hundred years might have passed. "Remember that," Zofia said to me. "It doesn't matter how cute a guy is. If he wants you to come back to his place, it isn't a good idea. It's okay to fool around, but don't spend the night."

Every once in a while, a woman from under the hill would marry a man from the village, even though it never ended well. The problem was that the women under the hill were terrible cooks. They couldn't get used to the way time worked in the village, which meant that supper always got burnt, or else it wasn't cooked long enough. But they couldn't stand to be criticized. It hurt their feelings. If their village husband complained, or even if he looked like he wanted to complain, that was it. The woman from under the hill went back to her home, and even if her husband went and begged and pleaded and apologized, it might be three years or thirty years or a few generations before she came back out.

Even the best, happiest marriages between the Baldeziwurlekistanians and the people under the hill fell apart when the children got old enough to complain about dinner. But everyone in the village had some hill blood in them.

"It's in you," Zofia said, and kissed me on the nose. "Passed down from my grandmother and her mother. It's why we're so beautiful."

When Zofia was nineteen, the shaman-priestess in her village threw the tiles and discovered that something bad was going to happen. A raiding party was coming. There was no point in fighting them. They would burn down everyone's houses and take the young men and women for slaves. And it was even worse than that. There was going to be an earthquake as well, which was bad news because usually, when raiders showed up, the village went down under the hill for a night and when they came out again the raiders would have been gone for months or decades or even a hundred years. But this earthquake was going to split the hill right open.

The people under the hill were in trouble. Their home would be destroyed, and they would be doomed to roam the face of the earth, weeping and lamenting their fate until the sun blew out and the sky cracked and the seas boiled and the people dried up and turned to dust and blew away. So the shaman-priestess went and divined some more, and the people under the hill told her to kill a black dog and skin it and use the skin to make a purse big enough to hold a chicken, an egg, and a cooking pot. So she did, and then the people under the hill made the inside of the purse big enough to hold all of the village and all of the people under the hill and mountains and forests and seas and rivers and lakes and orchards and a sky and stars and spirits and fabulous monsters and sirens and dragons and dryads and mermaids and beasties and all the little gods that the Baldeziwurlekistanians and the people under the hill worshipped.

"Your purse is made out of dog skin?" I said. "That's disgusting!"

"Little dear pet," Zofia said, looking wistful, "dog is delicious. To Baldeziwurlekistanians, dog is a delicacy."

Before the raiding party arrived, the village packed up all of their belongings and moved into the handbag. The clasp was made out of bone. If you opened it one way, then it was just a purse big enough to hold a chicken and an egg and a clay cooking pot, or else a pair of reading glasses and a library book and a pillbox. If you opened the clasp another way, then you found yourself in a little boat floating at the mouth of a river. On either side of you was the forest, where the Baldeziwurlekistanian villagers and the people under the hill made their new settlement.

If you opened the handbag the wrong way, though, you found yourself in a dark land that smelled like blood. That's where the guardian of the purse (the dog whose skin had been sewn into a purse) lived. The guardian had no skin. Its howl made blood come out of your ears and nose. It tore apart anyone who turned the clasp in the opposite direction and opened the purse in the wrong way.

"Here is the wrong way to open the handbag," Zofia said. She twisted the clasp, showing me how she did it. She opened the mouth of the purse, but not very wide and held it up to me. "Go ahead, darling, and listen for a second."

I put my head near the handbag, but not too near. I didn't hear anything. "I don't hear anything," I said.

"The poor dog is probably asleep," Zofia said. "Even nightmares have to sleep now and then."

After he got expelled, everybody at school called Jake Houdini instead of Jake. Everybody except for me. I'll explain why, but you have to be patient. It's hard work telling everything in the right order.

Jake is smarter and also taller than most of our teachers. Not quite as tall as me. We've known each other since third grade. Jake has always been in love with me. He says he was in love with me even before third grade, even before we ever met. It took me a while to fall in love with Jake.

In third grade, Jake knew everything already, except how to make friends. He used to follow me around all day long. It made me so mad that I kicked him in the knee. When that didn't work, I threw his backpack out of the window of the school bus. That didn't work either, but the next year Jake took some tests and the school decided that he could skip fourth and fifth grade. Even I felt sorry for Jake then. Sixth grade didn't work out. When the sixth graders wouldn't stop flushing his head down the toilet, he went out and caught a skunk and set it loose in the boys' locker room.

The school was going to suspend him for the rest of the year, but instead Jake took two years off while his mother homeschooled him. He learned Latin and Hebrew and Greek, how to write sestinas, how to make sushi, how to play bridge, and even how to knit. He learned fencing and ball-room dancing. He worked in a soup kitchen and made a Super-8 movie about Civil War reenactors who play extreme croquet in full costume instead of firing off cannons. He started learning how to play guitar. He even wrote a novel. I've never read it—he says it was awful.

When he came back two years later, because his mother had cancer for the first time, the school put him back with our year, in seventh grade. He was still way too smart, but he was finally smart enough to figure out how to fit in. Plus he was good at soccer and he was really cute. Did I mention that he played guitar? Every girl in school had a crush on Jake, but he used to come home after school with me and play Scrabble with Zofia and ask her about Baldeziwurlekistan.

Jake's mom was named Cynthia. She collected ceramic frogs and knock-knock jokes. When we were in ninth grade, she had cancer again. When she died, Jake smashed all of her frogs. That was the first funeral I ever went to. A few months later, Jake's father asked Jake's fencing teacher out on a date. They got married right after the school expelled Jake for his AP project on Houdini. That was the first wedding I ever went to. Jake and I stole a bottle of wine and drank it, and I threw up in the swimming pool at the country club. Jake threw up all over my shoes.

So, anyway, the village and the people under the hill lived happily ever after for a few weeks in the handbag, which they had tied around a rock in a dry well which the people under the hill had determined would survive the earthquake. But some of the Baldeziwurlekistanians wanted to come out again and see what was going on in the world. Zofia was one of them. It had been summer when they went into the bag, but when they came out again, and climbed out of the well, snow was falling and their village was ruins and crumbly old rubble. They walked through the snow, Zofia carrying the handbag, until they came to another village, one that they'd never seen before. Everyone in that village was packing up their belongings and leaving, which gave Zofia and her friends a bad feeling. It seemed to be just the same as when they went into the handbag.

They followed the refugees, who seemed to know where they were going, and finally everyone came to a city. Zofia had never seen such a place. There were trains and electric lights and movie theaters, and there were people shooting each other. Bombs were falling. A war going on. Most of the villagers decided to climb right back inside the handbag, but Zofia volunteered to stay in the world and look after the handbag. She had fallen in love with movies and silk stockings and with a young man, a Russian deserter.

Zofia and the Russian deserter married and had many adventures and finally came to America, where my mother was born. Now and then Zofia would consult the tiles and talk to the people who lived in the handbag and they would tell her how best to avoid trouble and how she and her husband could make some money. Every now and then one of the Baldeziwurlekistanians, or one of the people from under the hill came out of the handbag and wanted to go grocery shopping, or to a movie or an amusement park to ride on roller coasters, or to the library.

The more advice Zofia gave her husband, the more money they made. Her husband became curious about Zofia's handbag, because he could see that there was something odd about it, but Zofia told him to mind his own business. He began to spy on Zofia, and saw that strange men and women were coming in and out of the house. He became convinced that either Zofia was a spy for the Communists, or maybe that she was having affairs. They fought and he drank more and more, and finally he threw away her divination tiles. "Russians make bad husbands," Zofia told me. Finally, one night while Zofia was sleeping, her husband opened the bone clasp and climbed inside the handbag.

"I thought he'd left me," Zofia said. "For almost twenty years I thought he'd left me and your mother and taken off for California. Not that I minded. I was tired of being married and cooking dinners and cleaning house for someone else. It's better to cook what I want to eat, and clean up when I decide to clean up. It was harder on your mother, not having a father. That was the part that I minded most.

"Then it turned out that he hadn't run away after all. He'd spent one night in the handbag and then come out again twenty years later, exactly as handsome as I remembered, and enough time had passed that I had forgiven him all the quarrels. We made up and it was all very romantic and then when we had another fight the next morning, he went and kissed your mother, who had slept right through his visit, on the cheek, and then he climbed right back inside the handbag. I didn't see him again for another twenty years. The last time he showed up, we went to see *Star Wars* and he liked it so much that he went back inside the handbag to tell everyone else about it. In a couple of years they'll all show up and want to see it on video and all of the sequels too."

"Tell them not to bother with the prequels," I said.

The thing about Zofia and libraries is that she's always losing library books. She says that she hasn't lost them, and in fact that they aren't even overdue, really. It's just that even one week inside the faery handbag is a lot longer in library-world time. So what is she supposed to do about it? The librarians all hate Zofia. She's banned from using any of the branches in our area. When I was eight, she got me to go to the library for her and check out a bunch of biographies and science books and some Georgette Heyer novels. My mother was livid when she found out, but it was too late. Zofia had already misplaced most of them.

It's really hard to write about somebody as if they're really dead. I still think Zofia must be sitting in her living room, in her house, watching some old horror movie, dropping popcorn into her handbag. She's waiting for me to come over and play Scrabble.

Nobody is ever going to return those library books now.

My mother used to come home from work and roll her eyes. "Have you been telling them your fairy stories?" she'd say. "Genevieve, your grandmother is a horrible liar."

Zofia would fold up the Scrabble board and shrug at me and Jake. "I'm a wonderful liar," she'd say. "I'm the best liar in the world. Promise me you won't believe a single word."

But she wouldn't tell the story of the faery handbag to Jake. Only the old Baldeziwurlekistanian folktales and faery tales about the people under the hill. She told him about how she and her husband made it all the way across Europe, hiding in haystacks and in barns, and how once, when her husband went off to find food, a farmer found her hiding in his chicken coop and tried to rape her. But she opened up the faery handbag in the way she showed me, and the dog came out and ate the farmer and all his chickens too.

She was teaching Jake and me how to curse in Baldeziwurleki. I also know how to say I love you, but I'm not going to ever say it to anyone again, except to Jake, when I find him.

When I was eight, I believed everything Zofia told me. By the time I was thirteen, I didn't believe a single word. When I was fifteen, I saw a man come out of her house and get on Zofia's three-speed bicycle and ride down the street. His clothes looked funny. He was a lot younger than my mother and father, and even though I'd never seen him before, he was familiar. I followed him on my bike, all the way to the grocery store. I waited just past the checkout lanes while he bought peanut butter, peach nectar concentrate, half a dozen instant cameras, and at least sixty packs of Reese's Peanut

Butter Cups, three bags of Hershey's Kisses, a handful of Milky Way bars, and other stuff from the rack of checkout candy. While the checkout clerk was helping him bag up all of that chocolate, he looked up and saw me. "Genevieve?" he said. "That's your name, right?"

I turned and ran out of the store. He grabbed up the bags and ran after me. I don't even think he got his change back. I was still running away, and then one of the straps on my flip-flops popped out of the sole, the way they do, and that made me really angry so I just stopped. I turned around.

"Who are you?" I said.

But I already knew. He looked like he could have been my mom's younger brother. He was really cute. I could see why Zofia had fallen in love with him.

His name was Rustan. Zofia told my parents that he was an expert in Baldeziwurlekistanian folklore who would be staying with her for a few days. She brought him over for dinner. Jake was there too, and I could tell that Jake knew something was up. Everybody except my dad knew something was going on.

"You mean Baldeziwurlekistan is a real place?" my mother asked Rustan. "My mother is telling the truth?"

I could see that Rustan was having a hard time with that one. He obviously wanted to say that his wife was a horrible liar, but then where would he be? Then he couldn't be the person that he was supposed to be.

There were probably a lot of things that he wanted to say. What he said was, "This is really good pizza."

Rustan took a lot of pictures at dinner. The next day I went with him to get the pictures developed. He'd brought back some film with him, with pictures he'd taken inside the faery handbag, but those didn't come out well. Maybe the film was too old. We got doubles of the pictures from dinner so that I could have some too. There's a great picture of Jake, sitting outside on the porch. He's laughing, and he has his hand up to his mouth, like he's going to catch the laugh. I have that picture up on my computer, and also up on my wall over my bed.

I bought a Cadbury Creme Egg for Rustan. Then we shook hands and he kissed me once on each cheek. "Give one of those kisses to your mother," he said, and I thought about how the next time I saw him, I might be Zofia's age, and he would only be a few days older. The next time I saw him, Zofia would be dead. Jake and I might have kids. That was too weird.

I know Rustan tried to get Zofia to go with him, to live in the handbag, but she wouldn't.

"It makes me dizzy in there," she used to tell me. "And they don't have movie theaters. And I have to look after your mother and you. Maybe when you're old enough to look after the handbag, I'll poke my head inside, just long enough for a little visit."

I didn't fall in love with Jake because he was smart. I'm pretty smart myself. I know that smart doesn't mean nice, or even mean that you have a lot of common sense. Look at all the trouble smart people get themselves into.

I didn't fall in love with Jake because he could make maki rolls and had a black belt in fencing, or whatever it is that you get if you're good in fencing. I didn't fall in love with Jake because he plays guitar. He's a better soccer player than he is a guitar player.

Those were the reasons why I went out on a date with Jake. That, and because he asked me. He asked if I wanted to go see a movie, and I asked if I could bring my grandmother and Natalie and Natasha. He said sure and so all five of us sat and watched *Bring It On,* and every once in a while Zofia dropped a couple of Milk Duds or some popcorn into her purse. I don't know if she was feeding the dog, or if she'd opened the purse the right way, and was throwing food at her husband.

I fell in love with Jake because he told stupid knock-knock jokes to Natalie, and told Natasha that he liked her jeans. I fell in love with Jake when he took me and Zofia home. He walked her up to her front door and then he walked me up to mine. I fell in love with Jake when he didn't try to kiss me. The thing is, I was nervous about the whole kissing thing. Most guys think that they're better at it than they really are. Not that I think I'm a real genius at kissing either, but I don't think kissing should be a competitive sport. It isn't tennis.

Natalie and Natasha and I used to practice kissing with each other. Not that we like each other that way, but just for practice. We got pretty good at it. We could see why kissing was supposed to be fun.

But Jake didn't try to kiss me. Instead he just gave me this really big hug. He put his face in my hair and he sighed. We stood there like that, and then finally I said, "What are you doing?"

"I just wanted to smell your hair," he said.

"Oh," I said. That made me feel weird, but in a good way. I put my nose up to his hair, which is brown and curly, and I smelled it. We stood there and smelled each other's hair, and I felt so good. I felt so happy.

Jake said into my hair, "Do you know that actor John Cusack?"

I said, "Yeah. One of Zofia's favorite movies is *Better Off Dead*. We watch it all the time."

"So he likes to go up to women and smell their armpits."

"Gross!" I said. "That's such a lie! What are you doing now? That tickles."

"I'm smelling your ear," Jake said.

Jake's hair smelled like iced tea with honey in it, after all the ice has melted.

Kissing Jake is like kissing Natalie or Natasha, except that it isn't just for fun. It feels like something there isn't a word for in Scrabble.

The deal with Houdini is that Jake got interested in him during Advanced Placement American History. He and I were both put in tenth grade history. We were doing biography projects. I was studying Joseph McCarthy. My grandmother had all sorts of stories about McCarthy. She hated him for what he did to Hollywood.

Jake didn't turn in his project—instead he told everyone in our AP class except for Mr. Streep (we call him Meryl) to meet him at the gym on Saturday. When we showed up, Jake reenacted one of Houdini's escapes with a laundry bag, handcuffs, a gym locker, bicycle chains, and the school's swimming pool. It took him three and a half minutes to get free, and this guy named Roger took a bunch of photos and then put the photos online. One of the photos ended up in the *Boston Globe*, and Jake got expelled. The really ironic thing was that while his mom was in the hospital, Jake had applied to MIT. He did it for his mom. He thought that way she'd have to stay alive. She was so excited about MIT. A couple of days after he'd been expelled, right after the wedding, while his dad and the fencing instructor were in Bermuda, he got an acceptance letter in the mail and a phone call from this guy in the admissions office who explained why they had to withdraw the acceptance.

My mother wanted to know why I let Jake wrap himself up in bicycle chains and then watched while Peter and Michael pushed him into the deep end of the school pool. I said that Jake had a backup plan. Ten more seconds and we were all going to jump into the pool and open the locker and get him out of there. I was crying when I said that. Even before he got in the locker, I knew how stupid Jake was being. Afterward, he promised me that he'd never do anything like that again.

That was when I told him about Zofia's husband, Rustan, and about Zofia's handbag. How stupid am I?

So I guess you can figure out what happened next. The problem is that Jake believed me about the handbag. We spent a lot of time over at Zofia's, playing Scrabble. Zofia never let the faery handbag out of her sight. She even took it with her when she went to the bathroom. I think she even slept with it under her pillow.

I didn't tell her that I'd said anything to Jake. I wouldn't ever have told anybody else about it. Not Natasha. Not even Natalie, who is the most responsible person in all of the world. Now, of course, if the handbag turns up and Jake still hasn't come back, I'll have to tell Natalie. Somebody has to keep an eye on the stupid thing while I go find Jake.

What worries me is that maybe one of the Baldeziwurlekistanians or one of the people under the hill or maybe even Rustan popped out of the handbag to run an errand and got worried when Zofia wasn't there. Maybe they'll come looking for her and bring it back. Maybe they know I'm supposed to look after it now. Or maybe they took it and hid it somewhere. Maybe someone turned it in at the lost-and-found at the library and that stupid librarian called the FBI. Maybe scientists at the Pentagon are examining the handbag right now. Testing it. If Jake comes out, they'll think he's a spy or a superweapon or an alien or something. They're not going to just let him go.

Everyone thinks Jake ran away, except for my mother, who is convinced that he was trying out another Houdini escape and is probably lying at the bottom of a lake somewhere. She hasn't said that to me, but I can see her thinking it. She keeps making cookies for me.

What happened is that Jake said, "Can I see that for just a second?"

He said it so casually that I think he caught Zofia off

guard. She was reaching into the purse for her wallet. We were standing in the lobby of the movie theater on a Monday morning. Jake was behind the snack counter. He'd gotten a job there. He was wearing this stupid red paper hat and some kind of apron-bib thing. He was supposed to ask us if we wanted to supersize our drinks.

He reached over the counter and took Zofia's handbag right out of her hand. He closed it and then he opened it again. I think he opened it the right way. I don't think he ended up in the dark place. He said to me and Zofia, "I'll be right back." And then he wasn't there anymore. It was just me and Zofia and the handbag, lying there on the counter where he'd dropped it.

If I'd been fast enough, I think I could have followed him. But Zofia had been guardian of the faery handbag for a lot longer. She snatched the bag back and glared at me. "He's a very bad boy," she said. She was absolutely furious. "You're better off without him, Genevieve, I think."

"Give me the handbag," I said. "I have to go get him."

"It isn't a toy, Genevieve," she said. "It isn't a game. This isn't Scrabble. He comes back when he comes back. If he comes back."

"Give me the handbag," I said. "Or I'll take it from you."

She held the handbag up high over her head, so that I couldn't reach it. I hate people who are taller than me. "What are you going to do now?" Zofia said. "Are you going to knock me down? Are you going to steal the handbag? Are you going to go away and leave me here to explain to your parents where you've gone? Are you going to say good-bye to your friends? When you come out again, they will have gone to college. They'll have jobs and babies and houses and they won't even recognize you. Your mother will be an old woman and I will be dead."

"I don't care," I said. I sat down on the sticky red carpet in the lobby and started to cry. Someone wearing a little metal name tag came over and asked if we were okay. His name was Missy. Or maybe he was wearing someone else's tag.

"We're fine," Zofia said. "My granddaughter has the flu."

She took my hand and pulled me up. She put her arm around me and we walked out of the theater. We never even got to see the stupid movie. We never even got to see another movie together. I don't ever want to go see another movie. The problem is, I don't want to see unhappy endings. And I don't know if I believe in the happy ones.

"I have a plan," Zofia said. "I will go find Jake. You will stay here and look after the handbag."

"You won't come back either," I said. I cried even harder. "Or if you do, I'll be like a hundred years old and Jake will still be sixteen."

"Everything will be okay," Zofia said. I wish I could tell you how beautiful she looked right then. It didn't matter if she was lying or if she actually knew that everything was going to be okay. The important thing was how she looked when she said it. She said, with absolute certainty, or maybe with all the skill of a very skillful liar, "My plan will work. First we go to the library, though. One of the people under the hill just brought back an Agatha Christie mystery, and I need to return it."

"We're going to the library?" I said. "Why don't we just go home and play Scrabble for a while." You probably think

I was just being sarcastic here, and I was being sarcastic. But Zofia gave me a sharp look. She knew that if I was being sarcastic my brain was working again. She knew that I knew she was stalling for time. She knew that I was coming up with my own plan, which was a lot like Zofia's plan, except that I was the one who went into the handbag. *How* was the part I was working on.

"We could do that," she said. "Remember, when you don't know what to do, it never hurts to play Scrabble. It's like reading the I Ching or tea leaves."

"Can we please just hurry?" I said.

Zofia just looked at me. "Genevieve, we have plenty of time. If you're going to look after the handbag, you have to remember that. You have to be patient. Can you be patient?"

"I can try," I told her. I'm trying, Zofia. I'm trying really hard. But it isn't fair. Jake is off having adventures and talking to talking animals, and who knows, learning how to fly and some beautiful three-thousand-year-old girl from under the hill is teaching him how to speak fluent Baldeziwurleki. I bet she lives in a house that runs around on chicken legs, and she tells Jake that she'd love to hear him play something on the guitar. Maybe you'll kiss her, Jake, because she's put a spell on you. But whatever you do, don't go up into her house. Don't fall asleep in her bed. Come back soon, Jake, and bring the handbag with you.

I hate those movies, those books, where some guy gets to go off and have adventures and meanwhile the girl has to stay home and wait. I'm a feminist. I subscribe to *Bust* magazine, and I watch *Buffy* reruns. I don't believe in that kind of shit.

~~~~~~~~~~~~

We hadn't been in the library for five minutes before Zofia picked up a biography of Carl Sagan and dropped it in her purse. She was definitely stalling for time. She was trying to come up with a plan that would counteract the plan that she knew I was planning. I wondered what she thought I was planning. It was probably much better than anything I'd come up with.

"Don't do that!" I said.

"Don't worry," Zofia said. "Nobody was watching."

"I don't care if nobody saw! What if Jake's sitting there in the boat, or what if he was coming back and you just dropped it on his head!"

"It doesn't work that way," Zofia said. Then she said, "It would serve him right, anyway."

That was when the librarian came up to us. She had a name tag on as well. I was so sick of people and their stupid name tags. I'm not even going to tell you what her name was. "I saw that," the librarian said.

"Saw what?" Zofia said. She smiled down at the librarian, like she was Queen of the Library, and the librarian was a petitioner.

The librarian stared hard at her. "I know you," she said, almost sounding awed, like she was a weekend birdwatcher who just seen Bigfoot. "We have your picture on the office wall. You're Ms. Swink. You aren't allowed to check out books here."

"That's ridiculous," Zofia said. She was at least two feet taller than the librarian. I felt a bit sorry for the librarian.

After all, Zofia had just stolen a seven-day book. She probably wouldn't return it for a hundred years. My mother has always made it clear that it's my job to protect other people from Zofia. I guess I was Zofia's guardian before I became the guardian of the handbag.

The librarian reached up and grabbed Zofia's handbag. She was small but she was strong. She jerked the handbag and Zofia stumbled and fell back against a work desk. I couldn't believe it. Everyone except for me was getting a look at Zofia's handbag. What kind of guardian was I going to be?

"Genevieve," Zofia said. She held my hand very tightly, and I looked at her. She looked wobbly and pale. She said, "I feel very bad about all of this. Tell your mother I said so."

Then she said one last thing, but I think it was in Baldeziwurleki.

The librarian said, "I saw you put a book in here. Right here." She opened the handbag and peered inside. Out of the handbag came a long, lonely, ferocious, utterly hopeless scream of rage. I don't ever want to hear that noise again. Everyone in the library looked up. The librarian made a choking noise and threw Zofia's handbag away from her. A little trickle of blood came out of her nose and a drop fell on the floor. What I thought at first was that it was just plain luck that the handbag was closed when it landed. Later on I was trying to figure out what Zofia said. My Baldeziwurleki isn't very good, but I think she was saying something like "Figures. Stupid librarian. I have to go take care of that damn dog." So maybe that's what happened. Maybe Zofia sent part of herself in there with the skinless dog. Maybe she fought it and won and closed the handbag. Maybe she made friends with it. I mean, she used to feed it popcorn at the movies. Maybe she's still in there.

What happened in the library was Zofia sighed a little and closed her eyes. I helped her sit down in a chair, but I don't think she was really there anymore. I rode with her in the ambulance, when the ambulance finally showed up, and I swear I didn't even think about the handbag until my mother showed up. I didn't say a word. I just left her there in the hospital with Zofia, who was on a respirator, and I ran all the way back to the library. But it was closed. So I ran all the way back again, to the hospital, but you already know what happened, right? Zofia died. I hate writing that. My tall, funny, beautiful, book-stealing, Scrabble-playing, story-telling grandmother died.

But you never met her. You're probably wondering about the handbag. What happened to it. I put up signs all over town, like Zofia's handbag was some kind of lost dog, but nobody ever called.

So that's the story so far. Not that I expect you to believe any of it. Last night Natalie and Natasha came over and we played Scrabble. They don't really like Scrabble, but they feel like it's their job to cheer me up. I won. After they went home, I flipped all the tiles upside down and then I started picking them up in groups of seven. I tried to ask a question, but it was hard to pick just one. The words I got weren't so great either, so I decided that they weren't English words. They were Baldeziwurleki words.

Once I decided that, everything became perfectly clear.

First I put down "kirif"which means "happy news," and then I got a *b*, an *o*, an *l*, an *e*, an *f*, another *i*, an *s*, and a *z*. So then I could make "kirif" into "bolekirifisz," which could mean "the happy result of a combination of diligent effort and patience."

I would find the faery handbag. The tiles said so. I would work the clasp and go into the handbag and have my own adventures and would rescue Jake. Hardly any time would have gone by before we came back out of the handbag. Maybe I'd even make friends with that poor dog and get to say good-bye, for real, to Zofia. Rustan would show up again and be really sorry that he'd missed Zofia's funeral and this time he would be brave enough to tell my mother the whole story. He would tell her that he was her father. Not that she would believe him. Not that you should believe this story. Promise me that you won't believe a word.

Kelly Link lives in Northampton, Massachusetts, in an old farmhouse. She is the author of two short story collections—*Stranger Things Happen* and *Magic for Beginners*—and the editor of an anthology, *Trampoline*. She and her husband, Gavin J. Grant, publish a twice-yearly zine, *Lady Churchill's Rosebud Wristlet*, and were chosen by Terri Windling to succeed her as the new editors of the fantasy half of *The Year's Best Fantasy and Horror*. (Ellen Datlow remains as horror editor).

Her Web site is www.kellylink.net

Author's Note

I don't know whether I believe in faeries or not. I definitely believe in people, like Arthur Conan Doyle, who believed in faeries, but on the other hand, I've never been a big fan of Tinkerbell. The place I'd most expect to find faeries is Iceland, or else, of course, The Garment District. Some of my favorite faery novels are Elizabeth Marie Pope's *The Perilous Gard*, Diana Wynne Jones's *Fire and Hemlock*, Holly Black's *Tithe*, and Emma Bull's *War for the Oaks*. Joan Aiken's short story "The People in the Castle" was the inspiration for this story.

The Price of Glamour

Steve Berman

"[T]hese wonders and terrors have been lying by your door and mine ever since we had a door of our own. We had but to go a hundred yards off and see for ourselves, but we never did."
—Thackeray

London, 1844

Tup Smatterpit sat on the back of a chestnut seller's cart, his back warm from resting against the stove. Tup had sprinkled a pinch of powdered glamour over himself, and the old coster driving the wagon believed him to be one of the countless children that roamed Covent Garden's marketplace, rather than one of the Folk. As the donkey slowly pulled the cart through the crowd, the gentle sway and the constant *tick-tock*ing of his waistcoat was lulling Tup to sleep.

He ignored the sounds of vendors calling out their goods and decided to nap a little while. Tup nudged the back of his bent top hat, once a shiny pearl gray and now dingy as ash, so that it covered not only the tight curls of red hair but also his eyes. A chiming sound came from one of the many pockets of his waistcoat. He groaned at being disturbed and pulled out the right watch for the crime.

The sweeping hands on the enchanted dial not only showed him he had ten minutes to traverse the West End of London but also that the Dowagers, a pair of crones, were nearly through with a robbery.

If Tup was late meeting them, a rival bagman might collect the stolen goods. There were other fences in the city besides Tup's employer, but none as mean-spirited as Bluebottle. He was a spriggan, one of the worst of the fey, all bloated with spite and bile.

Tup didn't dare waste another moment and leapt down from the cart, nearly knocking over a woman with a basket of fresh flowers.

Slightly out of breath after dashing through side streets and avenues, Tup arrived near Hyde Park with time to spare. The watch stopped chiming a moment later, one of the slender hands pointing where to go next.

In the shadows of the alley, the Dowagers towered over a child shivering and huddled against the brick wall. They were an ancient pair and no one remembered their names. One's eyes were clear, her sister's blind and covered with a gray film. Otherwise they looked identical, tall and thin, almost brittle looking, with fingers that resembled twigs. Their long hair was touched with silver, and they had never abandoned their sackcloth clothing for anything contemporary, as had so many of the fey who dwelled in London.

The clear-eyed sister, clutching an armful of pretty new

clothes to her chest, snatched the bonnet from the head of the girl. The Dowagers, glamoured to resemble rosy-cheeked maids, lured children from the street with promises of sweets, only to strip them of everything of worth.

The blind one leaned down and tapped the girl on the forehead twice. "Leave us, child. Vex us not. We have taken enough."

"Enough," hissed her sister.

As the child ran past him, still crying, Tup nodded to the Dowagers and tipped his hat. "Ladies." He held up his sack, the mark of a bagman's trade.

"A frock, a bonnet, a petticoat." The first Dowager unceremoniously dropped the clothes into the bag. Her blind sister held up a glowing coin the size of a penny. "Stolen laughter. Bluebottle will pay well for a child's humor, no?"

"Five bags of glamour," hissed her blind sister.

"No doubt, m'lady. No doubt." He watched as she dropped the glittering piece after the fine clothes.

Tup reached into the bag and pulled out a wine bottle and drew the cork. The smell of the cumin lacing the wine filled the air. The Dowagers drew closer, their hands out, fingers curling and curling. Centuries might have passed since they plagued the children of the Celts, appeased only by such a spiced drink, yet their thirst remained.

"It's been so long, sister," the blind one whispered, a pale worm of a tongue wriggling over her lips.

"Give us the bottle." The other sister's fingernails swept close to his face.

Tup smiled kindly. "Oh, I shall, I shall. But I'm of a mind for that bit of laughter you threw in. Bluebottle will give you glamour enough for the finery." He let the bottle come close to their hands. "Agreed?"

As he had guessed, they did not hesitate. "Yes," they groaned, and the blind one took the bottle and drank deeply, her lips becoming stained with the wine. Her sister did not wait long before grabbing the bottle.

Humming a merry tune as he left them, Tup withdrew the laughter from the sack and slipped it into one of the pockets of his waistcoat. That bauble was worth a hundred petticoats.

The magic charm Tup had spoken before heading into the sewers had nearly faded, and the mire he stood on was beginning to stick to his shoes. But damn Cagmag would not stop digging through the surrounding filth long enough to say anything more than a few words at once. The slimy troll would tower over most fey if it ever stood upright, but down in the tunnels it could move about only on all fours. Cagmag dipped its hooked hands deep into the muck, then leaned forward to bring a nose that resembled a notched dagger low to sniff around. Tup was about to depart when the sewer-hunter pulled out a reeking handful and sighed majestically.

"What is it? A copper pot? A candlestick?"

"Pigsty sweepings." The troll opened its black-lipped maw and took a healthy bite of the muck.

Tup reached for the robbery watch and checked the crime. Nothing. He tapped the dial lightly. The hands still clearly indicated that something of worth was down there, seized by Cagmag.

"Ahh, here's a right bit." The troll lifted out more from

the filth. Its lamplike yellow eyes narrowed a moment. "Had to hide it, there's thieves about."

Tup leaned in closer, but the mass Cagmag pulled up looked no better than the sweepings. "Of course there's thieves."

"This one's too bold." The troll's dark tongue licked to reveal a fine riding boot. "Heard a leprechaun complaining some of his goods were stolen from his shop."

Tup stifled a chuckle. Leprechauns were crooked cobblers and deserved a bit of hardship. More than likely, 'twas a customer they cheated having a bit of satisfaction.

The troll finished cleaning off the boot and held it out to Tup.

"You stole that?"

"Aye." Cagmag tipped it back. "Oh, sorry, there's still a bit of foot left in it. Anxious, I was."

By sunset, Tup was weary from collecting all over London. He arrived late to his next appointment and looked around the emptying marketplace, trying to spot the cardsharp the "cheats" watch had led him to. He roamed the area to no avail. Desperate, he ventured into a nearby gin parlor.

Gas lamps that reflected off mirrored panes of glass brightly lit the crowded establishment. Tup did his best not to be jostled as he took a winding path through the room. He spotted the shabbily dressed hobgoblin with his mouselike whiskers and tufted tail beside a flavored liquor stand.

The hobgoblin, when he was sober, was skilled at broading—changing the faces of cards with a little bit of magic to cheat unsuspecting men. The faery rapped on the bar to get the server's attention. "Another Celebrated Butter, my good man."

Tup put a hand over the aromatic dram as the hobgoblin rose it to his wet lips. "Not thinking of drinking away all the pence are you, Rob—"

"Mr. Hobbes to you, sir." The hobgoblin nervously glanced around at the surrounding humans. His long whiskers had been oiled and curled at the tips to resemble a man's mustache. "At least, amid this company."

"Fine, then. There's the matter of your debt. Or shall I tell Bluebottle there's to be no payment?"

Hobbes blanched at the thought and licked his lips. "Oh no, not that. I nearly earned enough to pay what I owes. You have to put in a good word for me, Tup. Tell Bluebottle that without more glamour, I'd have to leave London." The hobgoblin moved the glass from underneath Tup's palm, careful not to spill a drop. "Come now, a dry swallow's a bad thin', we all knows." He rubbed his throat as if parched.

Tup could see that Hobbes was nearly drunk. Another few shots and his face would turn bluish and he'd pass out. "Where's the day's take?"

"On me person. It's not safe to hide anythin' anymore."

It took Tup a moment to realize what Hobbes alluded to. "The mysterious thief? Not you, too."

Hobbes nodded. "It's no tall tale. Quite a few of the Folk been robbed. Happened to that little portune that's been a thievin' carriages. And Jenny Greenteeth had brought in quite a haul from a body she . . . well, she said she found on the banks of the Thames. Kept it all in a cubbyhole by the docks but when Jenny went for it, was gone. Now who'd be so daft as to upset ol' Jenny?"

Tup felt bad for any fey foolish enough to steal from Jenny, one of the more mean-spirited of the Folk. The thief must be a shire pixie, new to the city, and ignorant of who not to cross. It hadn't been so long since Tup himself had come from Wessex, seeking his fortune in the grand chaos that was London. He hadn't been any wiser and was still paying the price.

The memory bothered him, making him anxious. He was tempted to buy a drink himself. "Enough of such talk." He held up his sack. "The coin."

The hobgoblin nodded and shook his right arm a moment before leaning in close and letting it drop over the mouth of the sack. Pence and groats and shillings tumbled out of Hobbes's sleeve. The hobgoblin's sharp fingers snatched the last coin, a guinea, before it fell.

"I'll be needin' this to stay warm tonight."

Sack heavy with the day's haul, Tup knew he should be heading to Bluebottle's, but made his way to the Royal Exchange, an immense stone building central to human commerce. The small shops along the front, little more than enclosed stands that offered books or newspapers or stationery, were closing for the night. Only a few people walked the Exchange's halls and if they bothered to notice Tup, thanks to a pinch of glamour, he'd seem nothing more than a lost youth.

On the upper floor of the northern side of the building

was a coffeehouse, nearly deserted at that late hour. He moved to the back and opened the door of a storeroom. Tup easily climbed over the aromatic sacks of beans to reach a forgotten trapdoor in the ceiling that led to a small attic and his home.

A man would have to stoop, but being just four feet tall, Tup needed only to worry about his hat being knocked off his head. At the far end of the room was a mound of goose feathers that served as a bed. As tempting as it was to relax a while, he could not afford the luxury at the moment.

He moved to the wall, his fingers finding and pulling free the loose stone. In the niche was a mound of treasure, the cream secretly skimmed from the milk of Tup's tasks over the past year. He reached into his waistcoat pocket, found the laughter he had bartered from the Dowagers, and added it to the pile.

Bluebottle, that artless plume-plucked maggot-pie, would be surprised at such a lovely hoard. Tup was especial-ly proud of the mourning brooch containing a lock of hair from a woman with the Sight. Took quite a bit of trickery to wrest the brooch from a dreary Irish ankou. What with all that wearing black and a gaunt face pinched like he was eat-ing something sour, no wonder the bloke found work as a professional mourner.

Tup's mind was often nimbler than his fingers, yet he was not so crafty as to have escaped servitude. He regretted again, for the thousandth time, being so impetuous when he first came to London.

He had been told there was but one source for good quality glamour, the fine powder that enabled any fey to disguise itself to humans without the Sight, a necessity to survive in London. All the iron the humans used to build and live in the city eroded a fey's natural ability. Tup, new to the city, lacked the coin or the goods to buy from Bluebottle, so there was only one recourse. He had thought himself up to the task, sneaking into the secondhand shop after nightfall and exploring the back rooms, only to be easily caught by the spriggan. Tup was lifted up by his shirt collar and saw that cages with frightened pixies hung from the rafters. Bluebottle would have dropped him into a massive grinder with rusty gears and teeth and made glamour out of him, if Tup hadn't been quick with his words. He begged and flattered, promising whatever services the spriggan desired. Bluebottle listened and made the little fey swear to serve as his bagsman, for twelve years, one for each of Tup's fingers that tried to steal from him.

He wondered how long before this thief would make the same mistake.

As he walked down the dingiest alley in all of creation, nearer and nearer to Bluebottle's rag-and-bottle shop, Tup's mood darkened. The door was two planks of wood nailed together and the outside had been painted a jaundiced yellow so that even the oldest and simplest scavengers could find the shop. Bluebottle traded glamour for stolen goods that he would sell back to humans. Nearly every fey in the city owed him, some far worse than others.

Tup walked in to find Bluebottle mending the frame of a wooden cage. The spriggan had a squat, lumpy body. His scruffy jowls and bald pate almost made him resemble a man, but the eyes were different, too small and shiny.

"Ah, my little coney's back." His voice had a rasp, one almost painful to hear.

Tup swallowed his rage at the insult. He hefted up the sack onto the counter. "A fine haul today."

Bluebottle narrowed his eyes. "We'll see." The spriggan put down the cage and snapped his fingers. On the counter to his right rested an immense ledger. The book opened and the pages flipped on their own.

Tup emptied the sack and Bluebottle began rummaging. He picked up a tin of tobacco and shook it near his small ear.

"One tin of Byer's Aromatic Cherry Tobacco. Full but dented along one side."

"From the glaistig," Tup mentioned.

Along the pages of the ledger ink blossomed, adding in the entry. A faint whisper of "seven pence," rose from the leather binding.

The spriggan reached for the young girl's clothes. "The Dowagers?" Tup nodded. "One bonnet, one frock, one petticoat, the latter with slight tear along the shoulder."

"Six shillings," said the magic ledger.

"That's not even a bag of glamour's worth."

Bluebottle shrugged.

Tup swallowed his worry that the Dowagers would dare tell the spriggan about his private deal with them for the laughter. He rattled off the names of the other fey who stole the goods he brought. Then he grabbed his sack and headed for the door, but was pulled back by a hand at his collar.

"A moment." Bluebottle tapped the pages of the ledger. "You filled your snuff box the other day with glamour, my coney. Are you paying for it now or shall your debt to me grow greater?"

Tup became flushed but kept his voice calm. "All I have left is a tuppence. You shaved my earnings down to a few pence."

The soft voice of the book spoke. "Tup Smatterpit. Owing eighty-one pounds to date."

"Heh, might as well be your weight in gold. You'll always be bound to me."

"Not true," Tup chirped.

"Oh?" The spriggan leaned over the counter. His breath was rank. "I'd free you from your service this very moment if you paid your tally."

Tup left the shop with Bluebottle's coarse laughter at his back. He ran all the way to the Exchange, giddy with the notion that, thanks to his hoard and the spriggan's ignorance, he'd soon be free. But there he found the stone that hid his cache had already been moved. The niche was empty, his treasure completely gone.

Tup choked back a sob. All his work, all his savings over the years, all gone. He'd be working for that artless clotpole forever.

In a sad daze, Tup wandered until he fell into a small crowd watching a street musician playing folk tunes on his hurdy-gurdy. Nearby, a young girl sold seedcakes from a basket. Tup found a halfpenny in his pocket, his last remaining coin, and bought one of the treats, nibbling it quickly and not leaving a single crumb on his fingerless gloves.

One of the watches began to chime, and he was tempted to throw it across the street. Why hadn't it rung for him?

Every theft by a fey should ring the magic watches. Out of instinct he looked at the dial, barely caring that a tiny boggan was picking pockets. It had only been a couple of hours since he had left for Bluebottle's. There might still be time to catch the thief and recover his goods. He needed help though, and there was only one of the Folk with the necessary gift.

Tup knew that the rook girl had an appetite for glamour. Though not truly a thief, she needed to cover up her bird feet if she wanted to charm men into buying her drinks and meals. He had been searching for her for over an hour, dashing through the better parts of London. He finally found her gazing at herself in the reflection of a jeweler's window. Her long black tresses flowed from beneath a dark, feathered hat that had seen better days.

She looked down at him with a sad smile. "I've nothing for your master, little one." As if to prove her poverty, she lifted up her dress to show not stockinged feet but scaly claws.

Tup reached into a pocket and withdrew his snuffbox. He opened the lid and showed her the glittering dust within. "Nearly full." Her eyes went wide and he snapped the lid shut. "Perhaps a trade is in order?"

A few moments later, her dark children, the ravens that spent their days at the Tower of London, were settling on his shoulders. Their eyes were the sharpest in the city and little escaped their notice. With raw cackles they told him the one he wanted was down on Cutler Street in the seedy neighborhood of Houndsditch.

When Tup rounded the corner onto Cutler, the only figure on the street was leaving a dilapidated building. Tup might have ignored the fellow, who seemed almost lost underneath a heavy coat, had he not flipped up a shining coin—easily recognizable as the stolen laughter—into the air a moment before catching it in his palm.

"You there," Tup called out.

The figure turned, a face going pale with fear. Then the thief ran, not down the street, but back into the hovel. Tup followed only a few steps behind him.

Inside was dank and smoky. The thief dashed up a rickety flight of stairs that groaned even under Tup's light weight. He passed open doorways of rooms with people crowded around tables with cards or throwing dice. On the next floor there were cries as the humans wagered on a pair of burly men boxing in a corner. Tup stifled his curiosity to look further and continued chasing his quarry.

Ahead of him, the thief threw open a trapdoor to the rooftop. Tup was almost nipping at his heels. Overhead, the London night sky was clouded from belching chimneys. The thief soon neared the edge of the roof but did not stop or slow. With a mad leap, arms swinging, he covered the gap to the nearest building. Tup easily jumped after him. The thief tripped on his coat and fell onto his side. Tup landed right on the rogue's back bearing him to the ground.

"Quite a chase," said Tup, trying to catch his breath. "But now there's the matter of what is mine."

When Tup turned the thief over, he expected to see the

slender features of an elf or a scraggly brown-furred boggart, not the face of a scared sixteen-year-old human boy. The faery drew back in shock.

A child, a human child! How could this be? Tup's mind whirled but could not disbelieve. It made sense, when he thought about it, explaining why his watches never chimed at any of the thefts.

The boy glared at Tup.

"So what are you, the seventh son of a seventh son?" Tup placed a foot on the boy's chest, keeping him down for the moment. "Have a water-bored stone?"

"What are you talking about?"

"What gives you the Sight?"

The lad gave an embarrassed smile. "Was only a bit of soot in me eyes. Back a few years I worked as a climbing boy. Served a right foul-mouthed sweep, I did, who'd threaten to burn me feet if I didn't climb chimneys fast enough." The boy shook his head ruefully. "One day found me in this tight bit. Something crawled above me but weren't a rat. You'd think that, well . . . maybe not you, sir. As it left, it dropped some soot on me face and as I blinked me eyes I saw a li'l fellow scrambling out the top. Ever since then, I see things."

Brownies, Tup knew, lurk in chimneys on cold mornings. Troublesome little ones that keep to houses. A scattering of ash from the heel in the eye was as good as any faery ointment.

Tup looked over the boy. He was thin, almost swallowed up by the overcoat. His hair was dark and his eyes were green like wild clover. A bit cleaned up and he'd be handsome enough for a Seelie Court plaything. "Do you have a name?"

"Lind."

"Right then." Tup offered a hand. The youth cautiously took it and stood up.

"So, what now? You're not going to be cursing me?"

"Now there's the problem. If it were known that a human had robbed the Folk," Tup grimaced at the thought. "Well, more than a few of your kind would find themselves at a horrid end." Tup removed his hat and scratched at his head. "If you return the things you stole from me, I'd be of a mind to let you go and keep this our little secret."

"If I could, sir, I would. Honest. But everything's sold or lost to cards. Could barely keep this coat and the bauble." He pulled out the shining penny. "Seemed so pretty I didn't have the heart to bet it."

Tup took the laughter from the boy's hand. "All that's left?" He choked out the words. It would take him years to amass enough again to buy his freedom. He was doomed to serve Bluebottle forever, running around sewers with trolls, consorting with the dregs of the city.

He turned to Lind. "You spleeny, reeling-ripe fool! I wouldn't worry about magistrates after we get through with you. Dancing 'til your feet bleed. Making your belly swell, your eyes pop." He poked the boy in the stomach.

"No, sir. Please, sir, a few days and I'll repay everything. I'm a fine cracksman, a master burglar," Lind said and puffed out his thin chest. "Ask any around Houndsditch or Whitechapel. There's not a house I can't break into. A few nights' work is all I need."

Tup considered a moment. In truth, he lacked the power to do more than annoy the boy for the rest of his days. He was surprised that Lind offered to make amends; he had always thought humans a rather dull, cowardly lot. Perhaps not all were so bad. "A fine cracksman?"

Lind grinned. "Aye. None better."

The boy's bravado amused Tup. In truth, he must have a good measure of skill to have pulled off the thefts. Perhaps there was a way. Bluebottle had to have a small fortune in coin after selling all the stolen goods to the humans. It would be fitting revenge to have the boy break in, swipe enough coin to pay off his debt, and then be free of service before the spriggan even realized the theft!

"If you do wish to make amends, meet me here tomorrow night."

Lind nodded and grabbed hold of Tup's hand, shaking it. "Thank you, sir. I won't be late."

Tup watched as the boy ran off. He told himself not to worry that he put so much faith in one who wasn't even his own.

Tup knew that every night, well past midnight, Bluebottle dined at the dustyards, where the city's dust and refuse was heaped and sifted for valuables. The spriggan would devour great handfuls of grit and grime.

So late the following evening, he led Lind to the closed rag-and-bottle shop.

"We're not going through the front door are we?"

"No. Did that years ago. It's warded—alarmed—and brings Bluebottle fast." Tup walked around to the side of the building. The wall facing them was crumbling brick and looked dangerous to climb. Old, closed shutters near the slanted roof blocked the only opening other than the front door.

The youth unbuttoned his great coat and withdrew his jemmy, the short crowbar made infamous by burglars. He gave the iron rod a bit of a playful spin in his hand. "An easy job."

"Maybe so. Until we're caught and ground to dust."

Lind's face grew serious. He slipped out of the coat. Beneath, he wore only a threadbare linen shirt and trousers. He thrust the jemmy into a back pocket and rubbed his hands together a moment for warmth before moving to the wall and finding a grip in the loose mortar above his head.

Tup watched Lind climb and admired the dexterity of the boy. Even when one of Lind's hands misjudged a crack and slipped, he remained quiet and recovered in an instant, swinging his weight onto his other side. Soon he was next to the shutters and carefully prying them open.

In the shadows, Tup leaned back against the wall and kept his eye on the street. While he waited, he idly considered how he would spend his new freedom. He might become a messenger or perhaps a guide to fey new to the city.

Then he heard the sound of muttering. He peered out from under the brim of his hat to see off in the distance an ungainly shape approaching. His ears caught the word "hogs," being mentioned again and again.

Tup realized then that sometimes pigs are let loose at the dustyards to feed on anything edible. No doubt Bluebottle's meal had already been well picked over by the hogs and he was returning home hungry and cranky.

Tup doubted Lind had had enough time to loot the dark shop. He was torn by the urge to run and leave the boy to his fate—one well-deserved, he told himself, after all, he did rob the Folk—and the urge to rescue him. The boy had been true to his word so far, and that could not be forgotten. As he started to climb the wall, Tup swore to himself that he should never ever have thought life in London among the humans would be thrilling.

He easily passed through the small window, and though he fell over ten feet, Tup landed like a cat on a thick table in the back room. The inside of the shop was pitch-black. He whispered out to Lind and heard a quiet answer next to him.

"Hurry, Bluebottle's returned." Even as he said it, Tup heard the sound of a key turning in the door's heavy lock.

"I haven't found a penny yet," came a whisper back.

"Damn," Tup said under his breath. His eyes had begun to adjust to the darkness and he got down from the table and found himself next to Lind. "Stay absolutely still."

The floorboards creaked as the spriggan moved through the shop, and a nearby door opened as Bluebottle entered the cavernous back room. He shuffled over to the far corner, at one point passing within inches of the pair, and lay down on a bed built into the wall. On a shelf near the spriggan's head was a familiar chest from which Bluebottle paid out Tup his pitiful earnings.

They waited, holding their breath, as Bluebottle shifted about on the bed, finally becoming still and loosing the occasional snore. Tup motioned toward the chest. Besides him Lind nodded but then went in the opposite direction, rooting quietly through the spriggan's personal effects.

Tup could not decide on a fitting curse for the boy as he got down from the table. He crept toward the shelf, pausing twice when Bluebottle shifted about in his sleep. Finally, he stood up on his toes to reach the shelf. As soon as his fingers touched the coffer, the robbery watch in his waistcoat pocket began to chime.

Bluebottle woke in an instant. Tup was grabbed roughly before he had a chance to flee and shaken about so that the many watchchains he wore jingled.

"A thief! My little coney never learned." Bluebottle brought his face close to Tup's. The spriggan's mouth opened wide, revealing many rows of dust- and grime-covered teeth. "So which grinder will it be?" He snapped his jaws in anticipation.

Tup closed his eyes, ready for the end, when all of a sudden Bluebottle was howling into the little fey's ear. He dared a look and saw the spriggan screaming in pain and, behind him, Lind stabbing at Bluebottle's foot with the iron jemmy.

Tup was dropped and, as soon as his feet met the floor, Lind grabbed and pushed him toward a small door. The boy followed, shutting the door behind them and jamming the crowbar into the frame. The wood rattled as Bluebottle pounded away.

The smaller room was faintly lit from the glow of cages hanging from the ceiling beams. There were no other exits; they were trapped. Tup remembered now where he was: the spriggan's glamour larder.

The imprisoned pixies, all no taller than Lind's forearm

even with their glittery wings, were woken by the noise. Thin, sad faces peered out between the bars. A few weak hands stretched out in silent plea.

Tup looked over at Lind, who held his chest tightly, as if hurt. "Are you all right?"

Lind gave a grin, the sort only a half-crazed fool who craved excitement wore.

"Good." Tup moved the table with the grinder beneath the nearest cage. "When I give the word, you'll let him in."

The boy looked a bit perplexed, but nodded.

Tup worked as fast as he could, always mindful of the curses and shouts of his former employer. Finally, he was done, and called out to Lind, who tore loose the jemmy and jumped back.

Bluebottle would have charged into the room if not for the wave of flying pixies that swarmed over him. His angry cries quickly changed to ones of shock and then screams of pain as the freed fey bit at his jowls, ripped his ears, and poked his eyes. Bluebottle collapsed backward and Tup and Lind jumped over him. The pixies continued to swarm over the spriggan, and their fingers were quickly stained crimson.

Off in the distance came the sounds of a whistle.

"The night watch," said the boy, tugging at Tup's arm. "A constable heard the screams."

Together they climbed back out of the shop, though the boy seemed oddly labored. Once they dropped down to the alley beside the shop, they fled. Tup led Lind through the twisted lanes of a slum the Folk knew well. They ended up at a small pub.

Tup took his seat at an empty table near the fireplace and lifted up two fingers. The serving girl nodded.

Lind looked around nervously. The other patrons were noticeably different from most Londoners. Some had slender ears ending in points, or noses longer than their drinking glasses, or delicate cricket wings that flapped in time to the fiddler playing near the fire.

The boy shivered, still clutching his chest. "So now what?"

Tup thanked the gal who brought the drinks and caught Lind staring at her back, which was hollow like a serving bowl. "The pixies won't leave much of Bluebottle for the coppers to find. I'm my own master once more."

"What of me? Planning on turning me over to them?" He glanced around him.

"The thought crossed my mind." Tup took a long sip of the mulled wine, enjoying its warmth and spices. "But you did save my life, and for that I'm thankful and forgiving. Your debt is paid."

The boy looked disappointed. "So that's it? After what we just did . . . bloody hell, after all I've seen of late—"

"Relax," Tup motioned toward the boy's untouched cup. "Have a drink." The fey was inwardly pleased at Lind's complaint. He had wondered if the boy would simply disappear after the night's adventure. He was surprised to find himself growing fond of Lind.

"At least let me pay for me own." The boy reached into his shirt and withdrew several small bags that he dropped onto the table between them.

Tup stared at the familiar bags a moment, utterly astounded. "Where did you get these?"

"Oh, a good cracksman never leaves without a little something. Found them in that back room." Lind reached for his cup and sniffed before drinking. He smacked his lips in appreciation. "Open them up. They're filled with gold dust."

Tup laughed and undid the ties to one. His fingers dug inside to lift up a pinch of glittering powder. "My boy, this isn't gold." He leaned in close. "It's glamour and worth a great deal to the Folk."

Lind's eyes widened. "So, what are we going to do with it?"

"We?" Tup chuckled good-naturedly.

"Aye." The boy hefted one of the bags. "We worked well together."

"And you'd want to be partners with one of the Folk?" Tup wrapped both his hands around Lind's. "It's risky, I warn you." He looked into the boy's eyes, almost mesmerized by their merry green.

Lind answered with a grin. "What's life without a little danger? Partners it is."

Steve Berman is from New Jersey and has had over sixty short stories and articles published since he began writing in his late teens. Urban fantasy, whether modern or historical, always intrigues him. Lethe Press released a book of his short fiction entitled *Trysts: A Triskaidecollection of Queer and Weird Stories*. Steve has edited an anthology of queer faery stories for Haworth Press entitled *So Fey* and has recently sold his first young adult novel, *Vintage*.

His Web site is www.steveberman.com

Author's Note

Some might think it odd for a suburban guy to dream about living on the crowded streets of Victorian London. But I do. Maybe I just read too much Dickens and Doyle. But to me, under the cover of fog and illuminated by gaslight, nineteenth-century London is a mysterious and magical place where anything can happen.

I asked myself what would happen to faeries of that time period that felt the same way: drawn to the city, curious about humans, and still as mischievous as ever. "The Price of Glamour" is what came to mind.

The Night Market

~

Holly Black

Tomasa walked down the road, balancing the basket of offerings on her head. Her mother would have been angry to see her carrying things like one of the maids. Even though it was night and there had been a heavy rain that day, the road was hot under Tomasa's sandaled feet. She tried to focus on the heat and not on the bottle of strong *lambanog* clinking against the dish of *paksiw na pata* or the smell of the rice cakes steamed in coconut. It would be very bad luck to eat the *parangál* that was supposed to bribe an elf into lifting his curse.

Not that she'd ever seen an elf. She wasn't even sure if she believed the story that her sister Eva had told when she'd rushed in, clutching broken pieces of tamarind pod, hair streaming with water. Usually, the sisters walked home from school together. But today, when it started to rain, Eva had ducked under a tree and declared that she would wait out the storm. Tomasa had thought nothing of it—Eva hated to be dirty or wet or windblown.

She kicked a shard of coconut shell out into the road, scattering red ants. She shouldn't have left Eva. It all came down to that. Even though Eva was older, she had no sense. Especially around boys.

A car slowed as it passed. Tomasa kept her eyes on the road and after a moment it sped away. Girls didn't usually go walking the streets of Alaminos alone at night. The Philippines just wasn't safe—people got kidnapped or killed, even this far outside Manila. But with her father and the driver out in the provinces and her mother in Hong Kong for the week, there was only Tomasa and their maid, Rosa, left to decide who would bring the gift. Eva was too sick to do much of anything. Rosa said that was what happened when an *enkanto* fell in love—his beloved would sicken just as his heart sickened with desire.

Looking at Eva's pale face, Tomasa had said she would go. After all, no elf would fall in love with her. She touched her right cheek. She could trace the shape of her birthmark without even looking in a mirror—an irregular splash of red that covered one of her eyes and stopped just above her lips.

Tomasa kept walking, past the whitewashed church, the narrow line of shops at the edge of town, and the city's single McDonald's. Then the buildings began to thin. Spanish-style houses flanked the road while rice fields spread out beyond them into the distance. Mosquitoes buzzed close, drawn by her sweat.

By the time Tomasa crossed the short bridge near her school, only the light of the moon let her see where to put her feet. She stepped carefully through thick plants and hopped over a ditch. The tamarind tree was unremarkable—

a wide trunk clouded by thick, feathery leaves. She set her basket down among the roots.

At least the moon was only half full. On full moon nights, Rosa said that witches and elves and other spirits met at a market in the graveyard, where they traded things like people did during the day. Not that she thought it was true, but it was still frightening.

"*Tabi-tabi po*," she whispered to the darkness, just like Rosa had told her, warning him that she was there. "Please take these offerings and let my sister get better."

There was only silence and Tomasa felt even more foolish than before. She turned to go.

Something rustled in the branches above her.

Tomasa froze and the sound stopped. She wanted to believe it was the wind, but the night air was warm and stagnant.

She looked up into eyes the green of unripe bananas.

"Hello," she stammered, heart thundering in her chest.

The *enkanto* stepped out onto one of the large limbs of the tree. His skin was the same dark cinnamon as a tamarind pod and his feet were bare. His clothes surprised her—cutoff jeans and a T-shirt with a cracked and faded logo on it. He might have been a boy from the rice fields if it wasn't for his too-bright eyes and the fact that the branch hadn't so much as dipped under his weight.

He smiled down at her and she could not help but notice that he was beautiful. "What if I don't make your sister well?" he asked.

Tomasa didn't know what to say. She had lost track of

the conversation. She was still trying to decide if she was willing to believe in elves. "What?"

He jumped down from his perch and she took a quick step away from him.

The elf boy picked up the *lambanog* and twisted the cap free. His hair rustled like leaves. "The food—is it freely given?"

"I don't understand."

"Is it mine whether I make your sister better or not?"

She forced herself to concentrate on his question. Both answers seemed wrong. If she said that the food was payment, it wasn't a gift, was it? And if it wasn't a gift, then she wasn't really following Rosa's directions. "I suppose so," she said finally.

"Ah, good," the elf said and took a deep swallow of the liquor. His smile said that she'd given the wrong answer. She felt cold, despite the heat.

"You're not going to make her better," she said.

That only made his smile widen. "Let me give you something else in return—something better." He reached up into the foliage and snapped off a brown tamarind pod. Bringing it to his lips, he whispered a few words and then kissed it. "Whoever eats this will love you."

Tomasa's face flushed. "I don't want anyone to love me." She didn't need an elf to tell her that she was ugly. "I want my sister not to be sick."

"Take it," he said, putting the tamarind in her hand and closing her fingers over it. He tilted his head. "It is all you'll get from me tonight."

The elf was standing very close to her now, her hand clasped in both of his. His skin felt dry and slightly rough in a way that made her think of bark. Somehow, she had gotten tangled up in her thoughts and was no longer sure of what she ought to say.

He raised his eyebrows thoughtfully. His too-bright eyes reflected the moonlight like an animal's. Tomasa was filled with a sudden, nameless fear.

"I have to go," she said, pulling her hand free.

Over the bridge and down the familiar streets, past the closed shops, her feet finding their way by habit, Tomasa ran home. Her panic was amplified with each step, until she was racing the dark. Only when she got close to home did she slow, her shirt soaked with sweat and her muscles hurting, the pod still clasped in her hand.

Rosa was waiting on the veranda of their house, smoking one of the clove cigarettes that her brother sent by the carton from Indonesia. She got up when Tomasa walked through the gate.

"Did you see him?" Rosa asked. "Did he take the offering?"

"Yes and yes," Tomasa said, breathing hard. "But it doesn't matter."

Rosa frowned. "You really saw an *enkanto*? You're sure."

Tomasa had been a coward. Perspiration cooling on her neck, she thought of all the things she might have said. He'd caught her off guard. She hadn't expected him to have a soft smile, or to laugh, or even to exist in the first place. She looked at the tamarind shell in her hand and watched as her fingers crushed it. Bits of the pod stuck in the sticky brown fruit beneath. For all that she'd thought Eva was stupid around boys, she'd been the stupid one. "I'm sure," she said hollowly.

On her way up the stairs to bed, it occurred to Tomasa to wonder for the first time why an elf who could make a love spell with a few words would burn with thwarted desire. But then, in all of Rosa's stories the elves were wicked and strange, beings that cursed and blessed according to their whims. Maybe there was just no making sense of it.

The next day the priest came and said novenas. And after that, the *arbularyo* sprinkled the white sheets of Eva's bed with herbs. Then the doctor came and gave her some pills. But by nightfall, Eva was no better. Her skin, which had been as brown as polished mahogany, was pale and dusty as that of a snake ready to shed.

Tomasa called her father's cell phone and left a message, but she wasn't sure if he would get it. Out far enough in the provinces getting a signal was chancy at best. Her mother's Hong Kong hotel was easier to reach. She left another message and went up to see her sister.

Eva's hair was damp with sweat and her eyes were fever-bright when Tomasa came to sit at the end of her bed. Candles and crucifixes littered the side table, along with a pot of strong and smelly herb tea.

Eva grabbed Tomasa's hand and clutched it hard enough to hurt.

"I heard what you did," Eva said with a cough. "Stay away from his goddamned tree."

Tomasa grinned. "You should drink more of the tea. It's supposed to help."

Eva grimaced and made no move toward her cup. Maybe it tasted as bad as it smelled. "Look, I'm serious," she said.

"Tell me again how he cursed you," Tomasa said. "I'm serious too."

Eva gave a weird little laugh. "I should have listened to Rosa's stories. Maybe if I'd read a couple less magazines . . . I don't know. I just thought he was a boy from the fields. I told him to mind his place and leave me alone."

"You didn't eat any of his fruit, right?" Tomasa asked suddenly.

"I had a little piece," Eva said, looking at the wall. "Before I knew he was there."

That was bad. Tomasa took a deep breath and tried to think of how to phase her next question. "Do you, um, do you think he might have made you fall in love with him?"

"Are you crazy?" Eva blew her nose in a tissue. "Love him? Like him? He's not even human."

Tomasa forced herself to smile, but in her heart, she worried.

Rosa was sitting at the kitchen table cubing up chunks of ginger while garlicky chicken simmered on the stove. Tomasa liked the kitchen. Unlike the rest of the house, it was small and dark. The floor was poured concrete instead of gleaming wood. A few herbs grew in rusted coffee cans along the windowsill and there was a strong odor of sugar-cane vinegar. It was a kitchen to be useful in.

Tomasa sat down on a stool. "Tell me about elves."

Rosa looked up from her chopping, a cigarette dangling

from her lips. She breathed smoke from her nose. "What do you want me to tell you?"

"Anything. Everything. Something that might help."

"They're fickle as cats and twice as cruel. You know the tales. They'll steal your heart if you let them, and if you don't, they'll curse you for your good sense. They're night things— spirits—and don't care for the day. They don't like gold either. It reminds them of the sun."

"I know all that," Tomasa said. "Tell me something I don't know."

Rosa shook her head. "I'm no *mananambal*—I only know the stories. His love will fade; he will forget your sister and she will get well again."

Tomasa pressed her lips into a thin line. "What if she doesn't?"

"It has only been two days. Be patient. Not even a cold would go away in that time."

Two days turned into three and then four. Their mother had changed her flight and was due home that Tuesday, but there was still no word from their father. By Sunday, Tomasa found that she couldn't wait anymore. She went to the shed and got a machete. She put her gold Santa Maria pendant on a chain and fastened it around her neck. Steeling herself, she walked to the tamarind tree, although her legs felt like lead and her stomach churned.

In the day, the tree looked frighteningly normal. Leafy green, sun-dappled, and buzzing with flies.

She hefted the machete. "Make Eva well."

The leaves rustled with the wind, but no elf appeared.

She swung the knife at the trunk of the tree. It stuck in the wood, knocking off a piece of bark, but her hand slid forward on the blade and the sharp steel slit open her palm. She let go of the machete and watched the shallow cut well with blood.

"You'll have to do better than that," she said, wiping her hand against her jeans. She worked the blade free from the trunk and hefted it to swing again.

But somehow her grip must have been loose, because the machete tumbled from her hands before she could complete the arc. It flew off into the brush by the stream.

Tomasa stomped off in the direction of where it had fallen, but she found no trace of it in the thick weeds. "Fine," she shouted at the tree. "Fine!"

"Aren't you afraid of me?" a voice said and Tomasa whirled around. The elf was standing in the grass with the machete in his hand.

She found herself speechless again. If anything, the daylight rendered him more alien looking. His eyes glittered and his hair seemed to move with a subtle wind, as though he was underwater.

He took a step toward her, his feet keeping to the shadows. "I've heard it's very bad luck to cut down an *enkanto's* tree."

Tomasa thought of the gold pendant around her neck and stepped into a patch of sunlight. "Good thing for me that it's only a little chipped then."

He snorted, and for a moment, he looked like he was going to smile. "What if I told you that whatever you do to the tree, you do to the spirit?"

"You look fine," she said, edging back to the bridge. He did. She was the one who was bleeding.

"You're either brave or stupid." He turned the blade in his hand and held it out to her, hilt first. She would have to step closer to him, into the shadows, to take it.

"Well, I'd pick stupid," she said. "But not that stupid." She walked quickly over the bridge, leaving him still holding the machete.

Her heart beat like a drum in her chest as she made her way home.

That night, lying in bed, Tomasa heard distant music. When she turned toward the window, a full moon looked down on her. Quickly, she dressed in the dark, careful to clasp her gold chain around her neck. Holding her shoes in one hand, she crept down the stairs, bare feet making only a soft slap on the wood.

She would find a *mananambal* to remove the *enkanto*'s curse. She would go to the night market herself.

The graveyard was at the edge of town, where the electrical lines stopped running. The moonlight illuminated the distant rice fields where kerosene lamps flickered in nipa huts. Cicadas called from the trees and beneath her feet, thorny touch-me-nots curled up with each step.

Close to the cemetery, the Japanese synth-pop was loud enough to recognize and she saw lights. Two men with machine guns slung over their shoulders stood near marble steps. A generator chugged away near the trees, long black cords connecting it to floodlights mounted on tombs. All across the graves a market had been set up, collapsible tables covered with cloth and wares, and people squatting among the stones.

From this distance, they didn't look like elves or witches or anything supernatural at all. Still, she didn't want to be rude. Unclasping the Santa Maria pendant from her neck, she put it in her mouth. She tasted the salt of her sweat and tried to find a place for it between her cheek and her tongue.

She wondered if the men with guns would stop her, but they let her pass without so much as a glance. A man on the edge of the tables played a little tune on a nose flute. He smiled at her and she tried to grin back, even though his teeth were unusually long and his smile seemed a touch too wide.

A few vendors squatting in front of baskets called to Tomasa as she passed. Piles of golden mangos and papaya paled in the moonlight. Foul smelling durians hung from a line. The eggplant and purple yams looked black and strange, while a heap of gingerroot resembled misshapen dolls.

At another table, split carcasses of goats were spread out like blankets. Inside a loose cage of bamboo, frogs hopped frantically. Nearby was a collection of eggs, some of which seemed too slender and leathery for chickens.

"What is that?" Tomasa asked.

"Snake *balut*," said the old woman behind the table. She spit red into the dirt and Tomasa told herself that the woman was only chewing betel nut. Lots of people chewed betel nut. There was nothing strange about it.

"Snake's tasty," the vendor went on. "Better than crow, but I have that, too."

Tomasa took two steps back from the table and then

braced herself. She needed help and this woman was already speaking with her.

"I'm looking for a *mananambal* that can take an *enkanto*'s spell off my sister," she said.

The old woman grinned, showing crimson-stained teeth and pointed past the largest building. "Look for the man selling potions."

Tomasa set off in that direction. Outside of an open tomb, men argued over prices in front of tables spread with guns. A woman with teeth as white as coconut meat smiled at Tomasa, one arm draped around a man and her upper body hovering in the air. She had no lower body. Wet innards flashed from beneath a beaded shirt as she moved.

Tomasa rolled the golden pendant on her tongue, her hands shaking. No one else seemed to notice.

A line of women dressed in tight clothing leaned against the outside wall of the tomb. One had skin that was far too pale, while another had feet that were turned backward. Some of them looked like girls Tomasa knew from town, but they stared blankly at her as she passed. Tomasa shuddered and kept moving.

She passed vendors selling horns and powders, narcotics and charms. There were candles rubbed with thick salves and small clay figurines wound with bits of hair. One man sat behind a table with several iron pots smoking over a small grill.

Steam rose from them, making the hot night hotter. Bunches of herbs and flowers littered the table, along with several empty Johnnie Walker and Jim Beam bottles and a chipped ceramic funnel.

The man looked up from ladling a solution into one of the empties. His longish hair was streaked with gray, and when he smiled at her, she saw that one of his teeth had been replaced with gold.

"This one has a hundred herbs boiled in coconut oil," he said, pointing to one of the pots. "*Haplas*, will cure anything." He pointed to another. "And here, *gayuma*, for luck or love."

"*Lolo*," she said with a slight bob of her head. "I need something for my sister. An *enkanto* has fallen in love with her and she's sick."

"To break curses. *Sumpa*, an antidote." He indicated a third pot.

"How much?" Tomasa asked, reaching for her pockets.

His grin widened. "Wouldn't you like to assure yourself that I'm the real thing?"

Tomasa stopped, unsure of herself. What was the right answer?

"What's that in your mouth?" he asked.

"Just a pit. I bought a plum," she lied.

"You shouldn't eat the fruit here," he said, extending his hand. "Here. Spit it out. Let me see."

Tomasa shook her head.

"Come on." He smiled. "If you don't trust me a little, how can you trust me to cure your sister?"

Tomasa hesitated, but she thought of Eva, feverish and pale. She spat the golden pendant into his palm.

He cackled, the sound dry in his throat. "You're more clever than I thought."

She didn't know if she should be pleased or not.

One of the *mananambal*'s fingers darted out to dot her forehead with oil. She felt wobbly.

"What did you do?" she managed to ask. Her voice sounded thick and slow as smoke.

"You're a fine piece of flesh, even with that face. I'll get more than I could use in a thousand brews."

It sounded like nonsense to Tomasa. Her head had started to spin and all she wanted to do was sit down in the dirt and rest. But the gold-toothed man had her by the arm and was dragging her away from his table.

She stumbled along, knocking into a man in a wide straw hat who was running down the aisle of vendors. When he caught hold of her, she saw that his eyes were green as grass.

"You," she said, her voice syrup-slow. She stumbled and fell on her hands and knees. People were shouting at each other, but that wasn't so bad because at least no one was making her get up. Her necklace had fallen in the dirt beside her. She forced herself to close her hand over it.

The elf pushed the *mananambal*, saying something that Tomasa couldn't quite understand, because all the words seemed to slur together. The old man shoved back and then, grabbing the *enkanto*'s arm at the wrist, bit down with his golden tooth.

The elf gasped in pain and brought down his fist on the old man's head, knocking him backward. The bitten arm hung limply from the elf's side.

Tomasa struggled to her feet, fighting off the thickness that threatened to overwhelm her. Something was wrong. The potion vender had done this to her. She narrowed her eyes at him.

The *mananambal* grinned, his tooth glinting in the flood-lights.

"Come on," he said, reaching for her.

"Leave me alone," she managed to say, stumbling back. The *enkanto* caught her before she fell, supporting her with his good arm.

"Let her alone," said the *enkanto*, "or I will curse you blind, lame, and worse."

The old man laughed. "I'm a curse breaker, fool."

The elf grabbed one of the Jim Beam bottles from the table and slammed it down, so that he was holding a jagged glass neck. The elf smiled a very thin smile. "Then I won't bother with magic."

The old man went silent. Together, Tomasa and the elf stumbled out of the night market. Once the music had faded into the distance, they sank down beneath a balete tree.

"Why?" she asked, still a little light-headed.

He looked down and hesitated before he answered. "You're brave to go to the night market alone." He made a little laugh. "If something had happened to you, it would have been my fault."

"I thought I was just stupid," she said. She felt stupid. "Please, end this, let my sister get better."

"No," he said suddenly, standing up.

"If you really loved her, you would let her get better," said Tomasa.

"But I don't love her," the *enkanto* said.

Tomasa didn't know what to make of his words. "Then why do you torment her?"

"At first I wanted to punish her, but I don't care about that now. You visit me because she's sick," he said with a shy smile. "I want you to keep visiting me."

Tomasa felt those words like a blow. Shock mingled with anger and a horrible, dangerous pleasure that rendered her almost incapable of speech. "I won't come again," she shouted.

"You will," said the *enkanto*. He pulled himself up onto a branch of the tree, then hooked his foot in the back and climbed higher, to where the thick green leaves hid him from view.

"I will never forgive you." Tomasa meant to shout it, but it came out of her mouth in a whisper. There was no reply but the gentle night breeze and distant radio.

Her hands were shaking. She looked down at them and saw the loop of gold chain still dangling from her fingers.

And suddenly, just like that, she had a plan. An impossible, absurd plan. She made a fist around the gold pendant, feeling its edges dig into her palm. Her feet found their way over brush and vine as she darted through the town to the tamarind tree.

The elf was sitting on one of the boughs when she got there. His eyebrows rose slightly, but he smiled. She smiled back.

"I've been rude," she said, hoping that when he looked at her he would think the guilt in her eyes was for what she'd done, not for what she was about to do. "I'm sorry."

He jumped down, one arm touching the trunk to steady him. "I'm glad you came."

Tomasa walked closer. She put one hand where the old man had bitten him, hoping that he wouldn't notice her other hand was fisted. "How's your arm?"

"Fine," he said. "Weak. I can move it a little now."

Steeling herself, she looked up into his face and slid her hand higher on his arm, over his shoulder and to his neck. His green eyes narrowed.

"What are you doing?" he asked. "You're acting strange."

"Am I?" She searched for some passable explanation. "Maybe the potion hasn't really worn off."

He shook his head. His black hair rustled against her arm, making her shiver.

She slid her other hand to his throat, twining both around his back of his neck.

He didn't push her away, although his body went rigid.

Then, as quick as she could, she wrapped the chain around his neck like a golden garrote.

He choked once as she clasped the necklace. Then she stepped back, stumbling on the roots of the tamarind. His hands flew to his throat but stopped short of touching the gold.

"What have you done?" he demanded.

She crouched down in the dirt, scuttling back from him. "Release my sister from your curse." Her voice sounded cold, even to her. In truth, she didn't know what she'd done.

"It is my right! She insulted me." The elf swallowed hard around the collar.

Insulted him? Tomasa almost laughed. Only an elf would let one girl stab his tree, but curse another for being insulting.

"I won't take the chain off your neck unless you make her well."

The *enkanto*'s eyes flashed with anger.

"Please," Tomasa asked.

He looked down. She could no longer read his expression. "She'll be better when you get home," he muttered.

She crept a little closer. "How do I know you're telling the truth?"

"Take it off me!" he demanded.

Tomasa wanted to say something else, but the words caught in her throat as she reached behind his neck and unhooked the chain. She knew she should run. She'd beaten him and if she stayed any longer, he would surely put a curse on her. But she didn't move.

He watched her for a moment, both of them silent. "That was . . ." he said finally.

"Definitely bad luck," she offered.

He laughed at that, a short soft laugh that made her cheeks grow warm.

"You really wanted me to come and visit?"

"I *did*," he said with a snort.

She grinned shyly. Balling up the necklace in her hand, she tossed it in the direction of the stream.

"You know," he said, taking one of her wrists and placing it on his shoulder, "before, when you had your hand right here, I thought that you were going to kiss me."

Her face felt hot. "Maybe I wish I had."

"It's not too late," he said.

His lips were sour, but his mouth was warm.

〜〜〜〜〜

By the time that Tomasa got home, the sky was pink and birds were screeching from their trees. Eva was already awake, sitting at the breakfast table, eating a plate of eggs. She looked entirely recovered.

"Where were you?" Rosa asked, refilling Eva's teacup. "Where's your pendant?"

Tomasa shrugged. "I must have lost it."

"I can't believe you stayed out all night." Eva gave her a conspiratorial smile.

"*Mananambal,*" Rosa whispered as she returned to the kitchen. Tomasa almost stopped her to ask what she meant, but the truth made even less sense than anyone's guesses.

Upstairs, Tomasa picked up the crushed tamarind pod from her dresser. His words were still clear in her mind from that first meeting. *Whoever eats this will love you.* She looked into the mirror, at her birthmark, bright as blood, at her kiss-stung lips, at the absurd smile stretching across her face.

Carefully separating out the crushed pieces of shell, she pulled the dried pulp free from its cage of veins. Piece by piece, she put the sweet brown fruit in her own mouth and swallowed it down.

Holly Black spent her early years in a decaying Victorian mansion where her mother fed her a steady diet of ghost stories and faery books. Her first novel, *Tithe: A Modern Faerie Tale* was the result. Published in 2002, it received two starred reviews and was named an ALA Best Book for Young Adults. Her collaboration with Tony DiTerlizzi on the *New York Times* best-selling *The Spiderwick Chronicles*, a serial novel for younger readers, followed. Her most recent book is *Valiant: A Modern Tale of Faerie.*

Her Web site address is www.blackholly.com

Author's Note

It is a great honor for me to be included in an Ellen Datlow and Terri Windling anthology, because one changed the direction of my career. I was planning on teaching and had already registered for my last semester of classes. That night, while leafing through a *Year's Best Fantasy and Horror,* I realized that all these writers and illustrators and editors I admired actually knew each other. They were friends. I immediately (and possibly rashly) dropped all my education classes and replaced them with literary ones.

I started "The Night Market" with some vague ideas about where I was going and found that various different elements crept in. Christina Rossetti's *Goblin Market* was the inspiration for the title and helped shape the marketplace itself, but most of the story came from tales of tree spirits that I'd heard from my Filipino mother-in-law and her friends. In fact, one of the most enjoyable aspects of writing "The Night Market" was being able to call someone in the middle of the night and get a description of the weeds in Alaminos or a line of dialogue translated into Tagalog. Then, of course, I would call a week later, tell her I scrapped that scene and make her describe something completely different. Thankfully, my mother-in-law seems to have forgiven me.

Never Never

Bruce Glassco

On the pristine white sand beside the harbor, the rotting carcass of the ship was as ugly as roadkill in a ballroom. Rotten timbers stuck out of the sand willy-nilly, rotten ropes fell away from rusted-through cleats, and bits of rotten canvas draped themselves at random around the whole rotten skeleton. Tiny crabs scuttled in and out of the mouth of a corroded, half-buried cannon nearby. A seagull hopped down from a spar to investigate the crabs. Then, hearing a high ringing noise drawing near, it flapped up to safety in a nearby palm tree.

Just above the surface of the shockingly blue water, there was a flash of light that might have been a spray-born reflection of the bright tropical sun. The bird, however, was taking no chances as it eyed the scene warily. The ringing sound grew louder as the sparkle of light circled around the ship once, twice, three times.

A half-buried timber twitched. Then, in a sudden rush,

all the beams changed their color from weathered gray to fresh-cut brown, swelling thick and square once more as they rose out of the beach in a shower of sand and fitted themselves into a perfect skeleton. Iron and bronze fittings shattered their way out of decades of rust, rose through the air, and riveted themselves into their proper places, now gleaming as if newly swabbed. A hundred stiff shreds of canvas lost their crusts of salt, flew together, and knitted themselves into great flapping sails, then reefed themselves neatly into place within the rigging that was racing hither and yon like a hundred shuttles in a hundred mad looms, binding up the entire ship in all its proud glory. For a moment the entire vessel hovered above the water, then it descended gently to float in the center of the harbor. An anchor rose to the surface from the harbor's bottom, and a rope from the ship's deck uncoiled itself, threaded itself through the anchor's eye, and knotted itself off. Then the anchor sank once more, and the ship floated serenely beneath the tropical sun as if it had never heard a rumor of the dust of time.

Round the entire harbor the flickering light sailed again, three times once more, and then vanished through the trees as suddenly as it had come. The gull cocked its head to one side. At first there seemed to be no further action. Then, from the verge where the trees met the sand, a dry white branch twitched. It began to roll down the beach, and as it came clear of the fallen palm leaves it became obvious that it was a not a branch but a weathered bone: a human thighbone, in fact. From different parts of the harbor other bones shot up to the water's surface and skimmed above the waves to a point just offshore. There the human skeleton assembled itself even more rapidly than the ship's skeleton had put itself together, rolling round and round above the waves as the bones fitted themselves into place with faint clicks.

Just beneath the surface of the water was a turmoil of frothing pink, like a person being eaten by piranha, only in reverse. The skeleton dipped once beneath the surface and rose again with its organs neatly tucked in place between pelvis and shoulder blades; dipped again, reappearing with muscles stretching from bone to bone and naked eyeballs staring from empty sockets; once more, this time reappearing with nerves and arteries and veins and fat knitting their way through the entire structure just as the rigging had knitted up the ship; and last of all the naked skin leaping from the water to wrap the whole grotesque form in its pink cocoon. Hair sprouted from the man's head as he sailed through the air and landed on the ship's deck. Trousers and a blue-and-white-striped shirt flew out of the galley and descended upon him. Then the force that had reanimated him released him, and he opened his mouth and screamed. The seagull, who had understood nothing of what had happened, understood that scream and took wing through the forest.

Now other skeletons were reassembling themselves above other parts of the harbor, sailing through the air and landing beside the pudgy form of the first man on deck. Last of all, a regal figure, taller than any of the other men by a good head and a half, came soaring out of the jungle at the lagoon's edge. He landed on the quarterdeck already clothed in a bright red greatcoat, his hair perfectly set and curled, his mustache waxed, his boots polished and buckled. As soon as he regained his footing he surveyed the scene calmly, then reached into one of his pockets and pulled out a black and white flag. He strode to the foot of the mast, attached it to a halyard, and began hauling away one-handed to raise it to the masthead. If the thought crossed his mind that the old sign of the skull and crossbones was more appropriate to this crew than to any other who had ever sailed beneath it since the days of the *Flying Dutchman*, he kept that thought to himself. With breathtaking grace he fastened the halyard to a cleat one-handed, then turned to face his crew.

"Well, my lads," he sang out in his silky, rich baritone, "Hook's back. Are you with me, or are you dogs ready to dance the frisky plank to Davy Jones where you all rightly belong?" The hook where his right hand should have been gleamed in the terrible sunlight.

James Hook appraised his crew keenly. Smee the bosun, always the sensitive sort, had begun handling the raisings worse every time. He still hadn't opened his eyes since that soul-piercing scream, and he was fingering his trembling chin and neck as if checking to make sure his head was still attached. Little Noodler was simply rubbing his hands together—they'd been put on backward during his first reassembly, and had never been right since. Bill Jukes suddenly sat down on the deck. Gentleman Starkey was leaning against the rail and staring into the water, breathing heavily. The rest were milling about uneasily.

Each time they returned to the island, Hook knew, the

first few moments were the most dangerous. On one such occasion Orinoco Jack, the second mate, had simply nodded to the assembled crew, picked up a cannonball, and stepped off the side of the ship, all without saying a word. He'd never come back on subsequent resurrections, either.

Hook needed to take their attention away from their own plight and reattach it firmly somewhere else. His usual method of doing so was to banish their terror of the unknown by replacing it with terror of something they could readily understand. Nothing fit that description better than the cold iron at the business end of his right arm. He began to scrape it back and forth across the brass compass housing, which he'd found produced the best acoustics. As the compass was nonfunctional at their current latitude, this was the only use the thing had.

The crew straightened up at the sound. In some ways he was a kinder Hook than he had been in his younger days, when he would have simply filleted one of them to get their attention. Alas, killing his own henchman no longer gave him the simple satisfaction he had once felt.

"Lads," he told them in the calm voice he'd trained them to know was his most dangerous, "as you can see, it's back again we've come. We don't know where this place is, we don't know why this keeps happening, and we don't know how it's done. But we know who is responsible, don't we lads?"

There was an uncomfortable pause. "The Boy," muttered Noodler petulantly, still staring at his hands. Some of the rest nodded.

This was bad. Hook had been hoping for a unified shout. His voice grew even calmer and more deadly. "And once we catch him what will we do with that primping popinjay, that crowing crustacean, that uncivilized menace to piracy and all the forces of wickedness, to say nothing of adulthood, eh, lads?"

Again there was a period of silence. Then, without getting up from where he sat on the deck, Bill Jukes spoke out in the bored tone of one who no longer cares whether he lives or dies. "I suppose we'll choose between getting stabbed by him and his gang again or walking the plank, sir. Just like every other time."

The crew seldom saw the red spots appear in Hook's eyes anymore, but they saw them now. "Is that so?" the captain whispered silkily, stepping over to where Jukes sat staring at the deck. A few pirates looked away. The hook flashed in the sun once, and Jukes toppled over. "Now again, men, I ask you, what are we going to do to that revolting child?"

This time the responding shouts were a bit weak, but undoubtedly prompt. "Run him through, sir!" "Give him the lash!" "Maroon him!" "Sit on his chest and make him say uncle!" That last was from Smee, who still seemed disconnected from things.

Hook nodded, satisfied. One must not think too harshly of him for his villainy. There was something of Milton's Satan in him that would always prefer reigning in Hell to serving in Heaven. Then again, there was the extreme value he placed on consistency. Without it he might have lost his mind years ago, and his crew soon after. On the island the game was surely rigged, but just as surely it was the only game in town.

After his crew had finished tossing Jukes's remains overboard, Captain Hook sent Mullins and Cookson out for some scouting. Besides a genuine wish to find out what had been going on in their absence, he also needed to reassure himself that they were all properly more terrified of his hook than they were of the savage beasts and other foes on the absurdly dangerous island. The report they brought back was not encouraging. Most of the paths had been changed, and in one clearing they'd come across three huge headless statues of blackened metal that looked like nothing they'd ever seen before.

"How long do you suppose he's kept us in the dark this time, Smee?" Hook ruminated. Smee was quite his favorite confidant; as one of the stupidest pirates, he never had the slightest idea what the captain was on about, which allowed Hook to soliloquize in peace. "Sometimes it's naught but a few days, sometimes it's a score of years. We'll need a better lay of the land than those two skugs can provide. How should we proceed, eh, lad?"

Smee gave the question due consideration. "Teach some parrots to sing, sir?" he suggested finally.

At length Hook decided on a bold but straightforward tactic. He would kidnap a Lost Boy. At worst this might provoke the boy's leader to a first confrontation, but it was still too early for that to worry Hook. There would always be at least two or three smaller skirmishes before the inevitable grand finale.

"You see, Smee," he explained as the two of them

watched the other pirates digging a pit in the forest, "hardly any of the Boys besides their leader ever know much wood-craft. The time between when Peter takes an interest in them and the time when they grow too old to stay is simply too short." Smee nodded and picked up a sugar cookie from a plate nearby, but Hook rapped it out of his hand with the hook's blunt side. "That's the bait, you fool!" Smee rubbed his bruised knuckles and kept quiet.

Time-worn stratagems such as this one often worked quite well on the island, and this occasion was no exception. They caught a Lost Boy that very afternoon. Of course there was a buried cage beneath the spread palm leaves, with a lid that latched into place to keep the little blighter from simply flying right out again.

The pirates were exceedingly merry as they rolled the cage back to their ship. Their victories were rare, and they savored them when they could. Hook, though, striding along beside the cage, listened to his new captive with growing dismay. Partly it was the language he used. Hook tolerated some swearing from his crew—they were pirates, after all—but he himself rarely mustered anything more blistering than "odds bobs, hammer and tongs." This child, though, seemed to show no hesitation at turning the air blue with his curses. What bothered Hook more deeply, though, was that Hook had never heard much of the child's vocabulary before in his life.

Once they managed to get the cage onto the ship, Hook gestured for silence from his crew and addressed the boy directly. He was a scruffy-looking sort, but then the Lost

Boys were always more or less scruffy, depending on their leader's most recent success in recruiting a mother for them. His hair was pale and wispy, and his skin was red with perpetual sunburn.

"Child," began the captain, "know that I, James Hook, have laid you low. Any moment now could be your last. At a word from me my crew might skewer you on the points of their swords, or hurl you and your cage overboard to let you be devoured by sharks or worse. Do you have any last words you wish to address to me, your captor—say, to plead for your miserable life?"

The boy stuck out his tongue. Hook smiled. This was the sort of behavior he was used to. Their leader might not always succeed in teaching his Boys much about woodcraft, or fencing, or most of his other areas of expertise, but he never failed to teach them bravery. This was a promising beginning.

"Don't think the Redskins will help you out this time, lad. Or the . . . the . . . " he drove his hook into the railing with impatience. "Smee, what was the name of those despicable German double-crossers we tried to ally with the last time we were here?"

Smee just nodded complacently, but Little Noodler called out "Natsees" in his usual laconic voice.

"Aye, Natsees it was. None of them are around about these parts anymore, d'ye hear?" Hook was fishing in the dark at this point. The political situation on the island was always complex, to say the least. Peter usually kept anywhere from two to six other factions on the island besides

his own, and tried to encourage as much making and breaking of alliances as possible to keep things interesting. Indeed,
he'd been known to switch sides himself in the middle of a
battle if he thought things were getting too stagnant. In his
times on the island Hook had known conquistadors, Aztecs,
headhunters, dervishes, pygmies, gypsies, cannibals, cow-
boys, samurai, and gangsters, to say nothing of the afore-
mentioned Redskins and Nazis. He'd even met an old con-
quistador once who told him that he could remember the
days when Saracens populated the island. Hook was hoping
that his captive would reveal which other groups he should
watch out for, but he got no satisfaction. The boy just spit.

Hook pulled his iron claw out of the railing and clanged
it against the iron bars, and was gratified to see the captive
move back a step. "You'd best be showing some respect to
your betters, child, or this right hand of mine may tickle you
between the ribs in a way you won't like!"

The boy seemed to regain some confidence and took a
step forward again. "Whatever. Hey, what's up with the
freakin' hook, dude? Are you supposed to be that psycho
from *Urban Legend*?"

"Urban wha . . . ?" Hook was nonplused. "I'm . . . we're
pirates, child. Surely you recognize . . . "

"Man, Pete said he was going to go fetch one of his old
enemies after we wrecked those giant robots, but I never
thought that any of Pete's bad guys would look like such a
dork." Hook took a step back, puzzled; he couldn't imagine
why someone would think he resembled a Doric column.
Besides, where could a Lost Boy have learned Greek? Still,

the child sensed that he had an advantage, and he began to press it. "And what's up with those curls in your hair, dude? You look like Cher in that video."

Hook's hand flew up to his carefully pressed Restoration-era locks. "What . . . ? I'm not sharing anything with you, you whelp!" He felt he was losing control of the situation.

The boy snorted. "Man, all you freaks look totally lame."

Taken aback, half the crew bent down to inspect their legs and make sure they hadn't accidentally crippled themselves. With his taunts not having their desired effects, the boy was looking frustrated now, too. Hook was fuming. This wasn't working properly at all. He was supposed to threaten, the captive was supposed to cower or act defiant, but the language barrier was ruining everything.

The boy decided to try again. "Listen, Jack, when my man Pete gets back from wherever he's gone off to, he's going to come out here and kick your—"

"What!" Hook roared, too put out to even notice he'd been called Jack. "You mean that whelp isn't even on the island! Why are we wasting time with all this nonsense, then!" With one savage blow he smashed the lock on the cage's lid and threw it open. "This whole exercise has been an absurd waste of my precious time."

The towheaded boy wasted no time in flying free of the cage. He hovered briefly above the deck, called out "What*ever*," and made a rude gesture before turning and soaring off over the forest.

The crew was looking confused, as if they weren't sure whether they had been bested or not. Smee was talking earnestly to his sword. Without a word to his cringing under-lings, Hook stalked across the deck and unshipped the ship's boat. Then he roared to Starkey and Noodler to lower him down to the water.

"Ahem, um, where are you going, sir?" asked Starkey.

"Somewhere I can think," bellowed the captain. "Starkey, you're in charge." The crew looked at each other nervously as they lowered the boat, for the captain never bellowed unless he was worried or confused or frightened. He fit his hook into the specially drilled hole in the right-hand oar handle and began pulling his way angrily to shore.

For a long while Hook simply walked at random through the island's trails. Normally he would have dreaded wandering alone on the island without a fair number of bodyguards, but at this point he was too upset to care. Once a puma growled at him from the underbrush, but he brandished his hook and glared at it until it slunk away abashed.

Then he stopped and sniffed the air. A thin cloud of smoke hung above the trees in a valley to the left of the path. A wolfish grin spread across Hook's features, and he left the trail and began to glide stealthily down the hillside.

The clearing was well hidden, but Hook could spot the faint trails that led to it. He circled around carefully until he spotted the inevitable sentry, who seemed to be dozing. A few quick steps and Hook had the man's arm behind his back, the hook at his throat. He pushed the man before him into the center of the circle of wigwams.

"Tiger Lily!" he roared. "You call this pitiful excuse for a brave your sentry? Come out now or I'll fillet him like a trout!"

At the entry to one of the wigwams a tall woman appeared, holding a tomahawk in one hand and a spoon in the other. It is one of the myths of Neverland that those who live there never grow up. The Lost Children do so all the time, though Peter does his best to try and stop them. When they've grown too much he has to kick out the whole gang and round up a new batch. Old age was a different story. That seemed to be even rarer on the island than death, and so Tiger Lily's growth had simply slowed down and stopped over the years. For many moons now she had shown the proud beauty of middle age, with faint creases just beginning to highlight the dark skin around her sparkling eyes, and a few faint threads of silver woven through her jet black hair.

Graceful as both of her namesakes she strode into the center of the clearing to stand before the pirate. Then as she recognized him, both of the implements she carried clattered to the ground, and she threw her arms around his neck. "James!" she cried. "It's been so long, I thought the Pan had forgotten you for good! Oh, welcome back to the island, James, welcome!"

Hook tossed the man he'd been holding aside and returned her embrace with his left arm, awkwardly, his hook raised high to avoid any accidental injuries. "Ah, Lily, it does my black heart good to see you. When I heard that the Boy was away and the truce in place, my first thought was to go and search out your camp. What say you we share some tobacco for old times' sake, eh?"

"Oh, come inside, James, come inside. Truly, truly I've

missed you." Hook followed her through the wigwam's flap and into the dim light inside. The great-grandchild that Tiger Lily had been feeding crawled out of the tent at her command, and the pirate seated himself on a lion skin, while she sat across from him on the skin of a black panther. She fetched a coal from the tiny fire in the wigwam's center and lit a pipe, and he got out a device of his own contrivance that held two cigars side by side. For a time the two of them sat and smoked companionably in silence.

Finally, with a great sigh, Hook spoke. "Lily, I fear I'm getting too old for this game."

The lovely chieftain put down her pipe and looked carefully at him. "Really, James? To me you don't look a day older than when I first met you. Some of us, you know, hardly ever get killed here and have to wait to see each and every sunset, while others . . ." She trailed off politely.

"Odds bobs, hammer and tongs, I know that my men and I spend twenty times the days on the bottom of the briny sea than ever we do walking beneath the sun! And mayhap measured in mere months and minutes, I may be no more than a few years older today than I was when I first landed on this pestilential outpost of the damned. But man alive, I feel old here!" He struck his chest with the flat side of his hook, ever mindful of the dramatic gesture.

Tiger Lily stroked her cheek meditatively. "What brought this on, old friend?" she asked.

Hook ground out his two cigars on the wigwam's dirt floor and flipped the butts out through the tent flap. "It was one of those miserable boys we captured this morning," he said. "I' faith, my men and I could barely comprehend his barbarous jabber. How many trips 'round the sun has the old world taken in our absence while we cool our heels here, Lily? We stay on this island and dance to the tune of that wretched juvenile's pipes, while in the world outside who knows what deeds petty or great are being accomplished? Fah, it's enough to drive one mad!"

"How many years since the last time you were here, James? Let me think. There were the Nazis, the secret agents, the aliens, the ninjas. . . ." She continued to reckon the various factions on her fingers for a while. Finally she said, "Nearly threescore winters, by my reckoning. Many, many moons."

Hook stared into the fire through the drifting smoke. "The first time we sailed here out of the mists, Lily, and the first few times he brought us back from the sea as well, if I remember rightly, we played by the rules he gave us and fought the battles we were supposed to fight. But after our fourth or fifth return, I gave my men the order to strike anchor and sail back through the mists to wherever we'd come from, even though the compass spun in its housing and the map made no sense and the sextant had gone amidships. I swore that it was better to go to the bottom of an honest sea than be marooned forever in this enchanted one. But no matter which way we set sail the same harbor would always open up before us, and I ceased giving the order before the men's hearts sank too low into their boots."

Tiger Lily nodded. "My braves never got much joy from the constant battles that settled nothing, 'tis true. And we had our whole village brought here, papooses and all, so we have much to distract us. It must be very hard for you and your men."

Hook rested his chin on his iron claw. "What is the world like out there, Lily? Even if we could find the right bearing, would there still be a place out there for an old pirate like me?"

Tiger Lily carefully placed her pipe on a clay dish on the rush-strewn floor. "No, James," she said softly, "I'm afraid there's no place left for one such as you, or, to speak truth, for one such as me either. In the last batch of boys that the Pan brought up there was one who was descended from my people. He was greatly interested in our village. Indeed," she chuckled, "far more so than the Pan himself, these days. He forgets about us for years at a time and leaves us to follow our customs in peace. Not to say that isn't all to the good, all to the good. . . ."

She rocked gently back and forth. "The boy spent time among us asking questions, and he answered some as well. In the world that he left behind, none of my people still live in skin houses like this one." She touched the taut side of the wigwam. "And no great ships with sails or cannons still cross the world's oceans, James. I'm sure that there will always be common sea-robbers, but you and your men are the last true pirates."

Hook groaned like a man marooned. "You know what's worst?" he cried, fingering his hook's iron tip with his left hand. "The worst is that I'm not even sure I remember who I was once, back when I could clap hands like other men. He gave me this name of mine at the same time he gave me this metal marlinspike, and when he did it I think he took my past away and buried it somewhere." He clasped his hands together so tightly that a thin line of blood ran down his left wrist. "Who was I, Lily? I know that I went to a good school, once upon a time. I remember playing cricket. I learned then that come hell or high water, I must never let the side down. Now I've seen both, and it's a hard, hard lesson, Lily! I'm like to go mad, I tell you!" Embarrassed, he turned away to dab at his eyes with his sleeve.

One of Tiger Lily's particular gifts was silence. She was silent now, picking up her pipe and puffing gently until her companion had regained his self-control. Then she said gently, "You won't go mad, James."

Hook sighed. "You speak true. I won't. But I envy the ones who do. It seems to be the only escape." He opened his cigar case and selected two more cigars, then in a sudden fury dashed them both to the ground. "It's not fair, I say! What could I have possibly done to deserve spending eternity as the plaything for some omnipotent juvenile godling?"

"Oh, he's not omnipotent," said Tiger Lily, blowing a smoke ring. "Not even close. That little strumpet does most of the work for him."

"Little strumpet?" Hook leaned forward. "Has he brought another sweetheart to keep house for him again?"

Tiger Lily laughed. "Oh, James, I fear you're desperately behind the times. You'll soon find out that the girls he recruits these days would much prefer killing pirates to being kidnapped and tied to masts. But it isn't the human girls I'm talking about. It's the fairies. One fairy, in particular."

Hook blinked. "Fairies?" he asked, bewildered. "Are you

telling me that such things truly exist? I've heard the children mentioning such things, but I had assumed they were merely playing one of their absurd games."

Tiger Lily shook his head. "You forget, I was born here, James. I can't see them now that I'm grown, but they're here all right. They make nests in the tops of trees. There is one who lives in the Pan's cave and looks after him. I think that she may have fallen in love with him, like many another foolish young girl has fallen for him in the past. Her name is Tinkerbell, and it is she who keeps resurrecting you again and again for the amusement of her young master. She is the one who helps guide all the visitors here from their far-scattered countries, and the dust from her wings plus pleasant thoughts are what enable the children to fly. If you wish to meet your jailer it is she, James."

"Jailer? A fairy? Preposterous." He leaned back against his pile of skins and thought about all the other preposterous things that happened daily on the island. "So if such a creature exists . . . which, mind you, I am not saying for a moment I believe . . . how did the Boy win such loyalty from her?"

"I think he saved her life once. At least, that's what the Pan says happened. We both know he's hardly the most reliable source."

"He makes things up," Hook agreed. "Regularly." He stood up abruptly and went to the entrance of the teepee, staring at two children in the center of the clearing who were laughingly throwing sticks at one another in the late afternoon sunshine. Presently he began muttering to himself, "If one such as he could do such a thing . . ."

Tiger Lily puffed out another smoke ring behind him. "I doubt you could even see a fairy, much less rescue one from death, James. And don't turn your back on people, it's rude. I'm not one of your crew, you know." Abashed, he turned to face her again. For the first time she looked him directly in the eye and held him in her dark brown gaze.

"What would you wish for, if you could find a fairy willing to grant your wish?" she said softly. "Would you wish to finally gain the revenge you have sought for so long against your ancient enemy? Or for escape for yourself and your crew, to sail once more on unenchanted seas?" He held her gaze without blinking, and she finally dropped her eyes. So soft he could barely hear her, she whispered, "Or would you just wish that you and your crew could finally sleep on the seabed undisturbed, forever?"

When she looked up again, the door flap to her wigwam was swinging, and the tall pirate was gone. He left behind his crushed cigars.

Hook's thoughts whirled as he strode back down the forest pathway through the gathering shadows. Assuming such a thing as a fairy existed, how could he establish a claim on something he couldn't even see? Could he put it in danger somehow, and then rescue it? Capture it and force it to do his will?

His mind had always been adept at coming up with plots and stratagems, but today it felt as if a long-lurking paralysis had gripped it. He tried desperately to find an idea he could grab on to. Could he trigger a rock slide somehow?

What about bird-lime? What could you possibly use as bait for a fairy?

A few feet off the right-hand side of the path was a brown bottle with a cork in it. There seemed to be some sort of golden liquid inside. Hook sniffed, and thought he could detect a faint smell of fermented molasses. "Rum?" he thought to himself. His crew could certainly use something to improve their morale. He stepped off the path to investigate, crashed through a layer of palm leaves, and tumbled to the bottom of the pirate trap that the Lost Children had just finished digging an hour earlier. A bell tied to a bent tree branch above his head began ringing wildly, and soon a whole flock of them had descended to circle the pit and stare at their new captive. Hook noticed that there were some girls with them as well, but he saw no pity in their hard, triumphant eyes. Their ringleader, of course, was the spiky-headed lad that Hook had captured earlier.

"Look at those curls," he told the others, pointing. "I told you he looked like a girl. Check out that coat-thing he's wearing. Did you know that every time they fight, Pete feeds him to a crocodile, so he always gets resurrected out of crocodile vomit? Look at that lame-o mustache. Hey, did a caterpillar die on your face, jerk?"

This and much more did Hook endure. It has been said that there is no sound more cheerful and uplifting than the carefree laughter of children. When that laughter is directed against you, however, there is no sentence of torture more disheartening, no long heart-hope's destruction more crushing, no joy forever flown more dire.

Look at that man waiting for a taxi on a busy street. He is pleasantly aware that his suit is impeccable, his coat ostentatiously expensive, his stock portfolio on the upswing. He contemplates a triumphant return to a pleasant home and a wife who adores him. Then, behind him, he hears that most unpleasant of sounds. Out of the corner of his eye he is aware of jeering and pointing, and he realizes with an indescribable sinking of his spirits that it can be aimed at no one else but him. At once all his self-satisfaction has vanished. Somehow he has missed the mark. Is there dog manure on his shoe? A Kick Me sign on his back? He is no longer a captain of industry, he is a miserable boy who wants nothing more than to run back home and crawl into bed and cry.

So it was with James Hook. After the children had finished making fun of him, they began throwing twigs and clods of dirt. Fortunately there were no large stones nearby. Eventually they grew tired of their sport and flew away. The last words that Hook heard them calling to one another as they left were, "Wait until Peter gets a load of this!"

The last shreds of evening faded from the island, and true night fell at last. A few curious stars peeked over the edge of the dirty pit, wondering at the shuddering heap of a man huddled at the bottom. Later, a crescent moon began to rise.

Much, much later, a few of the stars thought that the man might have said something, but being stars, of course, they were too far away to hear what it was. What he had called out, to no one in particular other than the trees and roots and the night creatures that surrounded him, was "Why do I always have to be the bad guy?"

Still later, when the moon had passed the top of her nightly climb and begun her descent, he cried again, so softly that even the earth could barely hear him, "Why do I always have to be the grown-up?"

Later still he was aware, through eyelids that were shut but not asleep, that the world outside was growing lighter. Soon it would be day, and his enemy would have him at his mercy. When you must always play the villain, it is no great dishonor to lose. Indeed, it is expected of you. But to fail utterly even to put up a good fight, that is unforgivable. Peter would scorn him, to be sure—and worse than scorn, there might be pity, which Hook did not think he could endure. Should he draw his cutlass and try to go down swinging, he wondered, or simply use the hook to end it all right here?

"Man," came a small voice from nearby, "why are you crying?"

Hook rolled over and opened his eyes. The light in the pit was coming from a tiny creature perched on a root, not much taller than the end of Hook's thumb. She seemed to be made of light, and at first it hurt the pirate's eyes to look at her. When he squinted and his eyes adjusted, though, he could finally make out her delicate features. She was wearing a shimmering slim garment that came down almost to her knees, and her entire body was so slim that she seemed almost sexless. A bluebell blossom was perched on her head at a jaunty angle. He tried to concentrate further to get a better impression of her face, but it was so small, and so overwhelmed by her shining eyes, that he could barely catch a glimpse of her thin nose and her tiny mouth.

"Man, why are you crying?" she asked again, a bit petu-lantly he thought. Her voice sounded exactly like small gold-en bells being shaken.

Hook shook his head and closed his eyes, but when he opened them again she was still there. "Tinkerbell?" he croaked through parched lips. "How is it that I can see you?"

The fairy threw back her head and gave a bell-like peal of laughter. "Yes, James Hook, I am Tinkerbell, and you can see me and understand me because I wish for you to do so. Why are you crying? Have you lost your shadow?"

Hook considered his answer, then said, "I am crying because I have lost my way, which is much harder to recover than a shadow. Can you help me find it again?"

"Had a rough day, have you?" The tiny creature put a minuscule finger on the corner of her mouth and cocked her head for a moment. "Yes, I think I can help you. But not down here." She looked around and wrinkled her nose. "Why on earth did you choose such an unpleasant place to be captured in? Silly. Come with me."

She unfolded sparkling wings and flew three times around Hook's head, spiraling upward, then shot straight up into the starry night, leaving a trail of glitter behind her. Almost unconsciously, Hook stretched his left hand after her, his fingers closing on nothing but starlight. Then she was gone, and he slumped back down onto the ground in disbe-lief. Had she, too, come only to mock him?

What had she said at the end, though? Come with her? But that was impossible, unless . . .

Suddenly, remembering what Tiger Lily had said about the dust from Tinkerbell's wings, Hook sprang to his feet. He stretched out his hand again and tried a small leap, but remained chained by gravity. What else had Tiger Lily said? Pleasant thoughts? What pleasant thoughts did he have? He would have to dig deeply indeed for them.

Finally, he laid his hand on one. A sunny day, a green field, a wicket to defend, and a stubby bat grasped in his hands. *Never, never, never let your side down, James.* He clenched the memory tightly until he could smell the grass, and when he opened his eyes, the ground was falling away beneath him and he was free, free as birds and dreams.

Hook had always known that at least a part of the reason he hated Peter so much was because of his flight. It is human nature to envy the rich, and Peter had all the riches that mattered most: eternal youth; absolute self assurance; and then, piled on top of them all, what an embarrassment of riches to possess this gift as well! Now, hatred and sadness both seemed to drop away behind Hook like forgotten gravity as he flew. He felt as if he could wrap his hook around a moonbeam and slide along it to anywhere he might ever wish to go.

Speaking of moonbeams, ahead on the one he was following was a small spark of light that could only be Tinkerbell, still guiding the way. Hook increased his speed until the cold stellar winds nipped past his ears, and the air grew thin and breathless. Then he realized what the fairy's destination must be.

The crescent moon in these skies was truly a crescent that waxed and waned, not an orb that rotated through darkness and light. It looked like a comfortable hammock, and it shone with a light brighter than Tinkerbell's and all the surrounding stars put together. The stars, Hook now realized as he passed by some of them, were about the size and brightness of carriage lanterns, with faces that turned to follow him upward as he flew.

Tinkerbell perched herself on the tiny horned tip of the moon, gesturing to him to stretch out on the large, comfortable curve of the crescent. Hook did so, glad after the wild ride to have something solid to hold on to. He looked down and immediately wished he hadn't, for the island that had become his home was barely a handkerchief on the vast sea below. Then again, what excuse was there for a fear of heights? He could fly!

Balanced on the thinnest sliver of the tip of the moon, Tinkerbell stood and pointed. All along the eastern horizon stretched the mainland, silver in the moonlight. Hook pulled his spyglass from a pocket and scanned it, then looked to the fairy again.

"That is no country built by mortal men," he said. "We have truly left our own waters forever, then."

Tinkerbell sat and hugged her knees. "We fairies have many responsibilities besides dreams and dancing, James. What you see before you is the Kingdom of Lost Things, and we are in charge of running it."

Hook slid his spyglass shut. "Lost . . . ?"

The fairy nodded. "Deep in your heart you must know, as all mortals know, that nothing you truly care about can be lost forever. Those things come to us here, and we guard them." She clutched the moon's tip and pointed. "Look there! You can see the Umbrella Forest beside the Lake of

Lost Laundry. In the morning all the lost umbrellas will open to greet the sun. The wind brings us all the kites and balloons and hats and ribbons that it takes away, and we store them over there. That shining white mansion belongs to my sister, who builds it from children's teeth she collects from beneath their pillows." She looked over her shoulder at Hook and shrugged. "Teeth, eh? Go figure. I guess there's no accounting for taste." Then she leaned out even further and pointed to vast structures that seemed so far away. Hook had thought them to be nothing more than haze on the horizon. "And those are the Palaces of Lost Dreams. The one on the left is for all the dreams you forget on waking, and the other one is for the dreams you never forget, but abandon as you grow. Nothing is ever lost forever, James. Never, never, never."

Hook dropped his gaze and looked down at the patch of land directly below them. "And the island is . . . ?"

Tinkerbell folded her arms and looked solemn. "I am the keeper of Lost Childhood. People think that they've left it behind them as they grow, but they haven't. I keep it safe for them here, always and forever. Nothing is ever truly lost, James. Not childhood. Not hope. Not even"—she giggled and flew over to brush his forehead with her wings—"pirates, James. I'm not sure I can promise you forever, but as long as children clap their hands and believe in pirates, you and your men can stay."

For once in his life, James Hook could think of nothing to say.

She hovered in the air before him, radiantly beautiful as the moonlight streamed around them both. "And now, James, did you have a wish for me? You've been a terribly good sport about all of this so far, and a wish is the least I can give you in return. What would you like?"

Captain Hook scratched his head with his hook and pondered. He thought of the three alternatives that Tiger Lily had laid out before him, and none of them seemed to make any sense to him now. Finally he said, "The next time you bring us back, could you put Little Noodler's hands on right way round again? They've been vexing him most terribly."

Tinkerbell stuck out her lower lip and pouted. "But he seemed so *boring*! I thought he'd appreciate having something to make him stand out." Then she smiled again. "All right, James. Now, Peter's on his way home, and I have to go guide him in. Will you be able to find your own way back down?"

"I think so. Yes." Hook looked around carefully until he found a moonbeam that seemed to be shining directly onto the harbor where his ship lay at anchor. He fitted his hook neatly around it, and slid.

The pirate crew was awakened by the clanging sound of the hook beating on the compass housing, and they leapt out of their hammocks to stand at attention. Smee was clutching a teddy bear he had received as a present from one of the Lost Boys, generations gone by. The sun was just appearing over the horizon and the moon was low in the sky. Just beyond the moon and sun, Hook could make out a pinprick of light speeding toward Neverland, second star to the right, straight on till morning. The island's master was on his way home.

"Lads!" he told the crew. "Your captain has discovered that the insufferable Boy who is our eternal foe will be returning this morning. I have devised a cunning plan, how-ever, that will ensure his destruction, once and for all. Are you with me?"

Something about his enthusiasm was contagious, and they yelled out an "Aye aye, sir!" that shook the waters of the harbor.

Hook leapt onto the lowest rung of the ratlines and wrapped his left hand into the rope. He leaned out over the side of the ship and smelled the wind picking up across the sea, and the wind was fresh and sweet. An island filled with beauty and danger lay before him to be conquered, and while the only game in town might be rigged, it was still a fine game after all.

"Lads," he called out to his men, knowing they would lose, "Lads, lads, I think we're going to win this time!"

This is the fourth Datlow/Windling anthology that Bruce Glassco has appeared in. (The first three were *Black Swan, White Raven; Sirens;* and the 1998 *Year's Best Fantasy and Horror.*) Six of his stories have been published in *Realms of Fantasy* magazine. He teaches English and Creative Writing at Virginia's Eastern Shore Community College, on a small spit of land between the Chesapeake Bay and the ocean. His most recent major accomplishment was writing and producing a sixty-player live-action role-playing game set in a mythical Balkan country in 1848. He is currently working on a novel in which fairies play a crucial role.

Author's Note

In the world of literature, the characters who get the least respect are always the villains. That isn't terribly surprising, of course, given where our sympathies as readers are supposed to lie, but still, when you think about it, it's rather sad. After all, why go into the villain business in the first place if obtaining respect isn't right up there on your top priorities list? It's not like you can realistically expect to take over the world, after all, so inspiring a little bit of respect before your inevitable demise seems like it should be the least you should hope for.

After all, what's a hero supposed to do if there aren't any villains around to fight? Be just another lazy couch potato, probably. If you're planning to crusade against injustice for a living, you need someone willing to go that extra mile to make sure there's enough injustice to crusade against. Villains make us come alive, give us a purpose in life, provide us with a sense of accomplishment when we dispatch them to their dooms.

So take a moment sometime to thank your local villain for making your local fiction possible. Try to see things from the other perspective. Because when you think about it, even the most upbeat fairy tales are often horror shows when you look at them from the other side.

Screaming for Faeries

Ellen Steiber

Oh, great. I've pissed off the faeries.

It all started when I babysat for Annalise and her friend Hillary, who was sleeping over. Annalise is my little cousin, and she got it in her head that there were faeries in the branches of the big oak tree right outside her bedroom window. Although she just turned four, Annalise is a very passionate person. She is not lukewarm about anything. She can't just talk to faeries or even call for them. She has to scream for them and then they appear.

Anyway, I was sitting for them on a Saturday night and, okay, I admit I was not paying such close attention to the girls. They were playing in Annalise's bedroom, and I was in the living room, watching a video and talking on the phone with Robbie Yarnell. Robbie and I had been seeing each other for exactly twenty-one days.

"So what time is good?" he asked, and I felt a little thrill go through me.

We had this plan. As soon as the girls were asleep,

Robbie would come over. "How about ten-fifteen?" I said. "The girls usually conk out by ten."

An eardrum-piercing scream rang through the house. "Gotta go," I told Robbie. Heart hammering, I dropped the phone and raced into Annalise's room, sure that one of them was mortally wounded. And all because I'd been the neglectful babysitter.

The two girls were standing in front of Annalise's open window, looking perfectly fine, screaming their little lungs out. "Hey!" I had to clap my hands to get their attention. "What is going on? Are you two okay?"

"We're fine," Annalise assured me. She was wearing a pale pink leopard-print top with a hot pink plaid skirt. It was a typical Annalise outfit. The pieces totally clashed yet somehow looked completely adorable. "We're screaming for faeries," she explained.

"You can't be here," Hillary said, twisting a strand of her white-blonde hair. Hillary is another enthusiastic four-year-old, but she's also angry as hell. If she doesn't get what she wants when she wants it, Hillary makes everyone miserable. "They won't come if they see you. You're too old."

"Gee, thanks, Hill." I wasn't sure whether or not to be insulted. I'm sixteen and have spent practically my entire life wishing I looked older.

I could see both kids were itching for me to leave the room. I glanced at my watch. It was barely nine, and I knew they'd have to be tired out if they were going to be asleep when Robbie showed. Besides, Annalise lives in a fairly secluded house in the Berkeley Hills. It's set a good ways back from the street, and there's garden on either side so you can't even see her neighbors' houses. Who was going to hear them? "Scream on," I said, and went to call Robbie back and tell him everyone was still alive.

They stopped screaming about two minutes after I got off the phone, and asked me to read them a story. Annalise handed me her favorite picture book, which is about a little pink girl pig who saves the circus. When we were done reading we talked about pigs and circuses. "Have you ever gone to the circus?" I asked them.

"No, but that's okay because I see faeries," Annalise answered. "And Hillary got boy faeries."

It occurred to me that maybe I should have looked out the window when I went into her room. "What do you mean, got boy faeries?"

"When I screamed girl faeries came. And they had wings and were wearing sparkly pink dresses. But Hillary screamed and got boy faeries and they were dressed in black leather," Annalise reported breathlessly.

It figured Annalise would deck them out in appropriate bad-boy apparel. I have never known a little kid who was so clothes conscious. Even though she'll only wear pink, Annalise changes her clothes at least eight times a day and keeps tabs on what everyone else wears.

"And they're stinky," Hillary added. "Because they sleep under stinky mushrooms."

That's when I realized there was a smell in the house, kind of like old Camembert cheese. This didn't upset me. Annalise's mother, my aunt Kate, works in the food business. She sells gourmet cheeses to restaurants, and her fridge is always stocked with the stuff. So I figured some of the cheese had gotten left out.

I checked my watch. Less than an hour till Robbie showed. I had to get them to bed. Still, I organized the girls into a quick game of Find the Cheese, and we checked between the sheets and under the bunk bed and couch, and even in the toy chest, but there was no cheese.

"It's the stinky boy faeries," said Annalise. "They came inside, but not the girl faeries because the girl faeries are shy."

"Is that what it is?" I asked Hillary. Based on nothing other than her charming personality, I was suspicious of Hillary.

"Yes," said Hillary. "And you better watch out."

"Why?" I asked.

Hillary looked at me like I was an imbecile. "Because the stinky boy faeries are mean."

It seemed to take forever but by ten the girls were both asleep. Robbie showed up right on time. He's amazingly prompt for someone who doesn't own a watch. He had his guitar slung across his back and was wearing his black leather jacket. The jacket startled me because of Annalise's story, but I reminded myself that Robbie has had his jacket a lot longer than Annalise has been seeing faeries.

We sat outside on the back deck, which looks out over San Francisco Bay, and drank some beer and Robbie picked out a tune on his guitar. And though the song sounded familiar, as if I'd known it all my life, I knew I'd never heard it before. The music started out soft and lilting, like a ballad from hundreds of years ago, and then the tempo sped up and became tense and insistent. It ended with a soft refrain full of longing.

The last chord faded into the night air. "That was amazing," I said. "What's it called?"

Robbie shrugged. "I don't know. I just made it up." He put down the guitar and gazed out at the view. "It's nice here. I like it when darkness covers all the buildings, and all you see are the lights going down to the water. It's about the only time the city seems peaceful."

"Mmmm," I agreed. We were one week into September, and it was one of those autumn nights without fog, and the lights of the city were like golden stars flung down from the sky, glittering against the soft black night.

The air still held the last of summer's warmth, and I was wearing a crop top. Robbie slid one arm around me. He drew me close and we started kissing. He smelled warm, like he'd been dusted with cinnamon and chicory.

He stroked the bare skin over my ribcage. Maybe because he plays lead guitar, Robbie has very sensitive hands. When I felt his fingertips stroking my skin I knew how a cat must feel when it arches under your hand. Everything in me just wanted to arch against Robbie, to keep his touch on me.

But then Annalise said loudly, "I can't sleep," and we bolted apart.

Annalise had come out onto the deck. She was wearing a white nightgown with pink stars on it and tiny pink satin slippers with wispy pink feathers and silver glitter on the toes.

"Hi, Robbie," she said, and climbed up onto his lap.

The weekend before, when my uncle was out of town, Robbie and I helped Kate move a dresser into Annalise's room. He and Annalise got on fine. Robbie has two younger brothers and three younger sisters, so he's used to little kids.

"Why can't you sleep?" he asked Annalise.

"Because the bad boy faeries came into my room and gave Hillary a nightmare. And they're making a mess."

Robbie grinned. "Don't give me that. Your room is always a mess."

This is true. Annalise loves to take things out of wherever they've been put away and leave them in little mounds all over the house. Her father, my uncle Eric, says she is chaos incarnate, but actually she's very organized. She knows exactly where everything is.

"Hillary is crying," Annalise said.

I sprang up, feeling another attack of the guilts. Even though Hillary is not my favorite person, I couldn't bear the idea of a four-year-old crying and me not noticing because I was busy making out with Robbie Yarnell.

Annalise had generously given Hillary the bottom bunk. I found Hillary huddled under the covers, sniffing loudly. I sat down on the bed beside her.

"You okay?" I asked.

"I had a bad dream." She sounded absolutely pitiful.

"Do you want to get up for a bit? I bet there's some cookies or ice cream in the fridge, and we could all have them out on the deck."

"I'm not allowed to eat sugar."

"Well, then how about a glass of milk?"

"I'm lactose intolerant," she informed me. "And I'm allergic to soy. I can only have rice milk or sugar-free sorbet. And no peanuts and my mother says nightshades give me mucus."

In Berkeley four-year-olds are very specific about their diets.

I kept my voice patient. "Do you want to see what we can find, or would you rather stay in bed?"

"Read me a story."

I debated a minute and decided that reading a book to her was probably easier than finding something she'd actually eat.

"Okay." I turned on the bedside lamp. Annalise was right. The room was a mess, a whirlwind of pink clothing, scattered toys, and little-kid jewelry. I picked up a rhinestone tiara with a striped sock hanging off its end, sure that the room hadn't looked like this when I put the girls to bed.

It took me a couple of minutes before I could find any of Annalise's books. Finally, I located one underneath an alphabet poster that had fallen to the floor. It was one of the Cicely Mary Barker books—beautiful little flower fairies, each with a rhyming poem. Very British, very sweet.

The moment I opened it Hillary screamed, "No, I don't want that one!"

"Well, what do you want?"

"No faeries!" she said.

I found a book about a little boy and his dinosaur, and Hillary settled down. When we were about halfway through,

Robbie came in. Annalise was riding on his shoulders, giggling. "Robbie's going to take me to where the faeries dance at night," she sang.

Robbie rolled his eyes. "I said I'd take her in here and tuck her in."

Hillary took one look at Robbie and stiffened. "Make him leave," she said.

"Now wait a minute—" I'd taken about all the Hillary orders I could stomach. "Robbie is a friend—"

"He looks like them!" she shrieked.

Robbie set Annalise on the top bunk. "Who's them?" he asked.

"The stinky boy faeries," Annalise explained matter-of-factly. "They're gone now. It just stinks a little."

I sniffed. There was still a cheesy tang in the room but it was very faint.

"Make him go away!" Hillary yelled.

Robbie raised his hands in surrender. "Okay, okay, I'm going." He was backing out of the room when I realized something.

"Wait." I nodded toward the open window. "Remember when we were moving stuff last weekend, and it was so hot in here, and we all tried to open that window—"

"Go!" Hillary shouted, holding her arm straight and pointing her finger. "You have to leave now!"

"Shut up, Hill," I said. "I need to ask Robbie about this."

Hillary's blue eyes went wide with outrage. "You can't talk to me that way!"

"I remember," Robbie said. "None of us could get it open because the paint around the edges was stuck."

I looked at Annalise. "Did your mom or dad open that window?"

"No," Annalise said. "It got opened tonight. By the faeries."

By now Hillary was working herself into a major meltdown, so Robbie left the room, and I worked on closing the window. It stuck every two inches. If the faeries had opened it, at least they could have greased the slides, I thought grumpily. Finally, I shoved it closed and read the girls another book, during which they both fell asleep.

Robbie was waiting for me in the dining room. He slung an arm around my shoulders and we went back out to the deck. The sound of traffic seemed hushed and distant. I could hear the chittering sound of a young screech owl.

"So, Cherr, when are your aunt and uncle coming home?"

I glanced at my watch. "About an hour."

The air was cooler now than it had been before, and I felt goose bumps rising on my bare skin. Robbie felt them too. He stood behind me, holding me against his chest, his arms warm around me. "Better?"

I nodded, staring out at the night as he rested his chin on the top of my head. Crickets were chirping in the yard below us, and a cat gave an outraged yowl.

I felt Robbie smiling. "I've been trying to get that sound—angry cat—with my guitar, and I come close but something's always missing."

"Is that for a song?"

"Not really. Just messing around." He kissed the side of my neck, giving me chills. "You're cold," he said. "Maybe we should go inside and take advantage of our hour."

We went in, and Robbie sat down on the couch and reached out a hand to me. I put my hand in his and let him draw me down beside him. I know holding hands isn't supposed to be a big deal. But it is. It's an act of trust to give someone your hand. When Robbie took my hand a ripple of warmth went through me, as if there were a sun hidden inside him that only I could touch.

I concentrated on that warmth and we started to kiss again. Some guys are predictable kissers. They start with your lips then want to move down your body. Or they start feather light then become intense and demanding. It's as if they follow some playbook for kissing. Robbie was never predictable. Robbie was a really talented kisser who somehow keyed into whatever it was I wanted. Hard, fast, slow, teasing—we were always perfectly, amazingly in sync.

So there we were on Aunt Kate's couch, stretched out against each other, kissing madly and completely lost in it. All I was aware of was the length of his body against mine, his hands sliding along my bare waist, his mouth hot on the side of my neck. My body arched away from him just so he'd pull me closer. His hand slid up under my top and I let my hand explore the smooth skin beneath his shirt. He felt so good. *We* felt so good. Every cell in my body was deliriously happy.

"I think we need to take this to another level," he said with a soft laugh.

And I felt my body tense, because we were suddenly on the border between exciting and dangerous, and there was the clear possibility that we'd go somewhere we'd never been before.

"What level?" I heard my voice catch.

I have a secret from Robbie. He thinks I've done it and I never have. Everyone in my school thinks I'm . . . experienced. This is because Maura McGuire, the biggest gossip in the Bay Area, spread the story that I did it with a college guy in San Diego. And I didn't deny it. (Okay, maybe it's sick but because I'm generally such a good girl, it was kind of a thrill to have everyone thinking I'm fast or at least semi-knowledgeable.)

I'm pretty sure this is at least part of why Robbie asked me out last month, that he thinks I'm open to a lot more than I really am. So far, though, he hadn't tried to push me or rush me. He'd been really nice, taking me out for pizza or a movie, giving me comps when his band played, even helping Aunt Kate move furniture.

And with his family and mine, his band, and school, we'd never had much time alone. At least not in the presence of a bedlike object.

"What level?" I asked again, this time attempting to sound cool and nonchalant.

He pulled back, his dark eyes amused. "You know what I'm talking about."

Actually, I don't, I wanted to say.

He pushed a shock of black hair out of his eyes. "Why don't you want to be together?"

"We are together," I said, knowing how lame it sounded even before the words came out.

"You know what I mean. Not like this. Like being lovers, when you're as close as you can possibly get to another person."

"Are you?" I asked, thinking of what I'd heard a girl in my class say. "Because sometimes sex just leaves you feeling sad and used and lonely."

His lips brushed mine. "That could never happen with us. You and me, we've got this connection. I think with you it would be really amazing."

Other times we'd been together there'd always been "limiting circumstances." It was like playing a game and knowing that the ref would step in or the clock would run out and no matter what, things couldn't get completely out of hand.

That night, though, we'd somehow left the safe confines of the game. I knew as well as he did that the rules were gone. Sometime during that last hour all the normal boundaries had dissolved, and it wasn't simply that the adults were gone and the girls were asleep.

Robbie's finger slid beneath my bra strap. "Will you let me look at you?"

Part of me desperately wanted to say yes, to find out just how amazing we'd be. The rest of me, the scared-out-of-her-mind virgin, blurted out, "No!"

Robbie sat up, putting some space between us but keeping a hand on my thigh. "What's wrong?" he asked gently. "I thought you liked—"

"I did."

"Then—"

"But I'm not ready," I said honestly.

He gently squeezed my kneecap. "Why not?"

"I—I don't know," I lied. "I just know I'm not ready. Yet."

The closeness between us was suddenly gone. "You're not going to turn into a tease, are you?" he asked, his voice still soft but now with something wary in it.

"Wait a minute. Can't I say I'm not ready without being accused of being a tease? Maybe I'm just not at the same *level* as you."

He drew back and shook his head slowly. "No. I don't believe that. You were right there with me, and you know it. It's something else. Maybe . . . something that scares you?"

That was the kernel of it but I couldn't admit it. Couldn't own up to what a total, immature, inexperienced virgin I was. How I wasn't even ready for him to touch my breasts because I was afraid that would lead to sex and I didn't really know what sex was or where it would take me, and how I wasn't at all sure I could handle that place. How I was afraid something inside me would change forever.

Robbie cleared his throat. "I have condoms if that's what you're worried—"

"I-I just can't do this tonight."

He sat back against the couch, blew out a breath, and studied my aunt's ceiling. "You're not making this easy, you know."

"I know," I said, suddenly filled with dread. This was it. Robbie wasn't going to want to see me anymore.

"Okay." He reached out a finger and ran it along the groove between my forefinger and thumb. "Don't worry about it. It's no big deal."

"It is." I was mortified to realize I was blinking back tears.

He leaned over and kissed my cheek then got up, put on his leather jacket, slung his guitar over his back, and started for the door. I followed him, feeling sick. "See you," I said.

At the door he turned and put his arms around me, folding me into a hug. Again, I felt that sun inside him. *I don't want to lose this*, I thought miserably.

"Listen," he said into my hair. "Being lovers . . . you should want it a hundred percent. It's not the kind of thing anyone should be pressured into."

"What if I'm never a hundred percent?" I mumbled into his chest.

Holding my shoulders, he pushed me away from him and kissed me gently on the lips. "You will be," he promised. "Wait and see."

Ever since I turned fifteen I've had this thing I do every night. Before I go to sleep I turn off the overhead light in my room and I light candles—one on my dresser, one on my night table, and one on the windowsill. Not to get witchy or summon spirits or anything. I just like the life in the flames, the way they flicker and dance. With the overhead on, everything in my room is the same, bathed in seventy-five watts of hard, bright light. With the candles, there's light and dark, and my room becomes a softer shadow place, with mysteries and secrets.

That night, after my uncle dropped me off at my house, I lit the candles and stared into the mirror before getting undressed. The low-rise jeans and short top showed the long line of my waist, the flat plane of my stomach. What was it guys were always saying? *A girl shouldn't dress hot if she won't put out.* Was my crop top hot? Was I sending the wrong signals, being a tease?

Okay, maybe it was a little hot, at least hotter than the loose T-shirts I usually wore. Yes, I wanted Robbie to be attracted to me and I'd dressed for it. But that wasn't the same as saying I was ready to go all the way. Was it?

With a shrug I changed into my nightshirt, the one Annalise picked out for my last birthday. It was pink, of course, with a large, goofy bunny rabbit down the front. I pictured Robbie in the room with me then: I wouldn't have to worry about sex. He'd be doubled over, laughing.

And then in the lower left-hand corner of the mirror, I caught a glimpse of something moving. My mom had seen a mouse in the kitchen that spring, so at first I thought it was the Return of the Mouse. But no mouse stands on two slender legs, has punked-out blond hair, and wears black leather boots, pants, and a black leather jacket.

I gawked in the mirror for a moment, knowing that candlelight can play tricks with your eyes, then I turned around slowly, expecting the hallucination to vanish.

He didn't. The little leather-clad figure leaned against my bedroom wall, arms folded across his chest, a sullen expression on his perfect, handsome face. Although he couldn't have been more than four inches tall, there was something, well, teenage about him. He wore tiny silver hoops in each ear and silver bands around his wrists. And I could smell him. It wasn't the stinky cheese smell from Annalise's house. He smelled both muskier and greener, as if he'd brought in the scent of redwoods and eucalyptus and loam.

"You can't be," I breathed, making no sense at all. "You—you're one of Annalise's faeries, aren't you?"

"Hungry," he stated flatly.

"You're hungry?"

He rolled his eyes. "Food."

"How long have you been in here?" I could feel my face going red with embarrassment. Had he been there when I was staring into the mirror contemplating my hotness? Had he watched me change? Had he seen me naked? I sat down on the bed and drew my bunny nightshirt over my knees.

"Modesty? Now?" he sniggered. I was getting the distinct impression that he'd decided I was only worth one-word sentences. His expression became serious again. "Food."

At least food was a safer topic than my modesty. "Well, what do you eat?"

I know, I know. I was having a conversation with something impossible, and yet he was so real, so demanding, that what would have felt truly crazy would be doing anything *other* than talking to him.

"Cakes," he said. "And ale."

"Oh, man, did you come to the wrong house. My mom's a twelve-stepper." At his blank expression I explained, "We can't have any alcohol in the house. And she's on another diet, so we don't have any cake either. How about . . . a granola bar?"

He wrinkled his little nose then looked hopeful. "Venison?"

I tried to remember what was in our fridge. Even when

she's not dieting, my mom is a pretty devout vegetarian. "Uh
. . . tofu burgers?"

"Ale," he insisted, and I had a vision of dawn breaking
and me still going round and round with this tiny, stubborn
creature.

"Apple cider," I countered, and he nodded grudgingly.

Closing the door to my room, I made my way into the
kitchen. The house was completely dark. Since my mom is a
sound sleeper and my dad hasn't lived with us since I was
six, I didn't worry much about anyone hearing me.

I turned on the light over the stove and glanced at the
clock. It was nearly one-thirty in the morning. No wonder
everything seemed slightly surreal. What, I wondered, was I
supposed to pour the cider into? All our glasses were at least
twice the size of the faery. I settled on a bottle cap, dripped
a few drops of cider into it, and brought it to him.

He didn't say thank you. He held the plastic bottle cap as
if it were a great bowl and downed the cider. He was an
extremely noisy drinker for such a little creature.

I waited until he put the cap down before asking, "Were
you in Annalise's room?"

He just grinned at me, revealing sharp, white teeth.

I once had a cat who could leap so effortlessly that I
never once saw him push off from the floor. One second he'd
be down on the ground, the next up on top of the fridge.
That's how the faery moved. From the carpeting to the top of
my dresser, and I never even saw him bend his skinny little
knees.

I think the faery jumped—or flew?—onto my dresser so

we'd be eye-to-eye. Because when he stood on top of it and still had to raise his chin to look at me, he scowled and stomped across the smooth oak top and kicked a bracelet I'd left there.

"Hey, stop that," I said. "If you're going to get all temperamental, don't take it out on my jewelry."

He whirled around. His face was livid and one finger pointed straight at me. I took a step back, feeling a prickle of fear. I wished I'd paid more attention when I'd read Annalise her stories. What was it faeries could do? Somehow all I remembered was their putting hexes on cows so they couldn't give milk.

At least we don't have a cow, I thought, trying to reassure myself.

The faery's glare faded as his eyes lit with malice. "Liar," he said softly.

"What—"

"Virgin," he went on.

I felt my throat tighten. "What the hell do you know about it?"

At this he smiled. "Watch," he said.

Then he sang out in a voice like the wind in the reeds. And the sweet spring scent of lily-of-the-valley wafted through my room. The flame on the windowsill candle danced higher, and in it I saw a faery girl.

She was exactly what Annalise described, dressed in a sparkly, gossamer dress. It didn't really have a color; it was more like a prism with all the colors flashing through it. Unlike the boy faery, she had wings, and she fluttered them open, gently lifting herself out of the flame. She hovered over the dresser for a moment, delicate and exquisite, then landed in front of the boy faery.

To my surprise she turned to me first. "Lily," she said, placing a slender hand over her heart.

"Cherry," I replied. (I'm always self-conscious about telling people my name—especially guys who think they're brilliant when they make crude jokes about it.)

"Cherry," she repeated thoughtfully. "Cherry blossom?"

"Yes," I said, though I didn't tell her the story. Apparently, I arrived nine months after my parents did it under a tree filled with cherry blossoms.

"Cherry jam?" she asked.

"Cakes and jam," said the boy faery, still looking belligerent.

I glared back at him. "How about a bran muffin and jam?"

He glanced at Lily who nodded and said, "Please."

I returned to the kitchen, leaving the two faeries in my room and wondering only briefly if I was losing my mind. From the second I saw the boy faery I knew he was real. I didn't know what it meant—that I was seeing faeries—or what to do about it.

Except feed them.

I spread some loganberry jam on a bran muffin, cut it into tiny pieces, and brought it to the faeries.

They ate like teenage boys, just about inhaling the food.

"When was the last time you ate?" I asked, curious.

"Mortals' food? April, eighteen-ought-eight," Lily said precisely.

I felt my jaw drop as I realized that meant she was nearly

two hundred years old—or older. Then I remembered another faery fact from Annalise's books. Time passed differently for faeries. They lived for centuries, and what might seem a long life for a human was only the equivalent of a few years for them.

The bran muffin demolished, they stood facing each other.

"Love," he said, in a voice like the ocean whispering in at low tide. The faery girl stepped toward him, placing her hands so gracefully in his, it was like a scene from a miniature ballet.

She moved closer to him and his arms went around her. And he was holding her close, caressing her, and they were both nearly rippling with pleasure and I was horribly embarrassed to be watching it.

I turned to leave, then caught myself. This was ridiculous. It was nearly two A.M. I was exhausted and I was leaving my room with my nice, cozy bed to give the faeries privacy.

I turned back. Now his hands cupped her face and they were kissing. I'd seen plenty of kissing—in school, on the streets, on screen. I'd even done some of it myself but never like this. These two went beyond intensity, maybe even beyond passion. They kissed as if the kiss were the thing keeping them alive, as if ending it would mean death. And I knew I shouldn't be watching something so intimate but I couldn't turn away.

After what seemed a long time they finally turned it down a notch. I cleared my throat. "Uh, excuse me."

Gradually, reluctantly, they drew apart.

"Do you think you two could take this somewhere else? I really need to go to bed."

The boy faery scowled again. "Sacred," he said.

"Probably," I said, trying to be agreeable. "Still, I'd like to sleep—"

"Gone," Lily said, and as soon as she said it they were.

I felt a pang of regret. I'd had something extraordinary—magic—in my room, and I sent it away so I could do something as boring as sleep. No, that's a lie. I sent them away because I couldn't watch. It was too much, too intense, too much a vision of what I was so afraid of.

I snuffed the three candles and shut my eyes. And I wondered what it would be like if Robbie touched me the way the boy faery touched Lily.

The next morning I walked into the kitchen to find my mother, in her bathrobe, staring bleary-eyed into the open fridge. "I don't understand it," she was murmuring.

"What?" I asked.

"My yogurt's gone bad and so has the milk, and I just bought them yesterday."

Maybe what faeries did was turn milk sour, though yogurt was already pretty sour. . . . I was going to have to take another look at Annalise's faery books.

"And look!" My mom gestured to the kitchen counter, where half a dozen large, smelly, yellow mushrooms sat in a green ceramic bowl. "I could swear I bought criminis, not those!" She kissed me on the forehead. "Good morning. Your mother is losing her mind."

"Maybe we should throw them out," I suggested helpfully. I was sure the mushrooms were left by the boy faery, which made them highly suspect.

"You can't throw out good food."

"Good, being the operative word," I reminded her. "Those things smell like sh—"

"Cherry!" She shot me a disapproving look then turned to the coffee machine, her expression tragic. "I can't drink my coffee without milk and I can't face the day without coffee. Any chance you'd take pity on your mother and go get some milk?"

"Okay. I'll get rid of the mushrooms when I go."

A few minutes later I headed out to the local deli for milk. I stuffed the stinky mushrooms in a neighbor's trashcan. It seemed a perfectly reasonable thing to do. At the time.

I didn't exactly forget about the faeries that day, as much as I told myself that they were gone. End of problem.

But maybe also the end of magic, a nagging voice inside me argued. Wasn't it ultra-amazing, a gift even, to be able to see and talk to faeries? Why was I shutting them out? Why couldn't I be like Annalise and at least be excited about them? *Because you're not four*, another voice inside me argued. I left it as a draw between the voices and concentrated on writing a history paper that was due the next day.

At about five that afternoon our doorbell rang. It was Robbie. Just seeing him standing on our porch made everything inside me light up. I'd been sure that after last night it was over.

"What's up?" he asked.

"Not much. I just finished Tressalino's paper."

"Oh, you're good," he said with a grin. "A girl who does all her homework on time."

"You don't do yours?"

"Just enough to get by. When our band gets signed, I'm going to leave school anyway."

I felt my throat tighten a little. I was just getting to know Robbie and already he was planning to leave.

Robbie peered around my shoulder, glancing into the house. "So can I come in or is this a porch date?"

"You can come in. My mom's at yoga class."

We stopped in the kitchen where, due to the profound lack of beer, we each grabbed a sparkling water then, without discussing it, headed for my room.

I felt a stab of nervousness. Was it going to happen this time? Did letting Robbie into my room count as teasing or, worse, asking for it? Had I just waded into waters way over my head?

None of the answers to those dramatic questions were in the cards that day. Robbie stepped into my room, and said, "Jesus, Cherry, this looks like Annalise's room."

I stood in my doorway, unable to form words. Ten minutes earlier, when I'd gone to answer the bell, I left my room relatively neat. Okay, the clothes I wore the night before were heaped on the floor, but my computer was on my desk, my books on the bookshelves, my quilt on the bed.

Now it looked as if a large, angry bear had ripped through the room. My computer monitor had toppled to the floor, and the screen was blinking with a weird greenish light. The miniature Calder mobile that sat on my desk was upended and jammed halfway under the bed, which had had all the sheets and blankets ripped off. A tangle of necklaces lay on the rug; an earring glinted beneath the chair. Weirdest of all, leaves in brilliant autumnal reds and oranges and gold lay scattered on every surface.

It was early September, the end of summer in Berkeley. The leaves hadn't begun to turn.

"What the hell happened in here?" Robbie asked.

"The paper I just wrote," I said stupidly. "I didn't back it up and now—"

Robbie gave me a long look. "I think that's the least of your problems." He glanced around. "Do you think anything was stolen?"

"I don't know yet."

So the two of us cleaned up. We didn't talk much except for me telling him where things went.

"Nothing's missing," I concluded as I slid the last of the books onto my bookshelf. "Someone just trashed the hell out of my room."

"You got any enemies?"

"Not the usual kind," I said, glancing at his black leather jacket. What would he say if I told him about the faeries last night or the mushrooms in the kitchen this morning? Instead, I picked up a red maple leaf and said, "Where do you think these leaves came from?"

He took the leaf from my hand and shook his head. "Pretty friggin' exotic. You think your vandal came down from the Sierras or flew in from Montana or something?"

"No. I think he—they—followed me back from Annalise's house last night."

Robbie's dark eyes look startled. "They followed you, even with your uncle driving you home?"

I realized I had to tell him the truth, mostly because I was too shaken up to lie convincingly. "Robbie . . . you know how Annalise and Hillary said they saw faeries last night?"

He nodded.

"I think they were telling the truth. Because when I got back here last night, I saw them, too. Two of them." I stopped, sure that sounded crazy enough. No need to get into details.

Something that wasn't quite disbelief flickered in his eyes. "And you think they—the faeries—are the ones who trashed your room and left the leaves?"

"I wasn't out of my room more than ten minutes when I went to answer the door. Who else could have gotten in and done so much damage without either one of us hearing a thing?" I hesitated. "I'm not sure how, but I think I pissed them off."

Robbie didn't say anything for a long while. He picked up one of the leaves and examined it intently, as if he might somehow read where it was from. At last he said, "I don't know about faeries, not for sure, anyway. But I know a little about energy. I've seen weird things happen when we play, almost like the music conjures up stuff that wasn't there before."

"I didn't have any music on."

"Doesn't matter. It doesn't have to be music. Certain people . . . I think unusual energy—you could call it magic—tends to follow them around. I think your little cousin Annalise is like that. And you may be, too."

"So . . . you believe me?"

He grinned. "Let's just say, I don't disbelieve you."

I felt wildly relieved and shaky all at once. It was good to know Robbie didn't think I was nuts. But everything was also one step scarier if what he said was true.

"I'm not normally a magical person," I assured us both.

"Aren't you?" He drew me to him and kissed me softly. I touched the smooth skin on his neck, felt the pulse there speed up. "Aren't you?" he asked, his voice hoarse. "What makes you so sure?"

My mom came home from her yoga class about two minutes after Robbie and I started kissing, so nothing went too far. We ordered in Chinese for dinner, and Robbie and my mom talked shop. She does publicity for a group of theaters in the Bay Area, so Robbie asked her questions about booking concert space.

"He seems very serious about his band," she said when he left.

"He is. He's pretty sure they're going to get signed. And then he's probably going to go off on tour."

"And you're afraid to care too much?" she guessed.

"Something like that."

"Have you been lovers yet?"

"Mom!" I wailed, mortified. The truth is, my mom's

always been far more upfront about sex than I am. She thinks it's something mothers and daughters should discuss openly. I think parents should make sure their kids get the facts straight—in fifth grade I firmly believed that women got babies by swimming with sperm whales—and then never be allowed to bring up the subject again.

"I like Robbie," she said, undeterred. "But if you haven't had sex yet, and I'm guessing you haven't, remember what I told you about protecting yourself. Condoms, condoms, condoms!"

"I know," I mumbled, wishing I could just say "gone," and disappear like Lily.

My mom touched my cheek, something she almost never does. "And make sure the first time is with someone who genuinely cares about you," she said more gently. "There can't be another first time, sweetie, so don't be too casual about it. When you give yourself to someone, it's sacred."

I felt the hairs along the back of my neck rise. "Um, I have some homework I really have to finish," I said, and beat a quick retreat to my room.

The boy faery was back, striding across the top of my dresser.

"Y-you," I sputtered, my embarrassment morphing into instant fury. "You're the one who trashed my room!"

He just stared back, his green gaze proud and unrepentant.

"What do you want?" I demanded. "What did I do to you? And why'd you follow me here?"

"Disrespected us."

I blinked. The faery knew about dissing? "How?"

"Lied. Called us stinky. Closed the window. Tossed mush-rooms."

"Well, if you were so concerned about your mushrooms, why did you leave them in our kitchen?"

"Gifts," he said.

"Gifts?"

"Gifts." He folded his arms again, and I could almost feel the anger lasering out of his green eyes.

I sat down on the bed to think. Living in northern California, where the psychedelic experience has never com-pletely gone out of style, my first thought was drugs. But I'd seen psilocybin mushrooms, and they didn't look anything like the bright yellow ones I'd thrown out. I glanced at the boy faery. "What kind of gifts?"

"Gifts of the earth," Lily answered. I have a teak box on my dresser where I keep my necklaces. Lily was standing in it, knee-deep in beads.

Seeing her made me smile. The boy faery was hostile and snarky. Lily was like a creature spun from diamonds, like a bit of Annalise's imagination come to life.

"Betimes mortals dream what is true," she said.

"And those mushrooms—"

Lily's wings opened and she lifted herself out of the jew-elry box and over to the boy faery. "They give dreams." She set down in front of him, still facing me. "Betimes dreams open doors."

"To what?" I asked uneasily.

The boy faery came up behind her, put his arms around

her, and began to kiss the side of her neck. Lily's eyes fluttered closed as she leaned back into him. His hands ran down the sides of her waist then moved to the front of her body, sliding up her shimmery bodice and cupping her breasts.

The way he touched her—how could such an angry creature also be so tender? I watched as Lily's eyes opened and she turned toward him. Desire flickered through her as though she had a flame inside her, dancing, moving toward then away from him, drawing him close to feel her heat. His green eyes grew emerald bright. In him it was like a wire, vibrating, resonating, everything in him taut and alert and connected to her.

Arms and legs, they wrapped themselves around each other with expressions so identical that for a split second they almost looked like twins. It was something I had no name for. But I understood: It was as if they were both at that moment part of a pulse older even than they were, something that's flowed up from the earth since time beyond memory. And watching them, I felt something inside me almost breaking, I wanted it so bad.

The sound of the phone ringing in the kitchen snapped me out of it, made me realize that I was once again spying on their intimacy. This time it didn't even occur to me to ask them to leave. "I'm sorry," I said, and bolted from the room.

In the kitchen my mom held the receiver out to me. "Kate wants to know if you'll sit for Annalise next Friday night, and Annalise wants to talk to you."

I told my aunt that next Friday was fine, then she put

Annalise on. Lately, Annalise has been very keen to talk on the phone. Her dad says she's four going on fourteen.

"Hi, Cherry," she said.

"Hey, Annalise. What's up?"

"You know what? Last night, after I went to sleep, I saw the faeries dance," she said.

I was getting a creepy feeling. "You mean, you dreamed about them?"

"No," she insisted. "I went to where the faeries dance. And it was a beautiful garden with pink flowers and there were orange and red and yellow leaves falling all around. . . ."

The week went by. Though I saw Robbie at school, we kept it casual. The faeries didn't show again, and neither one of us brought them up. Mostly, we ate lunch together and did some discreet necking. And we made a date for Saturday night.

Then on Friday night I sat for Annalise again. Thankfully, Hillary was elsewhere.

"So, Annalise," I said about two minutes after my aunt and uncle were gone. "I need to ask you about faeries."

Annalise tugged on the cuff of her pink flowered sleeve, revealing a strand of pink beads and little silver hearts fastened around her wrist. "I'm going to be a faery when I grow up," she told me solemnly.

A week ago I would have found that statement adorable. Now it seemed spooky. "Why do you think that?"

"Because I want to be. And the faeries like me."

"Have you seen them since last weekend?"

"No. I didn't scream for them," she explained.

"Annalise, I think that last Saturday night two of the faeries in your room followed me home. They showed up in my room."

She glanced out at the tree. "They don't let most big people see them. Maybe they like you, too."

That was not my impression. I told her about Lily and the boy faery.

Annalise pulled off her top so she could put on another. "His name is Flax," she informed me as she unearthed a pink fleece hooded sweatshirt from one of the mounds in her room. "He and Lily love each other. Flax sings to Lily, and then she comes to him and sometimes they hug and sometimes they dance."

"You told me on the phone that you went to a garden where the faeries danced." When I'd asked her more about it that night, she'd changed the subject.

She nodded, her small face serious.

"How did you get there?"

"The minivan." That made me relax a little. Kate drives a minivan. Clearly, Annalise was making up at least some of this.

"It's a pink pearl faery minivan," she went on. "It doesn't need gas. Two little white horses pull it, and it can hold six faeries plus me."

"Do the faeries have to be strapped in to little faery car seats?" I asked sarcastically.

Sarcasm is lost on Annalise. "No, they don't need them. The horses never have accidents," she told me. "And it has a moonroof because faeries like the moon. Will you make me an omelet with cheese and strawberries?"

I thought it sounded gross, but Annalise can get very fixated when she wants something, so I made her the omelet and she ate it. Then we built a faery fort with a blanket covering the dining room table, but the faeries didn't show. Annalise concluded that they were probably in their "beautiful pink diamond castle," and abandoned the fort to watch the *Mary Poppins* video for the ninetieth time. Later, she picked out a book for me to read to her. It wasn't a faery book. In fact, when I looked I couldn't find any of Annalise's faery books.

"What happened to all your faery books?" I asked.

She yawned. "I don't know. Maybe they're hiding."

So I read her a story about a young cat who wanted to be a firefighter. I was pretty sure I wasn't going to get any useful information, but I couldn't resist asking one more question before she fell asleep. "Since neither one of us has seen the faeries all week, do you think that means they're gone?"

"No," she said without a second's hesitation. "They're busy. But they'll be back."

By Saturday evening I was more nervous than ever about everything. I'd spent the morning at the library, reading up on faeries, and what I read was not encouraging. Some stories said faeries were the spirits of the dead. Others claimed they were fallen angels or a race of ancient gods. Sometimes faeries gave gifts, but mostly they seemed to drive humans mad or steal their babies. Faeries had a habit of luring mortals to their realm, and then the people would never be seen again. If the humans ever did make it back, hundreds of years would have passed and their whole world would be gone. The stories only seemed to agree on one thing: pissing off the faeries was not a good idea. And there was another pattern I noticed: Those mortals who survived their encounters with faeries seemed to spend the rest of their lives longing to see them again.

The other thing worrying me was, of course, Robbie. When he'd asked me out again, I realized that I was too curious to even think of saying no. What it came down to was that current, that alive thing between us that I couldn't turn away from.

So I took a bath and washed my hair and tried on six different outfits. Obviously, Annalise was rubbing off on me. I finally settled on a short lilac slip-type skirt, a black camisole, and a black crocheted cardigan, and strappy platform sandals.

I was leaning toward the mirror, putting on earrings, when I saw his reflection. Flax stood on the windowsill, watching me intently. All I could think of were the stories I'd read that morning, the ones that warned that things rarely went well for humans when humans and faeries met up.

"Why do you keep coming here?" I asked, trying not to sound as scared as I was, and also trying not to offend him. "Please tell me."

"Seasons change," he said.

I was half-tempted to say, *No shit. What does that have to do with anything?* But something in his eyes stopped me. For once there was nothing mocking or angry or demanding in them.

"Seasons change," he repeated. "Neither mortal nor fey may hold them back." He held out a hand and three bright autumn leaves—one red, one orange, one gold—began to spiral through my room. It was as if they were caught in a dance, never falling but whirling on and on, held by a spiral wind that only magic could summon.

"Oh, it's beautiful," I breathed.

"As it should be," Flax said. "Always."

Something about the way he was gazing at me made me ashamed of what I'd done. "I'm sorry I threw out your mushrooms," I said. Then a thought occurred to me. "If you gave them to me on purpose, was there some dream I was supposed to have?"

"That can't be told now." Lily had straddled the red circle on my mobile and was riding it as if it were an amusement park ride; it floated up and down beneath her as the mobile spun in a circle of bright primary colors. "Betimes dreams open doors," she said. "Betimes they are lanterns to show you the way."

"So now I'm going to be lost and stuck," I concluded, feeling a sad kind of dread. I thought of the stories of mortals who crossed the faeries and wandered lost for eternity.

Lily tilted her delicate head to one side, her eyes as cold and silvery as frost. "Mayhap."

I jumped as the doorbell rang then glanced at my watch. It had to be Robbie.

"Bring him to us," Lily said.

I got a sick feeling in the pit of my stomach. "No. I know I made you angry, and I'm sorry, but it's not fair to punish him for what I did."

Robbie rang the bell again and I thanked my lucky stars that I was the only one home and so didn't have to worry about my mom letting him in. I simply wouldn't answer the bell and he would leave.

"Doors must open," Flax said. Seconds later, I heard the front door open. Heard Robbie call my name. I didn't answer. Just sent him a desperate psychic message: *Don't come any closer! Please, just turn around and run as fast and far as you can!*

A lot of good psychic messages do when you're dealing with faeries. Robbie walked straight up to my bedroom door and knocked.

"I'm not ready," I called out desperately. "Actually, I don't feel so well. Robbie, we need to cancel. I can't go—"

"Liar!" Flax's voice was pure contempt.

Lily was no longer riding the mobile. I have a stuffed cat toy named Kenny on my bed. Lily sat cross-legged between Kenny's pointy ears. "Doors must open," she said, and my bedroom door, which had been firmly shut, swung open.

Robbie stepped in. He was wearing black jeans and a black T-shirt, his guitar strapped across his back. "Cherry? Are you okay? I—" His eyes went from me to Lily to Flax and the color drained from his face and I saw that thing flicker in his eyes again, only this time I knew what it was. Recognition. "Oh," he said, his voice barely a whisper.

Moving very cautiously, Robbie unstrapped his guitar,

leaned it against the wall, walked over to my bed and sat down. Both Lily and Flax came to light on the headboard, so they stood just above Robbie, almost as if they stood in judgment over him.

"I—" He drew a breath. "I've seen you before," he said to them.

"You what?" I demanded.

"When I was four," he said.

I felt betrayed, as if I'd found him with another girl. "You told me you didn't know about faeries."

"I was just about dying of pneumonia." His dark eyes were still locked on them. "All these years . . . I thought you were a fever dream."

"Betimes mortals dream what is true," Lily said.

"Did you call them the way Annalise did?" I asked accusingly.

He looked at me, and when he spoke again his voice had a tremor in it that I'd never heard before. "When I was four my parents had a huge fight. My mother was so pissed she left the younger kids with my dad, grabbed me, and drove straight to Yosemite. She'd grown up in the foothills, gone backpacking there all her life, so her first instinct was to take off for the back country, way off the trails. I don't really remember much about it. Except that the third night we were out there, miles from any road or camp, I came down with this fever. I was burning up. And there was no way she'd leave me and hike out to get help, and I was too heavy to carry that far. Most of what I remember is her rocking me in her arms, sobbing, saying I was dying and it was all her

fault, and praying to the trees and the mountains to help us."
He gave me a wry smile. "My dad's family is strict Catholic.
They pray to every saint you ever heard of, but my mom
prays to trees and rocks."

"And the faeries?" I asked.

Robbie took a breath, steadying his voice. "I must have
fallen asleep in her arms. Because I woke up in the middle
of the night and she was out cold and there was a full moon
high over the mountains. I don't know why but I climbed out
of the sleeping bag. We were in a little clearing of evergreens,
Douglas firs, I think, and the moon was so bright I could see
everything. I saw all these animals that night. A coyote, a
mink, a bobcat, a mountain lion, hawks and eagles and great
horned owls, a whole family of bears. All the animals were
out, all of them showed themselves to me, and none of them
made me scared. And then I saw them," he nodded toward
the faeries. "There were these two, and others. Lots of them.
I saw them, and I knew how sick I was and I thought—" He
shut his eyes, but forced out the next words. "I was out of my
head with fever. I thought they'd come to take me with them,
but somehow they'd leave my body, and in the morning my
mother would find me dead."

"Betimes we have done so," Lily said softly, "but not with
you."

"So you've come for him now?" I asked, completely terrified.

It was Robbie who answered. "They saved me, Cherr.
They worked their . . . magic, I guess, and the fever broke
and I'm still here."

"We couldn't let you die," Lily told him. "We have need of your music. You must play the songs of trees and the mountain, the songs of the wild ones who showed themselves to you."

"I owe you," he said to them, his voice steady but low.

"Don't say that," I pleaded with him. All the stories I'd read that morning were coming back to me in a panicked jumble. "That means they can collect. They'll take you under the hill to play for them and you'll feel like it's a ten-minute gig, but when you come back here a century will have passed and we'll all be dead and—"

"You're disrespecting us again?" Flax demanded.

I shut up. I was making it all worse and it was already very bad. Robbie and the faeries—and maybe the faeries and Annalise—they had ties with each other. The faeries had been in Robbie's life since he was a little boy, and it sounded as if they'd never really left. Would they always be with Annalise as well? And what was I doing in the middle of it? Maybe, I thought, I was in it because I could change things.

"Look," I said. "I understand you saved Robbie and maybe he does owe you for that. But isn't another deal possible? I mean, what if I give you—" I cast around wildly, searching for something to offer. "You can have anything in here," I said, realizing how little I had to give. "My jewelry? Or my mobile? You liked riding it—"

"We haven't come to take him," Flax cut me off. "No payment is owed. Yet you each must give something."

"You," Lily was speaking to Robbie now, "must continue to make music."

"I will," Robbie said. "I mean, playing guitar is all I want to do." He gave me a quick, shy smile. "Most of the time, anyway."

Flax fixed me with his green laser stare. "What of the girl?"

I tried to think of something to say in my defense. But they didn't want my things and I didn't know what else I had to give.

Without a word, Robbie got up and retrieved his guitar. He took it from its case then sat down on my desk chair. He began to play what he'd played the week before at Annalise's house. I recognized the notes, first gentle and lilting, the way they intensified. But then the song went farther than it had that night. He played the notes faster and harder until they rose and soared like something wild, then eased again to something so unashamedly tender I found myself blinking back tears. And all the while the leaves swirled to the music's tempo and the two faeries danced. They moved as if the music was inside them, the notes making their bodies curve and sway. Robbie was playing desire, and it seemed that what he played flowed into and through us all; the music became breath and pulse and blood.

Robbie finished and the last chord lingered, aching with longing. Lily stood in the curve of Flax's arms, resting against him, both of them looking completely blissed out.

"That song," Robbie said. "I got it from Cherry."

"What?" I asked. Was he lying to protect me?

"It's you," Robbie said simply. "Those chords are what I feel whenever I'm around you. That's as close as I can come to playing what I see inside you."

I felt myself trembling.

"That's what I think of the girl," Robbie said, his dark eyes meeting Flax's green ones. "She—" his voice had gone ragged "—she matters to me."

"You see beauty in her," Lily said.

Robbie nodded and drew a breath.

"And you see it in him?" she asked me.

"Sometimes I feel as if that's all I see," I confessed through a red haze of self-consciousness. To me Robbie was beauty and warmth and excitement and all I wanted was to always feel that sun inside him.

"That you can give," Flax said. "And you must give him your truth."

Robbie raised one black eyebrow. "What's he talking about?"

I hesitated. This wasn't a conversation I'd wanted to have in front of an audience but the faeries weren't giving me much choice.

"There's a reason I've been pulling away from you," I told Robbie. "I haven't been with anyone before."

"But Maura—"

"It's a lie. That I let her tell," I added. "That college guy I met when I went to San Diego—we played miniature golf. Big date."

"Really?" Robbie asked, a smile turning up one corner of his mouth.

I nodded. "I'm sorry I lied. And I'm sorry I don't know anything about sex, and so I want you but I'm not sure—"

Flax and Lily took to the air, Flax riding a red leaf, Lily a gold. We stopped talking and watched them, graceful, perfect creatures arcing through the room.

"Seasons change," Flax reminded us, his voice calling up the scent of eucalyptus. "Leaves fall. As they should, as they must."

"Since time before memory," Lily said as they spiraled toward the open window. "It's all a gift. So take good care."

We watched until they were out of sight. Robbie crossed the room to me and cupped my face with his hand. "It's okay," he said. "We can take it slow. Or not at all. Or—"

"I know," I said, and I did.

For Danielle Reed Lord, who screamed for faeries.

When Ellen Steiber was eight her aunt Dolly gave her *The Golden Book of Fairy Tales*, translated from the French by Marie Ponsot and illustrated by Adrienne Ségur. It cast a spell that's never been broken; she's been in love with fairy tales, myths, and folklore ever since. To date, she's published over thirty-five books for children and young adults, most of them drawing on myth and the supernatural. Her short fiction appears in various books in the Datlow/Windling adult fairy tale series as well as in *The Essential Bordertown*, edited by Terri Windling and Delia Sherman. She has won two Golden Kite Awards, and her young adult story "The Shape of Things" was reprinted in *The Year's Best Fantasy and Horror*. Her first adult fantasy novel, *A Rumor of Gems*, was recently published by Tor Books, and she's currently working on the sequel.

Visit her Web site at www.ellensteiber.com

Author's Note

Shortly after Terri and Ellen asked me to write a story for this book, I visited my sisters and their families in Berkeley, California, and found that all three of my nieces were into faeries. Samantha, then six, loved the Cicely Mary Barker books and had a little Flower Fairy doll that she carried with her everywhere. Mari, then three, had taken to wearing a pair of gossamer faery wings. And Danielle, then four, told me that she and a friend (who is much nicer than Hillary) screamed for faeries in the oak tree outside her window, and Danielle got the girl faeries and her friend the stinky boy faeries. And that, I realized, was the beginning of my story. I'm grateful to my sisters, their husbands, and my nieces for letting me freely borrow and adapt so many details from their lives.

As for the subject of the story, faeries have long been connected with the forbidden, which may be why so many of the old stories and ballads about them contain an element of seduction. In addition to being tricksters and babynappers, faeries are sexy. So when I saw that Cherry was stuck, afraid of her own sexuality and yet also feeling the power and the magic of it, I thought it would be interesting to see what the faeries might tell her.

Immersed in Matter

∾

Nina Kiriki Hoffman

I admit it, after fifteen years of denying it: I, Owl out of Ginger, am half human, more my father's son than ever I thought.

Everyone in my generation of faery has a human half. We all have the same human father. We never speak of it.

The race of faery was dying until our father came, sent as an ensorcelled emissary by our dead king. Before that, the only new children to enter the underground lands in three hundred years were those born of human women: half-bloods, never as gifted as their faery fathers. Most halfbloods stayed aboveground among humans, where their pieces of gifts could serve them well; the few who came to our lands were treated as lesser beings, servants, or sometimes slaves.

The faeries I knew my own age or near it were my half-brothers and sisters. The fraction of our human father in us was too small to show. We were all beautiful and skilled. We seemed entirely faery to everyone, with no stink or stamp of human. Most of us resembled our mothers; we looked different from each other, and our gifts were as strong as any among the purebloods. We were accepted as the next generation of faery.

Like everyone else, I never looked twice at the halfbloods who had been born aboveground, except to notice they were different, lesser. They smelled strange, and many were less than perfect physically. Fit for kitchen work, laundry work, work that involved dirt. Fit to pass among us as shadows.

My mother sang over my cradle when I was little about what kind of creature my father had been. She had loved him. She remembered him. She wished he would return.

I took it for a human tale and believed it not, just something with which to scare children. None of the other children I played with had mothers who sang such songs.

My generation was taught as previous generations had been—to pursue our own interests and gifts, choose our own teachers.

Mother taught me the basics of magic and survival, but my favorite teacher was Golden, who knew the languages and shapes of animals.

My mother was not happy with my choice of specialties— to shapeshift was to acknowledge our kinship with lesser beings, so the skill was disdained by the most prejudiced among us—but she indulged me, since that was where my gift lay.

Golden and I went up the tunnels and through the gates into the world above, where the lights in the sky changed and so did the temperature of the air, and water fell from the sky, as well as flowing in streams and springs. We wandered wild lands, swamps and forests, met animal people and saw what they could be persuaded to do. Golden had a gift for speaking with wolves and foxes. Bird language came more easily to my tongue. Golden taught me many lesser dialects, and together we learned cat language, though cats great and small ignored us when they liked, whether we got the accents right or not.

My greatest dream was to talk with horses.

I wanted to be a horse or own a horse. They related to people in a different way than other animals. They were so large and powerful, and yet they suffered humans to use them and ride them. I wanted to meet, know, and ride a horse. I wanted to discover the reasons for their cooperation with something they could trample.

Unfortunately, most horses lived with humans. Golden said horses ran wild halfway around the world, in places with lots of sand, but there was no gate that opened from our underground to that part of the world.

By choice, Golden would have kept me in the wilderlands always, but because I was fascinated by horses, I spent much of my aboveground time lurking near a road that led through the forest to a city. Traffic was frequent. Horses pulled carts of fruit, flour, and vegetables from the surrounding country to the city markets. Mounted messengers and soldiers passed on the road. Travelers in caravans rode horses or drove them, and guards traveled with them, on horseback. Traders and tinkers went both ways in horse-drawn wagons.

I listened to everything, to little herd dogs as they ran and nipped the flanks of goats and sheep, to cud-chewing cows and tinkers' cats, to humans even—but most of all I lis-tened to horses. I only half-understood their tales of travel and grass and water, fighting and running and carrying people. Their voices were low and wonderful.

Golden disapproved of my desire to know horses. They were too closely associated with humans. I had to sneak off to study them when he set me other tasks. Most often I went to the Feather Inn, a day's ride from the city, and watched the human boys who worked in the stables. They saddled and unsaddled horses, removed, repaired, replaced bits and reins, combed and brushed the animals, fed and watered them, and picked rocks and muck out of their hooves. They spread straw on the ground when it was too muddy, and mucked out the stalls, and slept above the horses in the hay.

At first I could not stand the stench of humans, but even-tually I became accustomed.

One frosty evening at the leading edge of winter, when Golden had sent me out to study the night habits of deer, I crouched under a bush with one of the inn yard cats. She was pregnant and hungry. I brought her a fresh killed rat.

"How can I get close to the horses?" I whispered.

"You won't be able to, not while you stink of faery," the cat said.

"What's wrong with how I smell?"

"We know your kind means us no good," said the cat. She had eaten the rat already and edged away from me as we spoke.

"I don't mean you any harm, or them either."

She flattened her ears. "All too often an incautious ani-mal disappears through a faery gate and is never seen again."

I hugged my green-clad knees and thought about that. I had seen animals underground: cats, dogs, even a tribe of foxes in one slowtime pocket where my aunt lived. The queen had a stable with horses in it, but it was fenced around with spell protections so strong I could never get near it. Whenever I tried, I found myself wandering the farthest reaches of the underground without any memory of how I had gotten there.

"I just want to talk to them. I don't want to steal them."

"I know the worth of a faery promise," said the cat.

Perhaps she was right. If I really wanted to speak with a horse, my best chance might be to find one of my own.

"Don't you think one of them would rather have me for a master?" I asked the cat. "Are humans so good to horses that horses want to stay with them? Humans hit them with sticks and straps. Humans make them work, even when they're too tired and old. Isn't there a single horse who would rather leave this place with me?"

"There might be," said the cat. "I don't generally speak with horses. They allow humans too much liberty. Get yourself inside and ask, but before you try, you'd better find a safer scent, or the cock will crow, the dogs will bark, and even the mice will squeak at you. Thanks for the rat." She slipped away.

A safer scent. Golden had taught me two transformations: owl and wolf. Sometime deep in the well of our history, there was a binding together with animals to acquire powers, and most of us shared some animal blood, though many tried to deny it, and many more never learned to work with it. At this stage in my magecraft, I could only transform into things that were part of my heritage, animals in my bloodline, and those were the only two who had left clear enough tracks for me to learn them—so far.

I melted back into the forest half a league, found a safe place up a tree, and called the owl out of me. The night shifted shape as I changed, became a place of lights and shadows, sounds and sights more intense, bright, and sharp. There was no solid darkness: I could see everywhere, and the sky was a place of many lights but no color. I spread silent wings and lofted, drifted through the air, scanned the ground beneath the trees for any sign of squeak or movement. Transformation always made me hungry.

Two mice and one vole later, I returned to the inn. Did I still stink of faery? I couldn't tell. I sifted scents. My relationship to them had changed too: many things smelled much more enticing to me, and things I would like as my faery self disgusted me. The stable appealed to me because it was home to mice and rats and possibly baby birds. I flew in through the open hayloft door, delighting in the rustles of mice in the straw, alert to the sounds and scents of human, horse, and jingling tack from the floor below. I found a perch on a beam where I could look past the hayloft down into the stables.

Below me, horses. Horses. Warm and huge and smelling of hay and sweat and their own less-than-leather wild scent, a scent of things that run. Did I have any horse in me? Until I could speak to them, see how deep their language ran in me, I could not tell.

A hoot flowed out of me, my delight in being closer to horses than I ever had before.

Below me, some boy looked up. "An owl," he said.

"A death bird! Scare it away," said another.

Two boys climbed up into the loft and pulled rocks from their pockets. They stoned me. "Get out of our stable! Go prophesy death somewhere else!"

I flew away, stinging where rocks had struck me. I found my tree again and roosted. An owl wasn't welcome, even if nothing knew it was faery. A wolf would be even less welcome. Dogs, the warped wolves who lived with humans, resented their wild cousins, and humans feared wolves. I had played tricks when I first learned wolf shape, sneaked up on humans camped in the forest and scared them from their fires, horses, and possessions. Golden made me stop. He said such actions put other wolves at risk.

Besides, horses hated wolves, too. Even when I'd chased off their humans, horses at campsites wouldn't let me approach them.

I climbed back into my faery self, dropped to the ground. I did a seek spell that took me to a place where deer were overnighting, and I spent the rest of the night watching them. Did my scent disturb them? It didn't. Toward morning I climbed down and approached them. None feared me enough to run from me or threaten me. The young one even let me touch it.

My sister-friend Henna was drawn to deer, though she couldn't take their shape. Her gifts lay in other directions: she could weave things into being.

I talked with these deer and couldn't understand why Henna liked them. So much of their orientation was fear; they knew they were food to many other things. Where was the fun in being something that ran away?

I went home at dawn, wondering why Golden made me study animals like these.

The answer was simple: he wanted me to study everything. He gave me raspberry tea with ambrosia in it, sweet, tart, and fortifying, and we sat by the green fire on his hearth, below bunches of drying aboveground herbs that hung from his ceiling. "You have time, Owl, ages and ages. You never know when something you learn today will serve you in the future. Just now we're living in peaceful times, but suppose there's a revolution or an invasion. It happens. You should know deer tactics as well as wolf and owl tactics . . . mole tactics, ant tactics, slug tactics. You don't know what the enemy knows; you never know what you'll need to know. Learn everything."

After tea and questions I went home to my mother's house under the unweathering sky of the underground, where time does not divide into days so easily as above.

How was I going to get closer to horses? Mice and rats could, but they could be stepped on. Chickens approached them, but people were too inclined to kill and roast chickens. Even if I could have turned into a mouse, a rat, or a chicken—and I couldn't—I didn't want to be a prey animal.

I had tried to learn cat transformation, but as far as I could detect I didn't have that heritage either. When I was older and had acquired knowledge, wisdom, and skills, per-

haps I would be able to transform into animals whose heritage I didn't own, but that might take a hundred years and
I wanted horses now.

I lay on my feathersilk mattress, the scents of aboveground herbs around me—Golden gave me some to sleep on,
for sharpening the brain, he said—and thought. What animal got closest to horses without being questioned?

Humans.

I had human in my heritage, though I'd spent my whole
short life trying to forget or deny it. I owned human heritage
with such a clear link that I could imagine the transformation without trouble.

If I accepted it . . .

I curled tight on my mattress and hugged my spider-
woven blanket to my chest. I had looked away so long. I
turned my eyes inward and saw the streak of self that had
come from my father. It lay along my spine. At first I thought
it was gray, but when I really paid attention, I saw that it was
shimmery and strange, all colors. It looked like no human
thing I had seen before.

I reached toward it, felt it engage me, then realized how
tired I was after a night of running and spying. I banished
the father self back to its hiding place and fell asleep.

Golden and I went aboveground again when night was
falling there.

Ice had formed along the edges of the creek, crisped the
surfaces of puddles, furred the dead leaves on the ground. I
pulled my cloak tighter around me. The first time I had seen
snow aboveground, I had fallen in love with it—its white-

ness, the way it packed into balls, and yielded and cushioned when I lay on it, the way it lay on everything and changed the look of the landscape, especially under the moon; I only noticed cold could hurt me later. Now I knew about frost and snow and ice; I knew to wear warm things and keep enough energy on tap to fire my blood when necessary.

"Tonight I want you to watch tree snakes," Golden said.

Snakes? "But Teacher, they're hibernating now."

"So? Spend a night watching them in their sleep. Note how they store and conserve energy. Another tactic you may find useful later."

"I want to try something else tonight."

"Oh?" Golden hunched nearer me, eyes aglitter. He wore a pelt with heavy fur over his shoulders, the fur the same color as his tangled wealth of red-gold hair. I had wondered often whether it was the pelt of an animal self he had shed or if he had actually killed something to gain it. "Have you found another heritage animal?"

"I have."

"What is it?"

I raised a shoulder in case he wanted to clout me, and whispered, "Human."

He stared, red fire in his eyes that shone in the shadow that was his face. At last, he said, "Ah."

I waited, then lowered my shoulder when he didn't raise his fist.

He took my hand and led me far through the forest, away from the gate. When we reached one of his work-spaces, a clearing with an underground chamber he had built where he stored baskets and the glass clippers he used to gather herbs, we stopped. It was a place only Golden and I knew.

"I've been expecting this," he said in a voice that was more growl than faery.

"You *have*?"

"Only from you, Owl. Any of the others who've come to me for lessons would never take this step. I know you haunt the roadways and the inn yard."

"I want to speak with horses."

"As fine an excuse as any," he muttered.

"What?"

"Never mind. Have you opened to your heritage?"

"Not yet."

"Do it now, where I can supervise."

I lay on the dirt floor of his underground lair and quieted my mind. I knew where to find the father self. I had only to glance at it, and it reached for me. *Wait.* "Golden, did you ever meet my father?"

"I did."

"What was he like?"

"A difficult question, young Owl. He was never the same twice. It depended on who looked at him and what she wanted. He came to my house once, when he was between women, a state I never saw him in again. That was the only time I saw him without a glamour on him. I gave him tea and fruitbread."

"What was he like?" I asked again.

"He was very young," said Golden.

"Teacher. What was he like?"

Golden laughed. "There were so many questions I wanted to ask him. Who was he? Where had he come from? How did the dead king choose him to be the father of our children? Why did he agree to this mission? Was it just that he was a young man with a reprehensible appetite for sex? Did that make him the right one to give us our next generation? Had he any qualities of character he could pass on to his children? This was before any of you had been born, but three of you were coming. I never found him free again."

"But what—"

"When I found him, he had just finished his time with Raven. I saw her hug him and kiss him good-bye and leave him in the common room of the queen's palace. She wove a black feather into his hair. For her, he had been dark and tall and strong, with silver eyes. She touched his cheek and left him, and he melted."

"Melted," I repeated.

"Melted into what he must have looked like before. A boy not much older than you, with brown hair and hazel eyes, handsome but not particularly interesting as humans can be interesting. He looked . . . like many other humans. He looked tired and sad. I took him home and gave him tea and watched him. His hands shook until after he had some of my fruitbread. I had all my questions ready, and I never asked a single one."

I lay silent. Presently, Golden said, "Fireweed came to my house to find him. She sat at my table and watched him finish his tea. He thanked me, then turned to her and smiled and changed into a tall white-haired giant with a beard to his waist and shoulders broader than mine. Her eyes filled with longing and delight. She led him away. I didn't see him again for three months, and at that point he was going off with Barley, and he had changed into a slender yellow-haired minstrel."

"What did he look like for my mother?"

Golden scratched his nose and studied me. "His hair was black and thick like yours, and his eyes were yellow, like yours."

My mother had peppery red hair and orange eyes. I was one of the few in my generation who didn't look like his mother. I had always wondered where my coloring came from, but had never asked. No one treated me as though I looked human. In fact, I looked a bit like Otter, a friend of my mother's.

"I resemble my father's glamour?" That didn't make sense. A glamour was for appearance, not for seed.

"Those of you who don't look like your mothers look like what your mothers desired of your father."

I had never heard of magic like that.

"Open to your heritage, Owl."

Which heritage? What my father looked like, or who he had been? I closed my eyes and reached for that pale many-colored place along my spine I knew came from my father.

I had thought it only a fraction of myself, a part I could ignore, but as soon as I opened to it, it threaded all through me, a faint and gentle warmth that tendriled out to my edges. I felt my organs squeeze and shift. My face tightened, and the bones of my skull closed in. The tips of my ears tingled, then shrank.

Too late, I thought, what if this change consumes me so

I forget how to restore myself? My animal changes had been governed by the much stronger part of my heritage I had from my mother. Even though everything in my body changed, my largest self remained intact.

My father had given me at least half of myself. What if his half was strong enough to swallow what my mother had given me?

The final tingles and spirals of change faded from my soles and palms and stomach. I lay with my eyes shut, sensing myself.

The air felt colder on my face, and the scents of the night were fainter. Sounds had faded. At last I opened my eyes and found the night was dark, darker than I had ever seen it. I was surrounded by shadows, and I couldn't see through them well enough to know what cast them. "Golden?" I whispered. Breath frosted as it rose from my mouth. My voice tasted strange. I had lost the edge that let me say things and make them true.

"Here." He was a large looming shadow above me. Terror thrilled through me, sudden, senseless. Golden opened his hands to let out yellow light, and I struggled to slow my heartbeat. This was my teacher. He would not hurt me. Slowly I remembered and believed.

I sat up and took stock. I smelled my hand. Though the scent was faint, it was human, not my own. My fingers were longer, but square-tipped instead of tapered, and I only had four fingers and a thumb now on each hand. My skin had darkened to a color of those who lived outside aboveground during the day.

I touched my cheek, felt my nose. Bigger. My eyebrows felt heavier, but my hair was finer, and there was less of it. "What do I look like?" I asked. My tongue against the inside of my teeth felt different too.

Golden sketched a circle in the air. It filled with silver, an air mirror that showed me my new self.

I looked like half the stableboys at the inn, human and nondescript. I touched my hair: no longer black and thick, some shade of brown I couldn't see very well with these eyes, and my eyes were a darker color than they had been, wider and not so slanted.

After a moment, recognition flickered through me. Somewhere I had seen this self before. I closed my eyes and chased the fragment of memory. There was a taste in it: peach. I had sat in my mother's lap when she was much taller than I, and a man with this clean-shaven face sat beside her, touching along arm and thigh. We were all on the big soft blue chair in my mother's bedroom, close enough that I could smell him. He smelled strange, different from everyone I'd met before, but I didn't think, then, that he smelled bad. He smiled down at me and gave me a slice of peach, ripe and sweet, which melted on my tongue and tasted of the above-ground season of summer and a sun I hadn't seen yet.

He kissed my forehead and stroked my hair, and my mother let him. He shared the peach with me and my mother until it was gone and we licked the last sweet, sticky juice off our fingers. We sat together like that for a long time, until someone else came and called him away. His eyes turned sad. He touched my hand and left.

"Oh, this is strange." I felt my face and frowned at the mirror.

Father. I *had* met him. I wore my father's face.

I turned from the mirror and looked at the night. Every direction I turned, I saw nothing but lighter darkness against dark, except when I looked up. The sky held stars, but they were smaller and dimmer than I remembered. "I feel blind and deaf and scent-deaf."

I struggled to my feet. I felt weak and clumsy.

In the other transformations I knew, I had gained things as I lost other things. Owl gave me flight, and night sight so strong the world looked as well lit as day, and hunting, and hearing so acute I could hear a mouse's footfall from the sky. Wolf had given me speed, strength, and a wild world of scents.

What was good about this change? I was the same shape I had been, almost, but weaker in every way.

Horses.

Now I could approach horses.

Why had I changed here, so far from the Feather Inn? It would take me ages to get there in this form, stumbling all the way over things I could no longer see or smell.

The easy answer was to change into an owl or a wolf and fly or run, then change back to this when I was nearly there. I held out my right arm and thought, *Wing*.

Nothing happened.

"Golden," I whispered. Had I changed myself so well I would never be able to change back? Was I trapped for the rest of my life in this form? How long a life could I lead, if I were truly human? Had I doomed myself to a short hard life and an early death?

"Oh, dear," he said.

I hated my father!

"Wait," said Golden. "Open to your heritage, Owl."

As a human, I couldn't summon up the instant change I had managed as myself. But perhaps . . .

I lay down again and closed my eyes, looked inside myself. For a long while I saw nothing, just the dark I couldn't see through with the senses I had now. Then something sparked and shone. A glimmer along my spine, a heat under my skin. The more I studied it, the stronger it grew. I opened to it, felt it wash away what I was and restore me to what I had been.

I owned my mother's nature too.

I sat up as my faery self, felt my ears and checked my fingers to be sure. But I knew: I could see and hear and smell again. I built my own air mirror, and summoned light to see myself, fingered my nose to make sure it felt the same as it looked.

I shifted to my owl self.

"Wait," said Golden. "Where are you going?"

"The inn."

"Haven't you done enough for one night?"

"No." I flew through the brilliant night to the Feather Inn, taking joy from everything about my owl self. Along the way, I feasted on mice I tracked by tiny sounds and slaughtered with talons and beak.

I perched in a tree outside the circle of torchlight by the inn.

I feared to make this change. First I let myself be the faery Owl I knew and had been since birth. *Remember.* I looked at my green clothes. Had I ever seen a human wear such a slashed-sleeve tunic, such an elegant mage-embroidered cloak with warmth spells sewn into it, and such trousers and shoes? No. While I still had my own skills and powers, I changed my garments' cloth so it was rough and brown, turned what was river leather about me into something coarser. I climbed from the tree, leaned against its trunk, took a last look and smell around, and sought my other self.

I opened my eyes to a muffled, hidden, freezing world. I shivered. Would the stable be warmer?

"Wait."

I glanced down. Something large, dark, four-legged, and furred stood beside me.

"You'll need money," my teacher said. He was a wolf, and he spoke wolf, but even as this foreign self, I could understand him. A mercy. He dropped a sack that jingled at my feet. "You must be cautious, Owl. Take a few coins out before you go among them. Offer only one at a time in exchange for food or shelter or whatever else you can buy. Never show them you have more; they kill each other for silver, even such false silver as this, which will last only a day. They won't know it is false, but remember, you must not be here when it disappears. Do you have your knife?"

I patted my sheathed dagger, which was made of fire-mountain glass.

"They will have iron," he said.

I shivered. I had seen what iron could do to us. A man I

knew had a shriveled hand because he had touched iron. One of my aunts had died of poisoning from brushing against an iron spike.

"It may not hurt you. It may be that your father has given you immunity, especially in that shape. If you see iron, test it. Put your hand near it. If you take no hurt of it, that's good to know. Tell them as little as possible. Don't trust them. I will wait here."

"Thank you." I took six silvers from the sack of coins, slipped them into my side pocket, and tucked the moneybag into my belt at the back, beneath my cloak. Stumbling a little, I made my way through the thin screen of trees into the muddy, churned, and torchlit inn yard. Most of the mud had frozen into ruts and peaks and hoofprints. It crackled as I crossed it. I went straight to the stable and peered over the half-door. No cock cried. No mouse squeaked. But a dog tied by the back door of the inn barked at me as I puzzled over the stable doorlatch.

Two stableboys came from the tack room, one chewing on something that smelled like bread and hot meat—half of it was still in his hand.

"What is it?" asked the other, who was taller but no less dirty. Both had straw in their hair.

I smiled, pleased that this, too, was a language I could still understand, even though I had changed into this lesser form. I had learned humanspeak along the roads. "I'd like to see the horses," I said.

"Why?"

Why? Wouldn't anyone? "Because they're horses."

"Are you daft?"

"No."

The boys looked at each other. "You just want to see them?" said the chewing boy.

"Perhaps touch them?" I said.

The chewing boy swallowed, peered at me. "Hank, you go on back to supper. I'll deal with this."

"All right, Robin," said the taller one. He went back into the tack room.

Robin came over and let me into the stable. "Where're you from, then?"

"The forest."

"And you want to see horses."

"Yes."

"You ever curried one?"

"Never."

"Would you like to?"

"Oh, yes."

He took another bite of his dinner, ducked into the tack room, returned minus what he had been eating, but with two brushes. "Show you on Bess, if you like. Got a stranger's horse here that needs tending after that, and I could use some help." He led me into a stall with a big brown horse in it. She was warm and smelled large and animal, sweaty and a little musty. She looked at us, lowered her nose to smell me. Her breath was hot and hay-sweet, and her whiskers tickled my face.

"Horse," I whispered. I held out my hand and she snuffled it. Her nostrils flared.

"You can touch her. What's your name, then?"

"Owl."

"That's a funny name. Here, Owl, stroke her nose like this, but then let's get on with it."

I ran my hand down the bony ridge of the horse's nose. She pressed against my hand.

"Come on." He handed me a brush and we moved farther back. He showed me how to brush Bess, how to look at which way the hair lay and brush with it instead of against it. It whorled some places and switched directions. "Don't be afraid to brush her hard. She likes it."

He left me at it for a moment, then came back with a wide-toothed metal comb and taught me to comb the horse's mane and tail. "Watch her back hooves. Don't pull too hard or she'll kick you. You follow?"

"Yes. Thank you, Robin."

"Eh. All right. You just keep working on Bess, and I'll finish my supper. When I'm done I'll show you the next job, eh?"

He went away and left me with the horse. I taught myself what she was as I stroked her. She let me touch her everywhere, so long as she knew what I was doing and I didn't startle her. She let me hug her around the neck. She taught me a few words of her language: *yes, no, oh, more of that, I like it!* Horse. At last. I brushed her until she shone, then leaned against her side, my head to her ribcage, and listened to her heart. Did I have horse heritage? Could I open to this? Could I *be* this?

"Here, now," said Robin behind me in a testy voice. "What are you doing?"

I straightened. "Resting." I had found no echoes of horse

inside myself. Maybe that was a problem with this shape: maybe I couldn't sense such things when I was in human form. Or maybe I had no horse in me to awaken.

I looked down at my hands. In one I still held the bristle-and-wood brush, but in the other I held the metal comb. My hand tightened on it. Was it iron? I let it fall, stared into my palm, which was whole, unmarked. I might have no horse in me, but I had enough human to protect me from the doom of cold iron.

Robin walked around Bess, nodding. "Good. You did good. You sure this is the first time you've touched a horse?"

"Yes."

"No fear in you, is there?"

I looked at him. I had many fears. What if I were trapped in this form? I had changed out of it once, but that didn't mean I could do it again. What if he attacked me? He was taller and had sturdier arms than I did. How could I fight when I could detect very little strength in myself? Could I use any of the skills I had learned underground when I didn't know the self I was?

"Ah," said Robin. "Well, not scared of horses, anyway, are you?"

"No."

"Good. Let me show you Bruiser."

I followed him to a stall at the end of the stable. We were greeted by a cascade of thunks as the horse inside kicked the walls. "Here's the thing. We've given him food and water," Robin said, "but we haven't brushed him. He doesn't like us. Come up here." He climbed up a ladder to the hayloft. I followed him. "Now take a look." We edged over to look down into Bruiser's stall, and he stared up at us, whites visible in his eyes. He was tall and dark, with a white blaze on his forehead and one white stocking. He screamed and kicked the wall.

"Hank was all for letting you in with him to start," Robin said.

I glanced at him and thought about that. Suppose this was the first horse I had tried to touch? What if it had killed me? I wouldn't have gone into that stall, though. I'd seen other creatures with bad tempers. I knew enough to stay away, unless I had skills that could protect me. In this form, I didn't think I had any skills. "Something hurts him?"

"Huh. Could be. Just figured he was a bad one, or has a bad master. He's old. Had a hard life. You can see it in his hide." He studied the horse, who stared up at us. "They don't pay us enough to take good care of one like this," Robin said. "It's as much as your life's worth to open that stall. We can leave him. He'll do."

The stable door opened. "Boys!"

Robin and I climbed down the ladder, and Hank came out of the tack room. An older man stood at the door, holding two horses by the reins below their chins.

"Well, here," said Robin, "a job. Get you some more experience, eh, Owl?"

"Oh, yes."

Hank snorted and tended to one horse, while Robin taught me the intricacies of bridle straps and buckles and saddle girths and blankets, how to rub a sweating horse down with a cloth before brushing it, and how to give only a little water at first to an animal that had been running, and add more later.

Everything we did satisfied something in me that had gone hungry a long time. I didn't understand it. And who was Robin? Why had he decided to be nice to me? With most of the people I knew, I had to claim kinship before they would even speak to me, and then we had to compare skills and powers so we would know who was above, and who below. Politics were thick in the air at the faery court. Many had nothing to do but jockey for favor. Since it was all they did, they took it as seriously as life.

Another reason I liked working with Golden aboveground was that we didn't have to concern ourselves with matters of status, except his as teacher and mine as student.

Golden had warned me to be wary of these humans. I tried to keep that in mind, but mostly I lost myself in the work, the wonder that I was finally able to touch a horse; its body heat and hair, solid strength, coiled power and speed and stamina, lay under my hands and brush.

When we had finished feeding, watering, and brushing the horse and stored his tack, we went back to the stall with Bruiser in it.

A cat walked along the top of the stall railing. "Who's this, who's this?" she asked, studying me with large yellow eyes. Bruiser kicked the wall below her, and she clung with her claws before she leapt to the straw near me. "What's wrong with you?" she snarled at the horse, who kicked the wall again.

I knelt and held out a hand to her. She came and sniffed, stared into my eyes, did not recognize me, though I knew her: she was the one who had told me to find a safer scent. "What *is* wrong with him?" I asked.

The cat blinked. She looked toward the stall.

The horse peered out at us over the top of the stall door.

Robin said, "Come on, Owl, there's nothing we can do for him, wild as he is. Want some tea?"

"You," whispered the horse to me. "You."

I rose.

"Where have you been? The old man took you away from me all those years ago, and you never came back! Where have you been?"

I walked to the stall, one slow step at a time.

"Boy," whispered the horse.

I held out my hand to him.

"Don't! He'll bite!" Robin cried, but the horse only smelled me. Then he screamed and whirled away and kicked the wall with both hind feet.

"Not my boy. Not my boy," he muttered, then stood, head hanging, breathing loudly, all his legs stiff.

I leaned on the stall door. "Did you know my father?"

Slowly his head rose. Slowly he stepped to the door, smelled me carefully, nibbled my hair. "Where is he?" he asked.

"No one knows."

"I'll take you, then."

"Will you?" I opened the stall door and slipped in, though Robin cried out to stop me.

The horse trembled as I touched him, but he didn't bite or kick me. His hindquarters were scored with whip marks. I still had a brush in my hand. I showed it to him, and he smelled it, then lipped it, then turned so I could brush him. "Who owns you now?" I asked. He had not been brushed in a long, long time. His hair was matted: layers of sweat, old shed hair, and the start of his winter coat made his hide a nightmare. Cold mud coated his lower legs. Scars old and new marred his hide. The corners of his mouth were thick with callus. Burrs were tangled in his mane.

"No one," he said.

Robin brought me a bucket with warm water in it, two rags, a comb, a hoofpick. The horse quieted as I cared for him the way Robin had taught me. Hank came to watch and jeer, but when the horse kicked the wall nearest him, he went away again.

"Who owns him?" I asked Robin.

"Owl, you spoke to him, and he made answers."

"Mm."

"Did you understand him?"

"Ah," I said. I thought, I had started to understand with Bess and the other horse, but everything Bruiser said was as clear to me as though I were talking to Golden or my mother. "Don't you talk to them?" I had watched all matters of the stable from a distance until now, but with the enhanced sight of the owl, the enhanced scent perception of the wolf. I had seen stable boys talking to horses, and men talking to horses as they rode.

" 'Course I do," said Robin. "They like the sound of a voice, if it's calm. Soothes them right down sometimes."

"Who owns him?"

"Who did he say when you asked him that?"

"No one."

"Hah!" said Robin. "Caught you."

"What?"

"He *does* answer, and you *do* understand. How is that?"

"Who owns him?" I asked for the third time. Underground, anyone who was asked a question three times had to answer with something like truth. There were many ways of turning questions away or changing subjects before the question could be asked a third time. Robin was skilled at this game too, I thought, but still, I had asked. Would he answer?

"A man in the inn brought him, but last I heard, he was offering to sell him for a fraction of his worth, could you but get the horse to cooperate. Now that he's cleaned up so nice, maybe the man will find a buyer."

"I'll buy him."

"Sure! A ragamuffin like you? Didn't you come here looking for work?"

I smiled at him. "I'll be back."

I had never been in a human building other than the stable, but I had seen people go in and out of the inn. Some went in through a door at the back, and some went in through the front. Most travelers, once they had handed their horses over to be taken care of or seen to their horses' stabling themselves, went in through the front door.

I took the brush, bucket, rags, and hoofpick back to the tack room and stowed them where Robin had gotten them from. Then I crossed the inn yard and went around the front of the building. My breath made white ghosts as I walked, and my face burned with cold.

The heat, smoke, and voices came out of the door when I opened it, and music—rough song and rougher playing on some instrument with strings, and the yeasty smell of beer, sharp overtones of wine, roasted meat, baking bread, smoke from fire and tobacco. People crowded around tables and a bar in a big, noisy, low-ceilinged, ill-lit room to the left. It looked more like the sort of party dwarves would throw than any I had seen underground; our gathering rooms were bigger, with taller ceilings, and the people wore better clothes and didn't smell so bad.

The entry hall led past the room, with hooks on the wall where people had hung cloaks, now gently steaming in the heat from two separate fireplaces in the common room; a closed door stood to the right, and there was a staircase straight ahead that the hall hooked past.

I had several moments to panic before anyone in the room noticed me. Here I was, inside a human dwelling, near a bunch of humans, most of them bigger than I was, and I had shed my skills and powers. What if they decided to kill me?

But mostly they seemed happy with their meat and drink and each other. Laughter boomed. The song the minstrel sang was a funny one, and many joined in the chorus. Nobody looked as though they were about to leap up and stab a stranger.

A thin man in an apron came to meet me. "Young sir, what's your pleasure?" he asked.

"I heard someone here wants to sell a horse, the big noisy horse in the stable."

"Gallo," he called over his shoulder. A large man in brown fur came away from the bar. "Horse buyer," said the innkeeper before he plunged back into the common room.

"Truly? You're interested in that brute of a—that wonderful creature of mine out back?"

"He looks strong."

"That he is, young sir. He can kick through a stable wall in—he can pull a heavy load. He only wants a bit of handling. Are you good with a whip?"

"How much do you want for him?"

"Thirty silver pieces," he said.

"Oh." I didn't know how many pieces of false silver Golden had given me, and he had told me not to show them in public. How was I supposed to count them out?

"Don't look so crestfallen, young sir. Tonight could be your lucky night. I've just had a good run of cards, and I'm feeling generous. How about twenty?"

I bit my lip and stared at the floor, wondering if he would go lower. It didn't matter to me how many he asked for, so long as I had enough. But apparently indecision was part of the game.

"Fifteen, then, but that's final."

"Hey, Gallo! Ten minutes ago you were saying you'd let the monster go for ten!" yelled someone in the room.

Gallo turned and snarled at the other man, then faced me again. "I'll give him to you for ten, though it hurts my heart to let him go so cheap."

"Ten," I said. "Excuse me a moment." I ducked down the hallway until it turned, took out my purse and counted out ten pieces of silver, then returned and handed them to him.

He bit them, studied them, smiled. "Will you want tack, then?" asked Gallo. "I'll throw in his saddle and bridle for another two."

Would the horse want to be saddled and bridled? I wouldn't, if I were a horse. But maybe I should take the tack anyway. I could always throw it away later.

"That tack he's got is only worth half a silver," called the same man in the common room.

I dug one silver out of my pocket and gave it to Gallo. "Will that do?"

"Yes." He tucked the silvers I had given him in his own pocket. "He's all yours, God help you. All of you are witnesses!"

The nearest people in the common room laughed and nodded and waved mugs of beer at us.

"Thank you." I had a horse. I had a horse. I ran out of the inn to the stables. I had a horse!

Now what?

"You did it?" Robin asked when I entered. "You bought him?"

"Yes. And his tack."

"His tack! Hah! It's worthless. The girth is nearly worn through, the saddle's scuffed to pieces, and the reins are almost past mending."

"Oh, well. I don't imagine I'll be using it much."

"What are you going to do with him?"

"Take him home." Would he come? Down through the gate and into the underground? What would my mother say if I brought a horse home? We had room in our house for a horse, but if my mother didn't like him, perhaps it was time for me to carve out my own living space.

If the horse wouldn't come through the gate, what *was* I going to do with him?

Hank brought me a very sorry saddle, a thin saddle pad,

and sad reins with tarnished buckles and a heavy, sharp bit. If I were a horse, I wouldn't want to wear any of this, especially that bit. It would cut the tongue.

I went to Bruiser's stall and opened the door. He glanced at me. "Did you eat enough?"

He went back to the food bin and ate the grain I had put there, drank deep from the bucket. How was I going to feed him?

"You want me to help you put the tack on him?" Robin asked.

I looked at the degenerate bits of things in my hands. "I don't think he'd like it."

"How are you going to ride him, then?"

"Ride him?" I hadn't thought this through. "But I don't know how to ride."

"I suppose it's just as well, that brute. Probably wouldn't let you stay on him anyway. What do you want him for, then?"

"I don't know." I walked toward the stable door, and Bruiser followed me. "Robin, thank you for everything."

"Hey. Come back if you want work, Owl. I'm sure they'd hire you. You learn fast, and you're good with the animals."

"Thanks." We passed Hank, who leaned, arms crossed, against Bess's stall door. Then we were outside in the flicker-torch dark and cold. I led my horse into the forest.

He snorted and reared when we came to where Golden waited.

"It's all right, horse. This is my teacher. He won't hurt you."

"Won't I?" asked Golden, who was still a wolf. "Why have you gotten this animal, Owl?"

"It's what I've always wanted, Teacher. You know that. This is my horse."

"This is my boy," said the horse.

"Oh, ho," said Golden.

"Horse," I said, "I'm going to change now so we can get home before daybreak. Only—"

"What'll you do, Owl? Fly off and leave the creature behind?" Golden asked.

"How far do you have to go?" asked the horse.

"A league and a half."

"Climb on my back," said the horse.

I studied the saddle, saddle pad, and bridle I held, wondered if they would help me. I climbed up into a tree and left them on a branch, then lowered myself onto the horse's back. He stayed steady. His back was broad.

It was strange to be shaped like I was and this high off the ground on top of something that moved.

"Boy, hug my neck," the horse said. "Wolf, lead the way."

The horse carried me through the night all the way to the gate. I clung to his huge hard warmth, my cheek pressed to his neck, his coarse mane whipping against my face and shoulders as he ran, my legs splayed wider apart than was comfortable. I was shaky and rattled by the time we reached our destination, but elated, too: the horse had let me ride him.

"Thank you," I said. I let myself down off his back and collapsed, my legs too wobbly to hold me.

The horse nibbled my hair. "You'll have to learn better than that," he said.

"You mean we can do it again?"

"Yes."

"Oh, thank you." I stretched out on my back and reached for my other self. It didn't take me long to find it this second time. I wrapped myself in change, felt the arcane strengths and skills come back. The world of scents came alive, and my hearing sharpened. I felt the breeze stroke my face and hands. Better. Much better. I ran my hand through my hair and sat up.

"Who are you?" cried the horse.

"I'm Owl," I said.

"You're not! You're not my boy's son anymore!" He reared, pawed the air, backed away from me.

"I am," I said.

"No! Nothing about you tastes or smells like him! Imposter. You tricked me!"

"Horse," I cried. I held out my hand. He danced away, plunged, kicked out. Golden dove and knocked me over before the horse could fell me.

The horse ran away into the frozen forest.

Light washed the edge of the sky. Winter's edge chilled the tears on my face. Golden shifted away from wolf, rose as his faery self, picked me up, carried me through the gate and home.

After I had slept, my mother made me dress in my best clothes and took me to a celebration in the queen's court. The warmth was just right in the spacious room, and all the colors bright and clean and pleasing to the eye. The work of artisans was everywhere, leaves woven into our clothes, flowers carved or inlaid on the tables, knotwork patterns painted on the floor and glazed onto the dishes. The smells were light and delicious, some of them flowers, some of them food; ripe fruit, light cakes. Minstrels played, and many danced; those of us who didn't dance sat by rank at tables, and ate and drank and talked.

All the children of my generation were there, seated beside their mothers, dressed well and looking like younger, less troubled versions of the elders.

Golden was not there. He hated affairs such as this.

I sat beside my sister-friend, Henna. The halfbloods, those who were not my siblings and wore their humanity openly instead of hidden against their spines, moved among us, offering fruit and sweets on green glass trays. Everyone ate. Everyone acted as though the trays floated past them unsupported by visible beings.

I touched one serving girl's wrist, and she paused, her yellow eyes wide, and looked at me. Her ears were as pointed as any of ours, her eyes as slanted, her chin as sharp; but she smelled human. She bowed so low her wrist slipped out of my grasp, and then she hurried away.

Henna stared at me.

We were not supposed to notice the halfbloods. We were not supposed to touch them. They were only allowed among us by grace. They should be thankful they were here in faery halls, instead of grubbing in the dirt above. These half-human lesser beings—

Half-human. Who was I to condemn them?

I blinked, gazed around the great hall, saw suddenly half again as many people present. Those of us who stood, carried trays, walked among the seated, slipped past the dancing ones—

More faery than I had looked when I saw my father's face in Golden's mirror.

I did not know the names of any of them. I saw the girl I had touched standing against the wall, whispering to an older boy with round ears. She glanced toward me, dropped her gaze.

Where did they go when they were not serving us? What did they do? Were they kind to strangers, as Robin had been kind?

If I wanted to talk to one of them, I would have to find her sometime when no one else was around. I didn't know if that was even possible, but it might be a thing worth trying.

It might be easier if I looked like my father.

It was one avenue I wanted to explore. And there was another.

I turned to my sister-friend. The skills Henna studied involved weaving: she wove light, water, air, and fire, and sometimes words and music into cloth, spells, food. Had she ever thought about our father? Had it ever occurred to her that he, too, had been a weaver, as he, too, had been a shapeshifter?

Did she ever realize he had been human under everything our dead king had done to give him the power to sire us? Had she ever asked her mother or her teacher what he looked like?

"Come aboveground with me tonight," I whispered to her during a burst of laughter. Henna was the best of my friends, my favorite sister. I wanted to talk to her about what it meant to be children of our father.

She did not answer me until some time had passed.

But at last she said, "All right."

Perhaps the horse would come back, and I could introduce him to another of my father's children. Perhaps she would smell right; I knew I could smell right again.

I did not know what to hope for, but I hoped.

Nina Kiriki Hoffman has sold more than two hundred stories and several novels. Her works have been finalists for the Nebula, World Fantasy, Mythopoeic, Theodore Sturgeon, and Endeavour awards. *The Thread That Binds the Bones* won the Horror Writers Association Bram Stoker Award. Her fantasy novels include *The Silent Strength of Stones*, *A Red Heart of Memories*, *Past the Size of Dreaming*, and *A Fistful of Sky*. Her third short story collection, *Time Travelers, Ghosts, and Other Visitors*, came out in 2003, as well as her most recent novel, *A Stir of Bones*.

In addition to writing, Nina works at a bookstore, does production work for a national magazine, and teaches short story writing through a local community college. She lives in Eugene, Oregon, with several cats, a mannequin, and many strange toys.

Author's Note

"Immersed in Matter" is a piece of a much bigger tapestry, part of the dreamweavings of night, the stories I tell myself on the edge of sleep. I talk these stories out to myself as I lie in the dark. Every once in a while, one gets captured in a poem or trapped on a computer screen or in my journal. This is the second one to make its way into print. ("Flotsam," in the anthology *Firebirds*, is another piece of the picture; chronologically, it happens later than this.)

Most of the children in Owl's generation track down their father eventually.

And I'm sure the horse comes back.

Undine

~

Patricia A. McKillip

All my sisters caught mortals that way. I have more sisters
than I can count, and they've all had more husbands than
they can count. It's easy, they told me. And when you get
tired of them you just let them go. Sometimes they find their
way back to their world, where they sit around a lot with a
gaffed look in their eyes, their mouths loosing words slowly
like bubbles drifting away. Other times they just die in our
world. They don't float like mortals anymore. They sink
down, lie among the water weeds and stones at the bottom,
their skin turning pearly over time, tiny snails clustering in
their hair.

Easy. When it was time for my first, my sisters showed
me how to find my way. In our deep, cool, opalescent pools,
our reedy, light-stained waters, time passes so slowly you
hardly notice it. Things rarely ever change. Even the enormous, jewel-winged dragonflies that dart among the reeds
have been there longer than I have. To catch humans, I
have to rise up into their time, pull them down into ours.

It takes practice, which is why so many of them die.

"But don't worry," my sisters told me blithely. "You'll get the hang of it. When you bring the first one home alive, we'll throw a party."

I had to choose a patch of sunlight in my water and swim up through it, up and up in the light until it blinded me, while I kept a vision of mortals in my mind. What mortals I knew were mostly my sisters' husbands and some mossy-haired, frog-eyed women who had accidentally fallen in love with my snarky water-kelpie cousins as they cavorted among the water lilies in human and horse disguises. But, my sisters assured me, as I moved from our time into theirs my hunger—and my loneliness—would grow. I would be happy to see the human face at the end of my journey. I should not expect to be in the same water there, but it would not be hard at all, they promised, for me to find my way back. I had only to wish and swim.

They gathered so sweetly around me in the water, all languid and graceful, their long hair flowing as they sang me farewell. The singing helped shift me across time; I felt as though I were swimming through their voices as much as through water and light. When I saw the trembling surface of strange water, I could still hear them, the distant singing of water faerie, so lovely, so haunting.

I should have turned at that instant, followed it back. But I felt the odd, shallow depths I had reached. My face and knees were bumping stones and I had to break the surface. I stood up, awkwardly, trying to find my balance in the rocky shallows and pulling my hair out of my face so I could see. I took a breath and smelled it first.

"Yark!" I shrieked. "Gack! What is it?"

I finally untangled the hair over my eyes and shrieked again. Dead fish. I was surrounded by dead fish. Big ones. Hundreds of them, in various stages of decay, wallowing in the water and reeking. They bumped me as I floundered through the stink, their eyes filmy with death where they weren't covered with flies. I wanted to screech again, but I had to breathe to do that. I was panting like a live fish by then, taking short little breaths through my open mouth, trying to get out of the river as fast as I could. The stones were slippery with moss. I flailed, terrified of stumbling and falling into the dead fish. Wearing what I did wasn't helping much; my long dress sagged, wrapped itself around my knees, caught underfoot. At every step, flies swarmed around me from the fish, buzzed into my eyes.

So, half blind, cursing furiously and gasping like a fish, I rose out of the river, and a mortal caught me in his arms.

"What are you doing in there?" he shouted.

I could feel his startled heartbeat, his dry shirt rapidly dampening with me. I opened one eye cautiously. I stood in mud now. I could feel it oozing up between my toes, which didn't improve my mood, but at least I could catch my balance. The mortal I had snared was very cute, with straight golden hair that flopped above one brow, eyes the gentle blue of our limpid skies rather than of the fierce blue-white blaze above our heads. He wore a shirt with a frog sitting on a lily pad and unrolling its enormous tongue to catch a tiny flying horse. A conversation starter, that would have been, if I hadn't just waded out of a river full of one.

I had to answer something, so I said, "I got lost."

"In that dress?"

I looked at it. My sisters had woven it for me out of mosses and river grasses, decorated it with hundreds of tiny bubbles. In this world, it looked like some kind of shimmering cloth overlaid with pearls.

"What's wrong with it?" I demanded, trying to kick away the ribbon of greasy fish scales decorating the hem.

He stared at me, goggling a bit, like the fish. Then his eyes narrowed. "Did you—did you, like, jump off something? After a party? Like a bridge, or something? And instead of drowning you came to in all this—this—" He waved at the appalling river, which was making a sort of gurgling noise as it drained through the fish jammed across it. "What was it? Some guy made you do this?"

I nodded cautiously after a moment. Some guy, yes. I pushed at my hair, trying to make it more presentable. A nasty odor wafted up from it. I couldn't cry—why bother with tear ducts if you are born in water? But I had seen mortals do it, and now I knew why. My first human, and here I was, sinking in mud and stinking while vicious little flies bit my ankles.

Extremely sorry for myself, I sniffed and whuffled piteously, "Yeah. And now I don't know my way home."

"Don't cry—"

"What did you do to all these fish?"

"Me?" he said incredulously. "I just came out here to throw a line in the water. Fishing's great here when the salmon are running. I could smell this all the way out to the highway. I've never seen anything like it."

"Fish can't run," I said crossly; he seemed more interested in them than in me.

"It's an expression," he explained with exasperating patience. "It's what they call it when the salmon swim upriver trying to get back to the waters where they were born so they can spawn."

"Spawn?"

"You know—lay their eggs and fertilize them. Propagate. That's when they're supposed to die." I nodded. That happened to mortals often enough where I lived. "Not like this," he went on. "Not halfway upriver before they've gotten home. And look at this water! It should be deeper and fast-flowing. It's like they couldn't breathe or something in this shallow water. This is all wrong."

He was still fixated on them, staring over my shoulder. I saw his point, though. I could never have dragged him under those pathetic shallows. I sniffed again, to reclaim his attention. His eyes came back to me; he touched my bare arms lightly with his fingers. "Ah, poor kid. What a nightmare. Where do you live? I'll take you home."

I had to think, then, which is not something my sisters warned me would be necessary. "Farther upriver," I said, pleased at my cleverness. I would make him take me to some deep pool where I could lure him under, steal him away from his world, take him back into mine. "But I can't go home like this. Reeking and covered with fish scales. Do you know a place where I can swim it off?"

He considered, torn between me and the dead fish. I rolled my eyes in mortification, hoping none of my sisters had followed to watch. But then, considering myself, I could hardly blame him.

"Sure." He bent down to collect his fishing gear. "I know just the place."

He took me in his truck to his home.

It was a little cottage not far away beneath some immense trees. His dog came out to greet us, wagging its tail politely until it caught a whiff of me. Then it bounded into my arms, howling joyously, nearly knocking me over.

"Whoa!" my mortal said. "Down, Angel. She loves company." Angel was big and golden, with a stupid grin on her face; she acted like she wanted to roll around on the ground with my dress. "Down! My name's Mike, by the way. Mike Taylor. What's yours?"

"Undine." At home we have our private names of course, but to mortals we are all Undines. "Ah—what are we doing here?"

"Undine. Pretty. Come on in. You can wash off in the bathroom; I'll give you some dry clothes to change into. Then I'll take you home. Okay?"

But he wasn't thinking about me as he led me into his house. It was sunny, cluttered and full of dog hair. He waved me into a tiny room which contained a tank, a basin, and a big porcelain mushroom. I had never seen anything like it. Luckily, he turned the water taps on himself. Some gunky water spurted out. And then it ran clear, so clear I had to reach out and touch it, smell it.

"Sorry I don't have a shower, just this tub. The pipes pick up dirt sometimes," he said unintelligibly. "You have to clear them out. There's lots of hot water though. I'll bring you some clothes in a minute. First I have to make a phone call."

I filled the tub to the top, managing to stop the flow before I made a waterfall over the side. As it was, I slopped plenty on the floor when I pulled my dress off and got in. I submerged myself completely, rolling and rolling in the warmth, my hair growing silky again, coiling around my naked limbs. I heard Mike's voice now and then when my ears came out of the water. Fish, he was talking about. Not the mysterious, enchanting young woman he had met on the river's edge.

Dead fish.

"I called the Forestry Department," he announced, breezing in with his arms full of ugly clothes. "And the Fish and Wildlife Department. And—" He stopped abruptly, the absent look fading from his eyes as I stood up in the water. "Oh," he whispered. "Sorry." He didn't move. I hummed softly, lifting my streaming hair away from my neck with upraised arms. The clothes dropped onto the floor. I held out my hand. He stepped into the water, forgetting even that he was wearing boots. The splash we made as I pulled him down hit the ceiling and pretty much emptied the tub, but neither of us cared.

But there was nowhere for me to take him except down the drain.

He lay in my arms afterward, spellbound, contentedly talking, even though he had to balance his drenched boots on the faucets and he was squashing me. I let him ramble, while I tried to think of a way out of our predicament.

"I don't make much," he said, "at the Sport 'n Bait Shop. But I don't need much to keep up this place, and my truck's paid for, and there's just Angel and me . . . I hunt and fish whenever I can. I love the outdoors, don't you?"

"Water," I murmured. "I love water."

"Yeah. . . . That's why this thing with the fish is so upsetting. Turns out it's all political, that's what Fish and Wildlife told me. The water that normally comes downriver got diverted fifty miles upriver. Can you believe that? To water crops in the Saskill Valley, which got hit by drought this summer. Dead crops or dead fish, take your pick. Well, fish don't vote." He had begun to fidget; in another moment he would realize he was lying with his pants down and his boots on in a bathtub with a stranger.

I kissed him, felt his muscles slacken. He babbled on, his voice dreamy again. "You don't have to go home right away, do you? I'll take you home later. We can build a fire, grill some burgers, go for a moonlight swim. . . ."

"Moonlight swim, yes."

"Well, we could have anyway, except that I doubt there's enough water anywhere along the river around here to do much but wade in." He was beginning to brood again. Then this noise rattled through my spell, some kind of weirdness clamoring for attention that made all his muscles tense. His boots jumped off the faucet; he rolled and floundered clumsily against me, groping for balance.

"Sorry, babe, gotta get that. It's probably Sam. She's always on top of stuff like this."

He sloshed out of the bathroom to go talk about fish

again, leaving me in a puddle on the bottom of the tub.

That was the last I saw of water until dawn.

Another shrillness woke me when it was still dark. I didn't remember where I was, and something moist was prodding my cheek and panting dankly. Then Mike switched on a light, and Angel, her grin inches from my eyes, licked my face.

"Garf," I said, wanting to cry again because this was not supposed to happen.

"Sorry, babe. Gotta go." Mike pulled a shirt over his head, popped out again, looking hopeful. "Come with me?"

"Will there be water?"

"Oh, yeah."

Which is why, an hour later, I was back with the dead fish, wearing Mike's clothes, standing on the riverbank with a sign in my hands that said PROTECT THE WILDERNESS IN YOU along with dozens of other dour, cranky humans, some wearing badges, others watching us through one-eyed monsters on their shoulders from a big truck labeled KXOX NEWS TEAM.

Mike keeps promising me that soon, soon, we will go out and find that moonlit pool, or that deep, deep sunlit lake, and we will float together, locked in one another's arms, our breaths trailing bubbles behind us as we kiss, and then we will swim beyond the boundaries of mortal love. Soon. But then, on our way to that magical place, the truck will suddenly detour to follow a creek that's turning all the colors of the rainbow and smelling like garbage. Or it will find the lake with the signs along its shores Warning of the Dangers of Swimming Here. Then he spends hours on the phone with Sam or Kyle or Vanessa, and then wakes me at dawn to walk in circles carrying a sign. And I still hope, because what else can I do?

But I am beginning to wonder if I'll be stranded here like a fish out of water for a mortal lifetime with this human, sweet as he is, before I can ever swim my way back to that deep, sun-stained pool where I was born.

Patricia A. McKillip's novels include *The Forgotten Beasts of Eld*, which won the first World Fantasy Award in 1975; The Riddle-Master Trilogy, of which *Harpist in the Wind* was nominated for a Hugo; *Something Rich and Strange*, which won the 1995 Mythopoeic Award; *Winter Rose*, which was nominated for a Nebula; *The Changeling Sea*; and *Ombria in Shadow*, which won both the Mythopoeic Award and the World Fantasy Award. Her most recent novel is *Od Magic*. She has also written a number of short stories, both science fiction and fantasy. She lives in Oregon, with her husband, David Lunde.

Author's Note

In Oregon, I can see water out of nearly every window of our house. We live very close to a bay, which, through my writing room window, looks like a lake with small, forest-covered mountains on the distant side. The bay changes constantly, sometimes into mud flats when the tide goes out, or into a misty, mysterious stretch of water without boundaries when the fog rolls in, or into a brilliant, moody, wind-tossed blue with rainbows stretching over it after a storm. Mermaids, kelpies, and undines live in such waters, I'm sure, which is probably why one surfaced in my head for this story.

The water I described as Undine's home came from the very detailed and romantic paintings of the Pre-Raphaelites. The water she finds herself in when she surfaces is a river in Oregon that made national news when huge numbers of salmon trying to get home to spawn were found dead in it. I left unanswered the question about whether my Undine, trying to find her way back to her watery birthplace as well, has better luck than the salmon.

The Oakthing

Gregory Maguire

Though the sky was a peerless blue, there had been thunder since dawn. Low thunder, ground thunder, leaving an acrid odor in twists of gray gauze that the wind pushed across the fields. As if a hand had rubbed a rod of graphite against the horizon, sketching vertical shafts of ghost in the warming day. It was the foot soldiers pushing, though, pushing the line, and it was the artillery behind them and flanking them that made such persuasive thunder.

The farm was not quite in their way. Not yet; it was off to one side.

A family had lived there for many generations. The place was called—with a light mocking of the habits of gentlemen farmers to name their estates—Sous Vieux Chêne—Under the Old Oak. To the villagers of Remigny, three miles east, it had been known only as the Gauthier place.

But at this point, there were few left in Remigny to call it anything. Most villagers, sensibly, had fled. The Gauthiers, capable farmers with farmers' stout common sense, were less practiced at dealing with invading armies. Though they did discuss the problem.

"We can't leave. There are the crops to bring in." The father was stubborn.

His wife more or less agreed, though she pointed out, "Your main crop is not wheat." She'd glanced sideways at their lovely child, their slightly dim, affectionate Dominique. Quite old enough to attract the eye of war-maddened soldiers. "Might it be silly to risk her safety for the sake of our wheat?"

It was a topic of discussion they had played with all summer, as one by one their farmer neighbors and the villagers of Remigny had fled to points south. Surely the line would shift? The Huns would not dare to drive their war machine through Gauthier fields!

That the Gauthiers held on to their convictions with such tenacity indicated a certain sort of family insanity. Neighbors had tried to reason with the Gauthiers, but the Gauthiers, back as far as any could remember, had not been a reasonable line. They had laughed and drunk their coffee with cow's milk and said, "But what means this *Schrecklichkeit*, this German frightfulness, to a Gauthier?" And said it over and over until there was no one left to hear it.

But with the dead and the starved animals all around, and the ruination of sugar beet fields, and the 42-centimeter howitzers pounding the center of the market town eight miles farther east . . . it was hard to concentrate on wheat.

Finally the Great Panic came home to the current crop of Gauthiers. They were interrupted at their praying of the Angelus by a cloudburst of cannonfire nearer than ever. At last they came to their senses, or lost their nerve, or both at once.

They cobbled together what they could. An agricultural wagon suitable for the transport of hay, a smaller cart that a donkey could pull. They spent the morning piling what supplies were left, and a few pieces of the better furnishings, as if, meeting a *caisson* on the road, they could barter for safety with a choice armoire or a nice tureen boasting swan heads for handles.

In the end, the thunder leaning more heavily upon them, the artillery nearing, their exit was undignified, disorganized, and incomplete. Madame Marie-Laure Gauthier and docile, sentimental Dominique had hitched up the team and left with the wagon, toweringly overloaded. Around its bulk and over the noise of the invasion they shouted revised plans for their rendezvous.

Hector Gauthier followed a few minutes later in the cart, taking the last of the cheeses. The cow had been dead for a week, likely of terror, and so no milk to sprinkle on the doorstep, to sour and keep the little people out.

And thus good-bye to Sous Vieux Chêne, good-bye, good-bye. *Au revoir,* we hope! *A demain,* with luck. Good-bye. The German armies, which had romped through Belgium and showed every likelihood of tromping through the boulevards of Paris, had managed at last to scatter even the stubborn and mentally giddy Gauthiers. *Incroyable.*

All of them, that is, except Madame Mémé Gauthier, the grandmother.

She had left her seat in the wagon because of an urge to

use the outhouse. Her daughter-in-law had bawled around the edge of the sacks of bedding that Hector would need to take his own feeble mother, she could not wait any longer, Dominique would not be safe! But the thunder of cannon had smudged the sound of her voice. Hector Gauthier hadn't heard the full message, nor could he see around the worldly Gauthier goods heaped high in the wagon. When Mme. Marie-Laure Gauthier left, her husband assumed his mother was safely on board, cursing and praying the rosary simultaneously.

When Mémé Gauthier emerged refreshed, the wagon was gone. The cart was gone. Since the cow was still dead, Mémé Gauthier was glad her sense of smell was largely gone, too. And her hearing was not what it had once been, so the cannon noise wasn't objectionable.

She was well into her eighth decade, and frightened by little. She'd been born in the 1830s, when this was just the Gauthier place, not Sous Vieux Chêne. The old oak was old even in her childhood, and just a tree, just an oak, not the name of a headache or a property. Still, though she'd cocked an eyebrow at news of uprisings in Paris, continental upheavals, even the invention of a steam engine to power a locomotive (she'd seen one once, too!), her life had been lived solely on the farm.

She was only mildly disappointed to have been forgotten by her son and his family. Indeed, she'd likely have forgotten herself, had she been in charge of the exodus.

Mémé Gauthier collected her walking stick—a nice bit of thorn with a smoothly knobbed head—and made her way through the forecourt of the barn buildings and around to the house's front door. Her son had locked it, but he'd likely have left the key in its usual place: a hollow in the eponymous oak. She had to think a bit about how to reach that high.

Finally she went and found a milking stool and dragged it from the barn where it was doing no one any good anyway. When she got to the oak, she saw that a number of its limbs had given up and fallen to the ground, like the spokes of a blown-out umbrella. What was left was a spiky pillar of old dead wood, knobbed with woody warts a century old.

But the hiding place was intact, and the stool afforded her enough height to grope in the hollow. Sure enough, she secured the key, an oversized iron thing from the days of her own father.

So she opened up the house that had just been closed against the invading armies. She invaded it herself. Well, why not, it was her own house. And she sat down on a chair with a rush bottom to think about what to do next.

Likely she dozed. She napped a dozen times a day. Sometimes she thought she must doze even while she walked, for she didn't always remember where she was, when she came to think about it, nor where she was going.

When she opened her eyes, the trapezoids of sunlight had shifted across the terra-cotta tiles. Their lines were more acute, the patches of light more slanting.

She squinted and rubbed her eyes. Was that a house cat in the sun? Surely not. All the house cats had long ago run out and drowned themselves from terror, so far as anyone could tell. Even the mice had gone *en vacances*.

The thing made a kind of a curtsey. Or perhaps it was a

rude gesture. At any rate, neither cats nor mice stood nine inches tall on hind legs. Unless some distant zoo in Louvain had been bombed and its monkey population scattered across the border into la belle France, this was a visitation by a little creature.

Where were her spectacles? She had given up needle-work in her seventies, and the more ripely adolescent her granddaughter had become, the less often Mémé Gauthier had wanted to look closely at her. "You wait right here, you," she said, and went to look in the chiffonier. But the chiffonier was gone. What a *cretin* her son was! Fleeing from an invading army with a chiffonier! Anyway, her spectacles were gone with it.

When she came back, the creature was still there. Mémé Gauthier took considerable pains to get down on her knees, the better to see. While she was there she prayed for peace, and then she prayed she'd be able to get back up again. First, though, she looked to see what manner of mischief this thing might prove to be.

It was, she decided, a tree sprite of some sort. In sorry shape. Sorely in need of succor, or attention, or perhaps concealment; she couldn't tell. It seemed an angular knot of twigs from one angle; and then again there were tines of thorn and froths of densely clumped root. Like pubic hair, or the hair in armpits, rangy, airy, and with a vegetable odor strong enough that even Mémé Gauthier could appreciate it. It was matted with mud that little by little was drying and falling in small clods on the floor.

But the thing—male, female, or neither, or both, or something else again, she couldn't tell—seemed to be, in the term used by those who practice the art of war, shell-shocked. It shook gently. If it had hands, it rubbed its elbows; if it had knees, or fetlocks, they knocked together. It did have something of a chin, and a yawp for a mouth, but its eyes were slitted closed like a newborn infant's, and its ears hung low, as if they'd died two separate deaths.

"And so a bit of company for Madame Mémé Gauthier," she said courteously. "It's thoughtful of you to call, when my kin have seen fit to abandon me."

The creature's shoulders, or high-slung hips, or airy ribs, shook, perhaps not at the actual sentiment but at the sound of a voice sent so obviously its way.

"You're in need of some comfort, but of what sort?" she asked. "And whatever enticed you to come in?"

The house had been vacated for no more than an hour. But then, because the cow was dead, she'd been unable to splash on the doorstep the customary sour-milk prohibition against intruders.

"I suppose you're welcome," said Mémé Gauthier. "But I can't sit around and play a hand of cards with you. It may take a day or two for my feckless relatives to realize they've misplaced me. And the Lord alone knows whether one of them will be able to retrace their steps to collect me, considering the advancing armies. I'm on my own—present company excluded—and must fend for myself."

It had been some time since she'd been able to say that, and the prospect gave her some pleasure. Let's see, what was needed first? To lock the doors, to secure the valuables, to tend to the animals, to water the vegetables, to clean the baby, to bank the coals?

There was no need to lock the doors, as it turned out, as there were neither valuables, nor animals, nor babies, nor coals, nor much by way of vegetables, for that matter. The kitchen garden offered some carrots, some kale in the act of bolting, potatoes in their secret graves, no doubt, and various herbs for savor. Though herbs were a bit difficult to savor on their own.

Mémé Gauthier scraped together what she could. The farm had never been electrified, and the portable oil lamps were gone. As the afternoon dragged on Mémé Gauthier's knees began to hurt, so she didn't trust herself to scale a chair and light the fancy ceiling lamp in the salon. She'd make just a small fire in the hearth, to lend some comfort and take the worst chill out of her fingers, and then she'd burrow under a blanket and wait till the gray dawn.

The creature's eyes hadn't yet opened, quite, but she thought it sensed her movements. When she went to the herb yard, it wandered toward that part of the property; when she went back to the pump, it retreated. But if she went farther—to the gate, to see if dim Hector or his Marie-Laure were hurrying back to save her—the oakthing was uncomfortable, and fidgeted like a dog or a worrying child. Having gained the house, it didn't want to leave, and it didn't want her to go either.

That's what it was, she decided, an oakthing. Evacuated from the battered tree that gave the farm its name.

"Scared out of your own home, you," she said to it, "just as Hector and Marie-Laure are scared out of theirs! Everyone packing up like tortoises and moving on. Well, I'm staying put, and let the Hun have it if he must. I'm too old to be of interest to a young soldier, in that certain way, I mean, and I'm too tedious and insignificant to detain an army in its mission. I've no food to steal and no virtue to protect, so I've nothing to lose. But what's your excuse?"

The oakthing collapsed into something resembling a sitting position, and put what it had of a face into what it had of hands.

"If it's the tree you're mourning," she said, "the old black umbrella that gives this farm its name, you're wasting your time. In its day it has sent out ten hundred thousand emissaries on its own behalf. Maybe more. Every spring, the acorns tumbled in the winds, and the oak tree has ten thousand cousins across Normandy and Flanders alone. If your particular hidey-hole has collapsed, well, the tree doesn't care. Its roots are in the future."

She peered down at the oakthing. "Its roots are in the future. As are mine, you thing. Dominique has loins as ripe as any old oak tree in springtime, and she will litter the future with her issue, which will be mine, too, if you look at it a certain way."

But perhaps the oakthing had no issue.

What should she do for it? Given that she could do little for herself, had she an obligation to put out more effort for an ambulatory clot of vegetable matter? If it were a baby or a cat, she would give it milk.

"The cats are all gone," she told it.

And that, she saw, was part of its problem. It may have lived in a tree, but it lived near a farm, and all farms had mice. So all farms had cats. And all cats drank milk.

In a desolate summer, even the mice were gone, and the

cats were dead, and the cows were dry or dead or gone, and the farm's slender economy no longer afforded a saucer of milk at the door for the cat. And while milk souring would keep an oakthing and its cousins away, the fresh milk put out for a cat was probably the oakthing's primary diet.

She would think about it in her sleep, and dream up a solution if she could.

But Mémé Gauthier had no sleep that night, for the artificial thunder of the German advance and the scattershot pebble-rain of feeble French resistance punched holes in her efforts to doze. When there was enough light to rise safely, she did, and rinsed the chamber pot by the pump, and then brushed her hair and cleaned her teeth.

The oakthing, it seemed, was gone, and she felt a sort of pity for it. Had it dried up in the night, or maybe reclaimed what was left of its tree? Had it found her unsympathetic? Had it abandoned her? Had she anything more important to do, as the invasion swept field by field from the northeast, than to worry about a twiggy figment of rural superstition?

Perhaps not, which meant her life had shriveled down to very little, too.

So she was glad when she found it, huddled under the overturned bucket. The overturned milk bucket. It seemed to be shedding more of itself, in scraps of bark and trails of blond dust. "You're wanting me to find milk for the cat," said Mme. Gauthier. "As if I haven't anything better to do."

But, in fact, she hadn't. So she put on her rubber boots and took an umbrella, as if its flimsy ribs and taut cotton skin could protect her from shrapnel, and she clutched at her walking stick, and went off down the lane.

There were four farms this way, two the other, and across the ditch and two fields was a one-room schoolhouse that had once had a goat tethered in its yard. The farms were farther but the ditch was a problem; she wasn't sure she trusted herself to maneuver across a plank. Still, she remembered that the goat had had kids rather late in the season, and though they might have been slaughtered or stolen or died of fright, if the goat had been left behind she might still have milk. And Mémé Gauthier had not lived on a farm all her life without learning how to milk a goat if a goat had milk to give.

"Are you coming?" she asked the oakthing.

It didn't answer, but spat at her as a child might: wanting the fruits of her expedition but resenting her for leaving anyway.

"Thankless," she told it, with some satisfaction.

And as she left the yard, she looked again at the sundered trunk of the oak tree. Had one of yesterday's thunder blasts been real weather from God, accompanied by vengeful lightning? Or had a snippet of bomb gone awry and curled the old wood into lazy scrapes as if it were made of butter? The bushels of leaves still turning in the breeze—still attached to their twigs, poking from branches, dividing from the stems of thick split limbs—the leaves didn't know they were dead yet.

She closed up the umbrella, enjoying a spit of rain on her brow, and used it as a second cane. Her arthritic wrists ached by the time she was halfway across the plank, edging sideways inch by inch, but the strategy worked, and she didn't overbalance. The meadow was full of sumptuous hay ready for harvest, and no one to do it. It would die, too.

Swarms of summer bugs insensible of the military action made a second weather of droning commotion at her shoulder height. She thrashed her way through, keeping her eyes on the roof of the schoolhouse in its thicket of poplars.

These trees, it turned out, were also splintered, and the east-facing wall of the school, once a rosy pink stone, was scorched with explosives and had buckled into the yard. The shutters were blown off their hinges or straight through the shattered windows. A few sets of uncollected wooden shoes lay marvelously undisturbed beside what remained of the door. No children had been here for a week at least, maybe more. But the goat, crazed with grief and solitude, was still there, bucking against its tethers, its forehead scraped bloody raw in its efforts to escape.

She had a need. She had the goat. The goat had milk. She had fingers gnarled with arthritis. What she didn't have was a bucket. She'd forgotten that.

"You, stop your barracking," she told the goat. "I've got a little baby at home that needs what you give. I can't think with all your noise, though."

She hunted about in the debris, poking with her walking stick and her umbrella. There wasn't so much as a single tin cup to salvage.

So in the end, with blistered hands, she milked the goat into the largest of the pair of wooden shoes. Then she loosened the buttons on her farm-dress and sank the shoes as best as she could, toe-end down, between what remained of her breasts. She tied herself up as well as she could. The milk slopped as she moved, but she would go slowly, and not all of it would slop, she hoped. It was the best she could do. She was eighty-six, or eighty-four, or something—what could the oakthing expect?

After a few steps homeward, she turned back: why not bring the goat with her? Could she get it across the plank? If it overturned her into the ditch she'd die there, damply.

She never got the chance to try. The goat shied at the first opportunity and twisted its tether out of her feeble grasp. Into the overgrown fields it disappeared, bleating in hysterical joy, which she imagined would be short-lived, given the panic of the times.

The wind smelled as if it was burning. The sun had gotten high the meanwhile, and it winked brassily now and then, colored by the smoke of gunfire. More of the meadow was thrashed down than she had managed by herself. She imagined stalking ogres with breath like roasting gunpowder, and the stink of hot metal. Feet larger than human boots could hold were responsible for the wreckage. If not gathered immediately, mold would set in, and rot, and the hay go useless, and the animals go hungry.

Only there were no animals, she remembered, so let the hay be stomped upon by ogres.

The return trip took her longer than she'd imagined. Well, she was tired with her efforts. The sun was already weaseling down the western skies, shimmying between big-bosomed clouds. One of the farms she'd thought about rooting around was, it seemed, on fire. The rutted track heading that way was muddy, torn up with iron-hooped wheels. Cannon had come through here, and horses, leaving their fresh stink.

But there was nothing at Sous Vieux Chêne for a scavenging corps, surely, nothing worth burning even?

And the oakthing—was it all right? Was it still there?

She couldn't go any faster than she could go. If the oakthing was going to die in the next four minutes for lack of fresh milk, it would just have to die. She had been inching forward in her life over all these decades at her own pace, and, as she well knew, things on farms died, in their time. Herself included, in her time, whenever that was.

But her breath came faster and, really, despite her farmer's philosophies, she *was* hurrying.

The door was kicked off one of its hinges and clods of mud were mulishly deposited on what had been a properly clean farmhouse floor. Beyond that, though, the house seemed intact. The advancing army had found nothing to steal, nothing to eat, and no one to rape, and perhaps the oakthing's need for milk had saved Mémé Gauthier herself. Taking her safely offstage at the right moment.

Not that she cared to be saved, particularly. Saved for what? To starve to death over the period of a week or two, watching the sun rise and fall, and hearing the crickets of late summer crisply gnaw through her last minutes, sounding like the merciless throb of a pendulum, until the pendulum finally wound down for good?

But she cared about the oakthing. After settling the shoes

carefully in a dry sink, and propping them up with some towels so they couldn't slope over and let the milk slop out, she went to hunt for it.

She found it clinging to the headboard of Dominique's low-slung bed. It looked more like a bug now, and its anxious movements were more twitchy than ever. It scrambled up and down the crudely carved post, inspecting the face of the man who lay with his head upon Dominique's thin pillow, adhering to it in a fracturing skin of dried blood and vomit.

"I *ought* to have managed that goat," said Mémé Gauthier. "But she managed me better than I could do her."

The man was a German soldier. A wound opened on the side of his neck like a red cabbage severed with a knife. For all her long life as a farmwife, Mémé Gauthier had never seen human anatomy laid quite this open to inspection. She was rather intrigued. The oakthing trembled in revulsion. It skittered down, looked at the wound, at the hideous mess of leakage, at the scorched brows and glossy burned temple, at the long elegant drawing-room nose and neat teeth, perfectly intact and as pearly as baby onions, not a brown one among them.

"It's the enemy," said Mémé Gauthier. "It's the German army."

The German army breathed in with long breaths, like a bellows with a leak, and when the German army breathed out, flecks of dried blood danced with a copper brilliance in the slanting afternoon light.

The oakthing twisted its fingers and pointed. There was a rifle on the floor, and a leather satchel.

"I know rifles," she said to the oakthing. "I've shot mad dogs in my day, and a horse who had to be done in, too. And I've fired over the heads of brigands and priests who had too much interest in the affairs of the household."

But she didn't touch the rifle. She pawed through the satchel instead, hoping to find some dried bread, some rations, some identification. There were a few documents in German; she couldn't read them. Whoever had left the soldier here, however, had already done what foraging there was to be done. She found nothing useful but a long needle and a spool of thread.

She lit the kitchen fire with some kindling and she threw in some wooden spoons to build up the flame, for she couldn't take the time to hunt for anything else. She held the needle in the heat for as long as she could, to guard against contamination, and when it had cooled so that she could handle it, she settled herself on the edge of Dominique's bed. She stitched up the wound as well as she could. Without her spectacles, she couldn't scrutinize her work. The edges didn't quite match, and the blood began to flow again, but not torrentially. She had a sense, perhaps a false one, that she was doing some good.

She was pleased. She wanted him well enough to be able to sit up in bed and look at her in the face before she shot him between the eyes.

The oakthing came down and settled on his shoulder, for all the world like the parrot on the shoulder of a pirate. "You belong to the oak, and the oak belongs to the farm, and the German army is a trespasser!" said Mémé Gauthier in disgust. "Get away from there, you. You traitor."

But the oakthing didn't attend to insults. It didn't care. It settled its twiggy apparatus of fingers against the fellow's wound as if, in the absence of milk, blood might substitute. Or maybe it liked invading armies who blasted its home, drove off the farmers it lived parasitically upon, turned the greens of the world into browns, and the late summer skies into boiling black hellfires.

There was still the matter of food, and Mémé Gauthier now had not eaten for more than a day. Though she was prepared to die of malnourishment, her fairly ample form would require her to starve for a while first, and she wasn't eager for that experience. Furthermore she didn't want to nurse a marauder into some semblance of health and then herself pass away before she had a chance to kill him.

Perhaps she ought just pull the trigger, get it over with? Why exact the vengeance of terror upon him? He was a young thing, and hardly more than a flea on the flank of Kaiser Wilhelm's brute force. His was a tender and suffering face, in its way. But his was the face of war, his was the presence of the enemy: that was what the war had brought her. And war would be her death at last, at her ripe old age, so he was as good as the Angel of Death. So it gave her a cruel pleasure and a sense of final accomplishment to consider slaying the Angel of Death before he could, in his time, slay her. She hadn't asked for his company, after all. Who does?

She decided to sleep on the matter, for now she was certain she would sleep. "Come away from him, you," she said to the oakthing, who pulled a face and—perhaps—stuck out a flaking tongue at her. But obeyed. It scrabbled down. Mémé Gauthier covered the soldier as best she could with a mangy horse blanket found in the stable. Then she settled herself in a chair. She was afraid to sleep lying down for fear she wouldn't be able to get up.

She hadn't bothered to pull the shutters to. She'd always liked daylight, and there was precious little of it left for her. The oakthing sat upon the sill of the window. After a while her eyes became accustomed to the dark and she could see the oakthing quivering. She didn't know if it was sleeping, or keeping guard, or merely waiting for her to get up and do something else. It looked more like a homunculus at night, when the light was poor, more like a little human or a sprite of some sort. She closed her eyes, thinking, It probably hasn't the capacity to see its own death as well as I can see mine. One doesn't need spectacles to see *that*.

She slept better than usual. Well, all that effort expended yesterday, at getting the milk. The milk! It was her first thought upon awakening. She'd neglected to give the milk to the oakthing. By now it would have found the milk, and drunk it, surely?

A warm rain drummed and let up, drummed and let up, against the glass. The oakthing was back on the bedstead keeping watch over the hostage. The soldier seemed no better or worse, though his sleep was even and his smell more foul. The milk, it turned out, was still there in the shoes. She put a finger in it to check. Already beginning to sour slightly.

"If you're to have this, a little breakfast, come and have it," she said, and prepared to tip the milk into a shallow dish and set it upon the floor. "Here, thingy."

Before she could manage, though—complicated movements, to reach down that far without toppling over for good—there was a sound through the windy rain in the yard. It was common enough, a farm sound, no different than any she'd heard any day of her long life in this same home. Simply the sound of someone pushing through the gate of the kitchen garden and coming along the pebbled path. She put her hand to her chest and gasped. So war does this to us, that quickly; it makes the most common of experiences foreign. "Yes, what?" she hissed at the noise. Surely it was the comrades of the soldier come back to fetch him. She would kill them, too, if she proved able to get to the chamber in time to get the gun. Damn, why had she left it on the floor by the bedside?

"Bring me the gun," she called to the oakthing, though she doubted it could understand her words, much less lift such a heavy thing and carry it.

The morning intruder paused on the doorstep. As if sensing the customs of the farm this century past, the intruder stopped and wiped the mud from boots against the granite stone set just so for that purpose. Then the door swung open and Mémé Gauthier stood up, reared her shoulders back, to face the next consequence of her fate and folly. "You!" she said, nearly spitting with irritation and, perhaps, relief. "You!" It was her granddaughter.

"I told them you'd be here," said Dominique in her airy way. She whipped a scarf from her head and sluiced the rain from her hair. "You old dog, giving them the slip like that."

"And they—they sent you back for me!" She trembled with rage at her son and daughter-in-law.

"They did not," said Dominique calmly, perhaps a bit proudly. "They didn't know I was leaving. If you could give them the slip, so could I."

"Girl, you're mad, madder than the rest of them. If they find out you've returned, they'll have to cross back through these treacherous reaches to rescue you! At least, when it was just me, they could shrug and say, *Alors*, it was her madness, God bless the bitch. But you have just consigned your parents to taking a terrible risk!"

"I left a note that I was going to Paris," she said calmly.

"Oh," said her grandmother. Maybe Dominique wasn't quite as slow as she always seemed. "Well, that was smart."

"And it wasn't all that hard to get through," said Dominique. "The roads were dry for half the night, and I kept to the shadows. I cut across the fields if I thought I heard the sound of boots thumping or horses. It was worse at the end, with the rain beating down, but that also kept early morning activity down, I think. So I had no trouble."

"You might have been raped, and beaten, and killed," said Mémé Gauthier. "Your parents struggle so hard to remove you from danger, and you thwart them. You taunt them. Why did you come back, *ma cherie*? And furthermore, did you bring any food?"

"You think I had time to market?" asked Dominique. "You think there is much more in the town than there is here? I came back because I didn't think you'd be able to manage alone, Grandmère. I couldn't see you foraging about the other farms for stores of dried food forgotten in corners of sheds, and the winter coming on."

"It's the highest of high summers!" said Mémé Gauthier. She had no intention of lasting into the early fall; the notion was laughable.

"I didn't come a moment too soon," said Dominique. "You've lost your mind even more than usual. I see you've got some milk from somewhere and stored it in your shoes?"

"I couldn't reach the pitcher on the high shelf. Don't be disrespectful." She was proud of having gotten that milk. "You'll have some for breakfast."

"I will, when I'm ready. First I need to lie down for an hour. It was an arduous walk, all the night long, and I'm exhausted from the excitement."

"No, don't settle in your room, come out here and lie on the floor, keep me company—"

"You want company, come sit in my room; I need to lie down," she said, and pushed through to the hall, and her voice went up and up.

Her scream woke the man.

"Now you've ruined everything," said Mémé Gauthier crossly. "He's not at all ready to kill. He wasn't even ready to get up yet."

The oakthing was sitting on the floor with its hands around the rifle trigger. It was unclear to Mémé Gauthier whether Dominique even noticed it. Perhaps it just looked like a scrap of broken branch to her; indeed, in the daylight, that's what it looked to the old woman.

"You've captured the German army?" said Dominique in wonder. "Grandmère, how capable of you. Rude, though, to give him my bed. Why not yours?"

"He took your mattress for himself, without invitation, and my bedding is all gone to town or to hell or somewhere. Come away, girl."

"He's very weak," said Dominique, who had had a way with the sick ewe and the lamb that wouldn't suckle. "Some moron of a comrade sewed up his wound with a pretty poor eye for style, I'll tell you that."

"You try it, with no lamplight and a spot of arthritis in your wrists!"

"Oh, Grandmère," said Dominique, "you did it? I'm proud of you." She moved forward, nearly stepping on the oakthing, stepping over the rifle. The soldier looked neither startled nor even particularly interested, but he was awake enough to track her with his eyes as she crossed the room and sat right down on the bed. "He needs a good washing, first, and then that milk, I think."

"I haven't gotten the strength to prime the pump yet," said Mémé Gauthier. "I'm only just awake myself." She corrected her tone. "Dominique, the man is a soldier of the invading army that scared your family from our home. You can't wash his wounds and set him out in the sun to heal as if this were a pavilion for invalids. We have to kill him and get rid of the body. For all we know, his comrades will come back looking for him within the day or so."

"He has nice eyes," she said. "Good morning, you. Can you hear me? Can you understand me?"

"*Imbécile!*" Mémé Gauthier didn't have words ripe enough to express her degree of astonishment. "Dominique, come away from him! I forbid this! Don't even talk to him!

That is aiding the enemy, a crime against your family, a crime against France!"

"He's a man who has been bleeding in my bed," said the girl. "I'm not proposing he be elevated to a monsignor of the church. Grandmère, please. *Guten tag?*"

The soldier blinked at the German greeting. His head lurched a bit on his neck as if he was feeling a twinge of pain, and thereby remembering he was alive. *"Guten tag?"* he mumbled back.

"Give me the milk," said the granddaughter. "Bring it here, Grandmère."

"I collected it for the tree sprite," said Mémé Gauthier, hopelessly.

"What tree sprite is that?"

Mémé Gauthier couldn't speak anymore. She just pointed to the floor. But her granddaughter wasn't looking. The oakthing lay down against the rifle, lengthening, matching its thorny limbs to the long steel shaft and the scratched and polished wooden handle. "It needs the milk more than we do," said the grandmother, but she knew her voice was too frail, and that Dominique wouldn't listen.

The farm is dead, she said to the oakthing.

And so are you, it answered, or nearly. But you have a child here who will find a way to live and keep life going, cost what it will, and I have nothing.

I will get you the milk myself, she told it.

It is not for me. The milk was never for me, it answered. It was for the life around me, and I lived on its edges.

"It's cold in here; the rain makes everything raw," said

Dominique decisively. "We'll build up a fire, Grandmère, and drag him into the kitchen for warmth. Don't worry," she added, at the grandmother's grieved expression. "I won't lose my head. I won't lose my heart to him, either. I'll keep my hands on the rifle." She swept the gun off the floor with one hand. With her other hand, she collected the litter of wood and leaves, for use as tinder.

Mémé Gauthier put her head in her hands and wished to die. But she was of strong country stock and, it seemed, life had not finished with her yet. So in time she straightened her shoulders and went to tend the fire, pour the milk, hector her granddaughter, confound the enemy, mop out the rain that seeped in under the door, and mourn, in a dry-eyed way, the living and the dead.

Gregory Maguire is a novelist who writes for adults and children. He now lives with his family outside of Boston, Massachusetts, though he has lived in Europe as well. His work for children includes the popular Hamlet Chronicles, the latest installment of which is *A Couple of April Fools*. For adults, his most recent work is *Son of a Witch*. His best-known work, *Wicked*, is the basis of a recent Broadway musical of the same name. Maguire has published fiction and criticism in *Ploughshares*, *The New York Times Book Review*, and other journals. He is also a founder and co-director of Children's Literature New England, Inc.

His Web site is www.gregorymaguire.com

Author's Note

The inspiration for the Oakthing is the drawings of Arthur Rackham, particularly those for *Peter Pan in Kensington Gardens*. While I didn't go back to look again at those color plates, I well recall the spiky, thorn-nosed creatures scrabbling about the hedges and hiding behind the palings of iron fences. They were very Edwardian creatures, those inventions of Rackham and J. M. Barrie. They were related both to the remnants of superstitious rural beliefs and to the Victorian craze for fairies-at-the-bottom-of-the-garden. For my story, I transposed one of them to the Continent, at the very close of the Edwardian age, when the first of the century's terrible wars blasted modernity into our faces. What simple rural creature could survive such an onslaught of blood and terror? And yet—look at this collection—in so many strange and clever ways, the small creatures have survived. They are hugely camouflaged, like the cleverest of chameleons. Despite the theme of my story, the fairy creatures have endured—sometimes in the pages of books for children, but elsewhere, too, if you know where to look.

Foxwife

∾

Hiromi Goto

Do not venture into the forest when the sun shines through falling rain. This is when the kitsune hold their wedding ceremony. It would be wise not to disturb them.

Yumeko stood in the stern of her small punt. The tan waters were quiet, only the buzz and whine of marsh insects filled the air. She held her paddle loosely in her coarse palm. The morning sun, penetrating shifting layers of clouds, cast a hazy light. To the north, a cluster of punts bobbed on rougher waters. She would not be joining them. When the girls and women mended nets and wove riddles between sisters and neighbors, Yumeko's name was never called. She cast her nets alone.

Yumeko stared up at her neighbor's domehouse. Perched on wooden stilts it rose high above the waterline. Her hard palm squeezed around her paddle. It was so difficult to ask a favor from Ikenaka, but she had little choice. With her cronemother sick, and her heartmother far away in the capital selling last season's bloodfish, Yumeko could barely manage. Ikenaka's home was perfectly thatched, Yumeko noted bitterly. Their own domehouse would be reclaimed by the swamp if her heartmother didn't return soon. Yumeko didn't know if her family could bear any more shame. Was it shameful, she thought, to be this unlucky? How long could she bear their censure?

Until the swamps dried up, her cronemother always laughed harshly.

A wet thud smacked into the small of her back, drops of water flying. Air whooshed from her lungs.

Coughed. Choked for air.

Clanless!

She dropped her paddle. Desperately groped for her gore knife.

"You're too late," a voice boomed. "If I was a beast or one of the Clanless, you'd be long dead and dissected!"

A dripping oar held loosely in her hand, Ikenaka stood short and solid in the middle of her own punt. The two boats bobbed closer together. The boards creaked loudly. A whisper in the moist air, a warm drizzle of rain broke through the rays of sunlight. Droplets slid down Yumeko's face, seeped between her lips.

A hot wave boiled in Yumeko's chest. Rose up her throat, to her eyes.

Ikenaka spat into the brown water. "I told Numa not to curse you with such a careless name! And look at your lot in life now, heh! Yumeko. Dream child! What nonsense! If your feet are not firm in your punt, you will drown!"

Yumeko swallowed the lump of pride. She bowed her

head grimly. "Thank you for your lesson, Ikenaka Obachan," she gritted. "I will take more care!"

"You," Ikenaka muttered. "You are One-who-Never-Learns. No matter how many lessons you are taught. Like your heartmother before you. No sense. No luck. You would be wise never to marry. Look at your poor cronemother, from a good clan, that one, nothing but ill luck since she knotted into your heartmother's home." The old woman's voice dropped. "I would have had you banished for what you did to my nieces!"

Yumeko hung her head. There was nothing she could say. It had been Yumeko's childish plans that had taken them far, far, into the center of the swamp. Lost in the Mists-That-Never-Lift. For three days. Until Tsuchi couldn't bear the screaming monkeyfrogs any longer. And had plunged into the waters. . . . Kaze would have plunged after her twin sister if Yumeko had not tied her to the bench. On the fourth day they had been saved.

But the cost. . . .

Yumeko would be paying the price for the rest of her life.

The rain, which had stopped, started drizzling again. Despite the warmth, Yumeko shivered. Strange weather, she thought, blinking the wet from her eyes.

Ikenaka's rough hand smacked her shoulder. Yumeko flinched, the small punt rocking.

"What do you want?" Ikenaka said grimly. The wrinkled skin hung heavily around her dark eyes.

Yumeko swallowed hard again. "I'm going out for blood-fish. Farther than the markers. We are overfished and my nets are empty. Could you look in on Kiri while I'm gone?"

Ikenaka blinked her small black eyes. Her rigid shoulders dropped. "Has she eaten yet?"

Yumeko shook her head, her cheeks burning. It was shameful not to be able to feed her cronemother properly.

"I'll take some sweetrice cakes."

Yumeko bowed her gratitude.

Ikenaka's hard hand clamped Yumeko's wrist. She held so hard that blood purpled in Yumeko's hand. She didn't try to pull free. Met the old woman's eyes.

"Dream girl," Ikenaka hissed. Her voice was low but the tightly coiled strength in her voice made Yumeko quake. "I gift you with another lesson. See how the sun shines through the rain? Stay in the waters. But don't go ashore. And don't go into the woods. Bad luck weather. Bad luck day." Ikenaka dropped Yumeko's wrist. And expertly swung her paddle back into the lock. Weaving the figure eight pattern, she cut through the weeds and water with hardly a ripple.

Yumeko rubbed the red marks on her skin. "Why," she called out. "Why is it bad luck?" And why did Ikenaka mention forests? Yumeko was going into the swamp, not toward the shore.

Ikenaka slashed her free hand diagonally through the air. Silence!

Yumeko sighed. Picked up her paddle to move into deeper waters well beyond the floating markers.

Yumeko bit her lip to keep back a jubilant shout. Arms weary, she gently lifted the heavy, wet scoop mesh. The muscles in her arms twitched and jumped, and sweat rolled down her face, stung her eyes. Her bucket was full to the brim with bloodfish and she'd even caught two large eels! She couldn't remember the last time she'd seen eels at the floating markets. She should have brought more buckets. But there was plenty to fill their bellies and enough left over for trade. She would come back this way tomorrow and the day after. It was so peaceful. So far from her people and their unforgiving looks, their harsh words. . . .

Yumeko cupped her hand and scooped a bloated fish. Without water to hold its form, the transparent body was a shivering lump. A tiny heart fluttered inside the bulbous red mass. Yumeko tipped back her head and slid the baglike fish into her mouth. She held it whole for a moment. The soft skin was cold and the fish quivered feebly against her tongue, the inner lining of her cheeks. She bit down. Salty liquid, rich and oily, burst inside her mouth. She was almost dizzy with hunger and relief. She gulped and gulped. Licked the salty juices from her lips. Kiri, she thought guiltily. Here she was eating while her cronemother waited, alone and hungry. But no, Ikenaka had said she would share her some food. Yumeko had caught plenty. She could eat a few more and then start back. The sun was several hours from the horizon and more clouds were scudding over the swamplands. Yumeko smiled, the oily juice of bloodfish staining her teeth pink.

The sudden screech of a monkeyfrog shattered the quiet. Yumeko jumped and the punt rocked beneath her feet. She looked all around, her heart booming inside her ears. That was a big one, she thought, nervously. But she couldn't see the subtle, rounded bulges of its head breaking the water.

Yumeko carefully slipped her hand into the bucket. Two

green ribbons of eels writhed between the fragile, bloated red bodies. *The second biggest*, Yumeko decided. *I'll save the biggest for Kiri.*

The punt heaved.

The stern burst upward. Impossibly, out of the water.

Yumeko windmilled her arms, swinging wildly for her center of balance. The skies shifted ninety degrees. *Our bloodfish*, Yumeko could only think as she sailed in slow motion through the air. *The eels—*

She sank heavily as the water poured into her waders. She might as well have been tied to anchors. The cold water sucked air from her body. She plucked at the buckles and ties of her boots with numb fingers. Her hands growing weaker and weaker. So cold. Her lungs burned. She looked upward. One arm raised. Tried to kick her feet. But they barely moved. The dim afternoon light receded into tan, umber. Darkness. *So deep*, she thought feebly, *Numa's going to be mad when she comes home. . . .*

No!

Yumeko would not leave the world like this. Fodder for monkeyfrogs. A tragic story told to children as a warning against foolishness.

Her gore knife! She groped at the sheath, clasped the handle. She swung her arm slowly in the torpid liquid and sawed at the straps of her waders. The leather finally gave and the deathly weight sank away from her like stone. In her loincloth and short tunic, she kicked with all the strength she had left. Desperate. Lungs on fire. Lights burst wildly around her in the inky waters. The need for air burned, seared her senses. She could barely keep from opening her mouth. She kicked desperately. And as she rose, the black depth grew slowly lighter. Tea-brown growing tan. But water tricked the eyes. What looked close was always farther. She wouldn't make it.

Yumeko breached the surface, mouth wide, gasping, choking. She floundered and, in her desperation for air, dropped her gore knife. When the panic for oxygen subsided, the cold penetrated. Teeth clattering, she scanned her surroundings. A blanket of mist hung over the water though she could see the brightness of the sun waxing and waning above it.

Mist.

What had flipped her punt?

Yumeko's eyes darted. Whatever it was, it had been big. She treaded water, her empty hands sliding through the bone-numbing liquid. Empty. No gore knife. She wanted to cry.

The punt had disappeared in the mist. Or sunk. Panic closed on her throat like a noose. What unknown beast lurked in the deeps of the swamp's belly?

She would succumb to the cold then drown if she didn't move.

A patch of mist felt warmer and brighter. Sluggishly, then more methodically, Yumeko swam toward the light.

She retched. The pain of the water forced through her nostrils was a white explosion behind her closed eyes. Coughing, pink froth slid down her chin. She dragged herself over stones. Stones, like the edge of a lake. Not like a swamp. They were warm. Yumeko pressed her face into the smooth rounded contours, bile stinging her throat. Yumeko blinked. Blinked. The mist pooled over the water, but not over the land.

Fat droplets of rain fell through the golden light of the evening sun. They plopped heavily onto the stone beach, on Yumeko's outstretched legs and arms. The droplets turned into a light drizzle. The sunlight turning rain into honey. She stared emotionlessly down the length of the beach.

In the distance was a sharp sound. It was familiar . . . but so out of place. She could not say where she'd heard it before.

The sound rang again, a farther echo retreating.

For a moment Yumeko didn't move.

Cronewives. Telling tales. Small, taut drums during the Autumn Moon Festival.

"Help!" Yumeko croaked. She staggered to her feet, fell back down on one knee. The sound was coming from an enormous forest just beyond the beach of stones. Through the glinting raindrops, the trees stood wet and resplendent.

The ceremonial drumbeats grew fainter and fainter.

"Cronewives!" Yumeko croaked. Licked at the rain on her lips to moisten her mouth. "Cronewives!" she shouted and broke through rough branches. Broad leaves clung, slick and cold against her skin. Between the trunks of trees, Yumeko caught glimpses of a train of figures dressed in sumptuous clothes.

The drums stopped beating. Yumeko panted as she crashed through the undergrowth. Perhaps she was disrupting a ceremony. Sometimes cronewives left their heartwives for seasonal rituals. Her own cronemother had gone away twice that Yumeko remembered. *They won't mind*, Yumeko babbled to herself. *They won't mind when they realize I'm in trouble.*

Yumeko burst through the last stand of trees into a beautiful tableau. The air was thick with an uncanny silence. The golden rain cast a beautiful light.

The long row of people stood as if frozen. Gowned in vibrant robes and silken waistbands the like of which Yumeko had never seen, some wore tall black hats; some held long staffs or spears in their pale hands. She stared at the column, at their very stiff backs. Six of the figures stood shouldering a thick, polished pole. From the pole was suspended a large, square woven basket. A curtain that covered a small window in the center of the basket twitched, then was still.

The tiny hairs on Yumeko's body rose, rippled, shivered. The last rays of red-gold sunlight played upon her skin. A patter of rain.

The figures snapped their faces toward her, a single motion, the sound of the stiff cloth rubbing against cloth swelled like a sudden deluge. Tawny eyes glittered fiercely in the copper-furred faces. Long pointed muzzles full of sharp white teeth.

They're wearing masks . . . just masks.

A blur of gold and red. She didn't even have time to cry out. Four guards clamped their human hands around her arms, her wrists, the nape of her neck. Their animal breath was sweet and sharp. She stared into their well-toothed jaws. *They look so real*, she thought. She gaped at their large triangular ears atop their heads. A white blur. Pain snapped sharply against the side of her face.

"Your foul gaze has ruined this wedding ceremony," a beautifully melodious voice murmured. "Sully us further and you will eviscerated."

Yumeko retched dryly. But she kept her eyes on her bare feet.

The rain stopped. Yumeko began to laugh. "Bad luck weather," she croaked. "Ikenaka said. Bad luck." Her guard slapped her again. Yumeko swallowed her hysteria and it sank, a rock in her belly.

The procession resumed its path through the forest, though the guards kept Yumeko well behind. Yumeko thought she heard whispering. Someone giggled. A voice barked, harsh and angry. Silence resumed. They played the drums no longer.

"They must be a secret theatrical group from the capital," Yumeko whispered to herself. "Performers for the nobles, perhaps, Numa said. All manner of people live in the capital. . . ."

There was a cough. Coughing. Tittering. Some of the creatures snickered behind hands held over their muzzles, others clutched their well-dressed middles and guffawed until tears rolled down their pointed snouts.

Yumeko stood stiffly. Her ears burned. She could bear no more shame. Enough that her own clan hated the sight of her. But to be laughed at by these—these—

"Humans," a creature laughed in her face. "What ridiculous things humans imagine to console themselves! How you have survived so long in this world is a joke of the gods."

It was more than she could bear.

"And what of you!" Yumeko hissed. "You have the look of

the Clanless. Banished to this remote place. With no home nor hearth you have no place in this world!"

The laughter stopped.

The guards raised their spears, ready to cut her down. But a creature barked from the head of the column and strode toward them.

"Be silent," she snarled, her voice deep. Tiny flecks of white speckled the deep red fur on her snout. Her eyes were golden, and the pupils large and black. "You know nothing. Our realms have existed long before humans walked upon this earth. And they will exist long after humans are gone. Your ancestors once called us gods. Now we are forgotten. But our powers and traditions remain our own. Speak nothing until you know enough to speak."

Her voice resounded with such power that Yumeko could barely breathe. It took all her self-control not to cower. The leader marched back to the front of the procession and they continued through the forest.

And as they marched for hours into the growing night, Yumeko uttered nothing.

A swollen, orange moon shone through a small window. The square of light fell on Yumeko's face and she frowned wearily. Batted at the glow, then opened her eyes.

Somewhere, a soft trickle of water slid over rocks. A night bird cooed, a dark and sad sound.

A bubble of hysteria tried to breach Yumeko's lips but she bit down.

How long they had marched, she didn't know. She couldn't even remember coming to this place. The scent of mold rose from the damp straw matting. Just like her domehouse. Her cronemother. Kiri would be distraught.

Yumeko pushed herself up. Her head spun. She closed her eyes and breathed deeply, willing the nausea to pass. When the rolling motion stopped, she rubbed her eyes.

A sweet, high-pitched giggle.

Yumeko spun towards the sound and promptly fell over.

The giggle turned into laughter.

"What do you want?" Yumeko muttered into the musty *tatami*. She slowly turned her head and stared at the square of mat lit up by the richness of the moon. The rest of the room lay in darkness.

A slender hand pushed a round, porcelain cup into the square of moonlight. The thick sleeve fell back from the wrist and rode up slightly, revealing a finely boned wrist, a thin arm.

"You must be thirsty," a soft voice whispered from the shadows.

Thirst roared into Yumeko's consciousness. She scrabbled for the cup and gulped the contents.

"Rather ill-mannered. Humans used to be more gracious." There was a pause. "But one supposes that it's just a reflection of their difficult times."

Yumeko didn't know how many were in the room. Was there only one who spoke to herself or were there many?

"Would you like some more?" the melodious voice asked.

Yumeko nodded. "Please," she muttered. She held out the small cup though she would have stuck her head into a stream and gulped like an animal if she could.

Two slender hands graciously poured the contents of a slim porcelain bottle into the cup. Yumeko stared. The hands were so human. So lovely. Her own hands were scratched and coarse. The color of chestnuts and lean with hard labor. Yumeko drank more carefully, then set the cup on the *tatami*. "Thank you," she murmured.

The voice giggled. Pleased. "It can learn manners," she said. "Clever," she whispered.

Yumeko cleared her throat. "I cannot see you in this darkness."

"Oh! So thoughtless," the sweet voice chided herself. There was a rustle of layered fabric. A luxurious sound. It whispered across the surface of the mat in a slow stately manner. The creature glided into the square of moonlight and slowly, slowly kneeled down, sat graciously back on top of her heels. Beautiful hands resting on one thigh. Gold and green threads glinted in her robe. She held her head downward, face shyly cast away from Yumeko's gaze, her dark black hair a thick curtain.

Yumeko gulped. How horrible, the human hair on the animal's head. Monstrous. Monstrous.

She slowly raised her head, her shiny black hair parting, sliding to reveal her face. Pale, moonlight skin. The bright red lines of her lips. Gentle sloping cheekbones. Her low bridge of nose. A tawny color glinted between her heavy half-closed eyelids. Her eyebrows were completely shaved off. Small black dots were painted high on her forehead. She was the loveliest woman Yumeko had ever seen.

The woman smiled.

The inside of her mouth was black as night.

Yumeko shuddered. Her teeth chattered, clattered, and she couldn't stop.

"Oh!" the woman breathed. "You are cold." She worked something at her waist and then drew off a golden overrobe. She was dressed in layers. The robe beneath was the color of dried blood. The young woman glided to where Yumeko lay curled upon the mat and draped the silky clothing over her.

The robe held the heat of the woman's body. The silky brocade smelled of clean animal fur.

"Are you a prisoner too?" Yumeko whispered.

The beautiful young woman sighed and shifted her weight. No longer sitting formally upon folded knees, she twisted slightly as she glanced at Yumeko from the corners of her eyes.

"You ruined my wedding ceremony." The young woman slowly blinked.

Yumeko gulped. The woven basket with the small curtained window. The young woman must have been inside it.

"I cannot be wed until the sun again shines through falling rain." The beautiful girl sighed rather deeply. "And who knows when that shall be?"

"I'm sorry," Yumeko managed. Then couldn't help herself, "Aren't you glad not to wed one of those—"

The young woman swiftly pinched Yumeko's cheek. Hard enough to bruise.

"You are slow-witted," the long-haired girl said sadly. "The Teacher gifted you with a lesson and yet you have heard nothing."

Yumeko's face burned. She held back her retort. For Yumeko was a prisoner and had no way of knowing if the girl cared for her own kind any longer. Who knew what her position was among the animal-headed outcasts? Yumeko rubbed her cheek with the soft inner lining of the robe.

"I'm sorry," the girl said gently. "Did that hurt?"

Yumeko didn't answer.

"Don't be angry," the girl smiled. The black cavern of her mouth. "I'll tell you my name," she teased, "if you tell me yours."

Yumeko said nothing.

"Ohhhh, this one is sullen," the beautiful girl whispered. Turning her face aside. "All these years I've waited for my hero, and I end up with a slow-witted swamptoad." She made a move to rise to her feet.

Yumeko rolled quickly, though her head spun, and clutched at the girl's sleeve.

"My name is Yumeko." Her heart pounded. "Are you a prisoner as I am?" she asked again hoarsely.

The beautiful young woman delicately tugged her sleeve out of Yumeko's dirty clasp. She smoothed the cloth with the palm of her hand.

"Yumeko," she said slowly. "How dreamy."

Yumeko pulled back.

"Truth be known," the girl carelessly said, "I hold no affections for my bridegroom." She rose gracefully to her feet in a fluid motion, as if her legs weren't made of bone and muscle. She glided to the window and stared out into the night. The direct light of the moon was not lovely upon her face. With her lips slightly parted, the black maw of her mouth seemed like the opening to an eternal pit.

Yumeko held her breath.

The young woman sighed, then turned to stare intently at Yumeko's face. The moon haloed the young woman's long hair with a blue light. Yumeko couldn't see her expression. Could only hear the cool tones of her voice.

"It's an arranged marriage, you see," the girl whispered. "The kitsune hold great powers, but their powers are maintained through traditions. I do not want to marry and I will not be bound by rules. The fox faery do not look kindly upon kin who break tradition."

"Kitsune," Yumeko muttered. "I have never heard of such people."

The beautiful young woman turned and spoke to the moon. "You see. She knows very little. What am I to do with the little I am given?" She pressed three slender fingers against her red lips.

Yumeko's face burned. She wanted to smack the young woman's face. Instead, she turned her back.

The girl was upon her before Yumeko had heard her move. An icy breath crystallized in the air beside Yumeko's ear, and gooseflesh rippled down her spine. She shuddered to think how close that black mouth was to her face. Her throat.

"Yumeko," the girl breathed, "I'm going to gamble with your life and mine."

Yumeko scuttled away from the girl's uncanny breath. "My life is not yours to gamble," she said bravely.

The beautiful girl giggled, her voice like chimes in the wind. "You're so very amusing. The kitsune, this very moment, discuss what is to be done with you. You've trespassed into their domain. You've disrupted a wedding ceremony. And then to insult them. You're very lucky you're still alive!" The last was hissed violently into her ear. The girl's mouth seemingly spreading wide, even wider. Her teeth. The deathly maw of her mouth. Each tooth was painted black.

Yumeko shuddered convulsively. "I'm sorry," she rasped. All she could manage.

The girl gracefully draped her slender arm along Yumeko's back. "Oh," she murmured, contrite, "it is I who am sorry for speaking harshly. I would like us to be friends. You see, I do so desperately want to be away." The girl smiled horribly.

Yumeko didn't pull away.

"My name is Hotaru. . . ." She trailed off. She sighed again, but this time, her shoulders sank from their casual assurance. Her arm slipped from Yumeko's back and she stared at the straw matting. "I'm frightened," Hotaru whispered. Without affectation. "The only way this might work is if you trust me." She traced the thread in the *tatami* with her forefinger. A rim of dirt was caked beneath her nail. Yumeko stared at the imperfection and some of the rigid tension in her spine dissolved.

"I don't trust you at all," Yumeko said, slowly. "But I will form a partnership with you until we've escaped from this place. Hotaru."

Hotaru's eyes glinted in the moonlight. Yumeko didn't know if they glinted with mirth or sorrow.

"Well," Hotaru blinked, "choose not to trust me, but you must believe what I say, else your disbelief will be our ruin, and I would be better fated to wait for another." The beautiful girl shivered. "So many years wasted already."

"Why didn't you run away by yourself?" Yumeko asked. Curious.

"Do you think I haven't tried?" Hotaru snapped.

Yumeko flinched. Then willed herself to breathe. "If this partnership is to succeed, you speak to me with some respect. You must not pinch me. You must not speak to yourself as if I'm not here. You must not expect me to know things you hold as common knowledge. Do you agree?"

"So." Hotaru's small painted eyebrow spots rose even higher on her forehead. "As you say," she acquiesced.

"Tell me where we are. Where is the fox faery domain? How can we flee?" Yumeko sat with her knees drawn to her chest, facing the lovely girl.

"The kitsune inhabit an island located in the middle of what you call the swamp. It's surrounded by mist that beguiles and bewitches. In that mist, there live communities of trollrats and monkeyfrogs. Though these creatures have no powers, they are closer in nature to our kind than yours. Some of the foxes hunt them for food. Some consider them to be unclean. If we manage to flee the foxes' den, we still have to get through the perils of the mist."

Yumeko's eyes widened.

"The odds are not in our favor." Hotaru shrugged. Then giggled with some of her earlier posturing. "But the risks make us look heroic, mmmmm?"

"And what if we stay?" Yumeko asked.

"I, I will be wed without my consent. You will die. Or you will be left to beg for death."

Yumeko gulped. "When do we leave?"

"The foxes are deciding your fate tonight. They will sleep during the day. We leave midday tomorrow." Hotaru slipped her hand into her sleeve and pulled out a pale rice cake. "It's not much, but it was the best I could do. Eat this and drink the rest of the water. Tomorrow I will signal you with the swampsparrow's song."

Yumeko snatched the delicate rice cake, then paused, remembering the girl's comments about manners. "Thank you," she said.

Hotaru smiled and a small dimple dipped in her round cheek. She stepped out of the moonlight and her form was lost in the darkness. Yumeko stared until her eyes watered.

"One more thing," the melodious voice whispered. "No matter what you see, do not make the mistake of underestimating the danger. Death can be found in the most benign places. Do not be tricked by the *appearance* of things. Look to their essence."

Yumeko, unable to control herself, stuffed the whole rice cake into her mouth. She chewed the salty sweetness, almost swooning with the flavors, the soft texture.

Hotaru sighed in the darkness.

A *whisk* of sound. Yumeko stopped chewing and tilted her head. "Hotaru?" she mumbled through the food in her mouth.

No one answered.

Yumeko shivered. Chewed quickly and swallowed. She drank the remaining water then curled into a ball in the corner closest to the window. She had no idea how they would make their escape. Hotaru, she thought. Firefly.

I do not trust you.

The sun glared, overbright, on Yumeko's face. "Kiri," Yumeko croaked. "I caught so many bloodfish." Yumeko dragged her arm over her eyelids and sat up. The night's events clicked rapidly through Yumeko's mind like beads on an abacus. She toyed with the idea that she was feverishly deluded. A silky robe slithered from her torso.

Yumeko scrabbled to her feet. The day was bright. How long had she slept? What if she'd missed Hotaru's signal? Yumeko stood next to the window. The tiny hut was in a small grassy glade. Enormous hemlock and cedar trees grew on the outskirts. She gaped. They must be thousands of years old. She had never seen their like. None near the domehouses were even half as large.

There was no sign of the kitsune.

The hut was rudely made, large cracks of sunlight shining between the boards. Yumeko quietly darted from wall to wall. She could see no guards around her prison. And there were no other houses. Where did the kitsune sleep? Yumeko sat in the middle of the *tatami,* her knees drawn to her chest. Just because she couldn't see them didn't mean she wasn't watched. Otherwise, why put her in such a flimsy shelter? She could push over a wall if she really tried. And Hotaru had said she was frightened. Yumeko was not used to the strange girl's ways. She was erratic, unpredictable. And possibly violent. If someone like Hotaru feared the fox faery, Yumeko didn't want to know what they had planned for her. And the talk of magic. She must mean rituals, Yumeko thought. Like the cronewives practiced.

Pweee chikka chik.

The call of the swampsparrow!

Yumeko's heart pounded.

Pweee chikka chik.

Casting a quick glance at the overcoat, she didn't pick it up. It would stand out in the woods and the weight was unwieldy. Flight now.

Yumeko scanned outside the window. No one. She gingerly crawled up and over, dropped softly to the ground. Which way? Where was Hotaru? She couldn't stand in front of the hut, waiting for her! Crouched low, she peered cautiously at the grass. The hut must have had a raised floor, because from the ground outside, Yumeko couldn't see the forest that surrounded the glade. The tall grasses towered well above her head. Maybe Hotaru was watching her and would follow after. She hoped.

Scurrying, she darted into the yellow-green stems. This is too easy, she thought. Where are the guards? Tall grasses soon hid her form, but she didn't feel safer for it—what hid her also hid others. Her heart tripped loudly in her eardrums. Where had the bog-rotted bird signal come from? She stopped short.

What if the bird song had come from a bird?

Yumeko clamped both hands over her mouth. She could barely contain her laughter.

The tall grass in front of Yumeko shivered. Hotaru slipped through the blades with barely a ripple, a small cloth bundle in her hand. "Silence, swamptoad!" she snapped. "You could be heard from ten *ri* away! I didn't signal and yet you flee. I don't have all of our supplies. Where is the overcoat?" Her quietly hissed words were like a dash of cold water.

In the brightness of day, the white powder on Hotaru's face was less ethereal, more tawdry. Creases underneath her eyes betrayed an age far greater than her sweet voice had suggested. The round eyebrow dots painted high on her forehead were so distracting. Yumeko stared.

"Overcoat!" Hotaru repeated. Gave Yumeko a quick shake.

"I left it behind. It's too heavy," Yumeko answered.

"Fool! When they see you are gone, they will know you've left with me!"

"Won't they realize that anyway?" Yumeko retorted.

"Any time they spend looking for clues is to our advantage. *Moh!* There's no point in talking! Follow me. Make no sounds."

Hotaru slid through the grass as if she was air. Her feet, Yumeko noted, were bare. Though Hotaru created a small path for her, Yumeko still lumbered through the grass like a swampbuffalo. She had never thought of herself as clumsy, but every blade she touched rustled, every leaf crinkled. She could feel Hotaru's back bristling with annoyance. The tips of the grass bobbed slowly back and forth above their heads. Yumeko's heart pounded. She hoped the fox faery were tired and slept soundly. The silence around them was thick. As if they were the only moving creatures upon the earth.

Hotaru suddenly stopped. Yumeko almost bumped into her back. Yumeko, slightly taller than her new ally, peered over her shoulder. Her heart plummeted.

They were back at the hut.

"Curse it!" Hotaru hissed. "They've bewitched the glade."

"Bewitched?" Yumeko repeated. "Like magic?"

Hotaru spun around. "You know not even that!" And then her face crumpled. Tears trickled down her face, ruining the white powder. Yumeko stared, horrified.

"What have I done?" Hotaru moaned. "All for nothing. And next they will take my ears." She squeezed tight her painted lips, but her shoulders shook with her sobs, her hands falling helplessly. The cloth bundle landed next to her dirty feet.

Awkwardly, Yumeko picked it up. The girl was so *unstable*. Vicious one moment, vulnerable the next. And while she wept, they were wasting precious time. Would the fox faery really cut off Hotaru's delicate ears?

Hotaru gasped.

Yumeko crouched. Ready to flee. Certain they had been discovered. Yumeko glanced at the girl. She was looking down at the ground.

Yumeko followed her gaze.

Three animals stood in a half circle. No higher than her knees, their thick fur shone reddish gold. Large pointed ears perched on top of their triangulated heads, and their muzzles narrowed and tapered to a point. Just like the kitsune-masked soldiers who had captured her. But these creatures weren't humans. They were only animals standing on four slender legs, on tiny paws. Their large bushy tails held upright. Tense. Perhaps they were pets. Or guard animals. They would make a wonderful winter coat, she thought. Yumeko glanced up at Hotaru's ashen face. The girl wove ever so slightly. As if she might swoon.

Maybe she had an exaggerated fear, Yumeko thought. Like how Numa was frightened of tiny spiders. Yumeko reacted as she normally did when she was bothered by animal pests or children.

"Sssssssssssssssssssss!" Yumeko hissed and swung the

cloth bundle with all her might. She walloped one of the creatures in the rump and it glanced off the heads of the remaining two. They yelped and darted into the trees.

The trees. . . .

The glade, the hut . . . all disappeared. As if they had never existed. Yumeko gaped at the trees that towered above her. The sun cast beams of golden light through the canopy. A squirrel chattered. In the distance, a crow rasped, low and hoarse. A stream trickled with liquid music.

"You're unbelievable," Hotaru said, wonderingly. "You drive away the kitsune with only a cloth bundle."

"Kitsu—what?" Yumeko squeaked. "Those doglets are the fox faery?"

Hotaru shook her head.

"Where's the hut? All the grass?" Yumeko spluttered.

"They were never here," Hotaru said carefully.

"You mean we've never been in danger?"

Hotaru grabbed Yumeko's arm as she ran down a faint trail. "We've never been out of it," she hissed. They darted through the trees as if demented Clanless were right behind them. Yumeko couldn't see anything of the fox faeries or the doglets, but she didn't stop running. She hoped Hotaru knew where she was going.

It felt like they ran for hours. Yumeko's bare arms and legs were scratched from branches, her face smudged with dirt and sweat. Long runnels of face powder trailed down Hotaru's cheeks, but she didn't pant. Yumeko had thought the girl had painted her brown face to look white, but if anything, her true complexion was whiter than the makeup.

"Stop!" Yumeko managed. "Can't run."

Hotaru glanced back at her. A strange expression flickered across her face.

"What?" Yumeko's voice, jagged. Afraid of the answer.

Hotaru shook her head. Her long black hair still rippled. Glossy. "Humans tire easily," she murmured.

Yumeko frowned, still gasping for air. "What do you mean, 'humans'? Like you're not one yourself. . . ."

Yumeko swallowed hard. No matter how she tried to shape some reason out of the events that had happened, nothing was as it seemed. The vertigo threatened to toss her to the forest floor. If there even was a forest. And Hotaru. What manner of creature was she? Who knew what lay beneath all the paint, all the clothing.

The strange girl tilted her head to one side, listening. Then she nodded and motioned for Yumeko to sit down. Yumeko dropped to the moss and panted noisily.

Hotaru laughed. Without her usual condescension. Yumeko smiled at the happy sound. She stared at the girl's eyebrow dots high on her forehead. They hadn't trickled away with her sweat.

"Must you stare?" Hotaru said snippily. "If you must know, the two bushy caterpillars above your eyes distract me no end, but do you see me gawping at you whenever there's a still moment?"

"*Keh!*" Yumeko sniffed.

A branch snapped somewhere in the distance. They both held their breath. But birds still chirruped in the trees. They lowered their guard. "How much farther must we run?" Yumeko said wearily. "Are we closer to the swamp? And what then, when we get there? Are there supplies in the cloth bundle?"

"You have so many questions and no answers of your own."

"Could you stop that?" Yumeko snapped.

Hotaru flinched. Then she raised trembling hands to pat at her hair, smoothing down the glossy length. She lifted her head. Her light brown eyes were flecked with gold and bronze. "I'm sorry," Hotaru said, soberly. "It has been years upon years since I have spoken with someone who might not hold ill intentions." Her voice dropped. "The kitsune behave on whim and fancy. They might love you and they might kill you. You just never know." Hotaru's words blurring fiercely. "Nothing is ever what it seems. They are wise and just. They are heartless and cruel. I no longer know how to behave."

Emotion welled at Yumeko's eyes. How long had the girl been a captive? Yumeko cupped Hotaru's small white hands. They were icy and Yumeko clicked her tongue, rubbed gently with her coarse palms. "Don't worry," Yumeko said. "We'll flee this place. We'll get back to my clan, then we can begin a search for your people. Perhaps in the capital." For Yumeko had never seen a person dressed or painted like Hotaru. Numa had said all manner of strange people inhabited the great city.

"You are kind," Hotaru whispered.

A sharp bark cut through the forest. Followed by another. Hotaru whimpered. "They have found us," she said hoarsely.

The afternoon turned into night. Suddenly and completely. As if a switch had been turned. The hair rose along Yumeko's spine and she clamped hard on Hotaru's hands.

"Is it a storm?" Yumeko asked desperately. "A storm has blown in," she pleaded. Hotaru's face was a wan gray mask in the darkness.

Yelps and barks, from all directions, drew nearer.

"No storm," Hotaru gulped. "The fox faery are trying to bewitch us. The afternoon sun still shines. We just can't see it."

"How can we fight them?" Yumeko moaned.

"I have so little left," Hotaru whispered low and fiercely. She pulled her hands out of Yumeko's desperate grip. "Listen. I'm going to create a light. It's all I can do. You must follow this light no matter what happens. You promise me!"

Yumeko nodded. Then realized it was too dark for Hotaru to see her. "I promise," she whispered.

A rustling of cloth. The small bundle of supplies was pressed into Yumeko's hands.

"You must keep this with you. I am nothing without it." Hotaru's voice broke.

"I will guard it with my life," Yumeko swore.

The barks turned into growls.

Kachi! Kachi! Kachi!

The sound of rock striking rock.

A small bluish light floated in the pitch black. Like a flame it flickered, bobbed, rippled. Then it started weaving away. Like a firefly.

Hotaru, Yumeko thought wonderingly. Firefly. That's why. Yumeko stumbled after the pale blue light. At first she tried to toe out tree roots, outcroppings of rock. But wherever the small flame went, the path was clear. Yumeko ran less cautiously. Clutching the bundle to her chest, she began to sprint.

And even as she fled the growls that seemed to snap at her heels, doubts bloomed inside her.

Swampfire, a cronewife's voice hissed. Swampfire is the unsettled souls of banished murderers and thieves. Follow swamplight and you follow death.

Yumeko shrugged the thought away.

Don't follow her. She is erratic, cruel. She leads you to the edge of a cliff!

Yumeko whimpered. But she still chased after the light.

"Hotaru is the mad one in their community. Everything she has said is a lie!" a voice hissed next to her ear. She batted at the voice. Felt nothing.

The sun, Yumeko chanted to herself. The sun is shining but I can't see it.

"Yumeko!" her cronemother cried. "You left me again." Kiri lay crumpled at the foot of a tree, her body twisting, writhing in pain. Blood ran out of both empty eye sockets and the gaping holes turned accusingly to her daughter. "The Clanless attacked while you were gone. Help me." Her wrecked cronemother raised one feeble hand.

Yumeko faltered. "Kiri," her voice broke. But the pale blue light flared brighter. Bright enough for her to notice. Why would her cronemother be the only one lit up when all else remained in darkness?

Yumeko sprinted even faster after the firefly light.

"How can you," her cronemother called out. "Your own cronemother." She started weeping. The sound almost tore Yumeko's heart in two. But she didn't stop. "Curse you!" Kiri screamed.

Yumeko sobbed as she ran, tears streaming down her face.

The black night air was ripped apart with the sound of rending cloth. Headless children tumbled to the ground, giggling from the mouths in their bellies. Their sibilant voices paralyzed, and Yumeko desperately clamped her hands over her ears. Spiders the size of domehouses clambered down the trees, their shiny chitinous armor clattering, stinking of phosphorous and ammonia. The monsterspiders reached with their eight legs, with curved, clawed hands to tear Yumeko into pieces. Babies without faces crawled along the ground. Their fat bodies translucent and red with bloody juices. They looked like bloodfish. . . .

Yumeko clasped her stomach. Retched.

"Yumeko," a sweet voice whispered. "Yumeko."

Her head turned slowly, as if tugged by invisible strings. Her feet growing so heavy she could barely lift them. Even as her mind screamed for her to flee, she turned back. Toward the voice.

"Ho-ta-ru?" Yumeko mouthed, the words stretching in dream distortion.

No.

Kaze swung gently from a rope tied around her neck. Her purple face tilted at an impossible angle, her body hung loose, almost boneless. Yumeko's teeth started clattering. She desperately tried to catch sight of Hotaru's bobbing light again, but she couldn't move. Horrified, she stared at the rope that ended in midair. Kaze, her friend, hanging for all eternity.

"Yumeko," Kaze sighed, her mushy lips still moved long

after the word was spoken. "I've missed you, Yumeko. I don't blame you, you know. It's not your fault that we lost Tsuchi in the Mist. You didn't make me kill myself."

Snap of branch stepped by a heavy foot. A figure came lurching toward them. With horrible determination. A faint glow of recognition in her bulbous eyes.

Tsuchi. Tsuchi, who had plunged into the swamp. She had been preserved in the water. Her copper skin striated with black markings. The marks writhed, slipping in and out of Tsuchi's water-swollen body. Eels, Yumeko realized in horror. Baby eels. . . .

"Look," Kaze sighed. "We're all together again. Let's play like we used to."

Yumeko crumpled. Desperately she squeezed her eyes shut. "No more," she prayed into the earth. "No more." She covered her head with her arms, pulling her body into an instinctive fetal curl.

With a howl of glee, the specters fell upon her.

The monsterspiders snicked pieces out of Yumeko's paralyzed body and the headless children gleefully licked her with tongues that unrolled from their stomachs. Kaze and Tsuchi stroked her head lovingly as the faceless swollen blood babies tried to open her mouth.

"Stop!" A word tried to penetrate the force that surrounded her. The monsters paused and Yumeko dropped one arm, sluggishly turned her head. Her eyelids felt as if they were sewn together. With the last of herself that was intact, she tore the threads that kept her eyes shut. Screamed.

A pale blue light wove all around her. Darting with a dizzying fury. Sound roaring, whining, shrieking, the specters flew off Yumeko's body and burst into pale yellow flames. So many and so fast she couldn't count them, the spheres of light dodged, leapt, chased after the small blue flame. They pounced on it from many sides, as if to extinguish it.

"Hotaru," Yumeko croaked. She could do nothing. Nothing but witness the fury of the burning specters.

The blue firefly, unable to fight the strength of numbers, desperately zigzagged between the trees. Small yellow flames joined together, merging their light into a large ball of fire. The glow crackled with electric snaps. The enormous flame chased the blue light, now wan and tiny. She would be consumed, Yumeko thought, horrified. The blue firefly was losing ground. The movements slowing as it wove between tree trunks, branches.

"Here," Yumeko cried. "Come to me!"

The blue light angled up, up, high into the false night. Yumeko's heart throbbing as the light grew fainter, fainter. The sphere of orange flames roared ever closer.

The blue firefly stopped. Mid-air. Then fell. Slowly at first, then gaining greater momentum. Hotaru's light plummeted straight downward, toward Yumeko's outstretched hands.

"Come to me!" Yumeko cried again. Lurched to her feet. Cupped hands raised above her head.

Hotaru's light raced downward. Landed in the sanctuary of Yumeko's palms.

The ball of orange flames crackled furiously, just a heartbeat away. It filled Yumeko's sight. In the last second, Yumeko clasped the firefly to her chest and closed her eyes as the orange fire consumed her from the head down.

The flames splashed around her, surrounding her upright form. Her hair rose with electric crackle, her exposed skin tingled madly.

The flames didn't burn.

Yumeko opened her eyes. She could see through the fire. Filtered orange and yellow, trees flickered as if she was seeing them from behind a curtain of water.

A circle of foxes. Sitting on their haunches. They stared intently at the girl standing with her hands clasped to her chest. The largest of the foxes tilted her head quizzically.

Do you know enough to speak now? A voice echoed in Yumeko's mind.

Outrage, anger, hate, swelled inside Yumeko. They flared briefly, then faded.

Why do you do this? Yumeko thought wearily.

The large old fox stared, unblinking. Then tilted her head the other way.

Because we can.

The flames that surrounded her vanished. It was afternoon again at the edge of a great forest. The forest with all of the chirps and creakings of its language. She stood near a shore surrounded by brown water. Just beyond the waterline floated a heavy mist.

The old fox lifted her speckled muzzle and barked once, sharp. The foxes broke their circle and disappeared into the trees as if they were never there.

A warm weight in Yumeko's hands.

She looked down.

A small white fox.

She still breathed.

"Hotaru?" Yumeko quavered. The small creature stirred, tried to raise her head. Managed to open her eyes. They were warm brown, streaked with gold and bronze. Small round black spots of fur were high on the fox's head. Yumeko couldn't see past her tears. She blinked desperately.

"They've left," Yumeko managed. "We're free." Yumeko could almost catch a strand of reason in this if she weren't so very tired. "We've come to the edge of the island." She stared fiercely at the misty waters.

On the shore was her punt.

Hotaru sighed deeply, then closed her eyes.

Yumeko walked to the small boat. Round stones crunched, overloud, beneath her bare feet. The shore was damp with the mist.

The small cloth bundle sat on the bench near the prow. Yumeko shifted the small fox into the crook of her left arm as gently as she could. The exhausted animal didn't wake.

Her heart tripped. The small white fox didn't have a tail.

"Hotaru," she whispered.

Hotaru had said she was frightened. That the kitsune had said they would next take her ears. Her beautifully pointed ears were still on her head. Why had they let her go? Perhaps they thought she had earned it. Yumeko didn't know. Perhaps she never would.

Yumeko, holding the white fox against her, pushed the punt off the shore. She wanted to be off the island. She sat on the bench as the sluggish water lapped them deeper into the mist. With her right hand, she untied the knots of the cloth bundle. There was no food or water. Only two worn scrolls. Folded red cloth. And something white. Yumeko reached with trembling fingers.

A small white tail. Not the bushy thickness of an adult, but thin and short. The tail of a kit. Yumeko carefully rewrapped the cloth bundle.

She stood in the stern of the punt and clasped the oar with her right hand. In the crook of her left, she cradled the sleeping fox with fierce tenderness. As Yumeko swung the oar in the twisting figure eight motion, she began to speak softly. "I live near the eastern shores of this swamp. We live in domehouses that stand on stilts above the brown water. My cronemother is Kiri and my heartmother is Numa. You will be a guest in our home for as long as you wish it."

The punt disappeared into the mist.

Hiromi Goto's novel *The Kappa Child* was the 2001 winner of the James Tiptree Jr. Award and was on the final ballot for the Sunburst Award and the Spectrum Award. She also published a children's fantasy, *The Water of Possibility*, that year. Her first novel, *Chorus of Mushrooms*, was the regional winner of the Commonwealth Writer's Prize for Best First Novel, and was co-winner of the Canada-Japan Book Award.

Her most recent publication is a collection of short stories called *Hopeful Monsters*, and she has a genre-bending horror novel pending with Penguin Canada. Goto is the mother of two children and currently calls British Columbia home.

Hiromi Goto gratefully acknowledges the financial assistance of the Alberta Foundation of the Arts.

Author's Note

The kitsune continues to slide elusively between realms magical, natural, and human. In Asian mythologies, the fox faery has left a long and meandering trail of deceit, grace, violence, and acts of great beauty. The complexities of the kitsune can beguile. A writer can become lost in seeking to know her. And in a sweep of a tail, a delicate leap, what you thought you saw is gone. The only sign of her passage is a droplet of water falling from a leaf, the brief glint of sunlight.

The Dream Eaters

A. M. Dellamonica

Mo Cottonsmith had just turned sixteen when she started Lopside Fashions, with cash she stole from a neighborhood fizz dealer. The money wasn't enough to sustain a business, but Mo counted on getting lucky. She believed in making her own luck, too—thanks to a roving copcam, her first creation just happened to debut on all the morning news shows.

The dress was daffodil yellow with simulated dewdrops on the bodice and a chain-mail hoop skirt. Mo's pal Juanita Jones was modeling, and the footage showed her fighting off a couple of deviants.

It wasn't much of a fight. When Juanita spun to face her would-be attackers, the blades hanging in a fringe at the bottom of the chain mail whipped around too. They took off Suspect Number Two's index finger at the second knuckle; then pinpoint blasts of pepper spray from the dewdrops finished him off. Sadly, his buddy fled before Juanita could deploy the tasers in her matching shoes. She fired them anyway, then pouted into the camera and strode off down the sidewalk.

So suddenly hoops were in again, and breezy, thieving Mo was a Person of Interest to someone besides Crimestoppers.

(They tried to stick her for hacking the copcam, but her lawyer got that flushed just before I joined the force.)

Lopside's next release was the A.D. Bodice, a bustier that padded out one of your boobs to a double-D while squeezing the other to a bud. It took off too, and at nineteen Mo began cashing the kind of checks the thought of which sends the rest of us running to the Scratch Lotto.

She spent it on a big expensive house, decorating the place in what she called Group Home Chic. I said there was nothing Group Home about it. She said Chic was not my subject. Back, forth, back again—it had been that way between us the whole time we roomed together at McMurty's, a civic dumping ground for girls who can't go home or get a foster placement.

Ignoring my input, Mo draped fabric all over her walls and furniture, then got herself the world's loudest stereo system. The basement she called the Hangar, because it was full of hammocks and toys for her various hangers-on.

She also built herself a new version of the nightmask she'd stolen from me years before, the last time she ran away from McMurty's. It had fancy green-tinted goggles, padded ones that fit comfortably, and heavy-duty hardware on the breathing filter. She slept in it, as I always had. People called this a charming eccentricity, and when they saw mine—the replacement I built after Mo filched the original—assumed I was copying her.

But that's ancient history—priors, you'd say in my trade. Here and now Mo's striding into the neighborhood policing office, scowling, clutching a shoebox. She's clad in a big-belly dress for an expectant mom—lime velvet in color, with boxy collars and cuffs. Panels peel away from its gut and something shiny and green hangs over her curved stomach.

"Constable Lizabette." She snaps her gum, all business.

"You pregnant, Mo?"

"It's for the fall show." She perches on a chair. "Wanna try it on? It comes with inflatable tummy."

"I'm working."

"Come on. I'll wear your uniform, march around in front of the door so nobody catches you screwing around."

"You wish." I cough to hide a smile. "What's in the box?"

"Don't know exactly."

Games. Stalling, I take a better look at the dress. The plastic moldings stretched over her belly are frogs and lizards, big-eyed, cartoonish, and friendly. "Someone's going to buy this?"

"I have preorders."

"What do you mean you don't know what's in the box?"

"Open it."

"You got it in the mail?"

"It's not a bomb, Liz."

I open it. Then I shut it again, stuff it in the bottom desk drawer, and close the window blinds before spraying every-thing with a disinfectant so strong it makes the eyes water.

"There's the girl I remember so fondly." Mo's voice is relaxed, but the room is darker with the blinds closed, and I see red marks on her mouth: she's been biting her lips. "You do know what that is."

"No," I say, but there's no strength in my voice.

"Know my motto, Liz?"

"Why earn something you can rip off?"

"Every puzzle has a solution. My genius is . . ."

"Yeah . . . knowing the person with the answer. So?"

"You sleep in a modified gas mask."

"So do you, Mo."

"Roommate see, roommate do. I know a survival tactic when I see it."

"Delusions. Everybody at McMurty's said so."

"Liz!" She kicks the desk hard. "You're not crazed."

I let out a breath. It's a victory, making her lose her temper. "The thing in the box is a fairy."

She falls back in her chair, spinning it with one foot. Her hands are trembling, and when she sees me noticing, her lip curls. "Is this where I flip out and say that's impossible?"

"Usually."

"A fairy."

"Yes. What does it look like?"

"Like an itty-bitty dead person with bird wings stuck to a slice of Wonder Bread."

"The 'dead' part is what should worry you. Fairies don't believe in mitigating circumstances."

"Kinda like you?"

"Shut up, Mo."

"Ooh, point for me."

Opening the drawer, I find the bread has worked its way loose from the box and is crawling up the inside of the desk. I pinch up the slice, avoiding the orange specks in the peanut butter that glues the little corpse there, faceup and splayed. "Time of death's around sunrise."

"How can you tell?"

"The size. It's just a baby."

"What's this?" She points to a green stem in its hand.

"A dream siphon."

"Which means?" She reaches to poke the body and I slap her hand. "Come on, what's a dream siphon?"

I fiddle with the papers on my desk, trying to hide how I'm pulled between what's right . . . and what I'm going to do. I should tell her this doesn't have anything to do with the police or my Commercial Drive beat; I should show her the door. But Mo stole my mask all those years ago. She cost me one of my last few dreams. It's hard not to feel owed, like I should grab this chance to get one of hers in return. Finally I ask, "Do you still have nightmares about weird bugs?"

"Maybe. So?"

"This is the cure." I push the green wand out of the fairy's dead hand with the tip of a pen. When I've got it off the bread, I raise it to Mo's face.

"Hey!" She rears back.

"You want to know about this stuff or not?"

"Yeah."

"Then relax. It's okay, I promise."

She stops wiggling and I lay the narrow point of the stem against the corner of her eye. "Think of a bug from your nightmares."

Mo grips my cheap, taxpayer-bought desk. Seconds later a tiny moth squeezes out of the wide end of the siphon. Shrunken and wet, it plumps out and starts flapping around on my desk. Drying as it grows to the size of my fist, it never manages to get airborne.

"This is it?" Its wings are covered in pink and yellow neon spots, and it looks like something from a kid's movie. "Big fearless Mo's afraid of this?"

"Not funny, Liz." The thing rattles its wings and she startles me by leaping to her feet, backing up against the wall. The siphon stem jiggles from its place in the corner of her eye.

"Relax," I say, grabbing the moth. It unfluffs defensively, shrinking to sleekness, becoming about the size of a plum.

"Is it dead?"

"It's too lovable to kill." This has turned out better than I guessed; I was expecting something horrible. I stuff the moth in my mouth and it dissolves like cotton candy, leaving a hint of dry sand between my teeth.

Mo turns away and retches. I'm surprised she's so affected—and petty enough to be pleased. After a second I relent, patting her back.

The dream I've swallowed starts to seep in. Moth-images flitter through my empty attic of a mind—dusty and hairy, gray and brown and green and orange and cartoon-colored, too. Powder-scented, with soft antennae, they have sharply jointed legs and perfect dots for eyes.

"You are so gross, Lizabette." Mo's reproach pulls me back. She's pale, and shadows edge beneath her eyes, which were bright and alert minutes earlier. Dream loss can do that.

"Get over it, Mo, and tell me what the dream-moth looks like."

"Why don't *you* tell me how it tastes?"

"Refreshing." I tug the siphon off her eye. "Humor me."

"Red. With . . . no, pink wings and . . ." Her eyes widen. "Ohmigod."

"It's like you dreamed it but now you can't remember?"

She nods, eyeing the yellow and pink dust on my palm.

"That dream is gone for good now."

"You mean . . . no more moth dreams ever?"

"Not for you; that's what a dream siphon does. Now, if all your questions are answered, how about getting out of my office?"

Instead she paces my tiny floor. "That's why you built the mask—fairies siphon off dreams and you were protecting yours?"

The few I have left, I think. What I say is, "Where'd you find the body?"

"The bread crawled over my hand this morning."

"I thought you don't eat wheat."

"Jesus, Constable, you keeping a file on me?"

"Was it your bread?"

"Of course not. And I don't want the lecture about caring for a juvenile. . . ."

My stomach flops. I get it now, why Mo's scared about the fairy instead of curious. Why she came to me.

"It was Peg's bread," I say.

Mo nods.

Seven years ago Peg was just a gaunt six-year-old with the most infectious laugh ever to ring in the drab hallways of McMurty's. Now, she's thirteen and one of Mo's hangers. She's a cute, good-natured kid, the kind who never gives you shit no matter what you catch 'em doing or who you're hauling them back to. Peg always gives you a smile and a cheerful word, even while her big eyes are speaking volumes: "Stop the squad car, let me disappear. . . ."

"Is Peg hurt?" My voice sounds like it's in a tunnel.

"She took off."

"She's gone?"

"She's *Peg*. She could be anywhere."

"Mo? Did you actually see her leave?"

Drooping, Mo squeezes her goofy lizard-covered gut. "No. And she left her things behind."

A familiar urge to smack her rises in me and then falls away. If Peg had been anywhere but Mo's, I'd never have known she was gone.

"Liz?"

"Peg's in trouble." Taken by fairies—I try to calculate how much she'll have aged. Nine minutes is a year when someone dreams in feytime. She could be in her thirties.

"Why, Liz? What do they want?"

"She killed a fairy." Pulling myself together, I indicate the corpse in its bready frame. "Exhibit A here was siphoning. One of Peg's dreams escaped, probably. It knocked her into the bread. . . ."

"They're allergic to bread, Holmes?"

"No. The siphoner got stuck in the peanut butter, struggled, and released a lot of pixdust."

"Pix—?"

I point at the orange specks in the peanut butter. "This. Pixdust."

"Looks like pollen."

"It's dander."

"Fairy dander." Despite what she's already seen, Mo's voice is skeptical.

"Magic fairy dander. It gave the bread the wiggles, and the slice folded over, strangling or squishing our victim. They're pretty delicate."

"And now? What's happened to Peg?"

"Taken."

"Where, to Fairyland?"

"Basically."

Mo rakes a shaking hand through her hair. "If she comes back, will she be like you?"

I pretend I don't know what she means.

"Great. What do we do?"

"Nothing." I peel the fairy corpse off the bread, and it withers into a husk. The bread I dunk in a cup of coffee, soaking it until it falls into crumbs, and then washing the mess down the sink. "Go home, Mo."

"You're going after her."

"No."

"You love that kid."

"Mo, she's gone."

"You're going, Liz, and I'm going too. Or else."

I squash the box and dump it in recycling.

"Or else—that's a threat. You're supposed to imagine dire consequences. Except you can't imagine, can you?"

"You'll have to spell it out."

"Come on. I could total your life—I know everything about you."

Unstrapping my sidearm, I unload it and open the office

safe, trading the weapon for a small pouch of pills and vials. "You'll be sorry if you come, Maureen Gonzich."

She bares her teeth.

"First off, you have to do everything I say. And no whining if you aren't up for a life-altering experience."

"Is that your idea of a briefing, Constable?"

"There's more. Pop out your contact lenses and put on your glasses. And take these."

Her eyes glitter as I dig out the pills. "What are they?"

"Antihistamines—totally legal. Sorry to disappoint you."

She tosses them back, sullen. It goes both ways—I know her teenage secrets, too.

"Now what?"

"The first time you go into a fairy city you have to offer a flesh tribute. We have to pull out one of your toenails."

I'm hoping she'll back out, but Mo doesn't even flinch. "Got anesthetic? Or do I butch it out?"

We don't talk as I set us up, do the surgery, wrap her bleeding toe. Pulling out a vial of aged pixdust, I mix it with saline. This gets trickled, one drop each side, into our ears.

"Hold the toenail up on your palm," I say.

It's already happening. My ears ring, so loud it hurts, and I point Mo toward the window so she'll see things slowing down—people freezing in mid-step, cars and trucks gliding to a halt. A thick, crumbly slop made of pixdust, discarded flower petals, and bits of opalescent eggshell comes into view, covering everything and everyone. Under its drifts, people turn into anonymous perches. It makes little hills of the cars and park benches.

Only the trees are clear of the slurr, fizzing air sweetly from their leaves to blow off the fragments and dust. They glow, making the daylight green.

Down here at ground level, fairies are few and far between. Only the flower-threshers are down in the pit of the city, drawing petals into their baskets with long multi-fingered rakes.

Something buzzes past, licking the toenail off Mo's upturned hand.

"Welcome to Kasqueam," I say.

Dusting the slop off of her shoulders and hair, Mo bites her lip again, this time so hard it bleeds. "I thought we were *going* somewhere."

I lead her out into the open air of the park. "The cities coexist—feytime's just faster. Kasqueam changes too fast for us to see . . . especially since we don't want to."

"It's like barnacles. . . ." She squints at the slurr-covered skyline of downtown.

"I guess." On the roofs, layered bulbs made of orange pixie wax cover the shingles in a crust. Six or seven feet tall, each bulb forms a chamber, and through their translucent walls we can see sleeping fairies and their various posses-sions. From time to time they crack open at the top, reveal-ing onion-layers of wax as a fairy emerges, buzzing wings adding to the general throb in the air.

One of the fliers bears down on us, and I have to grab Mo to keep her from dodging. The fairy swerves, clearing her by inches.

"No sudden moves," I lecture sternly. "They're faster—they'll always go around us if you don't skitter."

"They're so big," she says, stunned.

"They're older." Unlike the corpse on the bread, the fairies buzzing past us are teen-sized. Most are red-skinned with shaggy black hair, though a few lean toward Euro, Asian, and African heritage. They have long, angular limbs and wings like hummingbirds. The vibration of their wings makes my skin buzz and itch.

Sandy grains of dander are coming off their bodies in wispy orange clouds. Smelling of sugar and sweat, the pix-dust swirls in a fog along their flight paths.

"See?" I explain. "They eat flowers, they exude this."

"And they live in bulby waxy barnacles and they play chicken with the tourists. Got it."

"They do all sorts of things. Harvest flowers and sing songs and have wars with other cities. All the action is up higher."

"Where the air's clean?" She sniffles, despite the allergy pills.

"Cleaner."

"And they siphon dreams. I forgot to ask why."

"It's how they get stuff." I point at a bulb filled with odds and ends, a storeroom. We climb to the building roof and press our noses against the wax. Inside are ornate chairs, a dogsled, cartoonish paintings, a mushroom-shaped lamp, a bicycle, buckets, animal-head plaques. "They can't lift much, even when they're full grown, but dreams don't weigh any-thing. We're just a great big flea market as far as they're con-cerned."

"Fairies. They always seem so benign in the stories."

"You need to read older stories," I grunt.

"They got better publicists now?" The fear on her face had been fading, changing to curiosity and excitement. "So we're here, and Peg's here. Where do we start, Liz?"

We. I find I'm glad, for once, to have company in fey-time. I wiggle my foot inside my left shoe, imagining I can feel the missing toenails, my entrance tributes to four pix hives: Lundundown, Gayparee, Turanna, and Kasqueam.

Think, Liz. Peg. Brought here for killing the siphoner. But stashed where?

"We need a gossipmonger," I say.

"A what?"

One of the blurring forms swoops out of the flighted crowds above, wings driving a breeze that lifts our hair.

"The walls remember everything that ever happened for all the generations. Listen." I gesture at a layer of wax lying heavy on the side of a building, and Mo's eyes widen at the low murmur coming from it, a mixture of words that in Kasqueam are—I've been told—mostly Salish and Sto:lo. "It's like a database, a history. They know everything that happens here, and the gossipmongers speak the language."

"You're keeping Dogwood waiting." The swooping fairy had stopped just short of colliding with us. Arms folded over a skinny chest, she's wearing a sarong pieced together from dreamed dishtowels and rock T-shirts.

"We want to find a girl. Peg, a human girl. We know she's here but not where." Mo says it all in a rush, before I can make the request properly.

"Can you pay?"

I hold up the dream siphon, but the creature turns up her nose. "Newcomers talk, else you walk. So say the walls . . ."

"Don't rhyme at us," I say. "What do you want?"

The fairy's eyes flick down to Mo's stomach and the critters on the dress. "The name of your unborn?"

"No names," I say. "Besides, she's not preg—"

"Dogwood isn't addressing you!"

"I don't know anything worth trading," Mo says.

Dogwood points at me. "Tell me about *her*."

"About—"

"No names," I repeat weakly, and the fairy springs to my shoulders, bird-light despite her size. Her hands twist in my hair. "Tell me of your vexy friend," she croons.

Mo frowns and looks at me. "Vexy?"

I pry my hair free and check the fairy's hand for loose strands, letting go as soon as Dogwood vaults away. She lights on a lamppost, twirling.

"Vexy means troublesome, Mo."

"Troublecow." Dogwood trills ear-splitting laughter. Her wings throb, stirring up the orange slurr. "You have nothing?"

"She has a phobia," Mo says.

Dogwood's eyes widen. Her lips part, revealing small, glittering teeth. "Fears? Excellent coin!"

There's no help for it now. "You'll tell her where Peg is?"

"So pacted."

The magic words. "Go ahead, dammit," I tell Mo.

"She's afraid of needles." Mo looks at me sidelong, probably pleased that she's managed a trade but knowing not to gloat when I clearly want to clock her.

Dogwood shrieks again, pleased, and word goes out through the walls. I have enemies here. They may already be combing the dream-shops for hypodermics.

"Where's the kid?" Mo demands.

Dogwood pirouettes. "Fools. She's where you left her."

"What's that supposed to mean? Liz?"

I groan. "Your place."

We walk to Mo's house, Dogwood trailing us lazily. Sure enough we find Peg there, lying on a Hanger hammock. Pixwax has been dripped all over her like melted candles, encasing her body, cutting itself into diamonds where it hangs through the hammock mesh. The thin stem of a dream siphon drifts above her face, its open tip divided like a wishbone, its stems bent into the corners of her eyes. The siphon's tip pokes up through a small break in the pixwax, extruding set pieces from Peg's dreams—couches and books and xylophones. The dreams are brighter than a usual teenager's, as if Peg hasn't been thinned as much as most kids her age.

An acid-melted nightmask—my old one, I realize with a shock—is lying on the pillow beside her.

"That's why the dream that killed the fairy had so much kick," I murmur. "You've been masking her."

Fairies zoom in and out of the room, stripping any people-dreams of their clothing before shredding their bodies to dusty flakes, then picking up the objects and buzzing away.

"She's asleep?" Mo whispers.

"No," I say, relieved. "She's on the verge of waking."

"Sounds like the same thing to me."

"It's just different enough. When a human falls asleep in feytime, her body ages at fairy speed. You and I lie down now for a three-hour nap, we'd go home a couple of old ladies."

"Whatever. We're putting an end to it now, right?" Mo's voice is grim as she reaches for one of the passing fairies.

I grab her by the shoulders, slam her against a wall.

"You can't just flatten them. They'd put you down."

"You talk like we're fucking livestock."

"Smack one, honey—you'll find out."

Pulling free, she collapses onto a couch. "And you've known all about this for how long?"

"Always."

"How do you deal?"

I shake my head, having no good answer.

Finally she sighs. "What do we do?"

"Find some way to buy them off."

"With what?"

"I don't know yet."

She looks at Dogwood, who is crooning and twisting on one of the hammocks. "Any suggestions?"

The gossipmonger shrugs, making a gloat of it.

"Can you tell me why they grabbed her?" Mo asks.

"Perhaps."

"How much?"

"Mo, it doesn't matter," I say, but there's a Mountie's Stetson lying on the coffee table beside us, and Dogwood eyes it covetously.

"Dogwood could use one of those," she says.

"So pacted." Mo hooks the hat off the coffee table, tossing it like a Frisbee. It lands right on the fairy's head. Then it bears her, shrieking, to the ground.

"I told you, they aren't strong," I say as the fairy flails. The hat falls off before I can rescue her. Dogwood zooms into flight, buzzing Mo once and then hovering at a wary distance, wings thrumming furiously.

"Mo, they trade in dreams. Hard goods are useless to them."

"Okay. Fine. I understand. Where's that siphon?"

I hold out the stem we got off the corpse this morning. Mo wedges it into her eye.

"Look at the hat," I say, and a clean copy of the Stetson bubbles out of the stem and plumps up to life size.

Dogwood comes out of her snit, snatching it with a pleased screech and zooming out of the room. Mo wobbles. When I try to steady her, she nearly drags me to the floor.

"Take a breath—it can be tiring."

"She's gone." Mo's expression darkens. "Little shrike ripped us off."

"No. The economy runs on cascade barters. She'll trade the hat for something, trade that for something else. When she gets something she actually wants, she'll come answer your questions."

"You're sure?"

"She'll definitely be back. She's not hanging around because we're novelties."

"Why? What's she want with us?"

"Nothing I'm gonna let happen."

"Fine." She straightens up. "I had plans for that hat. Now I can't quite remember. . . ."

"It's what dreams do, Mo. They melt away."

"They're *taken*. Will we get an answer soon?"

"It'll be bad news," I say, and suddenly the gossipmonger is back, a satchel in her little hand.

She settles atop a bookshelf with a little curtsy. "The child is providing goods to the dreammongers as compensation for the death of Sundew and to punish the withholding of dreams."

Withholding . . . my eyes drift to the melted nightmask near Peg.

"It must have been an accident," Mo says, trying to reach past the pitiless black eyes. "Don't blame Peg. . . ."

"Dogwood pacted to answer a question, not to argue."

"How long will they keep her?"

"Until she's out of dreams, woman, just like the Trouble-cow." With that, Dogwood thrums up to the corner and presses her ear to a waxy bubble hanging from the ceiling.

Mo turns to me, desperate. "We could talk to someone else."

"No. She's speaking for them all. The only way we're getting Peg back is by making it a hassle for them to keep her."

She puzzles over that . . . then yawns. "I'm bagged."

"We're not built for this." I pass her a packet of caffeine pills.

"How long have we been here?"

"An hour, I think."

"I'm already tired."

"Take the pills."

"I shouldn't." She tosses two tablets back anyway, taking the ever-present gum out of her mouth temporarily as she swallows.

"Shouldn't . . ." My hand comes up over my mouth. "You *are* knocked up."

Her grin flashes. "I didn't lie. I just didn't answer when you asked. What's the big hairy problem?"

"You'll be lucky if the kid only has two heads."

"Stop making shit up."

"I don't have an imagination, remember? You have to leave."

"I'm not going until Peg's loose."

"It's not safe, Mo."

"Solve this problem and get us out of here, then."

Instead I dart up to her bedroom, looking for her mask. I find a box of them. Nightmasks, their tags read—the newest Lopside creation. Big bright goggles that seal around the eyes to keep the dreams in. The breather is trademark Mo, a thing that should be uncomfortable made perfect and cozy.

When I first escaped Turanna, I built my nightmask out of combat store scraps. I had escaped to humantime with only a few dreams left, and I couldn't bear the idea of losing them to the siphoners one by one.

And the joke on me, the unforgivable thing, was that when Mo stole the mask and started using it, she was preventing the normal dream-siphoning that happens to us all over the course of a lifetime. Masking made her a genius of sorts. At least, that's what they call her in the fashion community.

If this box full of masks is the real reason Kasqueam is making an example of Peg, then I'm the one to blame. Mo couldn't have known what would happen, couldn't know the fairies would see the masks as a first-stage attack on the foundations of their economy, of their very lives. They'd never understand how few people would actually sleep in the things.

"Did she speak true?" Dogwood's voice is a whisper, behind me. I whirl but she lands on my back, her legs locking around my belly, bare ankles crossing, grip firm. One hand claws at my shoulder. "Did your friend speak honestly, Troublecow?"

"I don't know what you mean. . . ." Then her hand comes around in front of my face, clasping a rusty, old-fashioned hypodermic.

Just seeing it makes me break into a sweat. I go still, because if I don't, I'm going to slam backward into a wall and crush her. And I don't dare. I want to live. Have to live if I'm gonna get Peg and Mo out of here.

I should close my eyes, but I can't look away from the dream needle.

"Go now," Dogwood says. "Leave them all—the girl, the woman, the babe. Do as I say and I pact to give them back by nightfall."

"In what kind of shape?"

"We can negotiate," she says.

"I can't."

"Truly?" Now her fingers are hooked through the steel loops of the hypo, her thumb rubbing its plunger. A drop of steaming brown fluid beads on the wickedly sharp point.

Don't run away. Don't scream. My voice, when it comes, sounds like a little girl's. "That can't hurt me."

She hisses. "Take the pact, Troublecow."

"I'm not leaving them." Moving slowly and gently, I unclench her hand from my shoulder, unlock the grip of her legs around my waist. Dogwood bursts into motion, letting go, her wings a loud and violent hum as she whips over my head and drives the needle into my mouth.

I try to scream for Mo, but sound doesn't come. The

point of the needle spears my tongue, going through painfully, and the dream-drug pools around my teeth. I try to spit it back, but the dream is already dissolving. My mind fills with nightmares—shots and punctures and stainless steel plates full of needles, dirty blood-tinged ampoules and sterile pointy shafts, the wide bores of blood donation needles, even the terrible metal slivers wielded by acupuncturists.

The fairy wafts backward to land on the box of masks. "Withholding dreams is forbidden. If your friend masks anyone else, we'll put her down."

I rub at my tongue, feeling for the puncture wound, but it is gone.

"It's a dream. I'll siphon it out," I say.

"Just you try," Dogwood crows, offering me a stem. It is long and thin and I cannot ignore—as I always did before—how its little openings are pointy and hollow. "You should have pacted with me."

Heart pounding, I pick up a brand new mask, staggering back down to the Hangar, and pull it over Mo's face. It fits a little strangely over her glasses, but she doesn't argue. Dogwood shadows me, grim but also pleased.

"How are we supposed to make keeping Peg a hassle?" Mo's voice is muffled.

I fall onto the couch, eyes locked on the wall, and put on my calmest cop voice. "It'll be okay. They've got power, yeah, but they're dumb and they've got short attention spans. We'll think of something."

Her hand clasps mine, warm and dry, squeezing. "What they're doing to Peg. It's what they did to you, isn't it?"

"More or less."

"And now they say you're trouble?"

"I've got a vengeful streak, remember?"

Her fingers trace a long scar running up her ulna. "But why not get rid of you, Liz?"

I open my shirt and show her the three orange circles around my collarbone, the ones that don't show in human-time. "I helped one of them, in Gayparee—that's their name for Paris."

"You in Paris? I can't see that."

"It was the fairy Paris, Maureen. I didn't go to Versailles or anything. The point is Cowslip put these marks on me, and the others can't kill me."

"You're her pet?"

"No."

"She's like an animal rights activist?"

"I'm getting tired of the cow analogy."

"Hey, it's not my fault the moo fits. You're just cranky because I'm in on your great big secret."

The funny thing is that I've wanted to tell Mo for years. But I don't say that. My skin prickles, and I try not to think of needles. "I'm worried about Peg."

"Cow cow troublecow, Lizzie is a troublecow. Cause a row, holy wow, Lizzie is—"

"Would you stop?"

"Cow!" It's a shout. "*Sacred* Cow!" Mo turns to Dogwood, eyes gleaming.

The gossipmonger makes Mo dream her a hairy blue jacket before admitting there is a way to make a human too holy—or something like it—for dream siphoning. She gives up the information without much fuss. There's a catch: we need a salve for Peg, an eyewash made from the leaves from something I've never heard of, a jester tree.

We troop from one end of Kasqueam to the other trying to find out about the tree. As the hours pass we get more and more drained, but the sun doesn't move in the sky. It beats down, merciless and golden, from the nine o'clock position. Twice we have to take more caffeine pills.

"How long is a day to them?" Mo asks. Dreaming things—chariots and spinning wheels and winking lightbulbs with legs—is making her ever more haggard, and I wish I didn't know about the baby.

"A lifetime," I say. "Spawn at dawn, mate at dusk. By twilight they're thirty feet tall."

"Thirty. And they can't lift more than a few grams?"

"I've heard up north in the summer they can make it to fifty feet tall. Long days, you know? They mate and their eggs pile up in the streets. Tiny little eggs, billions of them: in a city this big, they stack seven feet deep. And when the sun goes down, the fairies die."

"Billions of eggs." Her hand drifts up to the seven-foot mark as she considers this. "Liz, this doesn't look like billions of fairies. Don't all the eggs take?"

I tap the filter on her mask, trying not to notice how her eyes are hollow and bruised through the green glass of the goggles. "That's why the mask doesn't just cover the eyes. The eggs that live are the ones we inhale. They sit in our lungs through the night. Fairies hatch inside us, Mo."

Suddenly she's very busy checking her mask seals.

By now word is in the walls that Dogwood is vending

dreams to order, and we get into a complex four-way barter. An ancient fairy has a vial of jester salve, all prepared and ready, but payment comes dear. Mo has to make a skyscraper-high aquarium full of fish. I hold her steady while she pops her goggles and siphons it out of her mind. It grows to the clouds—an octagonal pillar, filled with shellfish and fantastic creatures. She cheats a little, filling it with pink lemonade so she won't lose her water dreams, throwing in more of the insects that have filled her nightmares since we were both girls. Even so, she loses some major dreams—sea horses and clams, sand dollars and smooth black pebbles and long thin reeds.

When she's done she pitches to her knees and I think for a second she's passed out.

This is what Dogwood is waiting for, why she's stuck close. I always pick up a greedy shadow when I speed into feytime. Dogwood wants us asleep and at her mercy. She'd catch Mo's baby and the dream-eaters would have Peg. We'd be mindless old women before they let us wake.

But Mo doesn't fall, just hangs there, head down, on her hands and knees, while the pact is declared complete. In exchange for the aquarium we get the salve.

"This better work," Mo says, trying to sound threatening. Her lips are bleeding.

I have my doubts, but I don't tell her that. "It'll be okay, Mo."

We stagger back to Lopside Fashions and hear a crackling sound that cuts off as we open the door. I light up incense, filling the Hangar with smoke until the dream siphoners are driven out. Only Dogwood refuses to go, retreating to the high corner of the room, waving the smoke away and then covering her face with one of her shirts.

I take up a pair of sewing shears and try to cut off the wax covering Peg's face. They slide over the barrier with a screech.

"Too hard to cut?" Mo asks.

Blinking, I look around. There are tiny basting brushes all over the floor and a drizzle of fluid—some kind of potion, surely—is pooled in the hollow of Peg's elbow. I touch the back of my fingernail to the liquid, which is clear but somehow brighter than water, almost lit from within. It dries fast, and when I flick at the fingernail seconds later, I find it is diamond-hard.

My eyes are welling up with tears. We were so close . . . and now we're out of time.

"Liz?"

Dogwood laughs shrilly through her shirt.

"They hardened her cocoon." I scratch my hardened nail over the wax uselessly.

"No!" Mo slides her hands over Peg, pressing, probing for soft spots and finding none. "We just have to bust her out."

"Time's up." I've lost my cop voice; it comes out a giggle.

"Dogwood'll tell us how to cut through—"

"Don't you see?" I lower my voice to a hiss. "She's screwing us deliberately."

"Someone else, then."

"You're dreamed out for today."

"I'd still try," Mo whispers.

I take a long breath, choking on incense, and make myself look away from Peg's face. "I'm sorry, Mo, but if we get caught here nobody will help her."

"So we leave? Come back once we've slept it off?"

Tomorrow. A fairy's lifetime. I nod anyway.

"The longer she's in there . . ."

"She won't run out of dreams in a day," I say. Mo wells up, and every urge I have to comfort her blows away as I wonder how she sees me. Harsh words rise from my belly and I barely hold them in.

"We aren't giving up, Mo." The thought of leaving the kid here feels like broken glass in my chest, but we're too close to getting lost ourselves. "Say good-bye."

"All right." The goggles have misted over, and she takes the nightmask off, leaning over to kiss Peg's forehead.

Then, with a glare, she spits her gum into the opening where the dream siphon extends above the wax.

"Mo!"

Dogwood howls, furious. Shoving me away with her free hand, Mo makes a seal with the gum over the vent before smearing the last drop of hardening potion over it. A single pink strand stretches between the siphon above Peg's face and Mo's thumb, thinning and breaking to fall in a sticky line down Peg's wax-cased chest.

"What can it hurt?"

I don't have an answer to that. I'm frozen, watching as one of Peg's dreams wells up the vent from her eye, then hits the blockage. It backs up the tube and emerges, somewhat flattened, from the other end. As the siphon jitters but fails to dislodge from Peg's eye, the dream unfurls into a frog.

Wax puffs up around it in a tiny bubble, and I poke the bulge with the shears. Still impervious.

Other things are already crawling out after the frog—a long thread of fern, a spray of little daisies. Each dream bounces off the one before, skating to a free space on her skin. They don't seem to have trouble bending the wax from the inside.

Soon Peg's face is covered in dreams—foliage I recognize from Burns Bog, hardware which mostly looks like school furniture.

People are coming out too, a handful of kids who are probably classmates. Under the wax they are protected from Dogwood. Helpless to destroy them, she growls down at us from the ceiling. The people dreams grow to a height of six inches, exploring the plants rooted in the dreamscape forming on Peg's body.

"Field trip," Mo whispers. "Look, there's a little science teacher."

"And a bus." The group putters over to the hem of Peg's nightgown, distending the wax. I test the surface again, fruitlessly.

A yawn splits Mo's face, and she shakes herself.

"We have to get you out of here."

"Always the fucking cop. Leave me alone."

A trio of tiny funnel clouds blows out of the siphon next, circling the wandering kids. Storm-cellar things appear: jam jars, spiderwebs, loose two by fours, hockey gear.

By now, Peg's body is half hidden by the crowd of dreams caught in the growing pixwax balloon. Peering in, I have a hazy sense of a story unfolding—the tornadoes drive the kids to the shelter, where they find a tunnel that leads to a helicopter. It seems like it all has something to do with trying to capture the whirlwinds in mayonnaise jars.

Watching it, I all but fall into a standing doze. I snap free and shake Mo. "We gotta go."

"Five more minutes," she pleads.

"No." I cast one last glance at Peg . . .

. . . and see the two of us.

The dream Lizabette is standing atop a pile of bone-shaped branches, wearing a uniform and explaining something. I can't hear the words, but I'm caught by how old I seem, how bossy.

But I'm tall, too, muscled and strong.

"Jesus," Mo says. Her Peg-dreamed self is a sexy dragon-girl, wild-eyed and gorgeous, snapping its jaws at everything. For a second I think I'd give a lot to be seen that way, but it's clear from Mo's face that this isn't at all the way she'd hoped Peg saw her.

"She trusts you," she says bitterly, looking at the little me. Then her expression changes, and she's pleading. "Liz, do something."

"I'll try." I pound on the wax membrane. All the dream-people pull loose from their scenery and look at me, a giant-sized thing rapping on the sky of their world. Dragoness Mo flies up to me, spraying fire, playful and beautiful. The flame thins the wax, but not enough. And then she's coiling off on another tangent, no help at all.

I look past her to the other me, pointing at the wax, at the weapon on her little hip. A yawn cracks my face, and even though I'm standing I can feel my eyelids sinking.

The dreamed me is still talking, talking too much, I must yak at Peg all the time, please shut up . . . and beside me Mo is wobbling.

"Okay, now we *have* to get out."

That's when the dream version of myself picks up a glass jar full of tornado and hurls it against the orange wax barrier.

There's a pop, just a tiny one. Then the whole balloon bursts. Dream-things tear around the room, and Dogwood gives chase, coughing. The whirlwinds set up conflicting currents; wind sucks at us one minute and blows us against the walls the next. One of the twisters blasts between my teeth, shooting down my throat and then dissipating, filling my mind with delicious long-lost shades of stormy weather.

Clear pockets of air are appearing in the cloud of incense. Just outside the room, I can hear rising fairy voices. The smoke in the air is still too dense, but they'll rush us as soon they can.

"The jester eyedrops," Mo shouts. She struggles to the hammock, twists her arm into the mesh so she can't be blown away, and pries up Peg's eyelids. "Liz, come on!"

I launch myself off the wall, opening the flask and washing the holy liquid into Peg's too-large eyes.

Just like that the fairies are keening, angry and cheated.

Still hacking, Dogwood falls on Peg's dream-people in a fury, slicing them to pieces. I just manage to grab the tiny version of myself, shoving it into Peg's mouth. The dragon dream turns instantly to follow, but Mo, catching her around the serpentine waist, looks speculatively at the gossipmonger and her shredding claws.

"Don't," I shout—too strongly, too much like a cop. It's

the wrong thing. All our history will drive her to do the opposite of what I say. "Mo, she adores you!"

She gives me a flinty, stubborn look.

"Can't you see? You have to be there—alive, inside her— if the way Peg sees you is going to change!"

Dogwood rushes forward, and I think, for an instant, that Mo will let her have the little spitfire. But no, a quick turn and dream-Mo flicks snakily down Peg's throat. Dogwood's hand stops just short of Peg's teeth.

"Can we go now?" Mo pulls Peg off the bed and staggers all of two steps before sinking to the floor, wax dripping into her velvet dress. She is oblivious to the tiny dreamed lightning bolt caught in her anklet.

Storm dreams, I think, savoring them—can't let her lose those. I snap the bolt free and squeeze its buzzing length between my fingers, press it past Peg's lips.

"Why isn't she waking up?" Mo demands fuzzily.

"She's falling asleep," I say. I can see the young face aging, ever so slightly. Mo sees it too and the reality of this place hits her again. Her eyes widen in fear even as she struggles to keep them open.

"It's okay," I tell her. "It's over."

Then I give them both a good pinch, squeezing the backs of their arms just above the elbow, catching the nerve there hard enough to bruise. Mo cries out, trying to yank free. Then her eyes widen and she starts to wake, slowing to statue speed.

Peg opens her eyes before she goes. "Lizabette," she says, smiling wide. "You came for me."

The look on her face leaves me breathless.

"*We* came," is what I say. I kiss her wax-sticky forehead and pinch her again, and she goes still on the floor beside Mo. Safe, both of them.

"My turn now." I turn to laugh in the face of the gossip-monger's fury, ignoring the voice inside that says I've barely come out even. Needle dreams, a fey-touched baby, Mo undoubtedly already thinking of ways to finagle more visits to Kasqueam, and who knows what the jester salve did to Peg. And me . . . I'm the responsible one.

But Dogwood just sees a loss for her side, so I smile as she yells curses at me in a language I don't speak. Imagining moths and thunder, I stick out my tongue at her, blowing a raspberry of triumph before pinching myself back to the slow world where I belong.

A. M. Dellamonica had the kind of action-packed childhood that most people dream of, featuring actual plane crashes and the occasional really long car trip. After catching her first fish at the age of six, she realized she was ready to fend for herself in the wild, though in the end it took her eleven years to pack her books and depart.

Her fiction began to appear in print in 1986 and, despite repeated washings, remains in circulation in a variety of print and on-line locales, including anthologies like *Mojo: Conjure Stories* and *Alternate Generals III*. Five of her works can be found anytime at SCIFI.COM. A prolific book reviewer, she teaches writing through the UCLA Online Extension Writer's Program.

Her Web site is at www.sff.net/people/alyx

Author's Note

Sleepers and abductees and time distortions—these motifs recur in old stories again and again. Rip van Winkle awakes to find he is twenty years older than when he originally lay down for a nap. Tam Lin, kept for generations as a slave by the Queen of the Faeries, is still young and beautiful when he is finally rescued. A musician plays for the Fey for one night, returning to the world years later. Meanwhile, Mr. and Mrs. Smith of urban legend see the lights of a UFO, and later notice that the dashboard clock says they are missing several hours.

I wanted to write an abduction story set in a fairy city, with magical urban denizens who were intimately involved with an unknowing humanity. Having conceived the fairies as rather parasitic creatures, it was easy to imagine that as human populations spread and grew—moving further from the forest and deeper into a world of concrete and steel— they would bring their unseen dream harvesters with them.

"The Dream Eaters" is set in my East Vancouver neighborhood, an endless source of energy and inspiring people. Of particular note are the stilt walkers, fire jugglers, and visual artists who make up Public Dreams, an organization that mounts the summer lantern festival, the Parade of Lost Souls, and several other events that edge this city and its people a little closer to feytime.

The Faery Reel

Neil Gaiman

If I were young as once I was,
 and dreams and death more distant then,
I wouldn't split my soul in two,
 and keep half in the world of men,
So half of me would stay at home,
 and strive for Faërie in vain,
While all the while my soul would stroll
 up narrow path, down crooked lane,
And there would meet a faery lass
 and smile and bow with kisses three,
She'd pluck wild eagles from the air
 and nail me to a lightning tree
And if my heart would run from her
 or flee from her, be gone from her,
She'd wrap it in a nest of stars
 and then she'd take it on with her
Until one day she'd tire of it,
 all bored with it and done with it.

She'd leave it by a burning brook,
 and off brown boys would run with it.
They'd take it and have fun with it
 and stretch it long and cruel and thin,
They'd slice it into four and then
 they'd string with it a violin.
And every day and every night
 they'd play upon my heart a song
So plaintive and so wild and strange
 that all who heard it danced along
And sang and whirled and sank and trod
 and skipped and slipped and reeled and rolled
Until, with eyes as bright as coals,
 they'd crumble into wheels of gold. . . .

But I am young no longer now,
 for sixty years my heart's been gone
To play its dreadful music there,
 beyond the valley of the sun.
I watch with envious eyes and mind,
 the single-souled, who dare not feel
The wind that blows beyond the moon,
 who do not hear the Faery Reel.
If you don't hear the Faery Reel,
 they will not pause to steal your breath.
When I was young I was a fool.
 So wrap me up in dreams and death.

Neil Gaiman is a transplanted Briton currently living in the American Midwest. He is the author of the award-winning *Sandman* series of graphic novels, and of the novels *Neverwhere* and *American Gods*. *American Gods* won the Hugo, the Bram Stoker, the SFX, and the Locus Awards. His most recent novel, intended for children of all ages, *Coraline*, won the Bram Stoker Award in the Work for Young Readers category, and was a finalist for the World Fantasy Award. His most recent novel is *Anansi Boys*. Gaiman's collaborations with artist Dave McKean include *Mr. Punch*, the children's books *The Day I Swapped My Dad for 2 Goldfish* and *The Wolves in the Walls*, and their new film *Mirror-Mask*.

In addition, Gaiman is a talented poet and short story writer whose work has been published in a number of the Datlow/Windling adult fairy tale anthologies, in *The Green Man* and *A Wolf at the Door*, and in several editions of *The Year's Best Fantasy and Horror*. His short work has been collected in *Angels and Visitations* and *Smoke and Mirrors*.

His Web site is www.neilgaiman.com

Author's Note

Most of the poems I've written are happy to sit on the page and be looked at. This one was written with the idea of a faery reel in mind, the beats of a dance that would make your feet twitch and set its measure in the back of your head, and so it was written to be read out loud. You could make up a tune for it, if you like. Proper faery tunes can fill your mind and your feet with their tune and their rhythm so there's no room left to think of anything else and you dance and move to the beat of the song until you collapse, exhausted, and never move again. Don't set it to one of those tunes.

The Shooter at
the Heartrock Waterhole

✥

Bill Congreve

ONE

The rifle kicked, and one of the creatures—the beautiful one—was dead. But the wyrde, as Dad would have called it, began long before then.

Two days ago, I shot and killed two sparrows, and a rabbit I'd called "Attitude." Right after, I buried them out in the deep sand away from the water.

At dawn yesterday, I smelled them as I woke. The sun filtered through the needles of a lone desert oak straight into my eyes. I rolled onto my stomach, lifted my head, and there they lay, just outside the tent flyscreen.

The corpses had been dug from their half-meter-deep holes and had been laid out on the orange sand and the leaf litter as neatly as you like, half a meter from where my head lay on the pillow.

I hadn't heard a thing.

It was an unusual waterhole. A gently sloping dome of granite the color of rusting iron, maybe fifty hectares in area, that the maps called "Heartrock," rose above the desert where I had camped. Millions of years of sparse rainfall—or a glacier in the last ice age—had carved the rock so that the water on that side of the dome all ran off in one spot. At that point there was a lip in the granite about five meters above the floor of the desert and, below that, a pristine rock pool surrounded by a bed of sand the color of red ochre.

From high above, the dome would look like a heart, with the high ground up near the point, aiming north, and the waterhole nestled in the heart of the V in the south.

From the edge of the water a dry sandy creek bed four or five meters across ran a half kilometer out into the desert, where it ended in a salt lake maybe a hundred meters wide. A once-in-a-decade flood would see the creek run for a couple of hours, the lake fill, and the whole place seemingly dry out two or three days later. And if some idiot were to walk out on the salt lake in the couple of months after the rain, they would crack through the crust of salt and drown in mud.

Stunted bloodwoods surrounded the water. The single desert oak grew amongst the spinifex fifty meters out along the creek bed.

I didn't even know what desert it was a part of, just that it was too far north and west to be called a part of the Nullarbor Plain. It smelled and sounded like the end of the world: empty, with an aftertaste of dust, eucalyptus, the soughing of leaves, and then silence.

The animals smelled like dead, wet fur, but with a gamey scent. I stared at them for a couple of seconds and then scrambled out of bed and into a pair of shorts and running shoes. My dad's Anschutz was where I had left it, in the tent at the foot of the bed, but the target rifle wasn't what I needed now. The Remington was in the Toyota: a pump-action shotgun instead of a single-shot twenty-two rifle. I grabbed the machete, pulled down the zipper on the insect screen, and bolted outside, running for the Toyota.

When I had the Remington in my hands, I shouted, "Hello!"

No answer.

I knew that, of course. Not another human being for two hundred kilometers in any direction. That was part of the job description.

But the birds' feathers had been brushed flat and the blood had been washed from the exit wound in the rabbit's skull.

Stunted eucalyptus and acacia scrub surrounded Heartrock's margins, living on what little water ran off the rock. Not enough bush to hide anybody—I know because I checked. As I stood on the peak, the binoculars showed me nothing but a mob of kangaroos resting in the lee of some trees a couple of kilometers away. I knew about them, they came down to the water every night. Kangaroos don't dig dead animals out of half-meter-deep holes and wash the bodies.

"Hello!" I shouted again.

After those first moments of surprise, I hadn't felt

threatened. But that was easy, I had a shotgun in one hand. Yet, somebody—somebody who enjoyed playing games—had dug up those animals. . . . I wasn't alone.

Back at camp, I leaned the Remington against a tree and fired up my small gas stove. I put enough coffee in the plunger for two. Perhaps the smell of coffee brewing might draw whoever was out there into the open. Some old Aboriginal, I expected. Or a prospecting crew playing silly buggers. My mate James was going to study geology when he got to university; this would be his idea of a joke.

But if a prospecting crew had been responsible, where were they? A half hour later I spotted bare footprints leading down into the water.

The first ten days I didn't shoot a thing. Since then each bird I'd shot, I'd buried in a separate grave. I would cut a couple of twigs, strip them of their bark, and tie them into a small cross. I called the corpse of the first sparrow, "An Insensitive Dependence on Bureaucratic Conditions," in a tribute to two favorite authors, wrote the name in pen on the wood, and put the cross at the head of the bird's grave. The second bird was another sparrow. It was "Trixie," after Dad's old Falcon utility. I chopped the legs off both of those and tied them to a tree branch to dry out, and for the ants to get to. I felt queasy at that, but my new boss in Eucla wanted trophies until he knew he could trust me.

A tiny flock of starlings interrupted breakfast one day in my third week. There were six in all. That was slaughter. I waited with the Remington loaded with buckshot till they were close, and then let fly. Five loads of buckshot in seven seconds, spinning from side to side like a maniac. Afterwards, I was a little disturbed at how much I had enjoyed it. When I buried those birds, I took special care.

I named the first rabbit I saw "Attitude," but missed the killing shot. It got away with a graze in its neck, but didn't go far. "Palm Tree," "Coconuts," and "10 Enderley Avenue" were buried alongside the birds. Now the plot of graves a hundred meters out in the desert measured six by three. Well, five by three with three holes, if you counted the bodies next to my tent.

I also had books, but I couldn't spend all day reading.

"Coffee's on!" I shouted.

Nobody came, of course.

I took the job a month ago, right after Dad's funeral.

The Western Australia Agriculture Department employed hunters in the desert to shoot birds—the non-native starlings, sparrows, doves, and shit they've got on the east coast which hadn't yet made it across the desert. Starlings were the big one. They were desperate enough to find people willing to live in total isolation fifteen hundred kilometers from Perth that they weren't worried I had just turned eighteen, only that I had my shooter's license.

In the desert the waterholes are hundreds of kilometers apart. A bird flies in, desperate for water. It goes anywhere else, it dies of thirst. It settles in for a couple of days, recovers a little, maybe moves on, maybe sticks around and dies of boredom. Think of the wider picture: a slow migration of non-native animals into what is still, even with all the wheat, sheep, cattle, grapes, bees, and shit, a fairly pristine environment. Add a hunter with a few loads of buckshot and you've got instant environmentalism. Either that or instant protection of commercial agricultural interests—I wasn't sure which.

Killing things to save others. Ironic, huh?

James and I had broken into the local kindergarten at midnight on James's sixteenth birthday to drink a couple of beers and watch *The Exorcist* on the school VCR. James loved doing things like that. He had spent the whole next day laughing.

Two years later, to the very day, it had been a bus with a load of kids from that same kindergarten that had killed Dad in a pedestrian crossing. More irony. Now here I was in the desert.

That was when I heard the flutter of wings. Weak, tiny wings, not like the small hawks which chased the insects at night, more like a thirsty sparrow.

About twenty meters up the rock slope from where I was camped, a clump of spinifex grew from a crack in the rock overlooking the waterhole. I found my keys, put the Remington behind the seat, and locked the Toyota for the first time in weeks. Then I grabbed the Anschutz from the tent and headed up the slope.

In the last few weeks I had spent hours every day lying beside that spinifex, just out of reach of the needles.

Why the Anschutz? Every weekend when I was a kid Dad would take that thing out to the Blacktown Pistol Club range in western Sydney for club shoots. While he was alive, he never let me use it, just bought me a little Winchester. When he died, I sold the Winchester and kept the Anschutz.

The target rifle wasn't designed for hunting: ring sights instead of telescopic, small bore, single shot with no magazine, floating barrel, the wrong ammunition, and as heavy as all shit—I had to use a sling wrapped around my arm just to hold the thing steady and give myself a chance—but I had only missed the once. And Attitude the rabbit had only bounced around out there in the desert a day or two before coming back to the water and his second bullet.

I began using the Anschutz because it was Dad's, and because the soft-nosed lead bullets it demanded made a mess of any small animal. I kept using it because of how I felt—hitting a two centimeter target with it at fifty meters in these conditions was more an art form than a matter of brute strength.

Sparrows, but *two* of them. I should have brought the Remington after all, and gone closer. Too late now.

I squirmed around until I was comfortable, put an extra couple of cartridges on the rock where I could reach them in a hurry, and waited.

The birds pecked at the sand and hopped down to the water. Aim a little high, the ring sights blotting out all but the small form of the first bird. Breathe out gently and watch the sights drift down across the target, hold the breath, take up the first pressure in the trigger, hold steady . . .

Of course I'd be sacked if the Department ever found out about the Anschutz.

. . . squeeze the trigger . . .

A brown smear across the sights. Slight recoil. A body dropped to the sand and the sparrows flew away.

I felt sick.

∿∿∿∿∿∿∿∿∿∿∿

She was a kind of dusky black, but not aboriginal. Her features were like nothing I've ever seen, even in the tourist markets in Fremantle: eyes slanting up, nictitating membranes, ears that were more like nubs surrounding a depressed pattern in her skull than human ears, webbed fingers and toes. She could have been fifteen, a little younger than me.

She was naked. She was dead.

Yin and yang, Dad had always said. Light and dark. A little bit of the light had just left the waterhole.

I had my father, Rudolf Cartwright, cremated. I took the official urn of ashes that contained a bit of Dad, a bit of coffin, and bits of a few other dead people and their coffins as well given how busy the crematorium was, to Bluff Knoll in the Stirling Ranges. The mountain was the first place Dad and I had stopped at for more than a few hours on our trip from Sydney after Mum went back to her family in Ireland.

October twenty-second at eleven fifteen P.M., four years ago, her plane took off. And despite all the promises, she never came back.

That was a confused time. Neither Dad nor I had wanted to stay in Sydney. He left his job and took me out of school. Both of us wanted a fresh start. We sold everything we couldn't fit in the car. Only when we drove away did we decide where it was we wanted to go.

Dad and I had fought tooth and nail for four days crossing the Nullarbor; by the time we had reached the Stirling Ranges northeast of Albany a day after leaving Norseman, we couldn't stand the sight of each other. He had climbed the steep, winding track below the cliffs and around and up to the back of the mountain while I sat at the base in a sulk. Then I had become afraid that he really was sick of me and would just keep on walking, down the far side of the mountain and away . . . or worse.

I ran up the mountain. On top we hugged and cried.

Burials and graves are for the living, not the dead. Bluff Knoll was where my memories of my father, and my impressions of place and time, were inseparable. Symbols. After I left Perth on my way out to the Agriculture Department's office in Eucla, I had stopped at the ranges. I climbed Bluff Knoll in the dark, and buried the urn near the crest about two A.M., a three-hundred-meter cliff on one side, a view across a hundred kilometers to the ocean on the other. It was windy and raining.

I don't know why I thought of her as *her*. She had no breasts, no nipples, and no genitals. Set in her navel was a dull chunk of black rock that wouldn't lift out. She could have been a boy but for the shape of her face and her rounded hips. The question only entered my mind as I carried her back to the Toyota and the first aid kit. I looked down at her in my arms and saw her full lips and her long, wet hair framing her face, and had no doubt. Perhaps it was her hair more than anything else—wild and long, straight and thick, the color of wild henna.

The bullet hole was in the side of her chest, below her left armpit, above her heart. There was no exit hole. At first, her blood had run freely; now it had slowed to a dribble. By the time I reached the campsite, it had stopped altogether.

I bandaged the wound, the scissors clinking against the stone in her navel. It was magnetized. I thumped on her breastbone in an imitation of the CPR I'd seen, and gave her mouth-to-mouth.

Nothing. So I did it all again, her body unfeeling under my hands.

I don't know how long it took me to stop. I fell back against the wheel of the Toyota and stared at her.

I stopped staring when I began shivering. It was night, the full moon at least a third of the way across the sky. Twelve hours since I'd shot her. I'd probably fallen asleep, but my head didn't feel like it. A bit like having a hangover without having the beers to get me there. I'd dreamt of water, but my eyes felt full of sand.

I wandered around the campsite in a daze, then staggered across to the waterhole to wash my face.

With the moonlight and the clear desert sky, I didn't need a torch. I'd walked this route a hundred times in the last weeks and knew every shrub, every twig, every boulder hidden under the desert floor. Heartrock loomed above. The trees rustled in a light breeze.

Then I tripped and fell on my face. I turned. Nothing. But it had felt like a branch coming alive under my foot . . . a snake? The sand lay bare under the moonlight, the nearest cover meters away. Perhaps a death adder sleeping *in* the sand? No, not in the cold at night.

I crawled forward to the water's edge, dipped my hands. Gasped. The water was freezing. Nothing in the desert in summer should feel that cold. I lifted my hands from the water, ice crackling from my fingers—not just my perception then, it *was* freezing.

Good. I splashed my face, opening my eyes to the water, needing to wash them out, needing to force myself awake. I gasped again, the cold driving under my eyelids.

I shook my head and wiped the ice and water from my face. For seconds I saw nothing through the moisture but the blur of bright moonlight to my right, then the blur shifted, and spun into a spiral of stars, twisting before my eyes, covering the whole of my vision, shifting until it was centered in front of me, dropping . . . I fell face first into the freezing water and bounced in shock to my feet, for seconds unable to force my chest to go through the motions of breathing.

Shaking with the cold, I stepped back. The moon was high on my right, back where it should be. Still water glinted with reflected moonlight; the dome of Heartrock loomed above.

A wavelet rippled across the surface.

Something was in the water—over against the rock-face, in the dark.

Some sort of native rat? A rabbit going for a swim? It'd freeze its arse off. I laughed nervously and stepped back again.

The next wave splashed across the sand and wet my feet. I turned and ran three or four paces, then looked back. The waterhole was only twenty meters across. There was no wind, how could it throw a wave a meter up onto the shore?

But the girl belonged here. That much I *did* know. She had deliberately taken a bullet to save the sparrows. She had dug up the dead animals and laid them outside my tent. She had obviously thought of herself as the protector of this place. I went back to camp and picked her up. Halfway back to the waterhole, my biceps stinging into agony, I switched her from my arms into a fireman's carry.

Yin and yang. Light and dark.

With the girl's body pressing against my shoulders, forcing my head forward, I didn't see the waterhole until I was only a couple of paces away, but then I swayed to a standstill and stared in terror.

The water glowed from below, a glow that I had once seen in a movie, as an orbiting spaceship moved from the shadow cast by a planet toward the emergent glow of an accelerated sunrise. Can you imagine it? That glow of promise before the spaceship moves into the light? Now turn that wondrous glow into a photonegative of absolute dark. Not so much the absence of light, though definitely that, but a covenant that wherever this darkness came, light would never return.

Above that darkness, myriad glints of light reflected like stars. And above the glinting light was the ice—ice on the sand, ice on the rock, ice weighing down the branches of trees and flattening the shrubs and the spinifex. Then I realized the glinting on the surface of the water was ice, too—a sterile reflection of the moon.

A tide of dead life lay at the water's edge—small fish, frogs, weed, reeds, freshwater shrimp, insects, a couple of crayfish—the life of the waterhole scoured out and left to die.

All this in just a couple of minutes.

I put the girl down, picked up a weakly struggling fish,

and tossed it in the water amongst the ice. Seconds later, waves pushed the frozen corpse back to shore.

The waterhole had become as sterile as the back side of the Moon; as ancient as the surface of this land before life began. Yet it held within it the threat of more sterility: I would be made as sterile and lifeless as the ageless atoms from which my body was formed if I ventured any nearer.

The sense of wonder remained, but the wonder had become a dreadful, bleak thing. This was the wonder of a raging fire, of acid burns, of the knowledge of *the* end—life destroyed and denied.

In a daze I picked up the girl. I had killed her, and she deserved better than a burial in this place.

TWO

Three days it took to reach the highway.

I left before dawn that same night. Broke camp, packed the tent, bedroll, and other stuff in the back of the Toyota, and then stopped and thought twice about what I wanted to do.

Just behind the cabin, the Toyota truck had a massive chest of half-centimeter-thick galvanized steel the width of the entire truck bed. For the firearms and ammunition, the chest had two heavy brass padlocks, each with different keys.

It was only when I discovered that her body fit neatly into this gun locker that I finally decided to leave. I put a pillow under her head, stood watching the dusky glow of her skin and her hair in the fading moonlight for a few seconds, covered her with a blanket, and locked her down.

The clock on the dash said 4:17 A.M. as I began bashing

my way south through the scrub and then across the gibber plain—a plain of loose stones of all sizes from pebbles to boulders lying on a strata of solid rock, in this case, granite. The stones squeezed up from under the tires and knocked against the chassis. Five hundred and thirty kilometers, the first third of it over open terrain, the rest over the kind of dirt track that carries a vehicle once a month.

By day, I drove. By night, I dreamed of water. Serene rippling pools under trees in the moonlight. Great ocean swells. Streams and torrents of water. All empty of life.

When I finally drove over the edge of the escarpment and down toward the Eyre Highway, I hadn't seen another human being—a living one at any rate—for weeks.

I stopped at the first roadhouse I came to—a combination petrol station, pub, and restaurant, with a couple of motel rooms, a parking area for caravans and trucks, a tent area, and a small zoo out back for the kids and the tourists. Four weeks ago I had stopped here and put up a tent amongst the cages. The pump attendant was a burly, irascible, middle-aged man who remembered me.

"Going home already?"

"They send me all the way out to this spot in the middle of nowhere, and some bugger's already there."

"Typical bureaucrats."

A little girl in a faded pink cotton dress and sandshoes with no socks carried a spade and dragged a dead wombat by the left rear leg past the petrol pumps. She looked at me curiously, like she was glad a stranger was present to witness this, and then turned to the pump attendant. "You can't wait until tonight, Daddy, he's starting to smell."

"Daddy"—the owner, obviously—looked embarrassed.

"Ah, the family pets . . . we've had a bit of bad luck recently," he said to me.

The girl dragged the wombat across the highway to a string of crosses planted in the verge on the far side.

The owner waved in the direction of the pet cemetery, "I want our customers to know we're doing the right thing. Lots of people used to stay here because of them."

"What's killing them?"

He shrugged. "Since the wife's gone, they've just . . . died. Grief, I guess. They miss her."

"They got names?" I looked at the girl dragging a couple of branches to cover the wombat. "Might make it easier for the girl."

"Ya reckon?"

"Yeah, I do."

"I reckon I'll do it my way. Less arguments."

A trail of blood followed the dead wombat across the roadhouse forecourt. Looked to me like it might have been a bullet in the head killed it.

I paid cash and got out of there.

The Eyre Highway is one of only two paved roads into Western Australia for the entire two-and-a-half thousand kilometers of border. It is a place where a half-dozen road-houses have their own time zone—one which differs to those on either side, not by one hour or a half hour, but by three-quarters of an hour, and which the owner of *one* of those roadhouses, being a patriotic West Australian citizen, refuses to use, preferring Western Standard Time instead. The center of population is the village of Eucla, of maybe fifty souls, most of them government and some of them with the same job of killing birds I have. When I finish at Heartrock, I'll be stationed there.

If I was to scrabble in the dirt at any of the rest areas on the highway, I would find the fossilized seashells of an ancient seabed. Fossicking for meteorites is prohibited, because they *can* be found, can be picked up off burning sand—providing a history of both the land and the solar system. In summer the daytime temperature can reach 55 degrees Celsius, or 130 degrees in the old scale Dad always used. The economy consists of selling fuel, beer, hamburgers, and a place to sleep to truckies, and to travelers who, for whatever private reason, would not catch a plane.

The land was empty, but driving through it I always expected to find something wonderful just around the next corner.

Heat shimmered off the highway ahead. The road followed the base of an escarpment—the shore of the ancient sea. I didn't know what brand the trees were. That was a word James used once in biology class: "brand." The teacher told him we were talking about a form of life, a species. "Not when some accountant sells 'em to you in a supermarket, you're not," James had replied. Whichever "brand" they were, the trees were stunted, dark green, all but identical, and scarce. It made me wonder what "brand" the corpse I had in the gun locker was. It was a horrible thought, but I still laughed.

A truck rose out of the heat-haze ahead. The shimmering flowed down the road toward the Toyota and surrounded it, floating up from the bitumen until it seemed I was looking through a sheen of water. Braking gently to keep control, I concentrated on staying on the road, on the white lines passing the edge of the Toyota's hood. Silhouettes of fish swam in the corners of my eyes. One swam at my face, and I flinched. A shadow passed overhead and I looked up at the massive roiling underside of a breaker rolling in against the shore.

The blast of a truck horn dragged my attention back to the road.

Waves? *Above* the road? The haze disappeared, as did all thoughts of "brand name" corpses. That kind of thinking worked in cities, not out here.

I felt haunted.

The tension I suddenly felt made concentrating easy after that. What was I doing touring the back roads of Australia with a corpse hidden in the vehicle? I had no answers. The police patrolled this road, pulling vehicles over at random to search for drugs. What if they stopped me?

Whatever this quest was that I had found myself on, I wanted it done.

That night I dreamed of water again. I was back at the roadhouse, standing in the middle of the highway, trucks roaring past in the night air. It rained, and the clean, healing water ran off the road, soaking deep into the verge amongst the graves.

Early morning twilight woke me. The ground was soggy, the tent wet. It *had* rained. Letting it all dry out a little before I packed, I put water on to boil for coffee and walked out of the scrub onto the highway. The trucks that had roared past all night had gone. The bloodied corpse of a kangaroo, crows picking at its flesh, explained a thump I had heard just before falling asleep the night before.

The glow of light where the highway met the horizon signaled dawn. The sunrise glinted off wet asphalt, four lustrous trails converging on the disk of the sun on the horizon, light reflecting from the sheen of water in the shallow furrows pressed into the road by trucks. Endless traffic, but a moment of beauty. I stared for a moment then went back to the gas stove and boiling water.

I needed to look at her.

Sipping hot coffee, I unlocked the tool chest. This was the morning of the fourth day in desert heat, and she hadn't started to smell yet. God knows what I would do when that happened. Pack her in ice? Drive the desert in a pickup truck weeping condensation? But she should smell! She was dead. No heartbeat. And it was my fault because I had shot her. I tried to imagine explaining her to the police, and couldn't. Was she even human? I wondered. Maybe that would get me off in a court—can you murder a nonhuman? But it didn't save me from knowing *I* had *killed*. I lifted the lid, and she was lying there in water a foot deep, her hair floating in a ring about her face like a dark sunrise.

I dropped the coffee and fell into the mud.

"You okay there, lad?"

Now I spotted the caravan back in the trees. Other travelers had come into the rest area overnight.

"Shit."

I managed to slam the lid. After that, I had no choice but to accept an invitation to breakfast, all the time thinking of what else I had seen there in the gun locker, other than a quarter ton of water that had appeared from nowhere: a fine patchwork of dark golden scales the size of pinheads covering the skin around her wound, and the black stone in her navel now shiny and smooth, like polished hematite.

I didn't try to figure it out. The wyrde was following me, and it wouldn't leave until this was resolved.

But now I was certain that I was haunted, and of what it was that haunted me—a halo of hair drifting in sparkling water.

Before leaving, I pulled out a map. The Stirling Ranges were not quite a thousand kilometers away, give or take fifty kilometers depending on which route west I took from Norseman.

The Stirling Ranges? I realized then where I had been heading since I had loaded the girl's body into the gun locker back at Heartrock. Bluff Knoll. I wanted to bury her beside my father. It had become that important.

And urgent—a thousand kilometers—I could do that in a day. Then I wanted to leave and never go back.

I made it onto the road a few minutes before eight A.M., estimated time of arrival: dusk. The day blurred into a drone of heavy 4 x 4 tires and a litany of places and names that I would never forget: Caiguna, and the hundred-and-forty-

kilometer straightaway; Norseman, where the tallest hills
are mine tailings and slag; the ghost town of Dundas where
I ate the cold chicken burger; the dirt road to Lake King,
with the most desolate and most desecrated roadside rest
area I had seen; Lake King itself, and Lake Grace, both of
them salt, but with townships made possible by damming
the runoff from outcrops of granite similar to Heartrock,
dams made by circling the rock with a wall of bricks four or
five courses high that slopes slightly downhill as it follows
the contour around the rock, trapping the water and guiding
it into a hollow on one side; the Pallinup River, the first
watercourse I had crossed that actually had water in it in
three thousand kilometers of driving—a genuine goddamned river that the map told me ran all the way to the
Southern Ocean.

I missed rivers. Western Australia just doesn't do running water like other places.

And that made me think of the waterhole at Heartrock—
a rare and wonderful place that wouldn't exist at all but for
an accident of topography in the bedrock millions of years
earlier. But the very scarcity of water also made the waterhole a trap.

How long had the girl been there?

By ten P.M., I was sitting on top of Bluff Knoll, Dad's urn
cradled on my lap. Once I had reached the peak, it had been
the work of minutes to find Dad's grave and dig the urn out.
I would never be able to fit both the girl and the urn among
the rocks in just that spot, and I wanted to see the urn again,
and feel it in my hands.

The stars were bright, and a stiff wind blew in from the ocean. A glow in the east signaled moonrise. The lights of Albany and Mount Barker shone to the southwest. Civilization. Six hundred meters below was the carpark, and the Toyota with its precious cargo. The gun locker was still full of water. The girl was still dead, the wound in her side a little more overgrown with the same scaly skin I had seen that morning. The big change was that the stone in her navel now glowed green.

Up here, I might be able to squeeze an urn between the boulders and cover it with a scrabbling of dirt and mud, but a body? And if I did find a spot, I would have to lug her all the way up, six hundred meters vertical like one giant flight of stairs. I wasn't looking forward to it.

The pause gave me time to think. She wasn't human, I knew that now, but her hair and her face haunted my every waking thought. I even wondered if she was truly dead. Probably not.

Something was expected of me, and I didn't know what it was. Had I done the right thing taking her away from Heartrock? I didn't know that either. But what was done was done, and I had to live with it.

I turned and aimed the torch up into the dark, at Alpha Centauri, and watched the beam disappear.

But Bluff Knoll wasn't the place for her, and that made me sad.

I dreamed of water.

Bright moonlight rippled into my eyes. The moon was close, the disk huge, white, and smooth.

A lake stretched for kilometers to my left. Just across the way, bare, jagged mountains reared from the water into the night. A meteor blazed across the sky, dimmed out, and thunder rolled across the water and echoed off the cliffs.

There were no trees, no grass, no bushes, no animals or insects. If life existed here yet, it was in the water or in the sky. Beside me, my father's urn rested on the coarse sand.

The place was sterile and reminded me of Heartrock after the waterhole had gone mad. But now I didn't feel threatened; instead, I felt old.

A hand thrust above the surface of the water. It looked human except it was covered in fine scales. A plain gold ring circled the forefinger. The hand held a naked baby above the water.

I was still and silent, unable to move, but I felt my presence there was sanctioned, as a witness.

The hand threw the baby up onto the shore, where it floated gently to rest beside the urn. The hand disappeared and a woman cried; my heart wrenched at the sorrow contained in that sound. A wake as of something swimming under the water drew away from the shore. The baby grew into a child and stood up on the sand. I recognized the features of the girl I had shot.

The girl picked up the urn and then waved good-bye to the lake. She disappeared, whisked away like a reflection between mirrors, toward the sheen of moonlight on a distant, much smaller, body of water.

When I woke, I picked up Dad's urn and climbed down off the mountain. The sun was just rising above the horizon.

Soon the first tourists would arrive.

I opened the gun locker and stood staring at her. Her wound had almost fully closed over, and dusky skin was growing over the scales. The stone at her navel blazed green in the sunlight.

I lifted her head clear. Water dripped from her hair. I kissed her gently on the lips, once, and lowered her back under the surface.

We were going back to Heartrock.

THREE

The void stood ahead in the night sky.

It was like the black glow I had seen in the water at Heartrock, but now it stood above the landscape like a signal fire, the promise of darkness and emptiness, the removal of life. It wasn't a blackness, I could see the stars through it and, during the afternoon driving across the gibber guided by the GPS system, I could sense it behind the sunlight, had been able to sense it ever since turning off the Eyre Highway. The feeling overshadowed my impatience as the Toyota bounced laboriously across the stony plain. I had become attuned to the wyrde.

When, as I got closer, the GPS went haywire—telling me I was in Rabaul, of all places—the void stood like a beacon above the horizon, both guiding me onward yet warning me away.

In the gun locker, the girl's wound was healed, waiting for her to come back to life. The water had drained away as inexplicably as it had come. Expecting nothing, but feeling an indefinable sense of what might be *possible*, I had nestled Dad's urn beside her head. Surely it couldn't work, he was dust. But she had healed, and I continued to hope, and the urn *had* been in my dream.

Whatever was happening would soon be over.

The attack began with the clunk of a stone. At first I thought it had been thrown up into the chassis by the wheels. But then the rattling clunk came again, from behind, against the side of the truck bed, and instinctively I swung the wheel away from the sound. The next one I saw in the headlights, silhouetted against the lee side of one of the great sand dunes that ran north-south through the desert, parallel to my route. A rock stirred from the gibber, hovered a moment, then came at the Toyota, accelerating, bouncing off the grille. I turned toward the dune and drove a little way up, where the sand was still firm, then drove along the side of it, away from the rocks on the desert floor. The Toyota leaned like a drunkard and the wheel twisted in my hands. Steering in sand is like steering a boat—the wheels acting like rudders pointed where I needed go. Keep the speed a steady forty kph, and no sudden moves. An easy target.

The stones came crashing in from the downhill side, aimed at the gun locker, a hail of stone out of the corner of my eye. But the locker was galvanized steel—the safest place she could be. The din was incredible. I drove hunched forward over the steering wheel. The window beside me shattered, showering me with glass, and I felt the passage of stones behind my head.

Then the gibber stopped, the stony ground at the base of the dune becoming covered in sand.

I slanted the Toyota down off the dune and drove on as fast as I dared, eager to cover as much distance as possible before the next assault.

Here I was, delivering a dead girl into the heart of a psychic storm that would strip my bones of . . .

I remembered once, sitting on the beach at Cottesloe watching the girls jogging past in their shorts and the sun setting behind the ships threading their way through the islands, James had asked if I believed in God. "No," I said. Then he asked if I believed in anything else, freedom, capitalism, terrorism, and I replied, "Just more dogma."

"You've gotta believe in something," he replied.

"Why?"

Then the sand began moving up around his legs. He looked at me and said, "Please help me. You've got to believe!"

I shook my head. The sand moved around his waist, then his chest, as if he were sinking into the beach.

"Please believe!"

"No!" I shouted. The sand covered his head, his fingers scrabbling at the surface as if he were trying to pull himself over the edge of a cliff.

"Please!" He disappeared in the sand. The surface bulged and then was still.

Please believe? James would never say that. I slapped my face, and night returned.

The false memory *had been* the next assault. What would be next?

I wanted to turn around and drive back to Perth, leave the girl lying on the sand and leave the waterhole to whatever it was becoming in her absence. Yin and yang.

A vision of long, henna-colored hair and a smiling face—
a smile I had never seen—drifted before my eyes. The vision
was followed by the memory of my father hugging me on top
of Bluff Knoll. I couldn't betray those images. I wasn't alone
in this.

The void became clearly defined against the stars. It was
nearer now, much nearer after the dream. The headlights
showed tire tracks I had made eight days ago.

Heartrock loomed ahead. I had been thinking of this for
days, trying to decide what to do, trying to plan, but not
knowing what I would face.

Once again the headlights showed stones stirring on the
desert floor. I twisted the wheel away from the tracks I had
been following, and aimed the Toyota at the rock slope. The
first rush saw me thirty meters up off the sand, but then I
geared back into low and concentrated on the slope. A boulder trembled ahead, and I swerved, letting it thunder past.

If I was at the peak, the goddamned waterhole couldn't
get at me with rocks or boulders.

It took five minutes to force the Toyota up the final two
hundred meters. I stopped the truck and got out. For a
moment I was fooled by the stillness of the night.

Then I looked up. The stars had gone out.

I pulled out the Remington and aimed at the sky.

The shotgun blasted into the darkness, the muzzle flash
unnaturally dim, the crack of the shots muffled, like shooting with a blanket wrapped around the barrel.

Shoot the sky? I laughed as I dropped the gun. Might as
well piss into the wind.

But I did it again, this time with the Anschutz. The bullet left a track like a meteor. I reloaded, fired again. Just fireworks. The only difference one of affect, of my emotions. Should *I* believe? *In what?*

I jumped back into the Toyota, switching on the headlights and letting it roll down the slope toward the waterhole. The quickest and easiest way to get the girl back into the water was to run the truck off the rock into the water. But could I walk out of here? Five and a half hundred kilometers of desert on foot? The desert would trap me, too. I needed the truck.

The headlights dimmed. I braked, slipped the Toyota back into gear. The headlights dimmed further. Then I couldn't see at all. I couldn't risk the vehicle.

Working by the feel of the steering wheel in my hands, I turned the Toyota so that it pointed across the slope and parked it. Then I climbed out, and worked around to the back. I could see nothing. The vehicle rocked as if buffeted in a high wind. I fumbled the keys into the padlocks, threw back the lid of the gun locker, and the nothing became tinged with green, centered on the jewel in her navel.

I felt inside the locker, found her, and pulled her over my shoulder. A fireman's carry again, leaving one hand free. Dad's urn was next. Again I felt that unreasonable, that impossible hope.

The Toyota rocked again. I found the edge of the truck bed, sat, felt down with my feet until they touched rock. I stood there for a moment, feeling her hair against my arm. The void had a faint green tinge, the jewel in her navel blazing against my shoulders. I felt no heat. I couldn't even see the urn inches in front of my face when I held it up, just the void like green silt in water.

I slid one foot in front of the other, feeling ahead for the surface. If I followed the steepest slope, I would find the waterhole. How far?

A rhythmic pounding came from behind me, and I scrabbled sideways. There was a rush of air, and the crashing of something massive through the soles of my boots. Another boulder.

It hadn't given up.

I had no time to be careful. I stepped out, and then jogged down the slope, feeling with my feet for clues, madly waving the urn for balance, desperately searching my memory. What had Heartrock looked like? The girl's weight slammed at my shoulders. My legs burned with the effort of staying on my feet.

Air blasted past my face. The temperature crashed. Ice formed inside my mouth. Was I still going down? I closed my eyes and stood still a moment to be certain. I didn't fall, so my balance was good. Down was *that* way.

The last of the air rushed past, and then I couldn't breathe at all. My lungs pumped in and out, but sucked at nothing. The void had become vacuum.

How far?

Another five paces and I stumbled and crashed to my knees. Pushed to my feet. Another ten paces. Soon I would fall and not get up.

Then my right foot fell, scraped rock, and fell again. My

left knee smashed into the edge of the rock and I tumbled forwards. A burst of white lit the green, and that was all.

I woke facedown on the sand, and shivered.

Lifting my head, I saw blue sky, the she-oak out in the desert, my little row of animal graves, the dry creek bed, my old campsite. . . . The void had gone. I rolled over and stood. The Toyota was in the most bizarre place. . . . If I'd driven any farther down the slope it would have taken a nosedive over a ten-meter cliff. How I had found my way around that, I don't know.

But I hadn't been alone.

The water was at my feet. I saw tadpoles duck behind some reeds. Less life than there had been before, but life, and already established.

Dad's urn had gone.

"Hey!" I shouted. No answer.

"Hey, what's your name?" I called.

Still no answer.

I waded into the water up to my knees. It was cold, but refreshingly so. "Where's my father?"

I saw a ghostly image of the girl against the wall of Heartrock, behind it a fading impression of other people: my father, an old woman, a boy, a pregnant teenage girl. How many people had been cremated that day? Only one mattered.

"I want him back!" I cried, and splashed further into the pool. I swam to the rock wall and tried to climb onto the slick surface, but fell back.

He is my price for what you did.

She was standing on the shore behind me. It was the first time I had seen her alive and whole, her hair falling past her shoulders, the stone once again a dead black thing in her navel. She was at once young, lithe and beautiful, but also old—geologically old. She didn't just live in this land, she was a part of it. I swam back across the waterhole, climbed out, and fell to my knees, unable to approach her, to touch her. How could I love something so old?

"I can't leave him here alone."

Look at them. She waved at the other ghosts. *None of them are alone.*

I stayed at the waterhole all that day, sitting on the sand, taking potshots with the Anschutz, watching the bullets flash into the water and minutes later wash up beside me on the sand. The game soured quickly, and I threw the rifle into the water in disgust.

Dad was gone.

That night, I dreamed of shooting her again, loading her back into the gun locker in the Toyota, and driving off, stealing the light away with me, leaving a decaying, ever blackening void in the desert. I would find some secluded stretch of river in north Queensland and let the water there bring her back to life. I would live bathed in light, and the void would never touch me until the day I died.

I woke in a panicked sweat long before dawn.

In the morning, I drove away. This time I headed north, farther across the desert and away from everything and everybody I had known.

Bill Congreve is a Sydney-based writer, editor, book reviewer, and independent publisher. He has received a William J. Atheling Award for genre criticism and reviews for *Aurealis*, Australia's longest-running and largest circulation genre magazine. He has acted as a judge for the Aurealis Award on five occasions. His stories have appeared in *Tenébrès, Event Horizon, Terror Australis, Aurealis, Bloodsongs, Passing Strange*, and *Cross-Town Traffic*, and he has edited the anthologies *Intimate Armageddons* (Australia's first modern, original horror anthology), *Passing Strange, Bonescribes*, and *Southern Blood*. A collection of vampire stories, *Epiphanies of Blood*, was published in 1998. Recent titles from his independent publishing company, MirrorDanse Books, include *Rynosseros*, by Terry Dowling; *Written in Blood*, by Chris Lawson; *Immaterial: Ghost Stories*, by Robert Hood; *A Tour Guide in Utopia*, by Lucy Sussex; and *The Year's Best Australian SF & Fantasy*, Volume One, which he co-edited with Michelle Marquardt.

Author's Note

I've driven across the Nullarbor about a dozen times, in one direction or the other. The Australian landscape is ancient, yet European settlement began only a couple of hundred years ago. Traditional European faery stories don't sit well in an Australian environment, yet there is magic here. For me, that magic lies in the sense of wonder I find in traveling the landscape, from the scarecrow in the passenger shelter of an outback tram line that hasn't been used for fifty years to the "dead boot" tree on the side of the Lasseter Highway near Uluru. In this story I not only wanted to find that magic so that others might also feel it, but to relate the magic to something as old as the landscape itself.

The Western Australia Department of Agriculture maintains teams of rangers at Esperance and Eucla to eradicate feral wildlife, and the few waterholes in desert regions are a key part of their strategy. However they don't send solitary rangers of the protagonist's age into the desert alone for extended periods. That's my artistic license. Thanks to those who helped with the story. All errors are mine.

The Annals of Eelin-Ok

~

Jeffrey Ford

When I was a child someone once told me that gnats, those minuscule winged specks that swarm in clouds about your head on summer evenings, are born, live out their entire lives, and die all in the space of a single day. A brief existence, no doubt, but briefer still are the allotted hours of that denizen of the faerie world, a Twilmish, for its life is dependent upon one of the most tenuous creations of mankind—namely, the sand castle. When a Twilmish takes up residence in one of these fanciful structures, its span of time is determined by the durability and duration of its chosen home.

Prior to the appearance of a sand castle on the beach, Twilmish exist merely as a notion; an invisible potentiality of faerie presence. In their insubstantial form, they will haunt a shoreline for centuries, biding their time, like an idea waiting to be imagined. If you've ever been to the beach in the winter after it has snowed and seen the glittering white powder rise up for a moment in a miniature twister, that's an indication of Twilmish presence. The phenomenon has something to do with the power they draw from the meeting of the earth and the sea; attraction and repulsion in a circular fashion like a dog chasing its tail. If, on a perfectly sunny summer afternoon, you are walking along the shoreline during the time of the outgoing tide and suddenly enter a zone of frigid cold air no more than a few feet in breadth, again, it indicates that your beach has a Twilmish. The drop in degrees is a result of their envy of your physical form. It means one is definitely about, searching for the handiwork of industrious children.

No matter how long a Twilmish has waited for a home, no matter the degree of desire to step into the world, not just any sand castle will do. They are as shrewd and judicious in their search as your grandmother is in choosing a melon at the grocery, for whatever place one does decide on will, to a large extent, define its life. Once the tide has turned and the breakers roar in and destroy the castle, its inhabitant is also washed away, not returning to the form of energy to await another castle but gone, returned physically and spiritually to Nature, as we are at the end of our long lives. So the most important prerequisite of a good castle is that it must have been created by a child or children. Too often adults transfer their penchant for worry about the future and their reliance on their watches into the architecture, and the spirit of these frustrations sunders the effect of "Twilmish Time"; the phenomenon that allows those few hours between the outgoing and incoming tide to seem to this special breed of faerie folk to last as long as all our long years seem to us.

Here are a few of the other things they look for in a residence: a place wrought by children's hands and not plastic molds or metal shovels, so that there are no right angles and each inch of living space resembles the unique contours of the human imagination; a complex structure with as many rooms and tunnels, parapets, bridges, dungeons, and moats as possible; a place decorated with beautiful shells and sea glass (they prize most highly the use of blue bottle glass tumbled smooth by the surf, but green is also welcome); the use of driftwood to line the roads or a pole made from a sea horse's spike flying a seaweed flag; the absence of sand crabs, those burrowing, armored nuisances that can undermine a wall or infest a dungeon; a retaining wall of modest height, encircling the entire design, to stave off the sea's hungry high-tide advances as long as possible but not block the ocean view; and a name for the place, already bestowed and carefully written with the quill of a fallen gull feather above the main gate, something like Heart's Desire or Sandland or Castle of Dreams, so that precious moments of the inhabitant's life might not be taken up with this decision.

Even many of those whose lifework it is to study the lineage and ways of the faerie folk are unfamiliar with the Twilmish, and no one is absolutely certain of their origin. I suppose they have been around at least as long as sand castles, and probably before, inhabiting the sand caves of Neanderthal children. Perhaps, in their spirit form, they had come into existence with the universe and had simply been waiting eons for sand castles to finally appear, or perhaps they are a later development in the evolution of the faerie phylum. Some believe them to be part of that special line of enchanted creatures that associate themselves with the creativity of humans, like the Monkey of the Ink Pot, attracted to the work of writers; or the Painter's Demon, which plays in the bright mix of colors on an artist's palette, resulting in never-before-seen hues.

Whichever and whatever the case may be, there is only one way to truly understand the nature of the Twilmish, and that is to meet one of them. So here I will relate for you the biography of an individual of their kind. All of what follows would have taken place on the evening of a perfect summer day after you had left the beach, and will occupy the time between tides—from when you had sat down to dinner and five hours later when you laid your head upon the pillow to sleep. There seemed to you to be barely enough time to eat your chicken and potatoes, sneak your carrots to the dog beneath the table, clean up, watch your favorite TV show, draw a picture of a pirate with an eye patch and a parrot upon her shoulder, brush your teeth, and kiss your parents good-night. To understand the Twilmish, though, is to understand that in a mere moment, all can be saved or lost, an ingenious idea can be born, a kingdom can fall, love can grow, and life can discover its meaning.

Now, if I wasn't an honest fellow, I would, at this juncture, merely make up a bunch of hogwash concerning the biography of a particular Twilmish, for it is fine to note the existence of a race, but one can never really know anything of substance about a group until one has met some of its individuals. The more one meets, the deeper the understanding. There is a problem, though, in knowing anything definitive about any particular Twilmish, and that is because they are no bigger than a human thumbnail. In addition, they move more quickly than an eye blink in order to stretch each second into a minute, each minute into an hour.

Out of the surf one day in 1999, on the beach at Barnegat Light, in New Jersey, a five-year-old girl, Chieko Quigley, found a conch shell at the shoreline. Its spiral form enchanted her. She took it home and used it as a decoration on the windowsill of her room. Three years later, her cat, Madelain, knocked the shell onto the floor, and from within the winding labyrinth, the opening to which she would place her ear from time to time to listen to the surf, fell an exceedingly tiny book, no bigger than ten grains of sand stuck together; its cover made of sea-horse hide, its pages, dune grass. Since I am an expert on faeries and faerie lore, it was brought to me to discern whether it was a genuine artifact or a prank. The diminutive volume was subjected to electron microscopy, and it was discovered to be the actual journal of a Twilmish named Eelin-Ok.

Eelin-Ok must have had artistic aspirations as well, for on the first page is a self-portrait, a line drawing done in squid ink. He stands, perhaps on the tallest turret of his castle, obviously in an ocean breeze that lifts the long dark hair of his topknot and causes his full-length cape to billow out behind him. He is stocky, with broad shoulders and calf muscles and biceps as large around as his head. His face, homely-handsome, with its thick brow and smudge of a nose, might win no beauty contests but could inspire comfort with its look of simple honesty. The intense eyes seem to be staring at something in the distance. I cannot help but think that this portrait represents the moment when Eelin-Ok realized that the chaotic force of the ocean would at some point consume him and his castle, While Away.

The existence of the journal is a kind of miracle in its own right, and the writing within is priceless to the Twilmish historian. It seems our subject was a Twilmish of few words, for between each entry it is evident that some good portion of time has passed, but taken all together they represent, as the title page suggests, *The Annals of Eelin-Ok.* So here they are, newly translated from the Twilmish by the ingenious decoding software called "Faerie-Speak" (a product of Fen & Dale Inc.), presented for the first time to the reading public.

HOW I HAPPENED

I became aware of It, a place for me to be, when I was no more than a cloud, drifting like a notion in the breakers' mist. It's a frightening thing to make the decision to be born. Very little ever is what it seems until you get up close and touch it. But this castle that the giant, laughing architects created and named While Away (I do not understand their language but those are the symbols the way they were carved) with a word-scratched driftwood plaque set in among the scalloped maroon cobbles of the courtyard, was like a dream come true. The two turrets, the bridge and moat, the counting room paneled with nautilus amber, the damp dungeon and secret passage, the strong retaining wall that encircled it, every sturdy inch bejeweled by beautiful blue and green and clear glass, decorated with the most delicate white shells, seemed to have leaped right out of my imagination and onto the beach in much the same way that I leaped into my body and life as Eelin-Ok. Sometimes caution must be thrown to the wind, and in this instance it was. Those first few moments were confused with the new feel of being, the act of breathing, the wind in my face. Some things I was born knowing, as I was born full-grown, and others I only remember that I have forgotten. The enormous red orb, sitting atop the horizon, and the immensity of the ocean, struck me deeply, their powerful beauty causing my emotions to boil over. I staggered to the edge of the lookout post on the taller turret, leaned upon the battlement, and wept. "I've done it," I thought, and then a few moments later after I had dried my eyes, "Now what?"

PHARGO

Upon returning from a food expedition, weighed down with a bit of crabmeat dug out from a severed claw dropped by a gull and a goodly portion of jellyfish curd, I discovered a visitor in the castle. He waited for me at the front entrance, hopping around impatiently: a lively little sand flea, black as a fish eye, and hairy all over. I put down my burden and called him to me, patting his notched little head. He was full of high spirits and circled round me, barking in whispers. His antics made me smile. When I finally lifted my goods and trudged toward the entrance to the turret that held the dining hall, he followed, so I let him in and gave him a name, Phargo. He is my companion, and although he doesn't understand a word of Twilmish, I tell him everything.

FAERIE FIRE

Out of nowhere came my memory of the spell to make fire—three simple words and a snapping of the fingers. I realize I have innate powers of magic and enchantment, but they are meager, and I have decided to not rely on them too often, as this is a world in which one must learn to trust mainly in muscle and brain in order to survive.

MAKING THINGS

The castle is a wondrous structure, but it is my responsibility to fill it with items both useful and decorative. There is no luckier place to be left with nothing than the seashore, for with every wave useful treasures are tossed onto the beach, and before you can collect them, another wave carries more. I made my tools from sharp shards of glass and shell not yet worried smooth by the action of the waters. These I attached to pieces of reed and quills from bird feathers and tied tight with tough lanyards of dune grass. With these tools I made a table for the dining hall from a choice piece of driftwood, carved out a fireplace for my bedroom, created chairs and sofas from the cartilage of bluefish carcasses. I have taught Phargo the names of these tools, and the ones he can lift, he drags to me when I call for them. My bed is a mussel shell, my washbasin a metal thing discarded by the giant, laughing architects, on the back of which are the characters "Root Beer," and smaller, "twist off," along with an arrow following the circular curve of it (very curious); my weapon is an ax of reed handle and shark's tooth head. Making things is my joy.

THE FISHING EXPEDITION

Up the beach, the ocean has left a lake in its retreat, and it is swarming with silver fish as long as my leg. Phargo and I set sail in a small craft I burned out of a block of driftwood and rigged with a sail made from the fin of a dead sea robin. I took a spear and a lantern—a chip of quartz that catches the rays of the red orb and magnifies them. The glow of the prism stone drew my prey from the depths. Good thing I tied a generous length of seaweed round the spear, for my aim needed practice. Eventually I hit the mark, and dragged aboard fish after fish, which I then bludgeoned with my ax. The boat was loaded. As we headed back to shore, a strong gust of wind caught the sail and tipped the low-riding craft perilously to one side. I lost my grip on the tiller and fell overboard into the deep water. This is how I learned to swim. After much struggling and many deep, spluttering draughts of brine, Phargo whisper-barking frantically, I made it to safety and climbed back aboard. This, though, my friend, is also how I learned to die. The feeling of the water rising around my ears, the ache in the lungs, the frantic racing of my mind, the approaching blackness, I know I will meet again on my final day.

DUNE RAT

The dunes lie due north of While Away, a range of tall hills, sparsely covered with the sharp forbidding grass I use to tie up my tools. I have been to them on expeditions to cut blades of the stuff, but never ventured into their recesses, as they are vast and their winding paths like a maze. From out of this wilderness came a shaggy behemoth with needle teeth and a tail like an eel. I heard it squeal as it tried to clear the outer wall. Grabbing my spear I ran to the front gate and out along the bridge that crosses the moat. There I was able to take the shell staircase to the top of the wall. I knew that if the rat breached the wall the castle would be destroyed. As it tried to climb over, though, its back feet displaced the sand the battlement was made of and it kept slipping back. I charged headlong and drove the tip of my spear into its right eye. It screeched in agony and retreated, my weapon jutting from the oozing wound. There was no question that it was after me, a morsel of Twilmish meat, or that others would eventually come.

THE RED ORB HAS DROWNED

The red orb has sunk into the ocean, leaving only pink and orange streaks behind in its wake. Its drowning has been gradual and it has struggled valiantly, but now darkness reigns upon the beach. Way above there are points of light that hypnotize me when I stare too long at them and reveal themselves in patterns—a seagull, a wave, a crab. I must be sure to gather more driftwood in order to keep the fires going, for the temperature has also slowly dropped. Some little time ago, a huge swath of pink material washed ashore. On it was a symbol belonging, I am sure, to the giant architects: a round yellow circle made into a face with eyes and a strange, unnerving smile. From this I will cut pieces and make warmer garments. Phargo sleeps more often now, but when he is awake he still bounds about and makes me laugh often enough. We swim like fish through the dark.

IN MY BED

I lie in my bed writing. From beyond the walls of my castle I hear the waves coming and going in their steady assuring rhythm, and the sound is lulling me toward sleep. I have been wondering what the name assigned to my home by the architects means. While Away—if only I could understand their symbols, I might understand more the point of my life. Yes, the point of life is to fish and work and make things and explore, but there are times, especially now since the red orb has been swallowed, that I suspect there is some secret reason for my being here. There are moments when I wish I knew, and others when I couldn't care less. Oh, to be like Phargo, for whom a drop of fish blood and a hopping run along the beach are all that is necessary. Perhaps I think too much. There is the squeal of a bat, the call of a plover, the sound of the wind, and they mix with the salt air to bring me closer to sleep. When I wake, I will . . .

WHAT'S THIS?

Something is rising out of the ocean, being born into the sky. I think it is going to be round like the red orb, but it is creamy white. Whatever it is, I welcome it, for it seems to cast light, not bright enough to banish the darkness, but an enchanted light that reflects off the water and gracefully illuminates the beach where the shadows are not too harsh. We rode atop a giant brown armored crab with a sharp spine of a tail as it dragged itself up the beach. We dined on bass. Discovered a strange fellow on the shore of the lake. A kind of statue but not made of stone. Composed of a slick and somewhat pliable substance, he bobbed on the surface. He is green from head to toe. He carries in his hands what appears to be a weapon and wears a helmet, both also green. I have dragged him back to the castle and set him up on the tall turret to act as a sentinel. Getting him up the winding staircase put my back out. I'm not as young as I used to be. With faerie magic I will give him the power of sight and speech, so that although he does not move, he can be vigilant and call out. I wish I had the power to cast a spell that would bring him fully to life, but alas, I'm only Twilmish. I have positioned him facing the north, in order to watch for rats. I call him Greenly, just to give him a name.

200 STEPS

I now record the number of steps it is at this point in time from the outer wall of the castle to where the breakers flood the beach. I was spied upon in my work, for the huge white disk on the horizon has just recently shown two eyes over the brim of the ocean. Its light is dreamlike, and it makes me wonder if I have really taken form or if I am still a spirit, dreaming I am not.

A MOMENTOUS DISCOVERY

Phargo and I discovered a corked bottle upon the beach. As has become my practice, I took out my hatchet and smashed a hole in its side near the neck. Often, I have found that these vessels are filled with an intoxicating liquor that, in small doses warms the innards when the wind blows and in large doses makes me sing and dance upon the turret. Before I could venture inside, I heard a voice call out, "Help us." I was frozen in my tracks, thinking I had opened a ship of ghosts. Then, from out of the dark back of the bottle, came a figure. Imagine my relief when I saw it was a female faerie. I am not exactly sure which branch of the folk she is from, but she is my height, dressed in a short gown woven from spider thread, and has alluring long, orange hair. She staggered forward and collapsed in my arms. Hiding behind her was a small faerie child: a boy, I think. He was frightened and sickly looking, and said nothing but followed me when I put the woman over my shoulder and carried her home. They now rest peacefully down the hall in a makeshift bed I put together from a common clam shell and a few folds of that pink material. I am filled with questions.

THE MOON

Meiwa, for that is her name, told me the name of the white circle in the sky, which has now revealed itself completely. She said it was called the Moon, the bright specks are Stars, and the red orb was the Sun. I live in a time of darkness

called the Night, and amazingly, there exists a time of brightness when the sun rules a blue sky and one can see a mile or
more. All these things, I think I knew at one time before I
was born into this life. Meiwa knows many things and some
secrets of the giant architects. The two of them, she and her
son, are Willnits, seafaring people who live aboard the ships
of the giants. They had fallen asleep in an empty rum bottle,
thinking it was safe, but when they awoke, they found the
top stopped with a cork and their haven adrift upon the
ocean. Sadly enough, her husband had been killed by one of
the giants, called Humans, who mistook him for an insect
and crushed him. I can vouch that she is expert with a fishing spear and was quite fierce in helping turn back an infes-
tation of burrowing sand crabs in the dungeon. The boy,
Magtel, is quiet but polite and seems a little worse for wear
from their harrowing adventures. Only Phargo can bring a
smile to him. I made him his own ax to lift his spirits.

A SMALL NIGHT BIRD

Meiwa has enchanted a small night bird, by attracting it
with crumbs of a special bread she bakes from thin air and
sea foam and then using her lovely singing voice to train it.
When she mounted the back of the delicate creature and
called me to join her, I will admit I was skeptical. Once upon
the bird, my arms around her waist, she made a kissing
noise with her lips, and we took off into the sky. My head
swam as we went higher and higher and then swept along
the shoreline in the light of the moon. She laughed wildly at

my fear, and when we did not fall, I laughed too. She took me to a place where the giants live, in giant houses. Through a glass pane, we saw a giant girl, drawing a colorful picture of a bird sitting upon a one-eyed woman's shoulder. Then we were off, traveling miles, soaring and diving, and eventually coming to rest on the bridge moat of While Away. The bird is not the only creature who has been enchanted by Meiwa.

150 STEPS

Magtel regularly accompanies me on the search for food now. When we came upon a blue claw in the throes of death, he stepped up next to me and put his hand in mine. We waited until the creature stopped moving, and then took our axes to the shell. Quite a harvest. It is now only 150 steps from the wall to the water.

GREENLY SPEAKS

I did not hear him at first as I was sleeping so soundly, but Meiwa, lying next to me, did and pinched my nose to wake me. We ran to the top of the turret, where Greenly was still sounding the alarm, and looked north. There three shadows moved ever closer across the sand. I went and fetched my bow and arrows, my latest weapon, devised from something Meiwa had said she'd seen the Humans use. I was waiting to fire until they drew closer. Meiwa had a plan, though. She called for her night bird, and we mounted its back. We attacked from the air, and the monsters never got within 50 steps of the castle. My arrows could not kill them but effectively turned them away. I would have perished without her.

WHILE MEIWA SLEPT

While Meiwa slept, Magtel and I took torches, slings for carrying large objects upon the back, and our axes, and quietly left the castle. Phargo trailed after us, of course. There was a far place I had been to only one other time before. Heading west, I set a brisk pace and the boy kept up, sometimes running to stay next to me. Suddenly he started talking, telling me about a creature he had seen while living aboard the ship. "A whale," he called it. "Bigger than a hundred Humans, with a mouth like a cavern." I laughed and asked him if he was certain of this. "I swear to you," he said. "It blows water from a hole on its back, a fountain that reaches to the sky." He told me the Humans hunted them with spears from small boats and made from their insides lamp oil and perfume. What an imagination the child has, for it did not end with the whale, but he continued to relate to me so many unbelievable wonders as we walked along that I lost track of where we were and, though I watched for danger and the path through the sand ahead, it was really inward that my vision was trained, picturing his fantastic ideas. Before this he had not said but a few words to me.

After turning north at the shark skeleton, we traveled a while more and then entered the forest. Our torches pushed back the gloom, but it was mightily dark among the brambles and stickers. A short way in, I spotted what we had come for. Giant berries, like clusters of beads, indigo in color and sweating their sweetness. I hacked one off its vine and showed Magtel how to chop one down. We loaded them into our slings and then started back. There were a few tense moments before leaving the forest, for a long yellow snake slithered by as we stood stiller than Greenly, holding our breath. I had to keep one foot lightly on Phargo's neck to keep him from barking or hopping and giving us away. On the way home, the boy asked if I had ever been married, and then a few minutes later if I had any children. We presented the berries to Meiwa upon her waking. I will never forget the taste of them.

THE BOY HAS A PLAN

Magtel joined Meiwa and me as we sat on the tall turret enjoying a sip of liquor from a bottle I had recently discovered on the beach. He said he knew how to protect the castle against the rats. This was his plan: Gather dried seaweed that has blown into clumps upon the beach, encircle the outer wall of the castle with it. When Greenly sounds the alarm, we will shoot flaming arrows into it, north, south, east, and west, creating a ring of fire around us that the rats cannot pass through. Meiwa kissed him and clapped her hands. We will forthwith begin collecting the necessary seaweed. It will be a big job. My boy is gifted.

100 STEPS

I don't know why I checked how far the ocean's flood could reach. 100 is a lot of steps.

WE ARE READY

After a long span of hard work, we have completed the sea-weed defense of the castle. The rats are nowhere in sight. I found a large round contrivance, one side metal, one glass, buried in the sand. It had a lethargic heartbeat, sounding off once every long while like a tiny hammer tapping. With each beat, an arrow inside the glass moved ever so slightly in a course describing a circle. Meiwa told me it was called a Watch, and the Humans use them to mark the passage of time. Later, I returned to it and struck it with my ax until its heart stopped beating. The longer of the metal arrows I have put in my quiver.

THE TRUTH, LIKE A WAVE

Magtel has fallen ill. He is too tired to get out of bed. Meiwa told me the truth. They must leave soon and find another ship, for they cannot exist for too long away from one. She told me that she had used a spell to keep them alive for the duration they have been with me, but now it is weakening. I asked her why she had never told me. "Because we wanted to stay with you, at While Away, forever," she said. There were no more words. We held each other for a very long time, and I realized that my heart was a castle made of sand.

THEY ARE GONE

In order to get Magtel well enough to take the flight out to sea on the night bird, I built a bed for him in the shape of a ship, and this simple ruse worked to get him back upon his feet. We made preparations for their departure, packing food and making warm blankets to wrap around them as they flew out across the ocean. "We will need some luck to find a ship," Meiwa told me. "The night bird is not the strongest of fliers and she will be carrying two. We may have to journey far before we can set down." "I will worry about your safety until the day I die," I told her. "No," she said, "when we find a home on the sea, I will have the bird return to you, and you will know we have survived the journey. Then write a note to me and tie it to the bird's leg and it will bring us word of you." This idea lightened my heart a little. Then it was time to say good-bye. Magtel, shark-tooth ax in hand, put his arms around my neck. "Keep me in your imagination," I told him, and he said he always would. Meiwa and I kissed for the last time. They mounted the night bird. Then with that sound she made, Meiwa called the wonderful creature to action, and it lit into the sky. I ran up the steps to the top of the tall turret in time to see them circle once and call back to me. I reached for them, but they were gone, out above the ocean, crossing in front of the watchful Moon.

50 STEPS

It has been so long, I can't remember the last time I sat down to record things. I guess I knew this book contained memories I have worked so hard to overcome. It is just Phargo and me now, fishing, gathering food, combing the shore. The Moon has climbed high to its tallest turret and looks down now with a distant stare as if in judgment upon me. 50 steps remain between the outer wall and the tide. I record this number without trepidation or relief. I have grown somewhat slower, a little dimmer, I think. In my dreams, when I sleep, I am forever heading out across the ocean upon the night bird.

GREENLY SPEAKS

I was just about to go fishing when I heard Greenly pipe up and call, "Intruders." I did not even go up to the turret to look first, but fetched my bow and arrows and an armful of driftwood sticks with which to build a fire. When I reached my lookout, I turned north, and sure enough, in the pale moonlight I saw the beach crawling with rats, more than a dozen.

I lit a fire right on the floor of the turret, armed my bow, and dipped the end of the arrow into the flames until it caught. One, two, three, four, I launched my flaming missiles at the ring of dry seaweed. The fire grew into a perfect circle, and some of the rats were caught in it. I could hear them scream from where I stood. Most of the rest turned back, but to the west, where one had fallen in the fire, it smothered the flame, and I saw another climb upon its carcass and keep coming for the castle. I left the taller turret and ran to the smaller one to get a better shot at the attacker. Once atop it, I fired arrow after arrow at the monster, which had cleared the retaining wall and was within the grounds of While Away. With shafts sticking out of it, blood dripping, it came ever forward, intent upon devouring me. Upon reaching the turret on which I stood, it reared back on its haunches and scrabbled at the side of the structure, which started to crumble. In one last attempt to fell it, I reached for the metal arrow I had taken from the watch and loaded my bow. I was sweating profusely, out of breath, but I felt more alive in that moment than I had in a long while. My aim was true; the shaft entered its bared chest and dug into its heart. It toppled forward, smashed the side of the turret, and then the whole structure began to fall. My last thought was, "If the fall does not kill me, I will be buried alive." That is when I lost my footing and dropped into thin air.

But I did not fall, for something caught me, like a soft hand, and eased me down to safety upon the ground. It was a miracle I suppose, or maybe a bit of Meiwa's magic, but the night bird had returned. The smaller turret was completely destroyed, part of it having fallen into the courtyard. I dug that out, but the entire structure of the place was weakened by the attack and since then pieces of wall crumble off every so often and the bridge is tenuous. It took me forever to get rid of the rat carcass. I cut it up and dragged the pieces outside what remained of the retaining wall and buried them.

A LETTER

The night bird stayed with me while I repaired, as best I could, the damage to the castle, but as soon as I had the chance, I sat down and wrote a note to Meiwa and Magtel, trying desperately and, in the end, ultimately failing, to tell them how much I missed them. Standing on the turret with Phargo by my side, watching the bird take off again brought back all the old feelings even stronger and I felt lost.

THE MOON, THE SEA, THE DARK

The water laps only 10 steps from the outer wall of the castle. Many things have happened since I last wrote. Once, while lying in bed, I saw, through my bedroom window, two Humans, a giant female and male, walk by hand in hand. They stopped at the outer wall of the castle and spoke in booming voices. From the sound of their words, I know they were admiring my home, even in its dilapidated state. I took back the enchantment from Greenly, so he would not have the burden of sight and speech any longer; his job was finished and he had done it well. I dragged him to the lake and set him in my boat and pushed it off. Oh, how my back ached after that. If the rats come now, I will not fight them. The dungeon has been overrun by sand crabs, and when I am quiet in my thoughts, I hear their constant scuttling about down below, undermining the foundation of While Away. A piece of the battlement fell away from the turret, which is not a good sign, but gives me an unobstructed view of the sea. Washed up on the beach, due east of the castle, I found the letter I had sent so long ago with the night bird. The ink had run and it was barely legible, but I knew it was the one I had written. I am tired.

THE STARS FALL

I have just come in from watching the stars fall. Dozens of them came streaking down. I smiled at the beauty of it. What does it mean?

A VISITOR

I saw the lights of a ship out on the ocean and then I saw something large and white descending out of the darkness. Phargo was barking like mad, hopping every which way. I cleared my eyes to see it was a bird, a tern, and a small figure rode upon its back. It was Magtel, but no longer a boy. He was grown. I ran down from the turret, nearly tripping as I went. He met me by the bridge of the moat and we hugged for a very long time. He is now taller than I. He could only stay a little while, as that was his ship passing out at sea. I made us clam broth and we had jellyfish curd on slices of spearing. When I asked him, "Where is Meiwa?" he shook his head. "She took ill some time ago and did not recover," he said. "But she asked me to bring this to you if I should ever get the chance." I held back my tears not to ruin the reunion. "She stole it from one of the Humans aboard ship and saved it for you." Here he produced a little square of paper that he began to unfold. When it was completely undone and spread across the table, he smoothed it with his hands. "A picture of the Day," he said. There it was, the sun bright yellow, the sky blue, a beach of pure white sand lapped by a crystal clear, turquoise ocean. When it came time for Magtel to leave, he told me he still had his ax and it had come in handy many times. He told me that there were many other Willnits aboard the big ship and it was a good community.

We did not say good-bye. He patted Phargo on the head and got upon the back of the large white bird. "Thank you,

Eelin-Ok," he said and then was gone. If it wasn't for the picture of Day, I'd have thought it all a dream.

THE TIDE COMES IN

The waves have breached the outer wall and the sea floods in around the base of the castle. I have folded up the picture of Day and have it now in a pouch on a string around my neck. Phargo waits for me on the turret, from where we will watch the last seconds of While Away. Just a few more thoughts, though, before I go up to join him. When first I stepped into myself as Eelin-Ok, I worried if I had chosen well my home, but I don't think there can be any question that While Away was everything I could have asked for. So, too, many times I questioned my life, but now, in this final moment, memories of Phargo's whisper bark, the thrill of battle against the rats, fishing on the lake, the face of the moon, the taste of blackberries, the wind, Greenly's earnest nature, the boy holding my hand, flying on the night bird, lying with Meiwa in the mussel shell bed, come flooding in like the rising tide. "What does it all mean?" I have always asked. "It means you've lived a life, Eelin-Ok." I hear now the walls begin to give way. I have to hurry. I don't want to miss this.

Jeffrey Ford is the author of the trilogy *The Physiognomy, Memoranda,* and *The Beyond,* as well as *The Portrait of Mrs. Charbuque* and *The Fantasy Writer's Assistant & Other Stories.* His most recent books are the novel *The Girl in the Glass,* a stand-alone novella, *The Cosmology of the Wider World,* and a second collection of short stories, *The Empire of Ice Cream.*

His short fiction has appeared in many magazines and in the anthologies *The Year's Best Fantasy & Horror, Year's Best Fantasy of 2002, The Green Man: Tales From the Mythic Forest, Leviathan #3, Album Zutique, Witpunk, The Silver Gryphon, The Dark, Trampoline, Thackery T. Lambshead's Guide to Exotic & Discredited Diseases,* and *Polyphony #3.*

His stories have been nominated multiple times for the World Fantasy Award, the Hugo Award, the Nebula Award, and once each for the Theodore Sturgeon Award and the International Horror Guild Award. He is the recipient of three World Fantasy Awards and one Nebula.

Ford lives in South Jersey with his wife and two sons. He teaches writing and literature at Brookdale Community College in Monmouth County, New Jersey.

His Web site is users.rcn.com/delicate/

Author's Note

When I was a kid growing up on Long Island, every Sunday my father would buy the *Daily News.* In that paper there was a color comics section with great features like "Dick Tracy," "Prince Valiant," "The Phantom," and so on. One of my favorites was a full-page comic, not broken down into boxes but one large illustration. It dealt with a diminutive race of people, each no bigger than a pinky finger, called "The Teenie Weenies." They lived as best they could in our giant world. I particularly remember an image from a certain week in autumn of one of them riding a wild turkey while his friends gathered huge acorns amidst falling leaves as big as flying carpets. Their courage and their community captured my imagination, for as a child, I too sensed the enormity of the wide world out beyond the safe limits of my life. I'm sure they had a hand, however small, in my writing of "The Annals of Eelin-Ok."

The other influence for this story was the ocean itself. Every summer I go out to the shore—specifically Long Beach Island off the coast of New Jersey. There is nothing like the ocean's vast power to put in perspective one's tiny physical presence in relation to the universe, and nothing like its natural setting to make one understand how vitally important each and every presence, no matter its size, is to that same universe. I think that is the secret to the appeal of faeries for me. They are a metaphor for the fact that every little seemingly insignificant corner of the natural world is alive, complex, and vital, and deserves the kind of respect we would give to our friends and family.

See you on the beach.

De la Tierra

~

Emma Bull

The piano player drums away with her left hand, dropping all five fingers onto the keys as if they weigh too much for her to hold up. The rhythms bounce off the rhythms of what her right hand does, what she sings. It's like there's three different people in that little skinny body, one running each hand, the third one singing. But they all know what they're doing.

He sucks a narrow stream of Patrón over his tongue and lets it heat up his mouth before he swallows. He wishes he knew how to play an instrument. He wouldn't mind going up at the break, asking if he could sit in, holding up a saxophone case, maybe, or a clarinet. He'd still be here at 3 A.M., jamming, while the waiters mopped the floors.

That would be a good place to be at 3 A.M. Much better than rolling up the rug, burning the gloves, dropping the knife over the bridge rail. Figuratively speaking.

They aren't that unalike, she and he. He has a few people in his body, too, and they also know what they're doing.

The difference is, his have names.

"*¿Algo mas?*" The wide-faced waitress sounds Salvadoran. She looks too young to be let into a bar, let alone make half a bill a night in tips. She probably sends it all home to *mami*. The idea annoys him. Being annoyed annoys him, too. No skin off his nose if she's not blowing it at the mall.

He actually *is* too young to legally swallow this liquor in a public place, but of course he's never carded. A month and a half and he'll be twenty-one. Somebody ought to throw a party. "*Nada. Grácias.*"

The waitress smiles at him. "Where you from? Chihuahua?"

"Burbank." Why does she care where he's from? He shouldn't have answered in Spanish.

"No, your people—where they from? My best friend's from Chihuahua. You look kinda like her brother."

"Then he looks like an American."

She actually seems hurt. "But everybody's from some-place."

Does she mean "everybody," or "everybody who's brown like us"? "Yep. Welcome to Los Angeles."

He and the tequila bid each other good-bye, like a hug with a friend at the airport. The waitress smacks the empty glass down on her tray and heads for the bar. There, even the luggage disappears from sight. He rubs the bridge of his nose.

Positive contact, Chisme answers from above his right ear. Chisme is female and throaty, for him, anyway. *All numbers optimal to high optimal. Operation initialized.*

He lays a ten on the table and pins the corner down with

the candle jar. He wishes it were a twenty, for the sake of the Salvadoran economy. But big tippers are memorable. He stands up and heads for the door.

Behind him he hears the piano player sweep the keys, low to high, and it hits his nerves like a scream. He almost turns—

Adrenal limiter enabled. Suppression under external control.

Just like everything else about him. All's right with the world. He breathes deep and steps out into the streetlights and the smell of burnt oil.

The bar's in Koreatown. The target is in downtown L.A. proper, in the jewelry district. Always start at least five miles from the target, in case someone remembers the unmemorable. Show respect for the locals, even if they're not likely to believe you exist.

He steps into the shadow that separates two neon window signs and slips between, fastlanes. He's down at Hill and Broadway in five minutes. He rubs the bridge of his nose again. *Three percent discharge*, says Chisme. After three years he can tell by the way it feels, but it's reflex to check.

The downtown air is oven-hot, dry and still, even at this hour, and the storm drains smell. They'll keep that up until the rains come and wash them clean months from now. He turns the corner and stops before the building he wants.

There's a jewelry store on the first floor. Security grills lattice the windows, and the light shines down on satin-upholstered stands with nothing on them. Painted on the inside of the glass is GOLD MART/BEST PRICES ON/ GOLD/PLATINUM/CHAINS & RINGS. Straight up, below the fifth-floor windows, there's a faded sign in block letters: EISENBERG & SONS.

Time to call another of the names. He massages his right palm with his left thumb.

Magellan responds. Not with words, because words aren't what Magellan does. Against the darkness at the back of the store white lines form, like a scratchboard drawing. He knows they're not really inside the store, but his eye doesn't give a damn. The pictures show up wherever he's looking. This one is a cutaway of the building: the stairwell up the left side, the landings, the hallways on each floor. And the target, like a big lens flare . . . at the front of the fourth floor.

They're always on the *top* floor. Always. He focuses on the fifth floor of the diagram and massages his hand again. The zoom-in is so fast he staggers. *Vertical axis restored*, Chisme murmurs.

The fifth floor seems to be all storage; the white lines draw wire-frame cartons and a few pieces of broken furniture in the rooms.

Not right, not right. Top floor makes for a faster getaway, better protection from the likes of him. Ignoring strategy can only mean that the strategy has changed. He probes his upper left molar with his tongue, and Biblio's sexless whisper, like sand across rock, says, *Refreshing agent logs. Information updated at oh-two-oh-three.*

Fifteen minutes ago is good enough. He thinks through the logs, looking for surprises, new behaviors, deviations in the pattern. *Nada*. His fourth-floor sighting will be in the next update as an alert, an anomaly. He's contributed to the pool of knowledge. Whoopee for him.

He stands inside the doorway, trying to look like scenery, but every second he waits makes it worse. If the target gets the wind up, a nice routine job will have gone down the crapper. And if the neighborhood watch spooks and the LAPD sends a squad, the target will for sure get the wind up.

But it's not routine. He knows it, he's made and trained to know it. The target is not where it ought to be. The names are no help: they follow orders. Just as he does. *No te pre-ocupes, hijo*. Do the job until it does for you; then there'll be another just like you to clean up the mess and you'll be a note in the logs.

Blood pressure adjusted, Chisme notes. Not an admonishment, just a fact. The names give him facts. It's up to him what to do with them. To hell with the neighborhood watch. He touches thumb to middle finger on each hand, stands still, breathes from the belly. Chisme isn't the only one who can do his tune-up.

He takes the chameleon key from his pocket, casual as any guy who's left something on his desk at work—oops, yeah, officer, the wife'll kill me if I don't bring those tickets home tonight. The key looks like a brass Schlage; he could hand it to the cop and smile. But when it goes in the lock . . .

He feels it under his fingers, like a little animal shrugging. It's changing shape in there, finding the right notches and grooves and filling them. When it feels like a brass key again, he turns it, and the lock opens easy as a peck on the cheek.

Thirty seconds on the alarm, according to the documents in the archives of the security service that installed it. Biblio tells him what to punch on the keypad, and the display stops flashing ENTER CODE NOW and offers him a placid SYSTEM DISARMED. This part is never hard. If a target showed up in one of the wannabe mansionettes on Chandler at four in the morning, he could walk right in and the home owner would never know.

If nothing went wrong after the walking in part, of course.

The stairs in front of him are ill-lit, sheathed in cracked linoleum and worn rubber nailed down treads. He smells dust, ammonia, and old cigarette smoke. But not the target, not yet.

He starts up toward the next floor.

The evening before, he got an official commendation for his outstanding record. He had to go to the Chateau Marmont, up the hill from Sunset, to get it, and on a Friday, too, so he had to pay ten dollars for valet parking to get his head patted. Good dog. If he could fastlane on his own time, it would solve so many problems. But hey, at least there was still such a thing as "his own time."

She was out on the patio by the pool, stretched in a lounge chair. From there a person could see a corner of the Marmont bungalow where Belushi had overdosed. He was pretty sure she knew that; they liked things like celebrity death spots.

Some of them almost anyone could recognize—if almost anyone knew to look for them. They're always perfect, of their kind. That's why so many of them like L.A., where everybody gets extra credit for looking perfect. Try going unnoticed in Ames, Iowa, looking like that.

She had wavy golden hair to her shoulders, and each strand sparkled when the breeze shifted it. She wore a blue silk halter top and little white shorts that showed how long and tan her legs were. She could've been one of those teen-star actresses pretending to be a forties pinup, except that she was too convincing. She sipped at a *mojito* without getting any lipstick on the glass.

For fun, he jabbed his molar with his tongue to see if Biblio could tell him anything about her—name, age, rank. *Nada, y nada mas.* None of them were ever in the database. Didn't hurt to try, though.

"Your disposal record is remarkable," she said, with no preface.

"I do my job." He wondered what other agents' records were. He was pretty sure there were others, though he'd never met them. She didn't ask him to sit down, so he didn't.

"A vital one, I assure you." She gazed out at the view: the L.A. basin all the way to Santa Monica, just beginning to light up for the night, and a very handsome sunset. No smog or haze. Could her kind make that happen, somehow? They'd more or less made him, but he was nothing compared to a clear summer evening in Los Angeles.

She turned to look at him fully, suddenly intent. "You understand that, don't you? That your work is essential to us?"

He shrugged. A direct gaze from one of them had tied better tongues than his.

"You're saving our way of life—even our lives themselves. These others come from places where they're surrounded by ignorant, superstitious peasants. They have no conception of how to blend in here, what the rules and customs are. And their sheer numbers . . ." She shook her head. "A stupid mistake by one of them, and we could all be revealed."

"So it's a quality-of-life thing?" he asked. "I thought the problem was limited resources."

She pressed her lips together and withdrew her gaze. The evening seemed immediately colder and less sweetly scented. "Our first concern, of course. We're very close to the upper limit of the carrying capacity of this area. Already there are . . ." (she closed her tilted blue eyes for a moment, as if she had a pain somewhere) ". . . empty spots. We are the guardians of this place. If we let these invaders overrun it, they'll strip it like locusts, as they strip their native lands."

A swift movement in the shrubbery—a hummingbird, shooting from one blossom to another. She smiled at it, and he thought, *Lucky damned bird*, even though he didn't want to.

"I still don't get it," he said, his voice sounding like a truck horn after hers. "Why not help them out? Say, '*Bienvenidos*, brothers and sisters, let's all go to Disneyland'? Then show them how it's done, and send them someplace where they can have their forty acres and a mule? They're just like you, aren't they?"

She turned from the bird and met his eyes. If he thought he'd felt the force of her before, now he knew he'd felt nothing, nothing. "Have you seen many of them," she asked, "who are just like me?"

He's seen one or two who might have become like her, in time, with work. But none so perfect, so powerful, so unconsciously arrogant, so serenely *sure*, as she and the others who hold his leash.

He's on the first landing before he remembers to check the weapon. Chisme monitors that, too, and would have said something if it wasn't registering. But it's not Chisme's ass on the line (if, in fact, Chisme *has* one). Trust your homies, but check your own rifle.

He holds his left palm up in front of him in the gloom and makes a fist, then flexes his wrist backward. At the base of his palm the tiny iron needles glow softly, row on row, making a rosy light under his skin.

He used to wonder how they got the needles in there without a scar, and why they glow when he checks them, and how they work when he wants them to. Now he only thinks about it when he's on the clock. Part of making sure that he can still call some of the day his own.

When he finishes here, he'll be debriefed. That's how he thinks of it. He'll go to whatever place Magellan shows him, do whatever seems to be expected of him, and end by falling asleep. When he wakes up the needles will be there again.

He goes up the stairs quiet and fast, under his own power. If he fastlanes this close, the target will know he's here. He's in good shape: he can hurry up three flights of stairs and still breathe easy. That's why he's in this line of work now. Okay, that and being in the wrong place at the right time.

Introspection is multitasking, and multitasking can have unpleasant consequences. That's what the names are for, *hijo*. Keep your head in the job.

Half the offices here are vacant. The ones that aren't have temporary signs, the company name in a reasonably businesslike typeface, coughed out of the printer and taped to the door. Bits of tape from the last company's sign still show around the edges. The hallway's overhead fluorescent is like twilight, as if there's a layer of soot on the inside of its plastic panel.

At least it's all offices; one less problem to deal with, *grácias a San Miguel*. Plenty of the buildings on Broadway are apartments above the first two floors, with Mom and Dad and four kids in a one-bedroom with not enough windows and no air-conditioning. People sleep restless in a place like that.

Which makes him wonder: why *didn't* the target pick a place like that? Why make this easier?

On the fourth floor, the hall light buzzes on and off, on and off. He feels a pre-headache tightness behind his eyebrows as his eyes try to correct, and his heart rate climbs. Is the light the reason for this floor? Did the target know about him, how he works, and did it pick this floor because of it?

Chisme gives his endocrine system a twitch, and he stops vibrating. He's a well-kept secret. And if he isn't, all the more reason to get this done right.

He walks the length of the hallway, hugging the wall, pausing to listen before crossing the line of fire of each closed door. He doesn't expect trouble until the farthest door, but it's the trouble you don't expect that gets you. Even to his hearing, he doesn't make a sound.

Beside the last door, the one at the front of the building, he presses up against the wall and listens. A car goes through the intersection below; a rattle on the sidewalk may be a shopping cart. Nothing from inside the room. He breathes in deep and slow, and smells, besides the dry building odors, the scent of fresh water.

He probes his right palm with his thumb, and when Magellan sends him the diagram of the fourth floor, he turns his head to line it up with the real surfaces of the building. Here's the hall, and the door, and the room beyond it. There's the target: shifting concentric circles of light, painfully bright. Unless everything is shot to hell, it's up against the front wall, near the window. And if everything *is* shot to hell, there's nothing he can do except go in there and find out.

At that, he feels an absurd relief. *We who are about to die.* From here on, it's all action, as quick as he can make it, and no more decisions. Quick, because as soon as he fastlanes, the target will know he's here. He reaches down inside himself and makes it happen.

He turns and kicks the door in, and feels the familiar heat in nerve and muscle tissue, tequila-fueled. He brings his left arm up, aims at the spot by the window.

Fire, his brain orders. But the part of him that really commands the weapon, whatever that part is, is frozen.

The *coyotes* mostly traffic in the ones who can pass. After all, it's bad for business if customers you smuggle into the Promised Land are never heard from again by folks back in the old 'hood.

But sometimes, if cash flow demands, they make exceptions. *Coyotes* sell hope, after all. Unreasonable, ungratifiable hope just costs more. The *coyotes* tell them about the Land of Opportunity and neglect to mention that there's no way they'll get a piece of it.

Then the *coyotes* take their payment, dump them in the

wilderness, and put a couple of steel-jackets in them before leaving.

He's done cleanup in the desert and found the dried-out bodies, parchment skin and deformed bone, under some creosote bush at the edge of a wash. The skin was often split around the bullet holes, it was so dry. Of course, if they'd been dead, there wouldn't have been anything to find. Some that he came across could still open their eyes, or speak.

Maybe in the dark this one can pass. Maybe she looks like an undernourished street kid with a thyroid problem. In the pitch-dark below an underpass from a speeding car, maybe.

She should never have left home. She should be dying in the desert. She should be already dead, turned to dust and scattered by the oven-hot wind.

Her body looks like it's made of giant pipe cleaners. Her long, skinny legs are bent under her, doubled up like a folding carpenter's ruler, and the joints are the wrong distance from each other. Her ropy arms are wrapped around her, and unlike her legs, they don't seem jointed at all—or it's just the angle that makes them seem to curve like tentacles.

And she's white. Not Anglo-white or even albino-white, but white like skim milk, right down to the bluish shadows that make her skin look almost transparent. Fish-belly white.

Her only clothing is a plaid flannel shirt with the sleeves torn off, in what looks like size XXL Tall. It's worn colorless in places, and those spots catch the street light coming through the uncovered window. The body under the shirt is small and thin and childlike. Her head, from above, is a big soiled milkweed puff, thin gray-white hair that seems to have worn itself out pushing through her scalp.

The office is vacant. An old steel desk stands on end in the middle of the room. Empty filing cabinet drawers make a lopsided tower in a corner. Half a dozen battered boxes of envelopes are tumbled across the floor, their contents spilled and stained. But the room's alive with small bright movements.

It's water—trickling down the walls, running in little rivulets across the vinyl flooring, plopping intermittently in fat drops from the ceiling. Water from nowhere. From her.

He hears the words coming out of his mouth even as he thinks, *This isn't going to work.* "I'm here to send you back." Once one of the poor bastards becomes his job, there's no "sending back." His left arm is up, his palm turned out. He should fire.

The milkweed fluff rocks slowly backward. Her face is under it. Tiny features on an out-thrusting skull, under a flat, receding brow, so that her whole face forms around a ridge down its middle. Only the eyes aren't tiny. They're stone gray without whites or visible pupils, deep-set round disks half the size of his palm.

She opens her little lipless mouth, but he doesn't hear anything. She licks around the opening with a pale gray pointed tongue and tries again.

"Tú es un mortal."

You're a mortal. A short speech in a high, breathy little-girl voice, but long enough to hear that her accent is familiar.

He's light-headed, and his ears are ringing. He needs adjusting. Damn it, where's Chisme?

Wait—he knows what this is. He's afraid.

She's helpless, not moving, not even paying attention. All he has to do is trigger the weapon, and she'll have a hundred tiny iron needles in her. Death by blood poisoning in thirty seconds or less—quicker and cleaner than the *coyotes'* steel-jacketed rounds would have been. Why can't he fire?

He tries again, in Spanish this time—as if that will make it true. "I'm sending you back."

Something around her brows and the corners of her eyes suggests hope. She rattles into speech, but he can't make out a word of it. He recognizes it, though. It's the *Indio* language his grandmother used. He doesn't know its name; to his *abuela*, it was just speaking, and Spanish was the city language she struggled with.

He can't trust his voice, so he shakes his head at her. Does she understand that? His left arm feels heavy, stretched out in front of him.

Suddenly anger cuts through his dumb animal fear. She's jerking him around. She found out somehow where his mother's family is from, and she's playing him with it. He doesn't have to make her understand. All he has to do is shoot her.

"You are not of the People, but you are of the land." She's switched back to Spanish, and he hears the disappointment in her voice. "You cannot send me back to something that is not there."

"Whose fault is that?" *Don't talk to her!* But he's angry.

"I do not know who it was." She shakes her head, less like a "no" than like a horse shaking off flies. "But the spring is gone. The water sank to five tall trees below the stone. The willows died when they could not reach it."

Willows and cottonwoods, they mark subsurface water like green surveyor's flags all through the dry country. He remembers willows around the springs in the hills behind his grandmother's village. "So you're going to move north and use up everything here, too?"

"*¿Que?*" Her white, flattened brow presses down in anger or confusion, or both. "How can I use up what is here? Is it so different here, the water and the land and the stone?"

There has to be a correct answer to that. Those who sent him after her probably have one. But he's not even sure what she's asking, let alone what he ought to answer. *Nothing, you moron.* And what did he expect her to say? "*Sí, sí,* I'm here to steal your stuff"? They both know why she's here. If she'd just make a move, he could trigger the weapon.

"We keep, not use. How to say . . ." She blinks three times, rapidly, and it occurs to him that that might be the equivalent, for her, of gazing into space while trying to remember something. "Protect and guard. Is it not so here? Mortals use. We protect and guard. They ask for help—water for growing food, health and strength for their children. They bring tobacco, cornmeal, honey to thank us. We smell the presents and come. Do the People not do this here?"

He tries to imagine that piece of blonde perfection by the Chateau Marmont pool being summoned by the smell of cornmeal and doing favors for *campesinos*.

The word triggers his memory, like Chisme toggling his endocrine system. He recalls his last visit to his *abuela's* house, when he was eight. She was too weak to get out of bed for more than a few minutes at a time. She was crying, yelling at his mom, saying that somebody had to take the tamales to the spring. His mom said to him, as she heated water for his bath, "You see what it's like here? When your cousins call you *pocho*, you remember it's better to be American than a superstitious *campesino* like them."

He'd grown up believing that, until *they* found him, remade him, and sent him out to do their work. In that hot, moist room he feels cold all over. To hide it, he laughs. "Welcome to the Land of the Free, *chica*. No handouts, no favors, no fraternizing with the lower orders."

Her eyes darken, as if a drop of ink fell into each one. Fear surges in him again. *You should have shot her!* But tears like water mixed with charcoal well up, spill over, draw dark gray tracks on her white, sloping cheeks. "Please—it is not true, tell me so. I have nowhere to go. The machines that are loud and smell bad come and tear the trees from the soil, break mountains and take them away. They draw the water away from the sweet dark places under the earth. Poison comes into the water everywhere, how I do not know, but creatures are made sick who drink it. I tried to stay by the spring, but the water was gone, and the machines came. There was no room for me."

"There's no room for you here," he snaps. But he thinks, *You're so skinny,* Jesucristo, *you could live in a broom closet. There must be some place to fit you in.*

She shakes her head fiercely, smears the gray tears across her cheeks with her fingers. "Here there are places where the machines do not go. I know this. The People here are *inmigrantes* from the cold lands—they must know how it is. They will understand, and let us help them guard the land."

Already there are . . . empty spots, the blonde by the pool had said. But just this one little one? Would she be so bad?

No. All of his targets were each just one. Together they were hundreds. "They're guarding it from all of you, so you don't use everything up. Like locusts."

She goes still as a freeze-frame. "Mortals use. The People guard and protect. Surely they know this!"

What is she saying? "The power. Whatever it is, in the land. It's drying up."

"The People let the magic run through us like water through our fingers. We do not hoard it or hide it or wall it in. If we did, it would dry up, yes. Who told you this lie?"

"They did. The ones like you." *Have you seen many who are just like me?* he hears the blonde saying, in that voice that made everything wise and true.

She hasn't moved, but she suddenly seems closer, her eyes wider, her hair shifting like dry grass in the wind. There is no wind. He wants to back away, run.

And he remembers that night in his grandmother's house, after the fight about the tamales. He remembers being tucked up in blankets on the floor, and not being able to sleep because it stayed in his head—the angry voices, his *abuela* crying, his *mamá* cleaning up after dinner with hard, sharp movements. Nobody's mad at you, he'd told himself. But he'd still felt sick and scared. So he was awake when the *tap, tap, tap* sounded on the window across the room. On the glass bought with money his mother had sent home. And he'd raised his head and looked.

The next morning he'd told his mother he'd had a bad

dream. That was how he'd recalled it ever since: a bad dream, and a dislike for the little house he never saw again. But now he remembered. That night he saw the Devil, come to take his mother and grandmother for the sin of anger. He'd frozen the scream in his throat. If he screamed, they would wake and run in, and the Devil would see them. If it took him instead, they would be safe.

What he'd seen, before he'd closed his eyes to wait for death, was a white face with a high, flattened forehead, gray-disk eyes, and a lipless mouth, and thin white fingers pressed against the glass. It was her, or one of her kind, come down from the spring looking for the offering.

"It is not true," she hisses, thrusting her face forward. "None of my kind would say that we devour and destroy. This is mortals' lies, to make us feared, to drive us away!"

He *is* afraid of her. He could snap those little pipe cleaner arms, but that wouldn't save him from her anger. It rages in the room like the dust storms that can sand paint off a car.

She has to be wrong. If she isn't, then for three years he has— He had no choice. Did he? Three years of things, hundreds of them, that should have lived forever.

"Your kind want you kept out," he spits back at her. "You don't get it, do you? They sent me to kill you."

He'd thought she was still before. Now she's an outcrop of white stone. He can't look away from her wide, wide eyes. Then her mouth opens and a sound comes out, soft at first, so he doesn't recognize it as laughter.

"You will drive us back or kill us? You are too late. Jaguars have come north across the Rio Grande. The wild magic is here. We will restore the balance in spite of the ignorant *inmigrantes*. And when we are all strong again, they will see how weak they are alone."

She moves. He thinks she's standing up, all in one smooth motion. But her head rises, her arms shrink and disappear, her bent legs curve, coil. He's looking into her transformed face: longer, flatter, tapered, serpentine. The flyaway hair is a bush of hair-thin spines. Rising out of it are a pair of white, many-pronged antlers.

Their points scrape the ceiling above his head. The cloud of tiny iron needles fills the air between him and her and he thinks, *Did I fire?*

But by then she's behind him. There's a band of pressure around his chest. He looks down to see her skin, silver-white scales shining in the street light, as the pressure compresses his ribs, his lungs. She's wrapped around him, crushing him.

Chisme will know when he stops breathing. When it's too late. The room is full of tiny stars. She's so strong he can't even struggle, can't cry because he can't breathe. He wants so much to cry.

The room is black, and far, far away. He feels a lipless mouth brush his forehead, and a voice whisper, *"Duermes, hijo, y despiertas a un mundo mas mejór."* The next world is supposed to be better. He hopes that's true. He hopes that's where he's going.

He lies with his eyes closed, taking stock. His ribs hurt, but he's lying on something soft. Hurt means he's not dead. Soft means he's not on the floor of that office in the jewelry district, waiting for help.

He listens for the names. Nothing. He's alone in his head.

He opens his eyes. The light is low, greenish and under-watery, and comes from everywhere at once. He's back in their hands, then.

At the foot of whatever he's lying on, a young guy looks up from a sheet of paper. Brown hair, hip-nerd round tortoiseshell glasses, oxford-cloth button-down under a cashmere sweater under a reassuring white coat. For a second he thinks he was wrong and this is a hospital, that's a doctor.

"Hey," says the guy. "How do you feel?"

Come on, lungs, take in air. Mouth, open. "Crummy." He sounds as if his throat's full of mud.

The guy draws breath across his teeth—a sympathy noise. "Yeah, you must have caught yourself a whopper."

This one's remarkably human, meaning damned near unremarkable. But the lenses in the glasses don't distort the eyes behind them, because of course, they don't have to correct for anything. He's never seen one of them so determined to pass for normal. Is there a reason why this one's here now? Are they trying to put him at ease, off his guard?

"Actually," he answers, "it was a little kid who turned into a big-ass constrictor snake."

"Wow. Have you ever gotten a shape-changer before?"

Bogus question. The guy knows his whole history, knows every job he's done. But there's no point in calling him on it. "Yeah."

A moment of silence. Is he supposed to go on, talk it out? Is this some kind of post-traumatic stress therapy they've decided he needs? Or worse—is he supposed to apologize now for screwing up, for letting her get by him?

The guy shrugs, checks his piece of paper again. "Well, you're going to be fine now. And you did good work out there."

Careful. "Any job you can walk away from."

"Quite honestly, we weren't sure you had. Your 'little kid' put out enough distortion to swamp your connection with us. As far as we can tell it took almost thirty minutes for it to dissipate, after you . . . resolved the situation. Until then, we thought you'd been destroyed. Your handlers were beside themselves."

Handlers—the names. He wonders what "beside themselves" looks like for Chisme and Biblio and Magellan, or whatever those names are when they aren't in his head. He's never heard emotion out of any of them.

He stares at the young guy, handsome as a soap opera doctor. He starts to laugh, which hurts his ribs. Has he dealt with shape-changers before? Hell, which of them *isn't* a shape-changer? However they do it, they all look like what you want or need to see. Except the ones, bent and strange, who can't pass. "I wasn't sure I killed her."

The young guy winces. "Killed" is not a nice word to immortals, apparently. "The site was completely cleansed. Very impressive. And I assure you, I'm not the only one saying so."

"That's nice." He's never failed to take out his target before this. He doesn't know what punishment it is that he seems to have escaped. For this one moment, he feels bulletproof. "I talked to her, before I did it."

Surprise—and alarm?—on the young guy's face. "By the green earth! Are you nuts? You must have been warned against that."

"She said her kind—your kind—aren't a drain on the local resources. Or aren't supposed to be. She implied you'd forgotten how it's done."

The soap-opera features register disgust. "Just the sort of thing one of them would say. They're ignorant tree-dwellers. They have no idea how complex the modern world is. You know what they're like."

He doesn't, actually. He's supposed to kill them, not get acquainted with them. "Her folks were here first," he says, as mildly as he can.

The young guy frowns, confused. "What does that have to do with it?" He shakes his head. "Don't worry, we understand these things. We know what we're doing. You can't imagine what it would be like if we let down our guard."

Pictures come into his head—from where? A picture of jaguars, glimmering gold and black like living jewelry, slipping through emerald leaves; of blue-and-red-feathered birds singing with the sweet, high voices of children; of human men and women sitting with antlered serpents and coyote-headed creatures, sharing food and stories in a landscape of plenty; of the young white-coated guy, on a saxophone, jamming with the piano player in the Koreatown bar while a deer picked its way between the tables.

"You'll be fine now," the young guy repeats. "Get some sleep. When you wake up you'll be back home. I think you can expect a week or two off—go to Vegas or something, make a holiday of it."

Of course, "get some sleep" is not just a suggestion. The guy makes a pressing-down motion, and the greeny light dims. He can feel the magic tugging at his eyelids, his brain.

The young guy smiles, turns away, and is gone.

It's a good plan—but not Vegas, oh, no. He'll wake up in his apartment. He'll get up and pack . . . what? Not much. Then he'll head south. Past the border towns and the *maquiladoras*, past the giant commercial fields of cotton and tomatoes scented with chemicals and watered from concrete channels.

He wonders if they'll be able to track him, if they'll even care that he's gone. For them, the world must be full of promising, desperate mortals. He'll lose the names, the senses, the fastlane, but he'll be traveling light; he won't need them.

Eventually he'll get to the wild places, rocky or green, desert or forest or shore. Home of the ignorant, superstitious peasants. That's where he'll stop. He'll bake tortillas on a hot, flat stone, lay out sugarcane and tobacco.

Maybe nothing will come for them. Maybe he won't even be able to tell if anything's there. But just in case, he'll tell stories. They'll be about how to get past people like him, into the land where the magic is dying because it can't flow like water.

Then he'll move on, and do it again. Nothing makes up for the ones he's stopped, but he can try, at least, to replace them.

Sleep, child, she'd said, *and wake to a better world*. He'd thought then she'd meant the sleep of death, but if she'd wanted to kill him, wouldn't he be dead? He relaxes into the green darkness, the comforting magic. When he wakes this time, it'll be the same old world. But some morning, for someone, someday, it will be different.

Emma Bull's first novel, *War for the Oaks*, is a contemporary fantasy about a rock musician who finds herself drafted into a civil war between the high courts of Faery. So she's been spying on the Fey for quite some time now.

Her third novel, *Bone Dance*, was a finalist for the Hugo, Nebula, and World Fantasy Awards. Her Bordertown novel, *Finder*, was reprinted for young adults in the summer of 2003. She's at work on *Territory*, a historical fantasy set in Tombstone, Arizona, in which magic affects the events surrounding the O.K. Corral gunfight.

She's a singer and guitar player, performing solo lately. Her last band, the Flash Girls, released *Play Each Morning, Wild Queen* on Fabulous Records a while ago. You can find more about her, them, it, and related people and critters (like her husband, Will Shetterly), on her Web site is www.qwertyranch.com.

Author's Note

In Sonora, Mexico, the Yaquis and Mayos say there are antlered serpents that live in the mountain springs and keep them from going dry. People make offerings at the springs, and ask the serpent for a good harvest.

If I still lived in Minneapolis, Minnesota, this story might never have occurred to me. But I moved to Los Angeles in 1996. Now I live in southern Arizona, which, as far as this story is concerned, is only more so. Someday, maybe, there won't be anyone to tell this story about.

How to Find Faery

Nan Fry

Watch and honor your cat
when his green eyes look through
and beyond you. Do the same
for your dog when she sniffs
and barks at invisible things.

Find a beech forest or even
one tree. Stand under it and listen.
The rushing you hear will be wind
in the leaves or the murmur of elves.

Take a bath in the moonlight.
Where moonbeams touch
the water's skin, sometimes
a nixie will swim.

Go to the shore and watch the tide
ebb at sunrise or sunset. Notice

how the wet sand holds the sky's
hues of mauve and coral.

Gradually the light brightens or fades,
and the sand returns to its own color.
Even so the world of faery washes
over this one, then recedes.
Here and there a shell gleams.

Pick up the shell and go home.
If it fades in the dry light of day,
shine it with your own spit
as a sign of the magic within you
that rises to meet the world's
darkness and flash.

Nan Fry is the author of two collections of poetry: *Say What I Am Called*, a selection of riddles translated from the Anglo-Saxon, and *Relearning the Dark*. The Poetry Society of America has placed one of her poems on posters in the transit systems of Washington, D.C., Baltimore, Maryland, and Fort Collins, Colorado, as part of their Poetry in Motion program. Her poems have appeared in several recent anthologies, including *Poetry in Motion®: From Coast to Coast* and *Opening a Door: Reading Poetry in the Middle School Classroom*.

Author's Note

As Robert Frost noted, a poem can say more than one thing at a time. When I wrote "How to Find Faery," I was thinking of those hints of magic that we sense in our ordinary lives, of how such glimpses can transform our view of reality, of how fleeting they are, and of how, ultimately, they come both from within us and from our response to the world.

Further Reading

Novels

Poul Anderson, *The Broken Sword*

Poul Anderson, *A Midsummer Tempest*

Gael Baudino, *Strands of Starlight*

Franny Billingsley, *The Folk Keeper*

Holly Black, *Tithe: A Modern Faerie Tale*

Holly Black and Tony DiTerlizzi, *The Spiderwick Chronicles*

Francesca Lia Block, *I Was a Teenage Fairy*

Herbie Brennan, *Faerie Wars*

Patricia Briggs, *The Hob's Bargain*

Kevin Brockmeier, *The Truth About Celia*

Emma Bull, *War for the Oaks*

Michael Chabon, *Summerland*

C. J. Cherryh, *The Dreaming Tree*

M. Lucie Chin, *The Fairy of Ku-She*

Marian Cockrell, *Shadow Castle*

Eoin Colfer, *Artemis Fowl*

John Crowley, *Little, Big*

Cecilia Dart-Thornton, *The Ill-Made Mute*

Pamela Dean, *Tam Lin*

Charles de Lint, *Jack of Kinrowan*

Charles de Lint, *The Little Country*

Charles de Lint, *The Wild Wood*

Diane Duane, *Stealing the Elf-King's Roses*

Lord Dunsany, *The King of Elfland's Daughter*

Alice Thomas Ellis, *Fairy Tale*

Raymond Feist, *Faerie Tale*

Neil Gaiman, *Stardust*

Lisa Goldstein, *Strange Devices of the Sun and Moon*

Hiromi Goto, *The Kappa Child*

Linda Haldeman, *The Last Born of Elvinwood*

Alice Hoffman, *Aquamarine*

Sarah A. Hoyt, *Ill Met by Moonlight*

Dahlov Ipcar, *A Dark Horn Blowing*

Kij Johnson, *The Fox Woman*

Diane Wynne Jones, *Fire and Hemlock*

Graham Joyce, *The Tooth Fairy*

Garry Kilworth, *A Midsummer's Nightmare*

Ellen Kushner, *Thomas the Rhymer*

Manuel Mujica Lainez, *The Wandering Unicorn*

Rebecca Lickiss, *Eccentric Circles*

R. A. MacAvoy, *The Grey Horse*

Juliet Marillier, *Daughter of the Forest*

Geraldine McCaughrean, *The Stones Are Hatching*

Eloise McGraw, *The Moorchild*

Dennis L. McKiernan, *Once Upon a Winter's Night*

Patricia A. McKillip, *Something Rich and Strange*

Patricia A. McKillip, *Winter Rose*

Robin McKinley, *Spindle's End*

Donna Jo Napoli, *Sirena*

Pat O'Shea, *The Hounds of the Mórrigan*

Elizabeth Marie Pope, *The Perilous Gard*

Kristine Kathryn Rusch, *The Sacrifice: The First Book of the Fey*

Midori Snyder, *The Flight of Michael McBride*

Midori Snyder, *Hannah's Garden*

Nancy Springer, *I Am Morgan le Fay*

Steve Szilagyi, *Photographing Fairies*

Tad Williams, *The War of the Flowers*

Patricia C. Wrede, *Snow White and Rose Red*

❧

Story Collections

Sylvia Townsend Warner, *Kingdoms of Elfin*

Terri Windling and Delia Sherman (editors), *The Essential Bordertown: A Traveller's Guide to the Edge of Faerie*

Jane Yolen, *The Faery Flag: Stories and Poems of Fantasy and the Supernatural*

❧

Faery Folklore

Katharine Briggs, *The Vanishing People: Fairy Lore and Legends* (and all of her other faery books)

Maureen Duffy, *The Erotic World of Faery*

W. Y. Evans-Wentz, *The Fairy Faith in Celtic Countries*

Thomas Keightley, *Fairy Mythology* (also published as *The World Guide to Gnomes, Fairies, Elves, and Other Little People*)

Diane Purkiss, *At the Bottom of the Garden: A Dark History of Fairies, Hobgoblins, Nymphs, and Other Troublesome Things*

Wirt Sikes, *British Goblins: Welsh Folklore, Fairy Mythology, Legends and Traditions*

Carole G. Silver, *Strange and Secret Peoples: Fairies and Victorian Consciousness*

William Butler Yeats, *Irish Fairy and Folk Tales*

THREE USEFUL REFERENCE VOLUMES ARE:

Katharine Briggs, *An Encyclopedia of Faeries: Hobgoblins, Brownies, Bogies, and Other Supernatural Creatures* (with an emphasis on British folklore)

Pierre Dubois, *The Great Encyclopedia of Faeries* (with an emphasis on French folklore)

Anna Franklin, *The Illustrated Encyclopedia of Fairies* (with faery lore from around the world)

NOTE: The books on the fiction list are contemporary ones, roughly defined as books published in the last twenty-five years. The exception to the rule is Dunsany's *The King of Elfland's Daughter*, which is just too good to leave out. It was recently published in a new edition, with an introduction by Neil Gaiman. The books on the folklore list range from nineteenth-century publications to contemporary ones. The older ones go in and out of print, so you may need to find them through your library.—T.W.

About the Editors

Ellen Datlow is editor of SCI FICTION, the fiction area of SCIFI.COM, the SCIFI Channel's Web site. Previously, she was fiction editor of OMNI for over seventeen years, and of Event Horizon, an award-winning Web site created with her former OMNI colleagues.

She is co-editor (with Terri Windling) of the six *Snow White, Blood Red* adult fairy tale anthologies, *A Wolf at the Door* and *Swan Sister*, both children's fairy tale anthologies, and *The Green Man: Tales from the Mythic Forest*. She has been editing the horror half (with Terri Windling, and now Kelly Link and Gavin J. Grant) of *The Year's Best Fantasy and Horror* for seventeen years. She and Terri also co-edited *Sirens and other Daemon Lovers*, an erotic fantasy anthology.

Solo, she is the editor of two anthologies on vampirism: *Blood Is Not Enough* and *A Whisper of Blood*; two anthologies on sf and gender: *Alien Sex* and *Off Limits; Little Deaths* (sexual horror); *Lethal Kisses* (revenge and vengeance); *Twists of the Tale* (cat horror); *Vanishing Acts*, an anthology on the theme of "endangered species"; and *The Dark: New Ghost Stories*.

Datlow has won the World Fantasy Award seven times, the Bram Stoker Award, the International Horror Guild Award, the 2005 *Locus* Award, and the 2002 Hugo Award, all for her work as an editor.

In addition, she is a consulting editor for Tor Books. She lives in New York City. Her Web site is at: www.datlow.com

About the Editors

Terri Windling is an editor, writer, painter, and passionate advocate of mythic arts. She has won the World Fantasy Award seven times, as well as the Mythopoeic Award for her novel *The Wood Wife*.

She has studied myth and folklore for many years, and especially loves tales of the faery folk. She had the privilege of editing *Good Faeries, Bad Faeries* by the English faery painter Brian Froud, and she's written numerous magazine articles on faeries and other mythological topics. She's also written three children's picture books about faeries, all illustrated by Wendy Froud: *A Midsummer Night's Faery Tale*, *The Winter Child*, and *The Faeries of Spring Cottage*. Her two books about faeries for young readers are *The Raven Queen* (co-written with Ellen Steiber) and *The Changeling*.

During the last two decades she's edited over twenty-five anthologies with Ellen Datlow, as well as several other anthologies, including one called *Faery*. She's been a consulting fantasy editor at Tor Books since 1985 and is the editor of the Fairy Tales series of novels and of the Borderland urban fantasy series.

Her paintings, which are based on folklore and feminist themes, have been exhibited at museums and galleries in the United States, England, and France. She divides her time between a four-hundred-year-old cottage in Devon, England, and a desert house in Tucson, Arizona.

For more information, visit her Web site, The Endicott Studio for Mythic Arts, www.endicott-studio.com.

About the Illustrator

Charles Vess's award-winning work has graced the pages of numerous comic books, and has been featured in several gallery and museum exhibitions across the nation, including the first major exhibition of Science Fiction and Fantasy Art (New Britain Museum of American Art, 1980). In 1991, Charles shared the prestigious World Fantasy Award for Best Short Story with Neil Gaiman for their collaboration on *Sandman* #19 (DC Comics)—the first and only time a comic book has held this honor.

In the summer of 1997, Charles won the Will Eisner Comic Industry Award for best penciler/inker for his work on *The Book of Ballads and Sagas* (which he published through his own Green Man Press) as well as *Sandman* #75. In 1999, he received the World Fantasy Award for Best Artist for his work on Neil Gaiman's *Stardust*.

He and Jeff Smith worked together on *Rose*, the prequel to Smith's *Bone*; his collaborations with his friend Charles de Lint include the picture book *A Circle of Cats* and the illustrated novels *Seven Wild Sisters* and *Medicine Road*. His other work includes the illustrations for Emma Bull's adaptation of the traditional English ballad "The Black Fox," in the anthology *Firebirds,* and the cover and decorations for Ellen Datlow and Terri Windling's *The Green Man: Tales from the Mythic Forest.*

His Web site address is www.greenmanpress.com.